PUPPET BOY

Visit us at www.boldstrokesbooks.com

PUPPET BOY

by

Christian Baines

2015

PUPPET BOY

ISBN 13: 978-1-62639-510-7

This Trade Paperback Original Is Published By
Bold Strokes Books, Inc.
P.O. Box 249
Valley Falls, NY 12185

First Edition: November 2015

CREDITS
Editor: Jerry L. Wheeler
Production Design: Susan Ramundo
Cover Design By G. S. Pendergrast

Acknowledgments

A huge thank you to everyone at Bold Strokes Books, including Radclyffe, Sandy Lowe, Cindy Cresap, fellow BSB authors, and others, for welcoming me into your creative family. Thanks especially to my editor, Jerry Wheeler, for giving me just the right balance of faith and tough love.

Thank you to authors Jeffrey Round, Kevin Klehr, 'Nathan Burgoine, Michael Rowe, Liz Bugg, Rob Byrnes, Michael Carroll, Geoffrey Knight, Ken Murphy, and others. Whether I see you frequently, rarely, or only on a screen, your encouragement, advice, advocacy, and friendship has been invaluable. The same goes for Scott, Graeme, Crusader, Rowland, and other LGBT booksellers. Thanks for all your support and the continued work you do for our voices and community. Please don't go anywhere.

Thanks to my writing tutors, particularly Tony Macris and Delia Falconer, as well as former editors, mentors, and fellow students who helped shape *Puppet Boy* through its early stages. Also to my acting teachers, Jeneffa and Lyn. Without your classes, this wouldn't be half the book it is.

To my friends and family near and far, you are the best cheer squad I could possibly want. There's no list of names I could make that would do you justice, and for that I'm extremely grateful. I will, however, give particular thanks to Tony and Adrian for being my beta readers for this project.

I have to give special thanks to my mother, because she's been my most tireless supporter and because the possibility of actually turning into Eric disturbs me.

Finally, thanks to the city of Sydney for your inspiration, beauty, darkness, and absurdity. You are an unending source of fascination, cynicism, intrigue, and love. Don't ever let anyone threaten or change your weirdness.

Chapter One

No price was too high for a good decorator who knew the value of soundproofing. This trivial certainty helped settle Eric's nerves as he cautiously descended the stairs to the theatre room's locked door. He could still hear his captive, the housebreaker he'd dubbed 'Joe,' crying out, and Eric wondered if the screams would cover the sound of the turning lock. He didn't want Joe to know he was in the room right away, or to yell at him directly. It would ruin everything.

At six days, one hour, and thirty-nine minutes, Eric knew he was no longer continuing this experiment out of interest or fascination but out of necessity. He didn't much like Joe's chances of leaving the house as something other than a prisoner or a corpse. If the man were to leave as a prisoner, there would be questions, from the police, from people at school, perhaps even from his mother.

On second thought, she probably wouldn't want to know.

If she came home at all, she would oblige the police with a good cry, during which she would insist she didn't know who her son was anymore—an ironic truth, all things considered—and board the next flight back to Los Angeles, where she had spent the last two months 'working,' as she called it, leaving Eric the house to himself.

For two whole months, Eric had felt almost self-actualised. At least, insofar as a seventeen-year-old within the confines of nominally Christian, North Shore private schooling could.

If Joe left the house as a prisoner, Eric's self-actualisation would come to an abrupt end. He'd be arrested, along with his captive. Fuck that. On the other hand, if Joe were forced to leave the house as a corpse, that would bring its own problems. Eric refused to entertain the idea—for now.

He turned on the MP3 recorder, his finger drifting over the controls almost subconsciously as he started murmuring the lyrics to an old Muppet song about being halfway down the stairs. He made only a half-hearted effort to stay close to the original tune, which was underpinned by his captive's whimpering. But Joe's voice soon roared one more barrage, and Eric refocused, erasing the recording.

Johansson, his music teacher, had told the class to be innovative in choosing sound sources for the digital editing assignment, and Eric would be damned before he passed up the chance to use a source as unique as the pleas of his bellowing captive. He had to get this right. Not to please Johansson, but to satisfy his own curiosity.

When the next scream came, Eric swiftly turned the lock, opened the door and dived through, closing it behind him as Joe went silent. He stood deathly still for a moment, his back against the wall, trying to steady his breathing as he listened for Joe in the perfect darkness of the room.

"Who's…who's there? Dude, is that you?"

Eric resisted the snarl that formed on his lips as he flicked on the recorder.

"Look, this isn't funny man, all right? They're gonna find me. You know that! They're gonna come looking for me! Just untie me, okay? I won't say anything. Please?"

Six days, and Joe hadn't stopped. Eric admired his tenacity, but surely it was clear by now the man wasn't going anywhere?

"Hello? Hello, dude? Are you there? Oh fuck, somebody help me!" The bellowing started up again. "Can somebody hear me?"

Eric smiled, even as the echo of Joe's voice, having now resumed its full volume, shook against the inside of his skull. This was better. He lowered the recorder's sensitivity as the levels spiked. For his many faults, Joe had an impressive set of lungs, which managed to keep screaming for a good four minutes of MP3 before Eric realised the time and shut down the recorder.

"Thanks," he offered, though he wasn't sure why. "I'll be back later."

"Hey! Hey, you're in here? You get back here and let me go, you—"

Eric closed the door behind him and relocked it, wincing as his captive called him the c-word. He replayed a segment of the MP3. It was perfect, crisply delivering every nuance of the man's cries. Eric went back upstairs and laid down on his bed, playing the track back one more time. He couldn't hear the real thing now, just the glorious swirls of panic from the MP3. He rolled over, deeply inhaling the scent of his pillow, the mixed aroma of slickly groomed hair, crisp linen, and chocolatey cologne. It was in this position, one leg crossed over the other, with Joe's screams filling the air, that Eric felt the newly formed erection inside his trousers. But jerking off now would have been terribly unprofessional. It was almost six. He had a client in less than an hour. Besides, he didn't know why the sound of Joe's screaming should make him hard. He swallowed down the vomit that threatened to repeat on him.

He stripped off his shirt, neatly folding it in half before putting it in the laundry basket. His socks and ugly grey school trousers followed in similar fashion until he finally stripped off his jock and turned on the shower of his ensuite bathroom, the smallest of three in the house. He paused a moment to inspect himself in the mirror. His thick mahogany hair needed trimming, and a few stray blades had materialised on his chest. They'd need to be plucked. On the other hand, he wasn't sure if his clients would really mind. Fuck them. He liked being smooth.

He plucked the hairs out, showered and towelled off, moisturising the three small, angry red spots that now protested the plucking of his chest hairs. A barely noticeable flaw, it annoyed him nonetheless.

Two shirts caught his eye, both of which had been gifts. The white one with the faint gold pattern from Margaret, and the purple one from Andy. Eric checked his iPhone to confirm Margaret was his client for the evening, before choosing the white and gold. Wearing her gift would please her. Besides, the silk and cotton blend felt good against his skin.

He needed to find cufflinks, as much as he hated them. They were expensive, fiddly, and somehow managed to make his otherwise slim, perfectly shaped wrists look clunky. But the shirt had French cuffs, and Margaret would expect cufflinks. Eric opened the top drawer of his dresser and examined his options. The topaz might work. It was classy enough to please his client, but understated enough to imply his own resentment of the accessory.

Another scream from Joe, barely audible from Eric's bedroom, broke his concentration. He accidentally knocked an empty Risperdal bottle off his bedside table. He quickly snatched it up and tossed it in the garbage. He didn't know why Joe bothered. The man wouldn't be heard by anyone outside, anyway.

Eric picked up the topaz links and tried to fasten them into the shirt's cuffs. Joe cried out again. Eric wasn't sure why, but the sound distracted and annoyed him. He finally gave up, finished dressing, and called a cab.

Chapter Two

Margaret was late in getting ready, which left Eric sitting on her Victorian sofa being eyeballed by her cat, a luxurious ragdoll with an elusive 'loving and beautiful' nature that Eric had yet to see. He liked cats in general. But apparently, Lady Persephone felt her affections did not come free with the generous three hundred and eighty dollars an hour plus expenses her owner already paid for Eric's company.

Eric hated waiting in here. The room was rarely used, and since Margaret had sacked her third cleaner in a year, the dust of the old world permeated the air like a virus, threatening to infect and antiquate the unwary visitor who inhaled it. The First World War-era clock that sat on the mantle above the bricked-up fireplace came alive with a loud series of chimes.

"Margaret, it's almost seven," he called. "Do you need a hand?"

When he got no reply, Eric drifted to the bottom of the staircase. Margaret stood at the top, her hair tied up, her makeup tastefully understated. She held a rabbit clutch purse encrusted with diamonds that caught the shimmer off her cerulean gown. She looked as regal, dignified, and prepared as any woman of forty-eight attending the opera with a man of seventeen could hope to be.

"No thank you, Eric. I believe I've managed." She smiled at him as she glided down the stairs.

"It was worth the wait," he beamed at her. "May I say that you look amazing tonight?"

"Thank you, dear. You're looking rather hands…"

Eric raised an eyebrow as her voice trailed off.

"Young man, your cuffs?" she asked.

He winced. "I'm sorry." "I was distracted."

"Distracted?"

"I couldn't choose."

Margaret nodded, her eyes narrowing. "Then, clearly, I must choose for you. Wait here."

Eric knew better than to argue when Margaret turned her back and started the return trek upstairs, a trek made with far less grace than her descent, as she was now a woman with a mission. He should have expected this. Given the choice between tardiness and appearing with a companion who wore open cuffs, Margaret would gladly miss the overture. The entire first act, if necessary.

She returned with a tiny velvet box, opening it for Eric's inspection as she reached the foot of the stairs. Topaz cufflinks.

"They'll do well with that shirt, Eric. Now, hurry up."

Eric cocked a half smile, fastening the links as his client turned out the lights and allowed him to escort her to the garage.

"The keys to your vehicle, Madam?" he asked.

Margaret returned his smile as she slid into the driver's seat of the Mercedes. He joined her from the passenger's side.

"Let's not be silly, dear."

"I've known members of the company's board for over twenty years. I simply cannot fathom what possessed them to hire a casting director who'd offer Tosca to Marie Breznik!" Margaret lifted her glass of Cabernet Shiraz blend in Andy's direction. "How soon we forget Salome."

"My dear, *no-one* could forget that Salome." Andy smiled, half-heartedly returning her gesture. "I'll give her this. She at least knows how to take firm hold of a part with both hands."

"And strangle it to death, you mean?"

"Well, it's a skill of sorts. Don't you agree, Eric?"

Eric shifted his eyes from Margaret to Andy uncomfortably before he remembered who was paying him that night. "She was... adequate."

"That's a very harsh rap, young man." A pained look crossed through Andy's smile as he took a sip of his wine. He held it up to the light and examined it as though it were laced with strychnine.

In Eric's experience, Andy rarely shared the same tastes as his peers. So the same red that was getting Margaret through three hours of Tropical Cyclone Breznik was all but unpalatable to him. He sipped at it nonetheless. Face was everything, after all. Even a face like Andy's, which seemed gaunt for a man of fifty-two.

Eric, for his part, had managed to spike his orange juice with an Absolut sampler as usual. He glanced around the Opera House foyer, scanning for faces he knew. Besides Margaret and Andy, who'd known one another for years, he'd seen three, perhaps four, current or past clients. There was Deborah Mills, who enjoyed treating Eric to a yoga class, followed by a long solarium session, topped off by an athletic two to three hours in the bedroom, or kitchen, or greenhouse, or anywhere else that took her fancy in her husband's absence. Carmel Roukstein, who he charged extra, as her appointments were unprofitably brief and typically involved feathered masks and scratchy Bowie records. He made a mental note to block her number. Gareth West, an otherwise very heterosexual and conservative member of state parliament, with five children and two alimonies, who enjoyed being jerked off whilst mummified in plastic food wrap, but only with his tie on, in a double Windsor.

"Eric!"

He snapped back to attention at Margaret's shrill summons, only then realising that the last few lines of conversation had been directed at him. "Sorry."

"I thought we'd lost you." She raised an eyebrow. "I was just saying to Andy that I might phone Elizabeth tomorrow and see if she can comp us in another night, perhaps when an understudy is playing. Are you free Thursday week?"

"Not Thursday week, Margaret. Eric has another appointment." Andy winked at him.

"Mmm? Well, can't you reschedule? The Merc' is in the garage until Wednesday and I'm expecting Gerald to be back sometime that weekend."

"Is he still in New York?" Eric asked, both to be polite and change the subject.

"London," Margaret corrected. "No, wait a moment, Hong Kong."

"I thought it was Tokyo?"

"No Andrew, Hong Kong. Tokyo was last week."

"I thought he was in New York," Eric prodded. "When was that, then?"

"Last month, Eric. Do try to keep up."

"And back to Hong Kong via London?"

"Yes."

"And Tokyo?"

"Yes."

"When was he in Paris, then?" Eric asked.

"Don't complicate things, boy. I'm his wife, not his diary. Right, next Thursday it is, then. I'll phone Elizabeth tomorrow first thing."

"Well if this flight's been overbooked, when can we reschedule, Eric?" Andy asked.

"Ah, well I don't really—"

"Andrew, you know as well as I that Eric does not discuss appointments *during* appointments. I'm sure he will be delighted to speak with you about this at a more convenient time."

"Speaking of which..." Eric muttered as the bell tolled for the second act.

Margaret shook her head, the wine having failed in its mission of mercy. "Come, dear. I think we've both had enough for one evening. Your artistic soul is far too delicate to be sullied so young. I'll get Elizabeth to schedule an understudy for Thursday week. Perhaps she'll leave an extra bottle of gin in Breznik's dresser or something like that."

"Margaret, that's evil!"

"There's no rest for the wicked, Eric, but they have occasioned to do God's work."

Eric knew rest was the last thing on Margaret's mind.

❖

"What was the matter with you tonight?"

Eric swirled the ice around his third screwdriver of the evening as he watched Margaret unfasten her hairpins. "Nothing."

"You arrive at my home in French cuffs without links on them, claiming that you couldn't choose because you were 'distracted,' and tonight, you seem near incapable of holding pleasant conversation with either Andrew or myself, despite having a perfectly sound knowledge of the topic under discussion. Which was?"

Eric stared at her, unable to recall.

"You see? You're normally so switched on, so fastidious, yet tonight you're the closest human relative to the goldfish. I would like to know why. I'm concerned about you."

"I'm fine. I promise."

"You're sure? You're not having any trouble at home? At school?"

"Nothing."

Margaret nodded, putting the hairpins away and removing the last trace of makeup from her chin. He could see her scrutinising him in the mirror.

"I suppose," she admitted, "if you were, it would be no business of mine. But you would tell me, wouldn't you, dear?"

He smiled, stepping forward and gently taking the foundation-stained cotton pad from her fingers. He held on to them as he placed his other hand on her shoulder. "Of course I would."

Margaret met his familiar gesture with her own cool touch. "You're a good boy, Eric. I hope you know that."

He shrugged, unable to resist a smile.

"Don't shrug, answer me."

"Maybe," he hastened, "to some people."

"That's enough. Not everyone deserves it, you understand. If someone's a perfect beast to you, you've every right in the world to be a perfect beast in kind."

He managed a polite laugh.

"What's funny, Eric? You've never been a perfect little beast? To anybody?"

He thought of Joe again. That was all right. Joe had been a beast to him first, breaking in and all. His moral choices were in perfect harmony with the gospel of Margaret, which only mattered while he was on her dollar anyway.

"I have my moments," he murmured.

"I hope you do." She got up, crossing to the heavy chest of drawers that sat largely neglected in the corner of her private bedroom. This was not the room she shared with her husband, but a very special chamber Margaret had crafted, almost as a shrine to herself. It was small, secluded at the top floor of the house and dimly lit. Much of the light came from bulbs around the mirror, a holdover from Margaret's long lost acting and, to a lesser extent, operatic career. She'd never lamented its passing. She had done *Cosi fan tutte*, *Our Town*, *My Fair Lady*, *A Midsummer Night's Dream*, *Entertaining Mister Sloan*, and countless others that were now just memories and rotting programs somewhere in her attic. Eric had seen her perform only once, as Frauline Schneider in a heavily cut-down production of *Cabaret*. It had been her last appearance on stage, before she loudly announced to the post-season cast party, that once one had redefined the role of Eliza Doolittle, it was hard to fill out Mrs Pierce.

"Eric."

He snapped his attention back to her. She was crouched down, rummaging through the bottom drawer of the chest, her brow furrowed with concern.

"Sorry," he mumbled.

"I need you to focus, boy. Wait for me in the sitting room. I'll be down in a moment."

❖

Margaret didn't keep him waiting long. She glided into the room, her steps even and confident as she turned a collar and lead over in her hand. "It's important to understand the human beast, Eric, however rarely you indulge it. There are quite enough people in this world who will treat you like an animal, particularly when you're young."

He nodded, swallowing the nerves that now fired through his spine and threatened to undo his carefully rehearsed composure. "Yes, I know."

"The problem is that many of us need it. Sad fact of life though it may be, we're not so far divorced from the human animal as we'd like to pretend, Eric. That's why you should always make it a point to use people's names.

"Yes."

"Yes?"

"Yes, Margaret."

"Much better. At their core, people are like dogs, Eric. They only catch on if they hear their names repeatedly and receive constant reinforcement."

Eric shifted uneasily in his seat as Margaret looked him up and down.

"Stop fidgeting, Eric. Good boy."

"Ummm...Margaret, I really don't do this. Animal play, I mean."

She ran a finger down the padded lining of the collar. It seemed soft enough, but Eric couldn't help but notice the ugly metal plate on the outer side. That didn't look comfortable.

"You're a good boy, aren't you, Eric?"

"Yes."

"Remove your jacket and shirt, then."

He obliged, feeling the pale, hairless skin of his chest ripple into gooseflesh as it was exposed to the archaic air and Margaret's curious gaze. "Better. Animal play is such a repugnant term, Eric. I expect you only to find the character within yourself. Come to me, Eric. Here, boy."

He took a step forward and instantly caught sight of his client, shaking her head from side to side. Eric swallowed, feeling as uncertain as he'd ever felt with Margaret. He glanced over at

Persephone, but the cat had her back turned, tail twitching in a rhythm that seemed strangely random against the regularity of Margaret's clock. He could do this. He'd read about it. Easy.

"Here, Eric."

He felt his knees begin to weaken, he thought at first, but that wasn't right. They simply started to bend. Bend and lower him of their own accord, until he was almost down on his haunches. Margaret took another step toward him, and he realised this wasn't right either. He straightened his legs a little, allowing them to push his body forward, until he found himself on all fours.

Margaret stood over him, staring down at his bare back and running a cold finger over the nape of his neck. "How silly of me," she laughed. "Your trousers, boy."

He nodded, sitting up on his knees and fumbling with his belt buckle.

"No," she snapped. "That won't do at all."

Eric lowered back to all fours again, eyeing her with curiosity.

"I know. On your back. Over there, on the rug."

He saw the rug out in the hall. It wasn't the cleanest of play spaces. In fact, to the best of his knowledge, it had never been taken out and beaten. Damn. This was going to make a dusty mess of his trousers.

"Go on."

He obliged her again, remaining on all fours and scrambling for the rug as instructed. He flipped over onto his back in an awkward crab-walking motion and went to lie down.

"No, that was far too human. Do it again."

Eric did as he was told, getting back up to all fours. He wasn't sure how to move at first. Did he bend one elbow first and let his body buckle in that direction or simply keel over? He realised he was thinking about this far too hard. When in doubt, there was only one course of action. Be cute.

He bent his left elbow and let the rest of his weight follow it, rolling into the rug, his face tucked under his front right paw. He straightened up a little, raising his back legs, all fours now airborne as Margaret approached.

"Much better. Good boy." She neatly removed his socks and folded them away inside his shoes before turning her attention to his belt.

It didn't come easily at first, stuck as it was under his weight. Margaret abandoned it after a few tugs, instead rubbing his tummy. Eric closed his eyes, allowing her touch to cool his skin as she petted it. It felt good, like a gentle massage that went through the very core of his body. He smiled, twisting and writhing to follow her hand as she started to tickle him. It was tempting to bring a paw down and stop her.

He lifted and tilted his butt as the assault of rubbing and tickling continued, and Margaret seized the opportunity to pull the stubborn belt free. She then unbuttoned his trousers and slid them off, followed by his jock, hanging them neatly in the hall closet. Eric watched carefully as he lay naked on the dusty rug. The trousers didn't seem too dirty, but it was difficult to tell in black and white. He rolled over, lying on his side as Margaret went to the sideboard to fix herself a drink.

"Wuff?" he asked.

She glanced over and smiled.

"Wuff, ruff ruff?"

"No gin for puppies, Eric."

"Arf?"

"No scotch either."

"Grrr..."

"Now, stop that. Go and wait for me in the lounge. I won't be long. Go on. Good boy."

He rolled back up onto all fours and shuffled his way into the lounge, sprawling in front of the plasma television. His front left paw brushed against something soft and rubbery. A ball. She'd actually bought him a squeaky rubber ball. He rolled it under his paw for a moment before hauling himself forward and batting it up under his chin, clasping it firmly in his mouth with a loud squeak.

"Oh good, you found it," Margaret exclaimed with delight as she appeared in the doorway, a gin and tonic in one hand and a stainless steel water bowl in the other. She gracefully crossed into the lounge and placed her drink down on a side table along with his bowl. She then took hold of the ball in his mouth.

"Give," she commanded.

"Grrr…"

"Eric, don't be naughty."

He opened his jaws and released the ball.

"Good boy." She tossed it into the hall.

Eric watched it bounce several times before it settled at the foot of the stairs.

"Go on," she smiled.

The pup got to his four feet and scrambled back into the hall, sliding clumsily on the polished wood floor until he reached the ball. With a couple of tries, he took it in his mouth and carried it back to his mistress.

"Good boy," she rubbed behind his ears. "Now, give."

Eric spat the ball out on the carpet. He tried not to drool excessively, preferring to stay an indoor pup.

Margaret took hold of the ball and threw it out into the hall again. It landed on the rug this time and was dusty when Eric brought it back. He obediently returned it, nonetheless.

"I hope you like it," Margaret beamed, taking the ball and putting it aside. "But that's enough for now. Come here." She sat down on the couch next to where she'd left her drink, picked up the bowl. and set it down next to her feet.

Eric followed her, sniffing the bowl carefully. He shot out his tongue and lapped at it, then looked up at her and grinned. Absolut Citroen. God bless, Mistress.

Margaret gave her knee a prim double tap, and Eric perched his chin on it as she continued to rub his ears. She raised the collar with a gentle metallic clink. He eyed it with suspicion.

"There's nothing to be afraid of. Chin up."

He didn't move at first. He just swallowed, watching the collar. It was big enough, he thought. It wouldn't choke him. All that metal just seemed harsh.

"Eric."

He lifted his chin and Margaret wrapped the collar around his throat, bending it until it was the right shape to fit his neck. She locked it closed with the clasp behind, and slipped her lead through the buckle at the front. Eric took a few deep breaths to make sure, but it was strangely comfortable—well-padded and snug around the base of his neck, while the rest of his body was bare. He returned his chin to Margaret's lap. She smiled at him, taking a sip of her gin and petting the back of his neck. He growled, but it was a contented, appreciative growl, as if sitting there at his mistress's feet, his head in her lap, was the safest, most natural position in the world.

Margaret let him lap at the bowl of vodka a few times before setting it down beside her gin. "There's a good boy," she said, beaming as she scratched behind his left ear. It felt surprisingly soothing. "Except your hair's getting too long."

"Wuff," he agreed.

She took another sip of the gin and offered him the vodka once more, tilting the bowl as Eric reached out his tongue to drink. He lapped some of the tart, citrus-flavoured spirit up his nose and began to cough. "Oh! Sorry, my dear!" Margaret pulled the bowl away and patted him on the back as he continued coughing. "Are you all right?"

Eric nodded, wheezing out the word "bathroom" between coughs.

"Of course, you know the way."

The pup scrambled to his human feet and headed swiftly there, Margaret's leash still hanging, cold against his exposed chest and stomach. He shut the bathroom door behind him and leaned over the sink, coughing out the last of the vodka and blowing his nose into his hand. He washed it off under the tap.

Eric looked up, staring into the eyes of his persona for the evening. Puppy Eric. Canine Eric. Ericus Canis. Eric, the Litter of One. The leash dangled limp and pathetic as he tugged at the collar.

Nobody owned him. This was bullshit.

"Eric, are you all right?" Margaret called.

"It's okay, I'll be right out!" He dried his hands on a towel and lowered himself to all fours, instantly regretting it as his knees hit the cold tiles. Satisfied as he was going to be under the circumstances, Puppy Eric returned to his mistress.

CHAPTER THREE

Jenny, very nice work. Callum, not bad."
As Johansson dropped each paper to its owner's desk, loudly voicing his opinion on each one as it fell, Eric found the image of some great paper cut opening the teacher's wrists and spurting blood over the pages too powerful to resist. If he wanted to share, he'd share.

"Julien…interesting. Very insightful."

A broad, stupid grin crossed Julien Davidson's face as he scanned the assignment. While Eric didn't exactly like Julien, he seemed decent enough. And despite being cursed with the lanky athleticism and nasal twang of a dumb, Central Coast jock, he was another arts freak. Another wannabe actor in the shark pool. That was okay. Not good, but okay. He was also tall, lithe, and deeply tanned. Like he had Mediterranean or Middle Eastern in him somewhere. Dark, tanned…attractive, in a guy kind of way. That made it less okay.

"How'd you do?" Eric asked him, managing to conjure up a smile he hoped looked sincere.

"Huh? Oh, uh…ninety-three."

"Nice." Shit.

"Mary, not quite what I expect from you."

Eric's eyes fell on the number as the paper landed. Seventy-eight. He watched Mary turn it over in small, white hands, her face incredulous as she scanned the small sea of red pen. Mary didn't do under eighty. Not since grade seven, when a sixty-eight average in natural science had sent her running from the classroom in silent tears. He'd found her at lunch, just past the tennis courts behind the groundskeeper's shed. He'd calmly taken the scrunched-up paper from her hand and explained why any school that based its curriculum upon literal six-day creationism and talking snakes was completely unqualified to teach the sciences. That was when Mary had told him how much she liked him, with the kind of nervous, sincere excitement only an eleven-year-old could put behind the word 'like.'

"I think you were robbed," he said. It was far from the articulate diatribe his twelve-year-old self had given her behind the shed, but it seemed more appropriate.

Mary turned the paper face down on the desk and offered him a smile. "It's fine."

"Eric."

He looked upward to meet Johansson's critical gaze. The paper flopped down, and Johansson moved on without comment.

Ninety-five.

His mind raced. Don't look at Julien. Don't even think about Julien.

"I knew it." Mary grinned, squeezing his arm.

"You barely know who Grace Jones is," he muttered, skimming over his assignment and its noticeable absence of red pen. This was crazy. Johansson would never let him off so easily. Such generosity and fairness could not possibly exist within the man's corroded void of a soul.

"I know a lot more about her now." Mary nodded at his paper, defensively.

"What'd you get?" Julien asked.

Eric looked up and saw him trying to sneak a look at his cover sheet. He passed the assignment over, satisfied the threat had been neutralised.

"Hey, congrats! Who's Grace Jon—"

"I'll tell you later."

Johansson really hadn't had much to say about Eric's assignment. He'd corrected some punctuation, at least one of which he'd gotten pointedly wrong, and a final comment at the end of the paper, which read only: '*A concise and well-researched commentary on Jones's career and her influence on contemporary pop. Your comments on her androgyny and gender identity are questionable, but adequately discussed in this instance.*'

Adequate? A score of ninety-freaking-five was *adequate*?

He managed to block out Johansson's droning, flipping through the pages again as the teacher handed out the remaining papers. Finally, the man said something that caught his attention.

"…your digital editing assignment, which is to find at least two sharply contrasted forms of sound and blend them. I hope you all remembered to bring in one of your sources for discussion today."

Eric turned the iPhone over in his hand. Here went nothing.

"Eric, since you've recently demonstrated such insight into mismatched art with your remarkable essay on Grace Jones—"

Remarkable? Adequate? Eric wished the moron would make up his mind. Wait a sec—

"Perhaps you'd like to lead us off?"

Crap. Not first. Anywhere but first.

"Do I have to?"

Johansson shrugged. "Somebody has to start. What's the problem?"

"Nothing." Eric got up, stepped to the front of the class and found the file on his phone. There was only silence at first, and then *Oh fuck, somebody help me! Can somebody hear me? Fuck! Help! Somebody help me! Please! God, just…somebody, please hear me?*

Eric saw Mary curling her lips into a smile. Then Julien. Then, Johansson's stare.

"What on Earth is—"

"Sorry about the swearing," he explained, sheepishly. "I'm going to edit it. I just haven't found the right effect yet."

"Right effect?" Johansson's protest was lost under Joe's cries. "Turn it off right now."

Eric obeyed, hearing more stifled laughs. Julien was grinning at him like an idiot.

"Quiet," Johansson insisted. "*Quiet*, now!"

Eric replaced the phone in his pocket.

"I like to think I'm very...open-minded when it comes to the projects my students want to pursue, Eric." A pimple at the edge of Johansson's receding red hairline seemed to flare an angry shade of pink with his words, like it had been squeezed by invisible fingers. "So, I am going to give you one minute to explain before I confiscate that phone."

"What's to explain? It's a guy screaming."

"We all heard that."

"It's from some old movie. From the 80's, I think. I got it off the Internet," he said, giving Johansson an innocent shrug. "We're allowed to use stuff from online, aren't we?"

"The source is not what concerns me, Eric. It's the content, and *why*."

"Because it's fear. Raw, simple, and undiluted. I thought I could match that against something really beautiful, really complex."

To Eric's astonishment, Julien raised a hand.

"I'll remind you that you're very new here, Mister Davidson. What would you like to add?"

"Well," Julien cleared his throat. "I kind of agree with Eric. It's about fear, right? I mean, the screaming? The guy's scared of being alone. So maybe, like, if you put it against something really busy, like an opera or something? You know, something pretty."

"Exactly," Eric agreed. Somebody got it. Yay.

"Yeah, and then you've got this guy screaming. It's like he's thinking, 'I'm always surrounded by people, all this pretty stuff that everyone thinks is so great, going on around me, and I still feel totally alone.' To him, it's all just noise, you know? And he hates it. He needs help. Like, he's so lonely, and he's surrounded by people who just don't care. They won't even stop for him to let it out, and the screaming is like, what's always going on inside his head. What's scarier than that?"

Somebody really got it.

❖

"Good morning, Linda. Is Ms Wagner in?"

"She's in a meeting at the moment, Eric. Is it urgent?"

Sure enough, the principal's office was empty. Should he wait? Eric considered the urgency of the detention slip in his pocket before remembering who'd issued it. "Not really."

He left the office and trekked through the immaculately manicured guest gardens to the small, brick chapel they surrounded. A clearing in the plants allowed sunlight to stream in through the stained-glass windows at any time of day. The pebbled pathway scrunched under his shoes as he approached. The door was already open, just as it always was.

Father Scott Callahan, a tallish, well-groomed, all-American looking Catholic of twenty-eight with dark, parted hair, darker eyes, a strong jawline and just enough stubble to look good without seeming trendy, looked up as the sound of Eric's footsteps broke his concentration.

"Eric," he acknowledged, returning to his work. "We don't have an appointment, do we?"

"No." Eric paused. "I just came to talk, if that's okay?"

Callahan nodded, tossing him a bound pile of folders. "If you don't mind helping me file."

"Uh, sure." Eric scanned the folders. Student counselling records. "Father, is this allowed?" He turned back a corner of one file.

"I didn't tell you to look *inside* them, did I?"

"Sorry." Eric couldn't resist a smirk. Seniors. He knew all the names. Callum Alford, Felicity Turner. Toby Brooker's file was especially thick. That confirmed it. Fag.

"Why aren't you in class?"

"Spare."

"No, you haven't. It's line four, senior music."

"Johansson threw me out. It's nothing."

"Uh-huh."

As priests went, Callahan was pretty cool. He kept it short at assembly, and he didn't jaw out the kids for not joining in prayers. But Eric knew a few parents and teachers, Johansson included, who hadn't been too pleased with the appointment of such a liberal chaplain. Some hadn't been too keen on the whole Catholic thing, either. Eric knew at least three spots in the school where 'What's the difference between Callahan and JFK? A bullet.' had been scratched into the wall, most likely by grade niners echoing the outspoken bias of their parents.

"He didn't like my assignment," Eric explained. "Thought it was too, I don't know, shocking or whatever."

"May I?"

Eric pulled out his iPhone, unable to suffer Callahan's bemused smirk. The screams filled the space between them, and the man's face became critical. Thoughtful.

"Take it back to the beginning," Callahan requested. "Play it again."

Eric did, the room now deathly still as the priest listened.

"There's a lot of fear in that man's voice. A lot of pain, too."

"Pain?"

"Where did you get this?"

"It's from a movie or something. God bless the Internet, right?"

"Are you sure?" Callahan frowned at him. "It sounds live to me."

Eric felt his stomach sink. "It could have been, originally. But I found it online, so maybe it was recorded straight onto the MP3 or something. Like a sound effect?"

"Okay."

"I really don't know. Like I said, I found it online."

"I said, okay."

"Do you think I should change it?"

"No."

Eric put the player away, thanking Callahan with a silent nod.

"How's your mum?" the priest asked.

"Okay, I guess. In LA at the moment."

"Working?"

"Her agent had her up for a two-liner on *Real Housewives* or something. Maybe it was just a photo shoot. I wasn't paying attention."

"You don't approve of your mother's work?"

"She can do what she wants."

"Even if that means spending months away from you?"

Eric resisted an indignant snort.

"Do you miss her?"

What was he supposed to say? That he missed his mum terribly and didn't know how he'd cope without her? Talk about his feelings? Make up some bullshit story about his latest episode? How would the truth have sounded? That he felt great, and those little green pills could go fuck themselves? It sounded good in his head. Did Callahan even know he was on meds? Like it was any of his business.

"I'm fine," he answered.

"How're you getting on with the American film schools?" Callahan asked.

"I'm putting a folio together. There's a couple that look good. New York would be my first choice. LA's got a few, but everyone does LA. Actually, Vancouver's got this great—"

"What about staying at home? NIDA?"

"I'm applying to NIDA too, for safety."

"Safety? Gutsy, mate."

"What do you mean by that?"

"I just meant…no, forget it." Callahan grinned. "I have faith in you, Eric."

"Thanks."

"And don't write off LA. You'd make some great contacts, and your mum could—"

"Can we talk about something else besides my mother?"

A defeated Callahan shrugged as the end-of-period bell terminated their conversation. Eric put down the files, spotting Julien's name on one as he left.

Too late for a look inside.

"So, as we discussed in the last class, Shakespeare's plays can be divided into three broad categories."

Miss Harley's words barely registered as Eric watched Julien, positioned two desks to his left in drama class, just on the other side of Mary. Music, drama, advanced English…Credit where it was due. Julien took his acting ambition seriously. Seriously enough for his parents to entrust him to Christian Fellowship. It was, after all, the institution of choice for well-to-do North Shore god-botherers, or at least, the ones unwilling to entrust their semi-talented spawn to an actual arts school, where the possibility of an acceptable six-figure salary would be silenced forever.

"Who can tell me what those categories are?" Harley asked.

Eric raised a lazy hand while his mind wandered back to its frequent preoccupation with whether Miss Harley's hair was truly as black as it seemed, or if the colour was a desperate attempt to cover a premature but inevitable strand of grey.

"Eric?"

"Histories, comedies, and tragedies." He decided the colour was probably artificial. It just seemed too glossy, somehow. Nobody had black hair that picked up that much light naturally. Joe's hair was pretty dark, though Eric hadn't seen it in the light since he'd clobbered the man unconscious in his kitchen, and even that moment had become a hazy memory.

"Excellent. So keep those categories in mind when you choose a play from the list."

Eric wondered which play would best match each of his classmates. *Macbeth*, starring Nerida White, la goth chick du freak. *That* black hair was definitely fake.

He raised an eyebrow as *Othello* went up on the board. Interesting choice, given no one in the class was black.

"History, comedy or tragedy?" Harley asked.

The question fell on apathetic silence until…

"Comedy?" Eric offered, trying to keep the sarcasm from his voice.

Harley shot him a deadpan look. "I assume that's a joke?"

"Depends on how you look at it. The guy gets tricked into killing his wife when she's really the only person in the world who's loyal to him."

"And you think that's funny?"

"The whole play is built on irony. Iago dearly loves Othello, but because he feels that love's been betrayed, he sets Othello up for the fall, and he does it through charm and honest observation. It's like he's hiding his agenda in plain sight, and he gets away with it right up to the end. From that perspective, in its own way, it's funny."

Harley tapped a long red nail against her desk as she considered his opinion, staring at him with piercing grey eyes as though he'd just called her out on the fake hair colour. "Has anyone else read or seen *Othello*?"

"I saw it once." Felicity Turner pushed a tress of long blonde hair away from her face, her gaze shifting uncomfortably between Eric and Harley. "I didn't think it was funny. I thought it was sad."

"It's black comedy," Eric explained.

"Because the guy's black? That's racist."

"Oh Jesus, grow a brain cell!"

"Okay, that's enough!"

He grimaced as *Hamlet* and *The Merchant of Venice* went up on the board. Grade nine stuff. Shakespeare's greatest clichés.

"You'd make a great Iago," Mary whispered to him.

Eric wasn't sure how to take that, particularly from his girlfriend. *Romeo and Juliet* went up on the board.

"God, kill me now."

"You don't approve, Eric?" Harley turned to face him with a gracefully raised eyebrow.

It wasn't just Harley, either. He started to regret sitting so close to the centre of the room as each pair of eyes turned, fixing on him with a sense of expectation he was in no mood to fulfill. He had to say something. Hell, why not *Othello*? But would that look too flippant? Would Harley think he was joking? Ugh. Would he wind up as Iago?

"No?" the teacher probed.

"*Titus*," Eric murmured.

"What was that?"

He looked her full in the face, polite but determined, as though the conversation had somehow charged him to now serve as defender of all things violently and joyfully perverse. "*Titus Andronicus*. It's not performed very often. It'd be great."

Harley took a deep breath, curling her lips in a smile. "That's not one of Shakespeare's more popular plays."

"Call it a cult classic?"

"So is *A Clockwork Orange*. The point being, I don't think *Titus* is an appropriate text for a high school production. It's not on the syllabus, and it's not considered one of Shakespeare's better plays to begin with."

"What's it about?" Julien asked.

"I'd be happy to discuss it another time, Jul—"

"Politics, revenge, rape, and cannibalism," Eric answered.

"Awesome!"

Harley was staring at him now, going slightly red around the dimples. "Eric, can I talk to you for a minute?"

With an obedient nod, he followed her outside and shut the door behind them.

"If you're doing this just for shock value, you'd better tell me now."

Eric tried to remember what he'd been thinking, first about *Othello*, how much he didn't want to play Iago, and then…"I just think it's kind of underrated. It'd be cool to see."

"Eric, I haven't seen a production of *Titus* in over ten years."

"That's my point. When are we going to get another chance?"

"Might I remind you that not everyone in this school or the general public shares your love of horror movies? That is what you're talking about doing. Shakespeare's horror story."

Shakespeare's horror story? Maybe that was enough. "Isn't that the point of good art? To get people talking?"

Harley crossed her arms, catching sight of Johansson across the quad. "I'll think about it," she muttered.

Chapter Four

Eric shifted uneasily, only now realising that his backside had gone numb from sitting on the stairs watching Julien, who'd just ditched Darren Worheimer and was now talking to Mary. Eric furrowed his brow almost subconsciously as his host, Nerida, kept talking.

"And like I said, I really respected what you did today, man. Was very cool."

"Yeah, thanks," he murmured.

Mary was still talking to Julien. Why was she talking to him? He'd never seen them talk at school. Nerida's parents had a thing for bonsai. Everywhere. He couldn't move for bonsai.

"I mean, I love acting," Nerida continued, "but when I see a play, I want to feel something, you know? I don't want to just choke on whatever crap somebody else thinks I should see just because they're getting some big kickback on it. I want to feel repulsed, like my flesh is being ripped open. Real intense. I get that from plays like *Titus*, man. And the Greek tragedies? They're all, like—"

"But you're not a cutter," he said. "You're real Goth. No scars on you, baby."

Mary looked ready to deep-throat the Bacardi bottle. Julien was laughing. Don't laugh at her, you bastard.

"Damn straight. So when you said 'let's do *Titus*,' I thought, 'Shit, yeah, that'd be cool. Totally different.' I read it about a year ago, right? And it was like, I couldn't stop, man. All done in one sitting. Boom."

Mary was laughing at Julien. Eric wished she wouldn't encourage him.

"Violence is an important part of who people are, you know? It's why I think people are still hard for Shakespeare. He really got what people are like. And you know what I think it is? He's writing for himself, but about us. About the people he saw. He didn't care about profit or sales or any of that shit they worry about now, and he didn't care who he pissed off."

"They? Who's they?"

"He wanted to understand people. Human beings."

"Probably. Give me the joint."

Nerida passed it to him. "That's why people still get off on him so much now. Human beings don't change, and they want to be understood. They long for that. They just want honest stories that really get them."

"Touch them?" he asked, inhaling long and passing the joint back.

"Yeah! Hurt them, even."

"Bite them."

"Consume them."

"Swallow them up."

"Tear their miserable guts apart because it's real. That's what I want to see."

"To rip your audience open? Force them to see what's inside? Do you write, Nerida?"

"Where are the playwrights who'll do that today, man?"

Eric saw Mary smile at him as Julien kept talking at her. "Think you could tear someone's insides apart with a bonsai? Even sew it back up inside them?"

"Nowhere is where!"

"Hypothetically, of course."

"They're all too busy doing this feel-good, post-modern, self-aware bullshit!"

"Do you *write*, Nerida? Like, poetry or about your cat or your parents in Iceland or wherever they are now?"

"I have a blog."

"Yeah. Excuse me."

"Where you going?"

"I have to go talk to a bunny." Eric got up off the stair and half-walked, half-wobbled his way into the kitchen for another Stoli.

"Bring me eggs," Nerida called.

❖

The fridge was empty, except for enough beer, wine, coolers, and post-mix to drop a small herd of elephants. The Stolis had somehow let themselves be pushed right to the back. To Eric, this could have indicated several things, including the fading popularity of vodka as a spirit of choice for the Australian youth market, possibly representing the cultural disconnection of Australia from Eastern and Northern Europe as a whole, or that he was the only one drinking them.

He also wondered what sort of drinks waiter Joe might make if he was tidied up a bit and dressed in a tux. Assuming, of course, that he could get Joe to shut up and accept his situation for an hour or two. The sensation of Toby Brooker's pelvis bumping against his backside did nothing to help his concentration.

"What can I get you, Toby?"

"Nothing."

"Then stop dry humping me."

"I wasn't. Geez!"

Eric pushed aside a Corona to reveal two remaining Stolis. He took one and twisted off the lid. Toby hadn't moved. Eric put an arm around the boy's waist, slid a hand inside the back of his jeans and nuzzled his neck. "You're not my type, sweetheart," he purred, laughing as Toby pushed him away.

"Jesus, Eric! I've got a girlfriend, okay? And you're drunk."

"I've only had two."

"Hey, *Titus* man!"

"Fuck off, Julien," Eric muttered, sipping his Stoli.

"That was awesome today, dude. I mean, in Music. Johansson's face was priceless!"

"You're welcome. Now please, go away." Eric wondered why he came to these parties. Maybe because people only knew your name if you showed up at as many as possible. Yeah, right. Nobody was using his name, except for Toby.

"I didn't know you and Mary were...you know."

"If I tell you we're going out, will you stop trying to fuck her?"

"If I stay here and talk to you, will you stop being such a hostile dickhead?"

Eric said nothing. His nerves tingled, as though Julien had just slapped him across the head.

"I have ears, dude, and you keep giving me dirty looks. You pissed off the fag and—"

"See? I'm not the only one who knows!" Eric called after Toby, who either ignored or didn't hear him.

"Now you won't even talk to me?"

Eric shrugged. "We can talk. Is that bonsai on the table getting bigger, or am I stoned?"

"Stoned?" Julien frowned. "You got some?"

"Nerida," he explained.

"Anyway, how'd you do that today? Get everyone to want to do your play?"

Eric smiled at him. They had Miss Harley to thank for that. Shakespeare's horror story? The pitch had practically written itself. "It's not my play. It's Shakespeare's."

"I guess," Julien said. "I'm just amazed that you managed to win people over like that."

"Why?"

"Okay, dude, don't take this the wrong way. You can be kind of a cu—"

"Watch it."

"Just being honest."

"No, I mean it." Eric glowered at Julien from under his thick eyebrows. "You can be honest. Call me whatever you want. I don't care. But do *not* use the 'c' word with me. You got that?"

"Uh, yeah, I guess. Okay."

"It's common. Thuggish."

"All right! Sorry, man."

"It's fine."

"All I mean is that you don't seem to like people much. It's like you're in this character *all* the time."

Eric took another drink. "You're okay. If that's what you mean."

"Sure. So why do I get the idea you're waiting for the other shoe with me?"

"Because you show promise, and I'm used to being disappointed. And who put on Kings of fucking Leon? Hey, Nerida?"

"Yeah?"

"Got anything a bit more indie?"

"Like who?"

"If I knew their names, they wouldn't be indie, would they?"

"Oh hah, hah! Will somebody just kill this bogan crap please?" Nerida snarled at nobody in particular. "Shit! My joint's gone out. *Darren!*"

"Tell the whole world, Nerida," Eric mumbled as the sound of Robyn filled the room. "That'll do."

"You're welcome," Toby sneered as he put the remote down and went back to his semi-discreet ogling of Julien's backside. Eric decided not to mention it. He owed Toby that much.

"Hipster, eh?" Julien asked.

"Pfft. Whatever."

"So what do you mean, I show *promise*?"

"Not sure," Eric said with a shrug. "Wrong word. Forget I said it."

Julien greeted Felicity Turner with a wide smile as their eyes met.

Eric shook his head. "Don't go there."

"Huh?"

"Turner. Do *not* go there."

"What? You're not with her too, are you?"

"No! Oh, look, on second thought? I don't care. Do what you want."

"What I *want* is to get to know you, if you'll let me," Julien slammed his beer down on the kitchen bench. "I thought if we were doing projects and stuff together, we could become mates. But you know what? Fuck it. And fuck you! Have a good one, Eric. Try not to kick any puppies on your way home." Julien picked up his beer and took a few steps toward Felicity.

"It's because deep down in every theatre snob there's a twelve-year-old watching all that blood and guts thinking 'shit man, that's cool!'" Eric said before he got away.

There was silence between them as Julien stopped and shook his head. "Huh? What the hell are you—"

"*Titus*. You wanted to know why everyone wanted to do it? Sometimes people just want to let go, lose themselves to sex and violence. And the fact that it's Shakespeare makes it all seem okay. Makes it feel cultural."

Julien nodded slowly, taking another sip of his beer. "I guess."

"How's it going, guys?"

Mary. Eric had almost forgotten she was there.

"Where've you been?" he asked.

"Getting supplies," she grinned, offering him a joint.

He took it gratefully and toked. It was fresher than Nerida's, or maybe the vodka was helping. He passed it to Julien. It seemed polite.

"Awesome," Julien took a puff, followed by more beer, then another toke before handing the joint back to Mary. "Even if it's a week at the gym fucked."

"Which gym?" Eric asked.

"FitForce, St Leonards."

Eric smiled and nodded. Okay. Just don't—

"Oh cool. Do you see Eric there?" Mary chirped.

Damn it.

"No. You go often?" Julien dabbed his tongue across his lips as he spoke. He looked like some slobbering dog. It was kind of endearing, in its way. Eric wondered if Margaret owned a spare collar. No, that was a very bad idea.

"Just weekends," Eric mumbled. "Kind of depends."

"More like four times a week!" Mary giggled. Eric hated it when she giggled. It didn't suit her. It sounded forced.

"Hey, great. I've been looking for a workout buddy. If you're interested, I mean."

Eric fought so hard not to roll his eyes, they practically ached inside his skull. "You're pretty fit. I'm not sure I'd be able to keep up with you."

"Don't be silly, man. You're in great shape. Besides, don't you want to see if I'm worth hanging out with? I show 'promise,' right?"

"You actually said that?" Mary's giggling had evolved into a cackle now, which was worse.

"Maybe," Eric muttered.

"Eric that is...so...so you."

"Thanks."

"How about Monday afternoon? You got anything else on?"

Eric shrugged. "Okay, I guess." What the hell? He was bored with the gym anyway. Having a workout buddy couldn't make it any worse.

"Great. After school then? Hey, I gotta piss. Watch my beer, okay?" Julien walked off before either of them could protest.

Mary put her arms up around Eric's shoulders. "You made friends with the new guy, Eric? *You?*"

"It's not that weird," he growled. He took an egg from the fridge and handed it to Nerida.

"I asked for eggs, plural," she called.

Eric didn't hear.

CHAPTER FIVE

Eric watched Mary silently count the houses they passed as the cab drove along his street.

"There's thirteen," he said.

She looked back at him and smiled. "Is that weird? Counting, I mean."

"Not that weird, I don't think."

"Anywhere here?" The cab driver flicked on the inside light.

"Yeah, I guess." Eric squeezed Mary's hand.

"You sure you don't want me to come in for a bit?" She squeezed back, smiling at him with her eyes, though her mouth didn't follow.

"It's not really..." he began. "Are you gonna be okay?"

"I know where I live," she replied with a shrug.

Eric suddenly felt foolish and took out his wallet.

"Thirty-three sixty," the driver mumbled.

"Come in for a bit. It's fine. Sorry, I'm a bit wasted." Eric ignored the driver's smirk in the rear-view mirror as he handed over the money.

"If you say—" she began.

"I do say. I'll call you another cab."

Joe had to be asleep. Or else he must have shouted himself dry by now. Mary wouldn't be there long, even if he asked her to stay. They got out of the cab in silence, the effects of alcohol wearing off as they gratefully swallowed the delicious night air.

"Come here," he whispered.

Mary stood still, watching him as he stepped behind her and put his arms around her pale, milky shoulders. Then, very slowly, they began the walk back to his house, in step together. One…two…one…like a slow waltz, as they neared his illuminated porch.

"Hey, watch my feet," Mary laughed as a wave of pot-induced nausea threw Eric off his balance.

He wrapped his hands around hers, intertwining their fingers as they held their arms outstretched and continued the stagger forward. "Grrrr…"

"Grrrr!" she replied, grinning.

"Grrrrrrarrrr!"

"Grrraarrr…braaaaaaains!"

"Braaaaaains!"

"*Braaaaiiiinnnnsss!*"

"*Braaaaains!*" Eric moaned. "Been to high school party—need braaaaaiins."

Mary broke apart from him, doubling over as she laughed.

"Exposed to jock! Need help!" He kept shambling toward her, arms outstretched, grabbing at the empty air. "Send braaaaainsssss!"

"Eric, that's mean!" Mary wheezed out between laughing fits. "Julien's just trying to be nice to you."

Eric shrugged, lowering his arms as he grinned at her. "He's okay."

She grabbed him in a hug before taking his hand and leading him up the steps to the porch. He held up a finger to hush her as he fumbled with the keys. Ugh, they all looked the same when he was stoned.

"Oooh, pretty things!" Mary cooed.

"You're drunk."

"I…am…not…woof!"

"Woof? I think you're pissed."

"Eric, I'll have you know I am in full command of ol' my fuggleties."

"Okay, now you're just trying to stir me."

"Is it working?"

"You always stir me," he smirked.

❖

Eric set the keys gently down on the sideboard before falling lengthways onto the couch. The room spun as he adjusted to his new sideways view of the world. His ears were ringing, too.

Joe…Joe was still downstairs.

He'd almost forgotten. Why had he brought Mary back here? Why tonight? Why drunk and stoned? Why did he endure that radio troll, Barry Weblock's bitter rage against the left-wing machine from ten past six every fucking morning? Why had Madonna swiped her babies from Malawi and not Cambodia? Did she think a Khmer adoption would look too trendy, or were her lips just too small after Angelina had set such unrealistic expectations?

"Got any red?"

Eric squinted against the light of the fridge, peering out from behind the outline of Mary's behind as she rummaged for a Shiraz, Pinot, or something similarly un-Merlotish.

"Not in the fridge," he mumbled. "Nothing open." His mind raced. He couldn't do this tonight. He had to get rid of her but not let her think she was being gotten rid of. Careful, slow, meticulous, relaxed.

"It's cool, found some!" Mary held up the bottle with pride.

Eric groaned and fell back into the couch, holding a pillow over his face. "That's Glogg."

"Glogg?"

"It's Swedish stuff. You mix it with…whatever, or straight or…" Fuck, no more alcohol. No more pot. Not now. Not ever.

Mary uncorked the bottle and sniffed the top, recoiling as the spicy aroma escaped into the kitchen. "Interesting," she took a swig straight from the bottle. "It's okay, I guess."

When Eric ripped away the pillow, she was standing over him, one knee pressed against his body on the couch, grasping the bottle neck in one hand.

"What the hell?"

"What?"

He tossed the pillow away and let her fall into his arms. She took another swig of Glogg as she collapsed into him and kissed his cheek. Eric held her tight against him, running his fingers through her long, mousy hair, down over her shoulder and the crook of her arm, past her modest breasts before settling on her svelte waist, pulling her even closer. She grinned with satisfaction.

"Did you have fun tonight?" she asked.

"Yeah, I guess."

"Good." She nestled deeper into his chest, kissing it through his shirt. "I sometimes worry that you don't have any fun."

"I have fun." He brushed her hair with smooth, even strokes. "I thought your dad didn't believe in fun."

"Ugh."

"Sorry."

"Can we not bring him up?"

Eric smiled, not forcing the issue as they lay there, cuddling in silence.

"I just feel," she finally said, "so happy right now. Dad doesn't believe in any happiness that doesn't come by the way of Hail Mary."

"And good ol' Jaysus."

"He died for your sins, Eric."

"But he rose for your *braaaaaaainns!!!*"

Mary dropped the Glogg bottle to the wooden floor with a loud clunk and snorted against Eric's chest. He stared at her, incredulous for a moment as she rolled off him and fell off the couch.

"You haven't heard that before?" Eric shrugged. "It's kind of old…"

She smiled at him from the floor, leaning back on her hands.

"What?"

"Have you…you ever thought what you want to do? With me, I mean."

He knew what she meant, of course. It was something he'd thought about every so often. Maybe more in the last year. It had been curiosity, mostly. "I just figured when you were ready, you'd tell me."

She frowned at him, almost offended as she crossed her ankles. "Are you saying I'm the one who needs to be ready?"

"No. Not necessarily," he corrected. "I just don't want to rush into anything." Rush? He couldn't think of another couple in school who'd lasted longer than a year.

Mary uncrossed her legs and brought her knees up to her chin, resting her head on them as she stared right back, her head tilted like an owl sizing up its prey. "I think I'm ready."

Eric swallowed, hoping he'd given her an understanding nod, though in his gut, he knew his head hadn't moved. "Yeah? Are you sure you want to do it now?"

"If you want to wait, I'm okay with that, too."

He suppressed a groan, rolling over onto his back and staring at the ceiling.

"What's wrong?" she demanded.

"Nothing, just…" He didn't want to tell her she was making him feel guilty. He'd had sex before, heaps of times. But this was Mary, and he didn't feel anything. And he didn't know why. Too drunk, too much pot, too much Joe. He heard a low moan.

"You got a ghost?" Mary asked.

Eric scrambled to his feet, trying to steady himself against the couch as he fought the natural lean of his body, which allied itself with gravity and inertia to pull him rapidly toward the floor. This had been a terrible idea. He didn't know what to say. Had Joe even made a sound? He had to be imagining this.

"Eric?" Mary prodded him again. "What's that noise?"

"I don't know."

"Is it…where is it?"

Joe moaned again. Eric lifted a foot to stomp on the floor before realising that this too, would be a terrible idea. "Next door," he lied.

"Oh my God," Mary whispered.

"Help…is somebody there? Can somebody hear me?" Joe said.

"Maybe we should call the cops. Do you think?"

"No!" Eric snapped. "No cops! We're both still high."

"What if the guy's hurt?"

"He's not hurt."

"How do you know?"

❖

As Joe's cries continued, Eric waited for a flickering eyelid, a shaking head, any recoil or sign of disapproval, but none came.

Mary just stared at him, waiting. The click of the door was so loud he wondered, in his drunken state, if he'd somehow shattered the lock.

"Hey!" Joe yelled. "Who's th—"

Eric darted across the room and clamped a hand tight over the man's mouth. Joe kept moaning, struggling and thrashing. Eric put a free arm around his captive's head and tried to hold him still. "Quiet," he hissed. "Just be quiet!"

"Oh my god."

Eric looked up at her in desperation. He couldn't hold Joe much longer. He felt the first beads of sweat form under his fringe as he tried to tighten his grip.

"Tape," he called.

"What?"

"Tape! Get me some tape! Kitchen drawers, second one down. Quick!"

"Eric—"

"Just get it!"

Eric felt Joe trying to force his jaws apart as Mary fled the room. He clamped down harder. The gentle thud of Mary's footsteps softened as she climbed the stairs. She was coming back. She wouldn't run. He was sure of that. He couldn't hold this vicious fuck much longer. He felt Joe's spittle as the man tried to bite his hand. A blessed relief surged through him as Mary's footsteps hit the stairs again.

"Give it here," he beckoned.

Mary shook her head as she neared his captive, electrical tape in hand. "Just hold him." She opened a strip of tape and broke it off with her teeth. "Move your hand."

"Huh?"

"Just move."

Eric let go of Joe and backed away.

❖

A fearful sweat poured from Joe's brow as he shook. "P—pl—please, don't—don't cover my mouth again. Please?"

"Shhhh," Mary hushed him quiet, holding the tape carefully in one hand as she brushed tears off his cheek

"Be careful with him."

"Please," Joe whimpered again.

Mary looked the man up and down with a curiosity Eric wasn't sure he liked. "Eric, he's so much bigger than you."

"He was in the house when I got home from school the other day. I hit him on the head with a wok," he answered truthfully.

Mary gave him a bewildered look before turning her attention back to Joe. "What's your name?"

"Joe," Eric said before his captive could answer. "I'm calling him Joe."

"Why Joe?"

"I..." the man choked out. "I need to, oh, God, shit!"

"What?" But Eric knew as soon as the acrid smell hit the air, along with a faint trickling sound. "Oh, shit, no. Shit, shit!"

"Eric, did your friend just piss himself?"

"Yes."

"It's been three days!" Joe snarled. "What the fuck am I supposed to do?"

"Three days?"

"Hey, you try taking this guy to the bathroom, then tying him up again. It's a big deal!"

"You've had him here for three days?"

Eric hesitated, leaning against a wall as if waiting for Joe to answer.

"Eric!"

"Nine," he admitted. "He's been here nine days."

"He hasn't pissed in *nine days?*"

"No, I've been...look, we need to get him cleaned up," Eric muttered.

Joe must have urinated like a racehorse. The theatre room was starting to smell like cats.

"Go back upstairs," Eric instructed. "In the third kitchen drawer, get two big knives and the blindfold that's in there."

"Blindfold?"

"Hurry up."

Again, he heard the sound of Mary's feet disappear up the stairs.

Joe stared at him warily. "She's right," he muttered. "Why Joe?"

"Because I said so."

"Coz you're a shit head?"

Eric balled his hand into a fist and slogged Joe hard across the jaw.

"Because I said so."

❖

Mary took a step back, her knife still trained on Joe as he straightened his legs and stood up to full height. The man's hands were free, though both ankles were still bound to the chair that had held him prisoner.

Eric coiled the ropes around Joe's wrists once more, lashing them together behind his back. Only then did he free his captive's ankles.

Mary pressed the tip of the knife against the top of Joe's stomach.

"Careful," Eric murmured. "If he bleeds to death, it's not a good look."

"I guess."

Eric picked up his knife, and they escorted Joe upstairs to the guest bathroom, finally untying the man's bonds.

"Get undressed," he ordered.

"What?"

"Do you shower with clothes on? Lose them."

"He doesn't seem very bright," Mary said. Before either Eric or Joe could move, she stepped forward and grabbed hold of Joe's flimsy cotton T-shirt, slitting it from bottom to top with her knife.

"Hey, what are you do—" Joe cried out.

"Shhhh." She slowly circled him and tore the ruined shirt off his back.

Eric looked Joe up and down. Mary was right. The man was considerably bigger than him, broad across the shoulders and solidly built too. He'd been lucky. Really lucky.

"You'll cut him if you try that on the jeans," he cautioned her.

"Probably."

Joe immediately opened his belt buckle and slid them off, fumbling over his shoes as he finished stripping. He tossed the stinking jeans aside, slowly removed his shoes, then reached for the blindfold.

"Leave it," Eric instructed.

Mary pulled back the shower screen and set the water running, taking Joe by the arm as she helped him step in.

"Have you considered a career in nursing?" Eric asked.

She flashed an angry look at him before storming out of the bathroom. Eric didn't know why. He took one final look at Joe, and then he followed her out.

❖

"What were you thinking?" Mary asked as the water stopped.

Eric hadn't thought this far ahead. He certainly hadn't thought he'd ever share his predicament with anyone, much less Mary. "Sociological experiment?"

Mary shook her head, squeezing her eyes tightly, like she was trying to block some horrible realisation.

"Don't do that. It'll be okay."

"Oh for fuck's sake, Eric. It is *not* okay, okay? What part of this is anyone supposed to think is *okay*? What? You keep him here? In the house, where you live? Where you sleep? What if he gets loose, Eric?"

"He won't."

"What. If. He. Does? You're fucked then, probably dead!" She took out a joint and lit it.

"I'll be fine. I can hand…What are you doing?"

"My best not to freak out," she mumbled, offering it to him.

Eric didn't need more pot, not with Joe loose. Not until the guy was safely tied up again. He took the joint anyway.

"Maybe it'll stimulate your imagination," she said. "Work out what to do with him."

"Sure it will."

They tightened their hands around the knives as the bathroom door opened a crack. Eric steadily got to his feet, passing the joint back to Mary as he exhaled, blowing grey smoke toward the opening door.

"Dude," a voice rumbled from inside. "There's no towels in here."

Towels? He wanted *towels*? Eric nearly choked on his own laughter.

Mary smirked as she took another puff of her joint.

"What's so funny?" Joe demanded, throwing open the door and standing, dripping wet and naked in the doorway like some underwhelming, red-faced colossus as they laughed at him.

"Nothing. Hey, hey, where's your blindfold?" Eric flicked the knife at Joe accusingly.

"Leave it," Mary grinned, "he has pretty eyes."

"What's that got to do with anything?"

"Well, he does."

Eric had to admit, Joe did have pretty eyes, in that Middle-Eastern sort of way. They looked scared.

He flicked the knife at Joe again. "Come on."

"You're not putting me back in that room?"

"Where else?"

"Eric, are they all that big?" Mary enquired.

"Huh?"

"His dick. I'm just asking."

Joe hurriedly lowered his hands to cover himself, but another flick of the knife, from Mary this time, forced them back up to their position of surrender, exposing his manhood for her inspection.

"I'm not really an expert," Eric mumbled.

"You've seen more than me. Are they all that big?"

"I don't think so."

"Is yours?"

"We're not talking about this now."

Mary took another puff of her joint. "Do you want some?" she asked Joe.

"Uh, no, thanks."

"Have some!" Another flick of the knife. Mary seemed to take odd pleasure in the elegance of it, the fluidity.

Joe grabbed the joint, which shook in his hand as he puffed at it.

"Keep going," she ordered.

"Mary," Eric cautioned.

"I said, keep going!"

Joe let out a violent cough as he forced the joint away from his lips. White smoke clouded around them.

"What are you doing?" Eric asked.

"I want him to pass out."

"Why?"

Mary wrapped an arm around Eric's neck, mauling him with wet kisses around his cheeks, chin, and throat. "Because I want it to be tonight, Eric. I want you to be part of me."

"Okay." Eric eased her away, careful to keep a knife trained on Joe. The man didn't move. He just watched their clumsy foreplay, wide-eyed, the joint still burning in his hand. "You want us to get the guy who broke into my house stoned enough to pass out?"

"Yes."

"So we can have sex?"

"Yes."

"No."

"No?"

"We're going to take him back downstairs, tie him up and—"

"No!" she snapped, pulling away from him. She seemed to be studying Joe now with a curious mix of sympathy and fascination. "I want him to watch. No, actually I want him with us."

"No way!" Eric couldn't tell if the wetness of Joe's brow was from the shower or nervous sweat.

"Eric, it's what I want!" Mary screamed, pushing at him.

Eric backed off to avoid the knife. "You're stoned! How do you know what you want?"

Mary steadied her breath as her eyes moved between Eric and Joe. "Kiss him," she murmured.

"Huh? Fuck off!" Joe cried.

"Smart boys don't tell the nice lady holding the knife to 'fuck off,'" she growled.

"Mary…" Eric said quietly, hoping his tone would connect with some half-sober level of reason inside her.

It did. Stepping back, Mary put her knife down on the floor where they could both see it. "Please? Kiss him."

"I don't think that's a good idea."

Joe backed away from them, vehemently shaking his head.

Mary folded her arms. "Then, I will."

"No."

"Eric! I'll do what I want."

Before either of the boys could move, she put an arm around Joe's neck and pulled him in to kiss her. Joe tried to pull away. "Dude, will you get your psycho girlfriend off me?"

"You do as you're told!" Eric gave the knife another angry flick in Joe's direction.

The man surrendered and met Mary's lips. Eric watched as she explored their captive's body, running her hands over his darkly tanned shoulders, chest and back, down his muscular stomach until she grabbed the shaft of his now erect cock.

"That's enough," Eric muttered, taking hold of Mary's arm.

She looked up at him, her eyes earnest and inviting as she caressed the curve of his hip. Joe grimaced as she tightened the hand that still gripped his penis. Eric kissed her, but it was a gentle brush over the lips. Not the deep, open exchange her kiss with Joe had been.

"Come on," she invited. "Please?"

CHAPTER SIX

Eric couldn't remember how Joe had ended up in his bed. Or Mary, for that matter. He clapped a hand over Joe's mouth, careful not to disturb Mary as he hauled the man out into the living room.

Joe hesitated as they passed the kitchen, but Eric was ready for that, grabbing a knife from the drawer. The man stared down at him like some predatory bird, thinking twice about whether the poised cobra it had hoped to make a meal of was worth the effort.

The theatre room didn't stink as much now. Eric made Joe move the chair to a dry area before tying him in it. Just to be safe, he picked up the electrical tape that had been left on the floor.

"Oh, fuck, man, don't…"

Eric taped Joe's mouth shut and left. He checked on Mary once more, then collected disinfectant and deodoriser from the kitchen.

Joe begged with his eyes. Eric hated that. But the man had stayed there all night. He hadn't run off. He also hadn't hurt Mary. At least, not that Eric could see.

"If I untape your mouth," Eric bargained, "you're gonna be quiet. No screaming, no moaning. I'll even let you talk, but quietly. Understood?"

Joe nodded, his movements as clamorous as his mute state would allow. Eric cautiously grasped the edge of the tape, tearing it off in one swift motion as Joe recoiled in pain.

"Are you okay?" Eric asked.

Joe was panting. "Yeah, I guess."

Eric sprayed the still wet patch of carpet with a generous mist of disinfectant. He felt Joe following him with his stare. It was annoying, like the faint smell of piss that still pervaded the room. He held up the bottle of disinfectant, aiming it directly at Joe's eyes.

"Hey! What are you doing, man?"

"I want you to answer me truthfully," Eric muttered. "Did you fuck her?"

Joe's entire body shook in the chair as he tried to jerk his head away. But Eric kept the nozzle trained on its mark.

"Did you fuck her?"

"No…no, I—"

Eric discharged the spray, sending it an inch wide of Joe's eye. Joe still winced.

"Did you fuck her?"

"Yes!" Joe sobbed. "I mean, yeah. I don't know, but I think so, yeah."

"*You don't know?*" Eric screamed. "*Did you or didn't you?*"

"I'm sorry, okay? She wanted it. You heard her! I only did what she wanted!"

Eric lowered the disinfectant, instead spraying deodoriser around the room.

Joe coughed as some of it fogged around his head. The door slammed, and the room returned to inky blackness.

Eric's phone was like a siren, tearing into the fragile tissue of his brain as it rang. He face-planted into a puddle of his own congealed drool, clamouring over the couch to try and grab the handset only to realise he'd grabbed the landline, and that the ringing was coming from his mobile.

"Yeah?" he sniffed.

"Eric?"

"Yeah?"

"*Eric!*"

"Fuck! I said 'yeah.' What do you want? What time is it?"

"It's after ten, dickhead."

"Who the hell is this?"

"It's Julien."

Eric couldn't speak for a moment. His throat was dry. "Oh, right. Julien. Sorry. Kinda hung over."

"Hahaha, yeah, tell me about it! Crazy night, man. You had fun though, right?"

Eric felt like his stomach was imploding, almost heaving up the remnants of his vodka binge as he forced himself to sit up.

"Hey dude, you there?"

"Yeah…last night…" he stammered. "Look, Julien this really isn't—"

"Haha, yeah. Was mad shit, eh? Listen, can you do me a couple of favours? Do you have Felicity Turner's number?"

"Huh?"

"Turner! Felicity Turner. Hot chick from drama, likes *Romeo and Juliet* and stuff, you know?"

"I know who she is," Eric growled. "Look, this isn't a good—"

"We talked for a bit last night at Nerida's, but I forgot to get her number. Don't suppose you've got it?"

"Who? Me?"

"No, the other eight guys I've got on conference call. Of course, you!"

Eric groaned as he collapsed back into the couch. "No, I don't."

"No?"

"I don't have Nerida's number!"

"Okay, but do you have Felicity's?"

"Shit, I meant Felicity! I've got Nerida's…I think."

"Oh. So, wait. Do you have her number or don't you?"

"Look! Felicity Turner, I do not speak to! Felicity Turner's number, I do not have! Felicity Turner is not in my particular sphere of discourse! Are we now clear on this?" The silence on the line lasted for all of four seconds. Eric counted.

"Jesus, mate. Take a pill or something! Fuck!"

Eric sighed. "Sorry, I'm not having a good morning. I *have* got Nerida's number, if that'll help."

"Already got hers. She's pretty handy. Getting me some—"

"Yeah, she knows people."

"So?"

"So, what?"

"*Turner*, dude. Felicity—"

"Look, I think I've got her on Facebook," Eric said. "If not, she'll definitely be on Darren's."

"Sick, man. Thanks."

"What else can I do for you?"

"Huh?"

"You said a couple of favours?"

"Oh, yeah. Have you got a copy of that play?"

"What? *Titus*?"

"Yeah. I mean, I checked the library, but get this! I ask the chick at the counter, right? And she just looks at me like I was some kind of freak. She's never heard of it!"

"Had you?"

"Dude, that's not the point."

"All Shakespeare is in public domain," Eric moaned. "I'll introduce you to a friend of mine. You'll like her. Lady Google?" The jibe came out snarkier than he'd intended. Mary was right. Julien was only trying to be nice. "I'll text you a good link. You can download the complete works."

"Ah, shit. Was hoping you had a hard copy. Hate reading stuff off a screen, you know? I get headaches."

"I'm not sure it's what Shakespeare had in mind either," Eric admitted, staggering to his feet and checking on Mary. She was still asleep.

"Hey, do you want to come over tomorrow? After church, I mean. Chill out, go to the beaches? Or I could meet you in the city. Maybe pick up a copy of the play?"

Eric half-smiled. Perhaps he could introduce Julien to Margaret after all. No matter how many times you pushed him away, he'd bound right back up to you and start licking your hand. A chill-out day with Julien? Why not?

"I'd like that."

"Let's see, I'll be done by…oh shit. Can't do it, dude. Got stuff on all afternoon."

"Huh? Oh, I see."

"But we're still on for the gym after school on Monday, right?"

"I guess. Catch you then."

❖

Eric tried not to stare as he watched Mary eat the bacon he'd overcooked. He'd offered to start over fresh, but she'd refused. Now she was nibbling at it like a fish.

"I told you, I screwed it up. I can make you some more."

"And I told you it's fine. Don't worry." She smiled at him.

He'd avoided the subject of Joe, and what had happened through the night. He was delaying the inevitable, but it was a discussion he didn't want to hear aloud. "Are you okay?"

"Yes. I am completely okay, Eric. Did you clean up downstairs?"

"Yes." Eric looked down at the burnt crumbs of bacon and toast that littered his plate.

Mary smiled at him. "Are *you* okay?"

"Huh? Sure, why wouldn't I be?"

"You know you never made it to the bedroom, right? You passed out on the couch first. We stripped you off and set you up with a doona to make you more comfortable."

Eric shivered at the mention of it. "Did it hurt?"

"A little, when he first started. He was very gentle with me, Eric."

Joe hadn't struck him as the gentle type.

Mary shrugged. "It's not a big deal. Chastity is an overvalued commodity."

"Who said that?"

"You, after that abstinence workshop at school last year, remember?"

"*That* guy was a freak."

"Who's arguing?"

He sniffed away a laugh. He probably had said something like that. "I'm just sorry it wasn't me. I know you wanted it."

"I would have preferred you, but like I said, it's okay. You're not like, upset or anything?"

"Why?"

She shrugged again, swallowing down the last scrap of bacon.

Eric shook his head as he reached across the table and squeezed her hand. "I don't care what you do, or who you do it with. Just be safe, be happy, and come back to me."

She grinned at him, squeezing back. "So, you're not jealous?"

"Oh, right. Because that worked out so well for Othello! Please."

Mary's laughter turned to coughing as she inhaled orange juice up her nose.

He finally managed to return her smile. "Do you want to go and get some real coffee?"

"Hell, yes."

"So go get dressed."

Eric lifted the handset of his landline and started dialling her home number. Her mother's dull, conservative tones came back like a feminised, Australian take on Sam the Eagle.

Hello. Thank you for calling—

A sense of faint relief washed through him as the message droned on. The last thing he needed this morning was to talk directly to Mary's father.

As we are currently unavailable to take your call, please leave a message, and may God's peace be with you.

His mind went blank. What was he going to do? Get Mary to leave a message? 'Hi Dad. Giving up chastity for Lent and fucking my way through Easter?'

He hung up. God owed him some peace after the night he'd had.

Chapter Seven

According to the wise, time-seasoned, artistic counsel of Margaret, as told, lectured or ranted to Eric on numerous occasions over a near-empty glass of thin, coppery theatre wine, a budding actor had several key rules to follow in building a successful career. One was to know the damn lines. This, Margaret swore, was a far less obvious point than it seemed. Two, don't ever, *ever*, become 'a model slash actor,' unless you intended to slash your artistic credibility to pieces or be unofficially retired by age twenty-five. Three, audition for *everything* until somebody who matters knows your name. And four, never ever accept a supporting role while the lead is being waved in front of you.

In that moment, rule four was noisily burrowing its way through Eric's skull. Miss Harley wanted him to play Titus. His audition hadn't even been that good, had it? He'd done a cold read for Saturninus, only to have Harley insist he try one of Titus's monologues.

His mouth was hanging slightly open. The teacher stared at him with a mixture of pride and confusion, as if her student had just received an Oscar, which had somehow morphed into a rubber duck upon reaching his hands. Every word of Kafka he'd ever read suddenly made perfect sense.

"Why don't you want to play Titus, Eric?"

Dozens of excuses swarmed his mind. That he'd been half joking when he'd suggested *Titus* in the first place. That his natural resistance to being the centre of attention made him completely unsuitable for the part. Though if that was true, why had he even opened his mouth?

"I really don't think I'm the hero type."

"Titus doesn't really fit the hero archetype as we understand it," Harley said. "That's what makes him such a dynamic character. He makes some terrible decisions."

"I just don't think he's me." The walls seemed to be retreating, like the room was breathing now. Or laughing at him.

"Why not?" Julien butted in. "This was your idea."

Eric felt his breath return to normal. Nobody was laughing. It was just Julien, Mary and Harley, staring at him, waiting for an honest answer. Honesty, he could do. "I just don't like being the centre of attention."

"I thought you wanted to be a director?"

"So?"

"So, you'd better get used to being the centre of attention."

He couldn't argue that.

Harley frowned. "It's just that, as an actor—which, as long as you're in my class, is what you are—that doesn't leave much opportunity for passion. It'd be a shame to throw that away, especially in a play like *Titus*."

"And I totally get that. But it's just not me. Sorry."

The teacher nodded slowly as she flipped through notes, her mouth twisted to one side in a thoughtful grimace. "Do you at least have a preference? I need something to work with."

"Not really."

"Okay," she sighed. "Just so you know, it wasn't easy to get this project approved. The state uses a standardised curriculum. I had to call in some favours."

"I appreciate that. Saturninus, maybe?"

"Thank you." Harley noted it down. "Mary, you're up."

Eric smiled as he left the stage, squeezing Mary's hand as he passed her. 'Good luck' was bad luck, and 'break a leg' was just cheesy. All theatrical tradition aside, did telling his girlfriend to break a leg constitute a threat of domestic violence? He recognised a few lines as Mary started her audition, but the words were soon lost under his own thoughts. He folded his arms and sat down beside Julien.

"Dude…why?"

"Because I don't want it." What else did they want to know? It felt so stupid, explaining himself over and over.

"Gentlemen!" Harley snapped. "Sorry Mary, go on."

Eric refocused on Mary's audition. A cold read for Tamora, Queen of the Goths, lead villainess and alpha bitch goddess of revenge, trickery and carnage. The perfect opportunity for Mary to show what she could really do.

"Who'd you read for?" he asked Julien.

"What's his name? The black guy?"

Eric looked Julien's somewhat dark, but still far from black complexion up and down with a half-smirk. "I think you mean Aaron, the Moor."

"Yeah. That dude."

"The bad guy. The one boning Tamora."

"Huh?"

Eric stifled a laugh. "Did you actually read it?"

Julien shrugged. "Kinda."

"Google kinda, or Wikipedia kinda?"

"Youtube."

"Oh, for fuck's sake."

"I'll pretend I didn't hear that, boys." The teacher stared at the now silent Mary for ten, maybe twenty seconds before she spoke again.

Mary kept shifting her weight uncomfortably. Had her audition sucked? No, that was impossible. She was great.

"I'm going to be honest with you, and don't take this the wrong way," the teacher began.

That was Margaret's rule five. Honesty in the theatre was never your friend.

"I think you've got great stage presence, but I'm just not seeing Tamora. You're a little too…sweet."

Eric remembered the image of her with Joe. Tufts of his captive's hair gripped firm within her fingers. Joe's muffled chokes and moans.

"You want me to play Titus's daughter?" Mary guessed.

"Come down here for a minute."

Mary obediently hopped down from the stage as Eric and Julien drifted closer. Eric hadn't thought of her in the part, but it kind of made sense. To the rest of the class, she was quiet, demure even. Only he knew better.

"I want you to consider Lavinia, yes. If you want her, that is. I'm not going to force you. It's an intense part. You've read the play, I assume?"

"Yes."

"So what do you think?"

It was hard for Eric not to stare, especially when Mary kept glancing over at the two of them, like she was about to implicate them in something, though he couldn't say what. He just knew he didn't like it. It reminded him of the way she'd looked at him on Friday night.

"Can she take some time to think about it?" he asked.

"Eric, it's fine." Mary faced Harley, suddenly confident and full of purpose. "I'll do it on one condition. I want Eric and Julien to play Chiron and Demetrius."

"Tamora's sons? Why?"

"They're the only guys I trust to rape me."

Eric felt like all his senses had exploded at once, his brain syphoned out through his ears. On some level, his consciousness had taken refuge high above the theatre and now soared beyond reach, unable to hear Julien's sudden fit of coughing or Harley's bewildered, shallow breaths. It finally returned to Earth, waiting for the comforting revelation of a sick joke that didn't come.

"Mary," Harley began. "Do you understand what you just said?"

"Yes."

"That's…not funny."

"I'm not trying to be funny. Sorry. I didn't mean to sound so dramatic."

"It's a drama class," a low voice muttered from behind them.

"Wait your turn outside please, Darren!" Harley snapped.

The voice's owner disappeared again with what, to Eric, looked like a sneer.

"It's just that I read that scene," Mary explained. "If I'm going to do something that scary, it has to be with guys I know and trust." She smiled at Eric and Julien. "I trust you guys."

Harley crossed her arms, darting glances between the boys. "Well, you're our best choice for Lavinia so far. But are you two okay with this?"

Eric shrugged. "I suppose so."

"Julien?"

"Umm…"

Eric was sure Mary had caught Julien's eye somehow. The sly curling of her lips. Perhaps even a wink, unnoticed by Harley. Whatever. It had been enough.

"Sure. I mean there are no small parts, right? Just small actors?"

Great. Now the ring-in jock was spouting consolatory stage advice.

"Fine." Harley remained deadpan as she scribbled in her notebook. "I want you off book in a month."

"Easy." Mary regarded Eric with an odd, conspiratorial smile as they left the theatre.

He smiled back. Suddenly, he wanted to do this, wanted to play something so dangerous, so intimate with her, in front of everyone. Hell, he wanted to help her piss off her father.

"Thanks," she whispered.

"Happy to."

CHAPTER EIGHT

Eric gripped the handlebars tighter as the weightless pedals spun round. Faster and faster, until the bike's circuitry re-engaged and the resistance hit his legs. His heart rate still read zero. Was there a prize for being the fastest clinically dead man on two wheels?

"Do you want to try another bike?" Julien asked. "The one next to me's okay, there's just this weird click in the gears."

Eric snorted indignantly. FitForce, the hallmark of fitness club quality. "I think I'm good." He kept pedalling. A heart, he could do without.

"So, you do three times a week?" Julien asked.

"I try." Eric suppressed his cursing as the strap around the left pedal broke loose.

"Jesus, don't they test this stuff? We should say something."

Eric didn't see much point. He knew the staff would sooner model the latest cheap looking logo towels, beach bags, and sunglasses while sucking back protein shakes than fix the equipment. Getting upset wouldn't solve anything.

"Hey mate," Julien called to one of the trainers. "We've got some problems here."

"Yeah," the man half replied, spearing Julien with a defensive glare. "They know about that one. It's getting fixed, okay?"

The trainer was gone before Julien could continue.

"What a dick," Julien muttered.

"He's with a client. How long have you been coming here?"

Julien shrugged. "A month. The one I went to in Coffs was never like this. Same chain, too. They just seemed to care, you know?"

"In Coffs? Of course they cared. They'd be lucky to get two members through the door."

"It wasn't that bad, mate," Julien grumbled.

"This is the North Shore. If they restock the disinfectant sprays, that's a good day."

"It's bullshit."

"Yeah, you get used to that." Eric didn't bother refastening the strap on the pedal. The club had started to swarm with the after-work crowd. Two cardio queens mounted a couple of treadmills. Their conversation could be heard from the bikes in front. Eric tried not to listen in. Instead, he focused on the skinny, middle-aged guy with the shock of bleach-blonde hair, who'd just sat down at the nearest rower. Having claimed his machine, the man sat idle, nattering on his iPhone in a nasal, gravel-strained voice about his latest call-back for a proposed revival of *Hello Dolly*, though nothing was set in stone yet and did Viola darling want he and Peter to bring a red or white tomorrow evening and was he sure John and Dorothea would be able to make it?

The gym's monitors were running the ad for liposuction again.

"See?" Julien moaned. "Why can't I look like that?"

Eric looked up to see the surgeon's smiling, wrinkle-free face, which every twenty minutes delivered the fateful news that all the running and sweating and pushing and rowing and pedalling and stair-mastering in the world wasn't gonna help your fat arse one bit, but never fear because Doctor Vacuum was here.

"Depends," Eric muttered. "How much do you enjoy blinking?"

"Huh?" Julien noticed the ad. "Not that, man. *Him*."

Eric glanced over at the trainer who now stood, talking to the queen at the rower. He'd noticed the slender, too taut body before, as well as the snugly fitting tank-top, the intricate snake tattoo that decorated his left forearm, and most of all, the skin. For all FitForce's drive toward the cult of the fake tan, CK, as Eric called him, was no slave to the sun. He was untanned, and untainted, with barely a mole or freckle in sight. That snake's habitat was spotless. Eric hated CK. Not a lot, but certainly a bit.

"Why? Is he your type?" Eric teased Julien.

"No! But I still know a good looking bloke when I see one. And that guy's ripped."

"Great," Eric smirked. Ripped? Did anybody still say ripped? "When he's done with Carol Channing's lovechild over there—"

"Carol who?"

"Go up to him and book a session. Get your Shakespeare on. Say, 'Oh CK, whose muscles are so firm and whose skin is so milky, perky, and bouncy, can you mould me to look like thee for a fee?'"

"Hey, what did you say his name was?"

"I don't know. I just call him CK."

"Huh?"

"Undies."

Squinting to see, Julien didn't notice the speedometer on his bike stop working. "Oh yeah. He could *model* for CK, you know?"

"I think he does."

"Yeah, his face *is* kind of familiar, you know?"

Eric grimaced. Careful, Jules. One foot on the slippery slope of the actor slash model.

"I don't think that skin's real," he said, keeping his voice low.

"Huh? What do you mean? How can you have 'not real' skin?"

"Botox. Or maybe…check out those lips. Collagen? What do you reckon?"

"I don't get it."

"Injections. Needles, skin refiners, that kind of stuff."

"Oh yeah. Ew! You think?"

"Who knows? But those lips? I reckon they're collagen," he mused, squinting at CK's lips. "Yeah, that's it. CK. All hail the Collagen King."

"The what? Are you high?"

"I just think Mummy and Daddy put a lot of money into helping Prince Charming look pretty. That's all."

"Well, he does," Julien admitted. "Something wrong with that?"

"Nothing at all."

"Right."

"If they can afford the perfect son, they should have him."

"Make him, you mean? Build him up like fucking Frankenstein?" Eric grinned. "If that's what it takes."

They dismounted the bikes and left the cardio floor, weaving their way through the now nearly impenetrable mass of people who'd invaded the gym and assumed between them, every muscle-straining, heart-raising, and limb-stretching position imaginable, plus a few new ones. Julien made a dive for an empty patch of carpet.

"Both your folks still at home?" he asked, offering his leg for Eric to lean against.

Eric took hold of the boy's calf and obliged him with the stretch. This wasn't a topic he was in the mood for. "Mum's in LA. Dad died when I was three."

"Shit, man, I'm sorry."

"*When I was three*. I'm over it."

"Guess so. But your mum's in LA? That's pretty cool. What does she do?"

"I'm usually on my own, okay?" The words came out much sharper than he'd intended.

Julien didn't bite. He just lifted one leg over the other, flattening it against the floor to stretch out his side. "She leaves you okay for money though, right?"

Eric felt the blood drain from his face as he saw CK talking to…Shit, it was! Six foot five, somewhere in his early thirties. The smooth, well-pumped chest, the powerful arms and floppy dark fringe.

Viktor. Andy's manservant.

He froze, ignoring Julien as his mind screamed at him to run. To get out of there, head straight for the locker rooms and not look back. Yeah, right. That would have led him straight past CK and Viktor. Better to do what he always did. Blend. Better to wait for them to move on.

"Dude?"

"Huh?"

"She leaves you okay for cash?"

Julien was looking at CK and Viktor now. Don't stare. Don't...
shit!

Eric offered Viktor a polite nod as the man waved.

"You know that guy?"

"No."

Maybe Viktor wouldn't come over. It wasn't like they were
friends. Maybe...damn it!

"Eric, how you doing?"

There it was. That low, eastern Euro-trash accent. Its owner
now towered over them both.

"I'm good, Viktor," Eric smiled. "You?"

"You're looking good. Don't see you here much."

"Been busy, you know? School?"

"Sure. Hey, how's it going?" the European extended a strong,
vein-stretched hand to Julien.

The boy introduced himself with a smile, allowing Viktor to
haul him to his feet. "Wow, you must, like, live here or something."

"What?"

"In the gym, I mean."

"Actually, I've never seen you," Eric interrupted. The last
thing he needed between Viktor and Jules was conversation. And
how many man-crushes at the gym did Julien need before it became
unhealthy?

"That's because you've been busy, Eric," the man grinned.
"Remember? School?"

"Yeah, that's right."

"You should make more effort. Bulk up a bit. I can e-mail you
a good plan."

Eric tasted blood on the tip of his tongue. "I don't want to bulk
up, Viktor. I like being slim."

"Sure. Can send you a plan for that, too. You looking for a
trainer?"

"*No.* Thanks."

"What kind of plan?" Julien asked.

Oh Jeee-sus.

But Viktor just flashed Jules a smileful of perfectly capped white teeth. "I'll see you later, Eric."

The man finally left them alone.

"Who was that?"

"He works for a client of mine." No sooner had the words escaped his mouth, than Eric realised his mistake. Idiot! How easy would it have been to tell Jules that Viktor had once been his trainer or…shit. Anything, *anything* else. He made a beeline for the locker room. Maybe Jules hadn't heard him.

"Client?"

No such luck.

"He's kind of a butler, handyman, bodyguard, that sort of thing."

"Right. So who's the client?"

"Nobody."

"What do you mean, 'nobody'? What sort of client is he? What do you do?"

Eric knew when he was cornered. Hell, it wasn't like Jules was going to believe him anyway. "I charge outrageous fees to service the wanton sexual depravities of the unreasonably rich. Happy?"

"Hahaha. No, really."

A lie would have been easy at this point, but no. Not now. He wasn't sure why, but he felt strangely liberated. 'Eric the escort' was out. He wouldn't deny it like some D-list celebrity whose sex tape had wound up on Perez Hilton. And a miniscule part of him, mischievous and vindictive with no sense of self-preservation, was having fun. Something about Julien's face, the disappearance of that ever-present wry smile, the faint shock that had invaded his friend's eyes. Was it almost titillating?

"No! You're shitting me!" Julien said.

This was it. If their tenuous bond didn't fall apart now, Eric doubted it ever would. And if it didn't, wasn't that something worth keeping? "Yeah, I sell my butt. Or my—"

"Dude, I don't need to know!"

"There are some hot, rich women in this town. Just because they've got money doesn't mean they're all wrinkled and gross."

"Yeah, but it's *weird*, isn't it? I mean, why? Just get your Mum to leave you more money! Jesus!"

"Look!" Eric snapped, instantly catching hold of his temper. "I have my reasons, okay? Anyway, it's not too bad. Kind of fun, actually."

"*Fun?*"

"Not the sex bit, but they take me out to the opera and symphony and plays. I get to see all the best stuff. Learn about the craft."

"But you...you sleep with them?"

"No. I never sleep over with a client. That's a rule. And I charge heaps extra for the ones I don't like."

Julien just shook his head, throwing his towel over his shoulder. He didn't even see CK pass by.

"Look, if you don't want to hang out anymore, I understand."

"Hey, I never said that!" Julien objected. "It's your life. Just... fuck me."

"If you want. Now, I like you, but you're a guy, which means I charge extra. Let's say three fifty an hour, plus expenses?"

"Three hundred and fifty bucks?" Julien clapped a hand over his mouth, suddenly realising this wasn't a conversation he wanted to have at the gym or anywhere in public.

Eric knew it, too. "I've got an appointment tonight. Want to come?"

"Yeah, right. Why would I do that?"

"They're loaded. We'll probably get three-fifty an hour each if we're together."

"Pass. I'm fine for cash, dude."

"Suit yourself." Eric lifted an arm and stretched out his tricep.

"Is she hot?" Julien asked.

"Can't answer that. Client confidentiality and stuff."

Julien just stood there watching him, oblivious to the noise that had enveloped them from across the gym floor. Eric didn't say a word, instead waiting for Jules to speak.

"Yeah, okay. I'll come along."

"Okay." Eric lowered his arms.

"I reckon you're making this shit up, anyway."

"If that's what you want to reckon. Appointment's in Edgecliff. Meet me at Town Hall steps at nine, okay?"

"Are you sure you want to do this?"

"You want to do it," Eric reminded him. "So, it's done."

CHAPTER NINE

Eric finished off the last of the teriyaki chicken he'd made and rinsed the bowl. His appointment tonight was a home visit. That didn't include dinner, but at least he'd had time to cook. He wasn't sure why he set aside food for Joe from the same meal he'd prepared for himself. But he'd done so each night he'd eaten at home for as long as he'd held the man captive. It just seemed more humane, though 'civilised' probably sounded better. That was what it was. Civilised.

He spooned the remains of the chicken into a bowl and carried it to the stairs. Something was wrong. He should have heard whimpering or moaning by this point. Surely Joe had heard the floor above creak with the weight of footsteps. By now, Joe should be protesting. Even whining. There was only silence.

Shit.

Had Joe gotten free? If he had, why wait so long? Eric had been home two hours now and not heard a word. Come to think of it, he'd heard nothing from the theatre room at all. Had Joe escaped? Had he just up and left? He seemed too tough for that, like the kind of guy who'd stick around for revenge if he got free.

The top stair creaked as Eric started his descent. He quickly reached the bottom and eased open the door to the theatre room.

Joe was still bound to the chair, blinking at him in the gentle light.

"Hey," Eric murmured

The man choked back a yawn.

Eric mixed the chicken as he approached his prisoner, leaving the door open to let the light in. Eventually, he'd replace the bulb in the room, maybe once it was less engaged.

"Smells good," Joe muttered as he opened his mouth to receive its first forkful.

Eric nodded, easing the food into the man's hungry maw, careful not to spill any. "There's a bit more garlic in it than I normally use. Not as much ginger. Tell me what you think."

Joe snorted at him through a mash of dinner. "Do you think I care about that shit?"

He returned the fork to the bowl, leaving it there as he pondered his unlikely food critic.

The man raised a quizzical eyebrow. "Dude? Some more?"

Eric shrugged.

"Oh, come on, man. Don't do this to me. I'm hungry."

Eric impatiently tapped his foot on the carpet.

"Can I have some more?" Joe asked.

Nothing.

"Oh, look! Dude, no games tonight! Please?"

"No, no games," Eric agreed, whispering.

Joe looked up at him, defiant at first. But it soon gave way to the gentle remorse Eric had been waiting for.

"I'm sorry," Joe mumbled. "It's good."

"Mmm? It's good, but...?"

Joe shuddered as he tried to keep his composure. "Maybe a bit more ginger?"

"Okay, cool. Thanks." Eric offered his captive another forkful of chicken, which Joe practically inhaled. Then another. Within minutes, the bowl was empty.

"Thanks."

Eric stretched out the fork and gently cleaned a stray piece of onion from the man's chin. Joe was still looking at him with those same remorseful eyes, but he ignored them. "I have to go. Got stuff on tonight. I'll check on you in the morning." He was halfway to the door when Joe's voice stopped him.

"That's the first time you've done that."

"What?"

"Told me when you'd be back. Sometimes it was hours. Sometimes it feels like a whole day or more."

"Do you care?"

Silence.

"Do you want me to come down more often?"

Joe snorted, but he wasn't indignant about it. To Eric, it sounded more resigned.

"Look, I don't have long. What's this about?"

Joe turned to him, now seeming almost comfortable, bound to his chair. "I want you to untie me, dude."

"Like hell!"

"No, you don't get it. I'm not gonna leave. I want to stay here, with you."

Eric suddenly realised that his research into Stockholm Syndrome, which had been practically nil, should have been much more extensive before commencing this experiment. This pointedly academic regret filtered through his confusion, amusement, fascination, and undeniable fear.

"I can't free you," he muttered. "You know that."

"Why not? I trust you."

"That's the point. I *don't* trust you."

"Aww, shit man! Where do you think I'm gonna go? Who am I gonna tell?" Joe wailed. "You don't know the first thing about me!"

"I know you broke into my house. You broke my trust before we'd even met."

"I told you I'm sorry!" Joe screamed.

"Keep it down, or I'll tape your mouth shut again." Eric paced around the chair slowly, his eyes fixed on Joe. This was something he'd never really considered. Where would the guy go? Where had he come from? Why hadn't he been missed? "You live with family?"

Joe shrugged.

"Don't shrug, answer me." He realised he was parroting Margaret and promised himself it would be the last time.

"Kind of," Joe said. "It's complicated."

Eric decided to try an easier question. "Do you think they're looking for you?"

"Don't think so."

"But you 'kind of' live with them, don't you? They give you food? Somewhere to stay?" Eric suddenly realised he'd no idea how old Joe was. Twenty, maybe? Could have been older.

The man looked up at him, dim light wavering against his dark eyes. Eyes Eric watched intently, determined to find the catch, the hidden agenda. The man who'd broken into his house. The man who would have cut him down, had he not struck first.

"That's what you give me," Joe said.

Every vessel and fibre in Eric's body bristled with protest, but his mouth wouldn't answer. He had no answer. Joe was right. How the hell had they ended up like this? "You're not having sex with Mary again, if that's what you're hoping for." He bit his tongue as soon as he'd said it, but it was too late.

"Fuck you, man!" Joe screamed, shaking in his chair. "Fuck you! *Fuck you!*"

Eric shrank back against the wall. Joe's entire chair shuddered, lurching off the ground as the man threw his weight around in furious, futile protest.

"Is that all you think I want? Fuck you, you nasty cu—"

Eric belted Joe hard across the jaw. He quickly backed off, but it had been enough. Joe sat there, slumped and silent, his head bowed. Eric grimaced as he saw the first drop of blood form in the corner of the man's mouth.

Joe was crying.

"Don't do that." His instruction came out more like a request. He heard Joe sniffing tears away. Fumbling in his pocket, he finally dug out a fresh tissue and wiped off the blood. The man flinched as Eric dabbed the wound. "It's okay. Try to relax."

Joe suppressed another sob, wincing as his captor mopped away the last of the blood.

Eric almost laughed. "Big baby."

He didn't get a response. Not even the flicker of defiance in Joe's eye. Eric put the tissue in his pocket and scrutinised his naked captive. Joe wasn't even looking at him now. He just sat there, his heavy breath the only sound in the darkness. Eric looked up at the projector that hung from the ceiling. "Do you want to watch a movie or something?"

Joe looked up at him, eyes wide, uncertain and mistrustful of what he'd just heard. Eric forced himself to keep a straight face. He wasn't sure why he'd made such an offer, but it had been genuine.

"I…I guess. If you want," Joe got out.

"Do *you* want to?"

After a long moment of hesitation, the man finally capitulated with a determined nod.

Eric moved past his prisoner and tried to make out the DVD spines in the dark. "What do you like?"

"Huh?"

"What kind of movies?"

"I dunno," Joe shrugged. "Funny stuff, I guess."

"Try again."

"Horror stuff's okay. I like *Saw*. You got *Saw*?"

Eric pretended not to hear the suggestion. "Horror…horror… horror I can do, yes." He withdrew a title from the shelf, smiling as he looked at Joe from behind. "If I asked you who Dario Argento was, I'd be wasting my time, wouldn't I?"

Joe didn't answer.

"Well, Dario Argento," Eric explained, removing the disc from its case and depositing it in the player at the back of the room, "may be the single greatest horror director Italy has ever produced. Him or Mario Bava. But I like Argento. Bava I find just so obsessed with melodrama. Know what I mean?"

"I don't really know directors and stuff."

"Of course you don't! I'm not flapping my lips at you just because I can. I'm trying to help you learn something so you can appreciate what you're seeing instead of just going 'What the fuck?' like some bogan who stumbled into the multiplex half pissed."

"I'm not dumb!"

"I never said you were dumb."

Another silence.

"What's it called?" Joe asked, finally.

"*Tenebre*." Eric shut the DVD player primly and took hold of Joe's chair from behind. "Blood, murder, lesbians, awesome score, crazy writers—you'll like it. Help me out here."

Joe lowered his feet and pushed against the floor. Together, they shifted the chair back until it was level with the couch, into which Eric promptly collapsed and hit play. After the first murder, about ten minutes in, Eric began to wonder if he'd lose Joe's attention. The movie was from the early eighties, older than either of them. While it was considered pretty brutal in its day, it seemed kind of tame now, and probably struggled to keep up with the kill quota Joe was used to. Eric didn't have time to sit through the whole movie. He tried to divide his attention between Joe and the screen. He'd seen *Tenebre* three or four times already.

He didn't know why he'd chosen it.

Another murder, the lesbian this time. Butchered while her lover waited upstairs. Andy, though understandably biased, had summed it up perfectly. Eighties cinema queers. Closeted fags, killing closeted dykes, titillating closeted bigots behind their obscene masks of mainstream tolerance. Sure, Eric could see why the fags and dykes got shitty. In *Tenebre*, the dykes were sliced up because the killer saw them as perverts, so Argento's audience could 'ooh' and 'ah' in shock and cluck their tongues in politically correct sympathy and outrage at the demise of such pretty muff divers.

Yet, according to Andy, nobody cared when a male deviant got chopped into pieces. In the microcosm of celluloid reality, it was a fag's occupational hazard. Only pretty girls earned the right to be deviants. Or boys who were so good at passing for girls, they were deemed acceptable entertainment for the self-proclaimed 'normal' majority. Only these fortunate few were allowed to live long, happy lives in moviedom. For the others, good fortune came in the form of dying young enough and horribly enough to see their bodies become communion wafers of the majority's oddly silent moral outrage. But only if no freshly bisected, pretty lesbians were available, preferably of the 'this one time at church camp and I hope my boyfriend doesn't mind' variety.

Joe's cock was hard.

Eric hadn't noticed it at first. Only now did Eric catch sight of Joe's attentive shaft in his peripheral vision. He closed his eyes. He could almost feel Argento's saturated reds slap his face as their reflection danced across the room, battering against his closed eyelids, threatening to force them open. He finally let them. Joe was still hard. The man's face was slumped, not watching the movie, but staring down at his erect sex which twitched at the action on screen. Eric looked up. The detective talking to the writer. Nothing spectacular. Another murder was coming up. He hadn't seen what had excited Joe. But Mary had been right. The man's cock was huge, bobbing its ugly head as the detective left the screen.

"Dude, do you have to look at it?"

Eric turned off the disc, returning the room to darkness, Joe's breath the only sound once more. The air seemed warmer now. More humid. Eric turned his nose up in revulsion. He could smell his captive. Not a bad smell, but one of sweat and fear. The smell of a helpless man.

"You can put it back on," Joe mumbled. "It's an okay movie."

Sure. Anything was better than this silent darkness. He set the player going again, and the projector's light filled the room. Joe was still hard. A blast of cheesy electronica hit the speakers as the scene changed. Eric muted the sound. "I'll put it back on when there's dialogue."

"Don't bother," Joe mumbled, his dick still twitching.

Eric couldn't help but keep watching it. This time, Joe didn't protest. It was the longest he'd ever spent, just watching, gazing at another guy's cock, twitching in its nakedness.

"If I untie one of your hands, do you promise you won't try to get away?" Eric disbelieved the words as soon as they left his mouth. Untie Joe? No way, no fucking way, not on his life.

"Yes. I promise." It was almost a sob, except Joe wasn't crying.

Eric dug his nails into his palms as he clenched his fingers tight. Why make a stupid offer like that? He couldn't go back on it now. Not now he had some level of trust with the guy. Bullshit! He didn't trust Joe so far as—

He untied Joe's right hand before the thought had even formed. He took a step back, waiting for the betrayal. The inevitable grabbing of the other restraint. The breaking free. His captive's sweet revenge. It never came. Joe looked up at him for a moment, but he didn't smile. He just nodded a solemn thanks, bringing his newly freed fingers around his cock, slowly stroking it as Eric watched.

Eric swallowed, tempted to look away. But what if that was exactly what Joe was waiting for? That one look away, and then, boom. Erection forgotten, and his captive was a free man. He forced himself to watch as Joe gently tugged, jerking his cock faster as the film's colours splashed around the room. The smell was back, the smell of Joe's sweat and fear and this time, arousal.

"Stop that." Eric's command had been quiet, barely a whisper. But Joe stopped immediately. Eric tilted his head, one hand over his mouth and nose as he regarded Joe with fascination. "Continue."

Joe returned his hand to his cock and began to pull.

"Stop."

The man instantly obeyed.

"Go."

And again. Eric grinned from behind his hand, but Joe wasn't watching him now. He was focused on the screen, pumping his fist, faster and faster. Eric hit pause. Joe was immediately still.

"I didn't tell you to stop!" Eric shouted. His own voice startled him, but it felt right as Joe immediately started jerking again, now watching Eric and ignoring the still screen.

"Stop." He set the DVD running again. A knife flashed. A woman screamed. All silent. "Go."

Joe masturbated faster this time. Eric shook his head. Could this be exciting the man so much? He opened his mouth to command 'stop,' but he was too late. The only sound was Joe's ecstatic moan as a wash of hot semen burst from his cock, spilling out over his smooth brown torso. The man gasped, trying to restore some regularity to his breathing as he looked up at Eric, his whole face quivering with embarrassment.

"I just…" Joe didn't have a reason, other than being horny. Eric knew that. "I'm sorry."

"How can I trust you if you show no self control?"

"I'm sorry," Joe whimpered. "I'll try."

Eric looked down at the man's pathetic, saturated form, one hand and two feet still tied to the chair. He picked up the blindfold and tied it around Joe's eyes again.

"Hey, what are you doing, man? I said I was sorry. No!"

"I'm going out," Eric replied, tying the blindfold tight. "You're not to move, and you're not to touch the blindfold. Understood?"

"Yes," Joe finally murmured after a long pause.

Eric unmuted the DVD and left the room.

CHAPTER TEN

It was ten past nine before Julien showed up on the steps of Town Hall, having ignored two text messages from Eric reminding him of the nine thirty appointment time and stressing that if he wanted to back out, sooner was better than later. But he finally arrived, dressed in a thin track jacket, a long-brimmed cap pulled low over his face like some low-rent incognito film star. Eric couldn't resist a sigh. Sure, it was Julien's first time, and they weren't exactly alone at Town Hall steps. But what was he afraid of? Being spotted? Doing what?

"Take it off." He grabbed Julien's cap by the brim and peeled it away.

"That better be the last time I hear those words tonight," Julien mumbled, trying to straighten his hair as Eric handed the cap back.

"Second thoughts?"

"I'm fine. But I thought, maybe I'd just watch. It's you they're paying to see."

"You think so, do you?"

"I reckon some women would get off on that, having another guy watch."

"You're not watching," said Eric. "It's all or nothing and now, we're late. Are you up for this or not?"

Julien looked around, licking his lips as the wind picked up. Besides the late hour, Eric just wanted to get inside. It was unseasonably cold for March. The kind of night that felt like it ought to be pelting rain.

"I'm here, aren't I?" Julien answered. "You got train tickets?"

"Have some dignity, will you?"

"Eric, I'm about to have sex for money. Money I don't *really* need."

"So, go home."

"No."

"Okay, then." Eric peered over his shoulder down George Street. Great, that was all he needed, a cab shortage. He finally managed to hail one down. "Last chance to back out?"

"Nup." Julien climbed in the back seat after him.

"Good."

Chapter Eleven

Eric! Glad you could make it. I must say, it's not like you to be late."

"Sorry, Andy. Had trouble getting a cab."

Andy waved away his excuse. "For the last time, you're to text me in future when you're ready to leave. I'll have Viktor come collect you in the Jag. If you're kind enough to come all the way here, I at least owe you a comfortable journey, understood?"

Eric barely heard him. He was too busy staring at Julien, whose mouth had locked open, begging some protest that came only in the form of a strange, choked, mewling sound. Eric was tempted to smirk, but he resisted.

"Also, young man, I wasn't aware you were bringing company?" Andy looked Julien up and down with admiring scrutiny. "Who's the frozen halibut?"

"Andy, this is Julien. He'll be joining us tonight."

Julien managed a nod. Barely. "H…hi."

"Andrew Felton. Lovely to meet you, Julien."

Eric could see his friend trying to choke down nerves as he accepted Andy's hand.

"My, what a nice, strong grip," Andy observed.

That was odd. Julien had barely taken Andy's hand with any strength at all. But these days it was getting harder to tell what Andy perceived to be strong.

"Uh, thanks, I guess." Julien stammered.

"Eric, I do wish you'd warned me. It's no bother to myself, you understand. But there are certain influential people not privy to my choice of lifestyle, and I would prefer that they remain so. Is that clear? You must be careful and discreet, the way you normally are."

"Yeah, I know. Julien's cool, I promise."

"Huh? Oh yeah, totally! Not a word from me, man. Mister Felton, sir, I mean."

"Mmm, I see. Are you gay, Julien?"

"Am I what?"

"You're at Eric's school, I assume? What are you, an actor?"

"Well, yeah, but—"

"Not that that means or has ever meant anything, you understand. Of course, I'm hardly in a position to stereotype."

"I'm not gay," Julien insisted. "Listen, maybe I should just go. Eric?"

Eric raised his hands defensively. "Hey, neither am I."

"No," Andy interjected. "You, young man, simply worked out that sucking the right cock gets you taken to the opera."

"Opera's not really my thing," Julien mumbled.

"Oh really? How many have you seen to come to this conclusion?"

"Well, none. But I just…"

"Then it is simply a matter of re-education and acclimatisation to life's finer pleasures, and the first step in that process, my awkward young voyeur friend, is a good glass of red. Shall we go inside?"

Julien swallowed, shifting uneasily between feet, fidgeting with his hands behind his back. Andy ignored his nervousness, leading the way inside through the narrow hall and up a short flight of stairs to the lounge. Eric beckoned for Julien to follow.

"No way, man. No fucking way."

"You can't back out now. We're here. He's met you."

"You didn't tell me your client was a dude! You didn't tell me the Russian guy worked for a *dude*!"

"You didn't ask. And he's not Russian."

"Coming inside, gentlemen?" a deep, accented voice chided them.

Eric looked up to see Viktor standing to one side to keep the way to the stairs clear. The man tended to get around Andy's house in an athletic singlet, shorts, and runners, as though domestic duties repeatedly interrupted some unending workout routine that could never be confined to the gym. They probably did.

"Hello again," the man grinned at Julien.

Eric couldn't remember if Viktor was of Croatian, Bosnian, or Serb stock, but he wasn't prepared to risk broken ribs for getting it wrong. Had Joe broken into Andy's house, the poor guy might not have made it out alive. Viktor didn't seem like the violent type, but still…

Julien didn't move.

"Come on," Eric smiled at him, putting a hand on his shoulder.

The boy silently nodded, not taking his eyes off Viktor's bemused stare as Eric led him inside. They went up the stairs to Andy's sitting room, Eric's favourite room in the house. He loved the sunken floor, the low coffee table with an always spotless teppanyaki plate at its centre. Immediately surrounding this were six cushions, which saw use only at Andy's thrice-yearly dinner parties, at which he and four elite guests—a number which, to date, had never included Eric, but had included Margaret on two occasions, so she'd said—would enjoy the most fashionable Japanese fusion cuisine, prepared by the latest chef hoping to make his name among Sydney's culinary untouchables. Andy had the contacts to put those dreams within a young chef's reach.

Surrounding this nest of potential gourmet excellence was a square formation of fawn-coloured couches, built into the walls of the depression on three sides, facing a wood-fire heater on the fourth. Three people could fit on each side, with lacquered food or drink rests built into each corner, and a flight of narrow steps leading down, opposite the fireplace. Eric hadn't given much thought to what his own house might eventually look like, but he knew he wanted a room like this one.

Andy smiled at the boys from one of the couches, a warm, open bottle of Pinot Noir and three glasses on the table. Eric took his usual seat, on the couch facing his client.

"Wow, man, your place is awesome," Julien murmured, only then remembering where he was and joining Eric on the couch. "I mean, Mister—"

"Andy. Just Andy. Thank you. I like it."

There came some louder steps as Viktor descended the stairs.

"Some wine?" Andy offered. "It's very good. New Zealand Pinot. An '09, I believe?"

"'08, sir," Viktor corrected, pouring the second generous glass.

"Even better. Julien?"

"Ah, I'm not really a wine drinker."

Viktor stayed his pouring, eyeing Julien with what looked like disapproval, though Eric couldn't be sure.

"No opera and no wine? Dear me." Andy was smirking at them now. "We do have a long way to go. Not to worry. I do have beer, or any spirits you might—"

"I sort of don't drink," Julien got out. "You know, seventeen? Underage and stuff?"

"Young man, preference is all very well, but if you're going to insult my intelligence—"

"He'll have a Heineken," Eric rescued. "Thanks, Viktor."

The Bosnian—Croat, Serb, whatever—took away the third wine glass with a respectful nod. Andy and Eric waited until he returned with a chilled Heineken before collecting their glasses.

"Gentlemen," Andy charged, "The Queen."

"The Queen," Eric grinned.

Julien lifted his beer half-heartedly.

"So glad we could reschedule to tonight, Eric. I was worried that I wouldn't see you before I fly out."

"Fly out?"

"South America, for four weeks. Rio, Buenos Aires, Machu Picchu, Lake Titicaca. I may even head down to Ushuaia if the mood takes me. Just to say I've been there, you understand."

"Sounds great," Eric said. "When are you going?"

"Three weeks from tomorrow."

"Awesome, but you've been before, right? I mean, you've been like, everywhere."

Andy shook his head, running a finger over the rim of his glass before taking a sip. "No, no. My first time. One last continent for me to conquer before I go, you might say. And before you say it, Antarctica? Come now, be serious."

"Don't talk like that. You're as healthy as I've ever seen you."

"Like an ox, thank you very much, and if I'm not as fit as I'd like to think, I'm sure the Inca Trail will have no hesitation in proving me wrong."

"I guess so."

"Where's Ushuaia?" Julien piped up, going a little red as Andy and Eric's focus returned to him.

"Oh good, you do talk. Eric, would you like to tell your friend?"

Eric hadn't expected that. He'd never heard of the place either. "Umm, I was going to look it up later."

"Slack, Eric. Slack! Ushuaia. The bottom of the world. The last stop before the great straits of Magellan."

"So you might get to Antarctica after all?"

"Young man, I've a travel bug, not a sub-thermal death wish. No, Eric. This will be the last trip, I'm quite sure. I've done better than most."

"Eric's mum's in the States at the moment."

Eric all but smacked Julien across the forehead with the fierceness of his glare. Chatting was fine, but Eric didn't bring his personal life into appointments with clients. He didn't appreciate Julien doing it, either. Especially not with Andy. And not about his mother. Not *ever*.

But if Julien had over-shared, Andy didn't seem bothered. "North America is a young man's journey. New Orleans, San Francisco, Montreal. Beautiful, all of them. Marvellous cities. But New York…Oh, there is London, I suppose. But everybody runs off to London. The great Australian cliché."

"What about LA?"

Jesus! Shut up Jules, just shut up!

"Los Angeles is a strange beast. Different for everyone. The most overrated, yet, at the same time, underrated city in the world. Are you sure you want to be an actor, Julien?"

"Yeah, of course!"

"Then what I think of Los Angeles doesn't matter. You must go."

The boys waited a moment as Andy shut his eyes, swirling his wine. Eric noticed Julien shift uncomfortably and looked around for Viktor, but the man had discreetly left the room, probably to go back to his weights.

"What about New York, Andy?" Eric prompted.

The older man opened his eyes a fraction as he lowered the glass. "That's where every young man should begin his journey. The beating heart of culture for the Anglophone world. Don't tell the British."

Julien looked confused. Eric smirked, but didn't interrupt.

"Until a man has tasted life there, how can he know his place in the world? Where he wants to make his home?"

"So much for 'See Venice, and die'?"

"Venice is the sewer of Europe, sinking with good reason. I shouldn't bother."

Eric wondered what his mother was looking for. Her place in the world? So far, she'd found 'her place' in Los Angeles, Amsterdam, Rome, Barcelona, Chicago, Miami…

"But what better way to spend life, don't you think?" Andy raised his glass to them both.

"So, you've always, like…known you were gay?" Julien asked. "You never got married and stuff?"

Eric felt his breath quicken, growing shallow as he tried not to look at Andy. Why had he done this? Why tonight? Why Andy? Why at all?

Andy's smile never wavered. "Let's not get into my life story. It's tedious."

"Sorry, just curious," Julien took another sip of his beer. "I'm not, by the way. Gay, I mean."

"Yes. You said so, though I'd keep that quiet if I were you."

"Huh?"

"All the best people are of indeterminate sexuality," Andy sipped more of his wine. "And preferably, parentage."

Eric felt the sudden urge to scull.

"Do you have a girlfriend, Julien?"

"Me? Nah. Eric does."

"Oh, really?"

"You don't have to sound so surprised," Eric muttered.

"Oh, I'm not surprised. Not at all. She's damn lucky to have you." Andy got this out with barely a trace of irony before draining the last of his wine.

"She's really nice. Smart too. Her name's Mary. Playing... Lavinia? It's Lavinia, right?"

"You're doing *Titus Andronicus*?" Andy groaned.

"Umm, yeah, it was Eric's idea."

Eric shrugged, finishing the last of his wine.

Andy looked at him like he'd just fired the first shot in a third world war. "I know I shouldn't be surprised, and yet...No, never mind. I'm sure it'll be a gory triumph."

Viktor reappeared with the bottle of Pinot. "Another Heineken?" he offered Julien.

"I'm still going, thanks."

"I don't suppose..." Andy trailed off, frowning a little before he continued. "Viktor, was Shakespeare ever very popular in Croatia?"

So Viktor was from Croatia? Eric had suspected as much. Something about the man's lips. They seemed fuller, in that bright, natural kind of way.

"I wouldn't know, sir."

Or not.

"But growing up, did you ever have to learn it?" Andy pressed.

"My parents moved to Australia when I was very young, sir. Too young to study plays." Viktor refilled Eric's glass. "I studied them in Australian school."

Eric had assumed that Andy knew all this. Viktor had been in his service for years. Had Andy not checked into the man's background?

Andy held out his glass as Viktor poured.

"So, what part of Croatia are you from?" Julien asked.

Viktor smiled as he answered. "Not Croat, I was born in Kiev."

Kiev? Ukraine? "You would have had Soviet schooling then?" Eric shuddered as Viktor scowled at him. The look was gone in an instant, but it had been there.

"When I was very young, yes," the man muttered. "Gorbachev years."

"You never told me that." Andy put down his wine and regarded his servant uneasily.

Viktor looked up as he withdrew from the table, his movements tentative, his expression confused. "You never asked about my schooling, sir."

"But I did ask about your background. You told me you were born in Croatia."

Eric could feel Julien's eyes burrow into him. Andy hadn't lifted the glass. He just stared at Viktor.

"No, sir. Grandmother was Croat. I told you. But not my parents. Not me."

"I see."

"So," Eric said. "Kiev. What was that like?"

"It was fine. Don't remember much."

"Do you still speak Ukrainian?"

"A little."

"Russian?" Julien asked. "They're pretty similar, right?"

Viktor grunted at him, looking up at his employer. "If that will be all?"

Andy watched the man in silence, allowing the question to settle. When he finally spoke, it was almost in a whisper. "That will not be all, Viktor. You're...you're Ukrainian?"

"Yes, sir. Born in Kiev, sir."

"Do not *sir* me, Viktor!"

"I thought you knew."

"I thought I knew *you*, Viktor. I thought we were open with each other."

"Andy, does it really matter?" Eric tried to soothe his client.

"So, where's Ukraine again? It is *near* Russia, right?"

Eric hushed Julien with a look. Andy's face was going pink, his confusion now sinking into a scowl as he stared at Viktor. His lips quivered as he picked up the glass and took another sip of wine. A drop spilled onto the coffee table. Viktor instantly produced a cloth.

"Leave it!" Andy set down his glass with such force, Eric was amazed it didn't crack.

Viktor rose again to his full height. His face was stoic, unchanging as he stared at the wine spot on the table.

"You told me you were born in Sarajevo, Viktor. Capital of *Croatia*, remember? You lied to me, Viktor. You *lied* to me. Or did you just forget to mention it? Is that it, Viktor? Did we just *forget*? Lose a few brain cells when Chernobyl went up, perhaps? Well? That would explain a hell of a lot, wouldn't it?"

The boys exchanged grim looks. Andy's voice had taken on a mocking Russian accent mid-spiel, and the insults hung in the silent air like sprayed poison.

"If that will be all, *sir*?"

"Do *not* call me sir!"

Eric clawed at the couch as Andy spat out the words with a pronounced, spiteful hiss. Julien had sculled his Heineken and now inched his way to the edge of the couch. But Eric couldn't leave yet. He couldn't let Andy lose Viktor over something so trivial.

"Bosnia," he pointed out. He didn't know if the change of subject would help, but he had to do something. "Sarajevo's in Bosnia. The Croatian capital is Zagreb."

Andy snapped around to face him, eyes burning. "Must you know everything, boy? It's fucking tiresome!"

"I think we should go. Eric?" Julien grabbed his hand.

"No! You two stay." Andy turned his furious gaze back onto Viktor. "*You* go! Get out and take your weights with you!"

"Andy, this is stupid!" Eric protested.

"Get out!" Andy sculled down his wine. "Get *out*, Viktor!"

Eric flinched as Andy threw the glass at his manservant. But he was astonished when Viktor shot out a hand and caught it. Still, the glass cracked, breaking in the man's sudden, strong grip.

"See?" Andy shrieked. "Clumsy oaf! I brought you into my home!"

"Shit! You're bleeding," said Julien.

Viktor shook his head, returning the broken pieces of glass to the table as he tried to hide his bloodied hand. "It's okay. I go."

"Andy, are you crazy?" Eric implored. "What difference does it make?"

"Do you want to get paid, young man?"

"Look, at least get something on his hand." Julien stood up, moving to Viktor's side. "I'll help."

"No, you sit down!" Andy growled.

"Fuck you, you grouchy old cocksucker!"

These were the words that silenced the room. Eric barely noticed Viktor withdraw as he watched his client and friend eye each other off, locked in some silent battle he wasn't privy too. He jumped when Andy finally spoke.

"There are two things I will not tolerate in my home, Julien. One is lies. The other is vulgarity. Do you understand?" The voice had been even and quiet, and something about its gelatinous liquidity made Eric want to sink back in his seat.

It worked on Julien, too. The boy slowly sat down. "I was just gonna help put a bandage on his hand."

"Viktor can take care of himself. Thank you."

Seconds later, the sound of a closing front door echoed through the house. Eric shook his head. Their visit had gone far enough. "Andy, I think we should go."

"Why?"

"Well, you seem…upset." Eric knew his word choice was feeble, but it was the only one he could think of that didn't translate to 'crazy.'

"I'm not upset. I have the company of two nice, handsome, *truthful* young men. Why should I be upset?"

"Andy, we've really got to go. This one's on the house, okay? Thanks for the wine."

"If you must. But on the house? Nonsense," the man protested. "I won't hear of such a thing. Viktor? Viktor! Bloody hell, built like Hercules and deaf as a post."

"Andy—"

"No, no. Eric, your services have, as always, been completely satisfactory and it has been a pleasure to meet your friend. Goddamn it, *Viktor*!"

"Andy—"

"Fetch my wallet, will you? The boys have to leave."

"Andy!" Eric barked. "He's gone."

The man stared back at him, face quivering with disbelief. "What?"

"You fired him."

Andy gripped the edge of the couch with shaking hands, frowning as he considered Eric's words. He finally pushed himself up out of his seat and left the room.

Julien let out a sigh of relief. "Fucking hell."

"Sorry."

"For what?"

"He's never like this."

"What? Totally insane? Are they all like that?"

Eric hushed him quiet as Andy returned, fumbling with his wallet and taking out a wad of cash.

"No. Andy, I mean it. This one's free."

"Listen, Eric, how about you give me a discount, and we'll call it even, okay?"

"Okay. A discount, if you like."

"Two hundred, then."

"Okay." Eric agreed.

"Each."

"Oh, Andy!"

"I insist."

"Yeah, Eric. He insists," Julien muttered, taking his two hundred dollars.

Andy laughed at him. "I like you, Julien."

"Eric, are we done?"

"Yeah. We're done."

The house felt cold as Andy escorted them out. Eric shivered, wondering where his jacket was before remembering he was still wearing it. Julien didn't hesitate as he bounded off Andy's porch to the street, but Andy placed a hand on Eric's arm, holding him back. "Did I…did I really fire Viktor?"

Eric nodded, and his client's face sank with dejection.

"I shall miss him. Good night, lovely one."

Eric leaned forward and let the man kiss his cheeks. He didn't say a word as he left the house, and soon caught up with Julien out front on the silent street.

CHAPTER TWELVE

As they passed the line of imposing, eastern suburban houses that overlooked the walk back to the train station, Eric watched his companion closely. Julien didn't look back at him. He didn't seem disturbed or upset either. He just walked, hands thrust deep inside the pockets of his jeans, his only communication the odd, dry cough. It was getting late. The air had cooled enough to draw a thin fog from their breath as they kept walking.

"Sorry if that freaked you out." Eric didn't know why he was apologising. Julien had asked to come. Still he didn't answer. All Eric heard was the steady tap of steps against concrete. "Andy's a nice guy, really. I don't know what happened tonight."

"Seemed like a freak to me."

"Are you okay?"

"Dude scared he's got reds under the bed or something? He would've grown up with all that shit, right?"

"Will you stop it? That wasn't the issue. Besides, Andy's a leftie. "

"For real?"

"Old Labor Party. Used to work for Hawke, years ago. Knew a heap of socialists back then. I don't know what was wrong with him tonight."

Julien shook his head. "If you say so. But he's so *old*, man. I mean, the idea of you and him…yeach!"

"We never have sex."

"Huh? For real?"

"Yep. That's why I thought he'd be a good one for you to meet. Andy just likes to talk. Don't know why. Lonely, I guess."

"Yeah, I can see why. Hey, wait a sec." Julien grabbed Eric's arm and spun him round. "You didn't think to tell me this? You didn't stop to think that maybe, just *maybe* that bit of information would make me feel a bit better?"

"I thought you did really well," Eric said with a smirk.

Julien shook his head, slowly letting go of Eric's arm. "You're a twisted bastard."

"You knew that already."

The air was warmer as they neared the arcade leading down to the train station. Eric stopped, took out his phone and checked the text he'd received late that afternoon.

Will collect you from the bus stop outside Edgecliff Police Beat at eleven. Be on time, Puppet Boy.

"So, what now?" Julien asked.

"I've got another appointment."

Julien almost unhinged his jaw. "You're kidding me. Tonight? You do two in one night?"

"My record's four."

"What are you, Santa Claus? How do you…no, never mind. Fuck, man!"

"It's easy when one of them is Andy. Kind of nice, actually. I get a rest."

"Yeah, get a rest and stay for the psycho show."

Eric ignored him.

Julien studied the train timetables above them. "I can't do another one, mate. I wasn't expecting this. Mum's gonna—"

"You can't come to this one. It's not like Andy. This one's the real thing."

Julien's dark brown eyes quivered with nervous curiosity, even concern. "Are you gonna be okay?"

"Yeah. Why wouldn't I be?"

Julien licked his lips, avoiding Eric with his eyes now, as he tried to play cool. "I don't know. It's late. I'm not sure I like this, man. I'm not judging you or anything, but…you know. What happened back there kind of freaked me out."

Eric half smiled. The cold had made Julien's lips seem darker, more pink, somehow. Or perhaps it had just made his skin seem paler. Even more noticeable was the contrast to the distinguished, short stubble that lined the boy's jaw. Eric wanted to reach out and run his fingers over it, though he didn't know why. It seemed a kind of novelty. Like a toy, just sitting there, begging him to play.

"Look, dude, come back to my place, okay? We'll put a Blu-Ray on. I got some fresh gear off Nerida."

Eric realised he'd been staring at Julien's face for almost a minute without saying a word. His friend's offer was tempting. But he hated to reneg on an appointment, and he couldn't afford to lose this one. This was a client who made him *real* money. He smiled, putting a hand around the nape of Julien's neck, though again, he didn't know why. "No. Sounds like fun, but I can't."

Julien regarded the friendly hand with a faint, sceptical smile. He gently removed it, giving it a squeeze as he let it go. "Okay, dude, okay. You know what you're doing. Have it your way. I'll see you at school, yeah?" With that, the boy turned and headed for the trains.

"Hey," Eric called. "We're still cool, aren't we?"

"If you get any trouble tonight, you call me, straight away. You got that?" Julien instructed.

"Okay, I will. If there's any trouble, which there won't be."

Julien broke into a grin, happier than Eric had seen him all night. He disappeared into the concourse as the blast of a train horn filled the arcade from the station below. Eric watched him go until Julien disappeared to the lower level. The beep of Eric's phone broke his concentration.

A little early, if you can make it, Puppet Boy.

Eric sent back a text to confirm. A little early was perfect. He pulled his jacket tighter around his body and briskly walked the half-block to the bus stop. Someone had scrawled *Help me you white cunts* in dark, red-brown graffiti on the cop shop wall again. The letters, slick and wet with rain that had already stopped, stood out like pronounced bruises under the blue light. Eric ignored it and sat down at the empty bus shelter.

"Eric."

The low, Slavic voice startled him. He looked up to see Viktor, who smiled as he sat down to wait for the bus. The man was still dressed in the same flimsy singlet and runners, his wallet and phone bulging from the pockets of his training shorts. At least his hand had stopped bleeding in the cold air.

"Hey," Eric murmured. "Are you okay?"

"Don't I look okay?" Viktor did look suspiciously happy for a man who'd just been fired for such ridiculous reasons.

"That was shitty, what he did to you. I know some people who might be looking for help, if you want."

"No. Andy is...not himself right now."

"What? What do you mean?"

Viktor smiled at him, a broad smile, full of spotless white teeth and cheek. "I just called my wife. I tell her I stay at home for a few days. And she tell me that makes her very happy. Then, in two days—you will see—I get a call from Andy. 'Oh, my poor Viktor, I'm so sorry. My house is filthy. Can you come clean and cook? I pay you for days you missed.' Blah, blah. He might not even remember. Maybe I turn up to work in a few days and he wonder where I've been? This is nothing. Is the fifth time, in two months."

Eric didn't know what to say at first. How long had this been going on? Two months, or even before then? He couldn't help but laugh as Viktor yawned.

"What?" the man asked.

"He's done this before?"

"Sure, and is always my background. He can't remember, you see? And something in his head tells him I lie, then he freak out. He yell at me. Now, I tell him different country each time. He not even notice."

"So, you *are* lying?"

"Not at first. But after second time, I get sick of it. So I play game with him. He doesn't know what to believe. He's very sick, Eric."

"And you're lying." Eric grimaced. "You're making fun of him. The biggest thing he wants from you is loyalty. Honesty. And you're lying."

Viktor's grin broadened even farther. Eric wondered if the man's lips were going to split at the edges. "There are things I want from him too. They all lie, Eric. All they understand is lying."

Eric wasn't sure what to say, or if Viktor had meant to include him in his cryptic and damning use of the word 'they.' The beeping of the former and, apparently, soon to be reinstated manservant's phone spared him from comment. As Viktor read the message, Eric caught sight of the sender's photo. A redhead, whose confident expression belied her fragile, porcelain features.

"Your wife?" Eric asked.

Viktor nodded as he returned the text, his grin suddenly more sincere. Less frightening now.

"She's very pretty."

"Thanks." Viktor put the phone away.

"So, where are you from, really?" Eric asked.

They were interrupted by a black Mercedes pulling into the bus stop. Eric's ride. The one he couldn't keep waiting.

"Here." Viktor shrugged as Eric got up. "Always been here."

"Great," he muttered. "That's great, Viktor. Fucking great."

CHAPTER THIRTEEN

The Majesty Apartments loomed over Potts Point like the defiant middle finger of local money, determined to rise above the insatiable white-collar hoard of latte-sipping, self-declared up-and-comers. A monument to permanence. To money that would always be money, against all impertinent challengers. It reminded all those who passed its imposing wooden doors of their place in the world, as though the building itself had graciously withdrawn from the waterfront to allow the mortal citizenry to share its harbour views from ground level.

This left The Boy entirely unsure of his own place within the hierarchy. After all, he'd been granted the rare privilege of access to its lowest underground, lined with the symbols of vanity's empire. BMW, Mercedes, Lexus, Jag, two Rollses that never seemed to move, perhaps because their owners couldn't? The Boy's mind swam with the stories behind every vehicle, of the modern fiefdom to which these were crucial symbols.

He'd been granted the unique privilege of having the emperor be not only his client, but his personal chauffeur. No middle man. That was how The Master liked it. No conversation. That too, was at The Master's request, though The Boy was thankful for it. What would they talk about? The weather? Religion? Politics would only end in blows and a lost client.

He didn't face The Master's gaze in the elevator, instead offering just the faintest smile in the corner of his eye, enough to suggest anticipation and fondness. On reaching the top floor, he was swiftly escorted through the opulent wooden doors, up the stairs to The Master's living room. He stripped off his clothes, graciously accepted a glass of champagne, the brand of which he couldn't pronounce, and looked out over the still, black waters of the harbour. He raised his nose a little, allowing his face to take on a well rehearsed look of disinterest, without seeming entirely bored.

"I'm glad you could make it tonight, Puppet Boy." His host downed the champagne faster than was probably healthy for a man his age. Not that it mattered. Just as long as The Master didn't die on The Boy's shift. That would have been awkward. "School going well?"

"Yes," he replied with the one syllable The Master permitted.

"Good. Good."

The chilly autumn air felt good against The Boy's skin. He closed his eyes, breathing deeper as the fold of silk covered them, the thin elastic strap around the back of his head carefully tucked under his hair. Neatness was important to The Master.

"And how's that sweet girl of yours? What's her name?"

The Boy swallowed his annoyance, both at not being able to answer within the allowed syllables, and at the very rudeness of the question.

"Jane."

"No, no it isn't. I'm sure of that. Are you lying to me, Puppet Boy?"

"Yes."

He cried out as the hard strap came down over his shoulder. Shit! That had been a belt. It had to be. The thickness, the weight of the leather. The psycho was using...*starting with* a belt.

"Don't," he gasped, forcing a faint whimper into the word, hoping it would speak to The Master's guilt.

"I beg your pardon?" The Master's words were smooth, warm, and confident, with years of grammar school tuition, then teaching, rounded by the clipped tones of a Cambridge degree. They might have been comforting, in some way, though he knew The Master was not usually inclined to nourish the comforts of others.

"Hurts."

It did hurt. He felt the searing glow of a welt on his shoulder before The Master finally remarked on it and gave his version of an apology. "I understand."

The Boy raised the champagne to his lips once more, only to have it snatched from them when The Master's phone rang.

"Hello? Jesus Christ, Phil, do you know what fucking time it is? What do you—Oh, look, no. No, no. Because I'm not *doing* it! I thought we were clear today. I don't care what Deborah's doing on her show. She can piss off to the bleeding hearts on ABC or go back to community radio where she belongs. Yes, you can tell her I said that, and if it's a problem for her, she'd better get extra comfortable with it, because it might just be a reality for that bitch very soon. No, I'm not *doing* a 'refugee' story! Look, if she wants to do it, let her. Make it one for the mid-morning dole queue crowd if you really care what the wankers think. Of course it's not bloody personal! Where's your brains? My show's for the everyday listener. You do understand that? The working man and woman in the street and the fact is they couldn't give a shit if the boat sinks on a bunch of muzzies. What do you mean, don't I think it's racist? Who gives a toss? I'm talking about the listeners, and *they* don't want them bloody here! Have you got that, Phil?"

The Master had begun tying The Boy's hands behind his back by this point. The ropes were cutting into his skin. The Boy decided then and there, no more ex-Scout Leaders as clients.

"We went through this song and dance last year for that World fucking AIDS Day. *AIDS*, Phil! What does she think this is? 1990? Nobody's scared of that shit anymore, and…Hey, you know who does care, Phil? Poofters and junkies, and that's all! So why don't you go bitch to them?"

The Boy bit his lip.

"Tell Deborah she gets ten minutes, *ten minutes* for her bit on the illegals and tell her she can thank me tomorrow. Talking that crap makes us all look like a pack of stray cats and the listeners go elsewhere. That means the sponsors *go elsewhere*. Now, do you understand *that*, Phil? Good. And get that email off to the Premier's office. Remind those fuckwits that her interview's for eight and not to be late. I'm not having another Jefferson fiasco."

The phone snapped off. The Boy finally stopped clenching and unclenching his fists.

"Always the way, Puppet Boy. Work, work, work."

"Yes."

The Master was close now; he felt the push of the man's suit against his bare skin, warm, musty breath swirling over his face. He felt the dry, leathery lips kiss his cheek. Never on the mouth. On this, The Boy had been very clear. It had been the one concession The Master had granted.

He swallowed again, loud enough for The Master to hear. The man chuckled at him.

"You think I'm too harsh, Puppet Boy?"

Shrug.

"What do you think of the muzzies? Speak freely."

Now, finally afforded the luxury this one time, The Boy didn't know what to say. "They're kind of hot, some of them. I keep one tied up in the basement."

The Master let out an imperious laugh. "Come on," he took The Boy by the arm, "you little bleeding-heart slut."

Chapter Fourteen

Eric wasn't expecting Joe to still be awake when his client dropped him home. It was almost one. He barely managed to stay awake as he lazily flicked on the lights. And pain. So much pain, he could barely walk. Part of him wondered if fifteen hundred a time was worth it. But for four appointments worth of income in one hour, he'd deal.

He tossed the money into the dresser and unbuckled his belt, stripping off his pants and shirt. His mind drifted to the man tied to the chair in his theatre room. The man he'd half-untied before he'd gone out, then left there. Would he still be waiting? He'd had a chance to escape already, in plain sight. But he hadn't. Freak.

Eric swallowed the dry lump that had formed in his throat as he descended the stairs. Leaving Joe a free hand had been a bad idea. Trust be damned. There was no trust here.

The light of the stairway spilled into the theatre room. Joe was still there, silent, but awake. Eric examined his captive. He still had the blindfold on, and his cock was still semi-erect, aided by the occasional stroking of its owner's free hand. He could have taken the blindfold off at any time and freed himself, but he hadn't. The man just sat there, blindfolded, gently massaging his penis in the dark. Eric coughed as his dry throat finally got the better of him.

Joe instantly dropped his cock, lifting his head with a start. "Is that you, dude?"

Eric nodded, then realised Joe couldn't see him. "Yeah, it's me."

"What time is it?"

"Nearly one. Have you slept?"

Joe shook his head. "I didn't know if you wanted me to."

"Why wouldn't I want you to?" Eric scoffed. "If you're sleeping, you're not going to run off."

"I already told you, I want to stay here, *sir*." The last word was said with what looked like a sneer in the dark.

Eric resisted the urge to hit the man again. "Don't call me that."

Joe shifted to face him. "Okay."

Eric hesitated, moving behind his captive and taking the DVD out of the player, replacing it in its case and sliding it back into the shelf. "Did you like the movie?"

There was silence at first, then, "It was okay."

"See, the writer's so given over to the fantasy, to his stories, that he lives them."

"Right."

"He doesn't even know he's the killer."

"Yeah, I got that."

"What do you mean, would I want you to?"

"Dude, I get it now. You're in charge. I broke into your house, so in a way I attacked you."

Eric swallowed. In a way, he'd attacked Joe. At what point did the self-defence line wear thin? "So?"

"And you beat me. I attacked you and you beat me. You won. I'm yours, dude. You own me now."

Eric choked out a forced laugh. Now his captive was going genuinely crazy. "I don't own you. I just—"

"Can I leave, then?"

"No!"

"Then I'm still a prisoner. I'm still *your* prisoner."

He couldn't argue that.

"Can I please take off the blindfold?" Joe whispered, his logic getting no answer.

"Yeah, I guess."

The man eased the blindfold off, jostling his hair as he tossed it to the floor.

Only then did Eric notice the smell of stale sweat and sex in the room. His acquisition needed a wash. But he was too tired tonight. Then again, why did *he* have to wash Joe? "If I let you come upstairs, do you promise to behave?"

"I'll do what you want."

Eric was unarmed. Hell, he was standing there in nothing but briefs. Exposed. Powerless. But Joe made a tempting offer. If the guy was telling the truth, it would take a massive burden off his shoulders. If it was a lie, he was fucked.

"You can untie yourself."

Joe didn't waste time, working the other rope until he was free. The ankle ties quickly followed. He carefully tilted forward in the chair, gradually shifting the weight to his feet. "Can you help me? Please?"

Eric could feel his breath quickening. He couldn't move. The possibility that he'd made a mistake, that Joe was just waiting for him to get close enough—

"Dude, please?"

"You'll be okay, just take it slowly," Eric urged him.

Joe grimaced, wobbly on his feet as they took his full weight. He eased himself off the chair, slowly rising to full height, then suddenly falling forward.

"Woah, careful!" Eric darted forward and caught the man before his legs collapsed.

With some effort, Joe regained his footing. "Thanks."

"Do you need a drink or anything?"

"I'll be okay. My feet hurt. Pins and needles."

Eric smiled, ignoring the pain his own body was in. As they reached the light of the upper level, Eric could feel something was wrong. He felt the warmth against his leg.

"Shit, man! You're bleeding!"

Eric groaned at what seemed to be that night's theme. "I'll be okay. I just need a shower."

"Dude, you need more than that. Wait for me in the bathroom, yeah?"

Eric frowned, annoyed that the self-proclaimed humble servant had suddenly taken charge of his care. He didn't need to freak out.

Eric knew what the bleeding was. Yes, it hurt like a bitch, but it would stop soon enough. Still, part of him was curious as to what Joe had in mind.

Joe, meanwhile, had gone straight for the kitchen. "Where do you keep your first aid stuff?"

"Over the fridge." Eric retreated to the bathroom. Didn't everyone keep it either above the fridge or under the bathroom sink? He wished Joe would get out of the kitchen. Away from the knives that until now had served as Eric's protection. But Joe ignored them, taking the first aid kit from its cupboard and two fresh icepacks from the freezer.

Eric held up a cautionary hand as the man came near. "I can do it. It's okay, thanks."

"Just let me make sure. Fuck man, you're bleeding out the arse!"

"It's nothing!" Eric snapped. "Now, will you please leave the kit and the ice here and get out?"

"It looks kind of serious, dude. You want me to get an ambulance?"

"Just go to my room, sit on the bed, and wait for me there."

Joe took a step back, his eyes almost mournful.

"Use my ensuite and have a shower," Eric said. "I'll be there in a minute."

The man did as he was told, and Eric set about checking the damage. The bleeding had already stopped. He couldn't do much about it. The tear would heal on its own. Occupational hazard, if you wanted one and a half grand a time, at least.

He cleaned off the blood and put a bandaid near the edge of his arsehole to keep Joe off his back. Not that he was going to see anything. What did the guy care if he was bleeding? Even the pain had stopped now.

He returned to his bedroom, placebo bandage in place. Joe was sitting obediently at the foot of the bed, a fresh towel wrapped around his waist, hair still wet from the shower.

"What now?" the man asked.

Eric shrugged. He didn't have a plan here. No schedule to follow.

"Umm, this is gonna sound stupid," Joe said, timidly. "But I want to make sure."

"Go ahead."

"I don't want to have sex, okay? I'm straight."

Eric snorted indignantly. "So am I. You know that."

"Yeah, I guess. Mary, right?"

"You don't get to talk about her. And I will beat you to a broken and bloody lump if you touch her again. I mean that."

Joe nodded. "Okay. What do you want me to do?"

Eric tilted his head, pulling back the sheets on his preferred side of the bed, watching Joe, just as Joe watched him. "Get down on all fours."

The man did as he was told and looked up at Eric, obediently.

Eric climbed into bed, pulling the sheet up tightly under his chin as he looked down at his prisoner. His project. "Jump up."

Joe did, sitting at the foot of the bed, hands tucked between his knees, awaiting further instructions.

"You sleep there."

Joe turned in several circles, chasing a non-existent tail as he settled on the bed beside Eric's feet. The man's weight pulled on the sheets. They felt uneven, like Eric was being pushed to the edge of the bed.

"That's not going to work. Get down."

"Huh?" Joe grunted.

"I've changed my mind," Eric said. "Not on the bed. *Down.*"

Joe nodded and hopped down, repeating his tail chasing ritual as he settled on the carpet. Eric watched, fascinated as the man curled into a ball with a faint shiver. Eric took a spare blanket from the foot of the bed and tossed it to him.

"Thanks."

"Excuse me? What was that?"

"Wuff."

"You're welcome."

And for the first time since they'd met, the two of them fell asleep in the same room.

CHAPTER FIFTEEN

"Eric, where are we going?" Mary giggled as she ran to keep up with him.

"Harley said we could rehearse where we wanted, and the script says 'another part of the forest.' Come on!" He took her hand as they jumped over rocks and fallen branches, heading deeper into the wild parkland that backed onto Christian Fellowship's grounds.

"Have you been back here before?" she asked.

"No."

"We could get in a shitload of trouble."

"For taking a walk?" Eric pulled Mary close to him and clasped her hands in his, bearing down on her with an evil grin. "The trouble starts when I cut thy tongue and ravish thee!"

"Jules? Come on! You're missing the fun!"

"Oh yeah." Julien almost tripped over a rock as he staggered toward them. "Because I don't want to miss the tongue cutting. That shit's ace."

"Fine, you cut the tongue, and I'll ravish." Eric knew Jules hadn't been thrilled with the change of part or the lost opportunity to play Felicity Turner's lover, but nobody had forced it on him. Eric was happy to do it for Mary. Who'd twisted Julien's arm?

"Come on! Get with the ravishing already!" Mary snapped playfully, pulling down her blouse to show off three inches of modest cleavage.

"You mean you actually have breasts? Oh sweet and terrible temptation," Eric mocked, taking out the script and flipping pages. He skimmed the text as she pulled down her blouse some more. "You know, when Shakespeare was around, they'd have tossed you out as a whore for doing that."

"When Shakespeare was around, they'd have Jules playing Lavinia."

"Fair call."

"Huh?" Julien frowned.

"They usually didn't let girls on stage." Eric enlightened him. "Relax. She's stirring you up." After their encounter with Andy, Eric wasn't prepared to cast further doubts on Julien's masculinity. At least, not yet.

"Yeah, I know all about that. You know that's where the word 'drag' comes from, right? Boy enters 'DRessed As Girl?'"

"Umm, yes."

"So, is that what you want your dad to think?" Julien asked Mary.

Eric gritted his teeth, wishing Julien would shut up. But the stupid jock wasn't looking at him.

"What?" Mary asked.

"That you're a whore?"

Mary smirked at him, and Eric relaxed, unable to resist a smile of his own. Everyone needed a goal. Topping Mary's father's shit list was more satisfying than most within their immediate reach.

"Okay." He found the page they needed. "So if we skip the bit where Tamora's sons kill Bassianus—"

"Who?" Julien asked.

"Lavinia's husband. Saturninus's brother."

"Saturn...huh?"

"The young, new emperor..." Eric offered, seeing his friend's clueless face. "Look, let's not get into the rest of it just yet. One scene at a time, okay?"

"Cool," Julien approved.

"Now, Mary—"

"Yes, Mister Director?"

"What?" Eric looked up from the script, his eyes fixing on her. "What do you mean?"

"You're totally directing us."

"I am not."

"It's what you want to do, isn't it? This play was your idea, so we're all yours."

"I don't want it to be like that," he grumbled. "Not with you."

Half truth, and they knew it. Something about taking the play and making it his own appealed to him. Didn't he have the right to some creative control? Hadn't it been his crazy suggestion to do this play, and hadn't he somehow convinced the entire class to go for it? Didn't he get Harley to go against the state curriculum for them? And fuck it, if he could control Joe, he could control a bunch of high school actors. All his idea. All his.

"Do you want Chiron or Demetrius?" he asked Julien.

"Huh? The brothers, you mean?"

"Yeah, which one do you want? Harley wants us to decide." He looked to Mary for an opinion, but the girl was silent.

"What's the diff'?"

"Demetrius gets more lines, just. Chiron's younger, a bit more out there and fun. I think Chiron would suit you better."

"Cool."

"So, act two, scene four?" Mary pulled the sleeves of her blouse down over her hands, covering them in the makeshift 'stumps' of her cuffs.

"That's the first scene where it's just the three of us, so I guess. Wait, you've got it memorised already?"

Mary shrugged away his disbelief. "Actually, it's not the three of us. It's just you two. I don't have a tongue by this point, remember?"

"Oh yeah, right."

"Or hands."

"Right."

"You just cut them off."

"Yes, I remember. Thanks."

"Ymoa're mbelcumb," the girl mumbled, her tongue folded back inside her mouth to simulate its removal.

"What was that?"

"Ymoa're *mbelcumb!*"

"Oh! You're *welcome*. Shouldn't talk with your mouth full, darling."

"Bewy punnhy."

"Or empty, in this case."

"Phuck yiew, 'itch!"

Eric flashed a grin and went back to the script. "So, now go tell, an' if thy tongue can speak, who 'twas that cut thy tongue and ravish'd thee." He pulled her close, his arms tight around her waist.

Mary screamed, an empty, muted sound, from behind her folded tongue as she turned her face away in feigned disgust. Eric wasn't sure how a tongue-less mouth muted its sound, but they could work that out later. The two of them stood in silence, waiting for the next line.

"Jules?" Eric asked. "*Jules?*"

"Y'ul'en!" Mary shouted.

"Huh? Oh, it's me?"

"Where's your script?"

"Oh shit. I left it in class. Distracted. Sorry!"

Eric shook his head, throwing Julien his copy. "Page fifty-one."

"Right." He fumbled awkwardly until he found the right page. "Ah…Write down thy mind, bewray thy meaning so, An if thy stumps…"

Eric had to admit Julien's cold reading was spot on for a guy who hadn't read the script. "See, how with signs and tokens she can scrowl."

"Go home," Julien answered. "Call for sweet water, wash thy hands."

An anguished cry pierced the air as Mary threw herself to the ground, beating at it with her cuff-enclosed fists, screaming the same muffled screams as she pounded the rocks and grass.

"Shit! Are you okay?" Julien asked.

She looked up at him with furious, mad eyes, a trail of spittle bubbling over her lower lip and down her chin before she spat it to the ground. Julien fell back as Mary's vengeful screams levelled on him. She threw herself at him with unhindered fury.

"What're you...? Hey!" he yelled as she beat her fists against his chest and clawed at his arms with clenched fingers. "What the...? Eric! Arrgh!" A searing pain ripped down his forearm. He whipped it back, catching Mary across the jaw with a loud crack.

The girl screamed as she clutched her stinging face. For an instant, the temptation seized Eric to throw himself at Julien, to wrestle him to the ground and start bashing his head. But it had been an accident. Nobody's fault. He hoped his friends would see it the same way.

Julien finally tore his eyes away from the blood that was trickling over his arm, in time to see Mary's eyes, the hatred that had filled them before, now intensified. "Shit! I'm sorry! Are you o—Hey!" He stumbled back again as she spat in his face.

Eric stepped forward, grabbed her hair from behind and yanked it back. Mary screamed in agony, twisting her head around as though he'd pulled it with all his strength. "She hath no tongue to call nor hands to wash," he recited, suddenly releasing the hair and launching her head forward. More spittle. More anguished moans. "So let's leave her to her silent walks."

Mary scrambled across the ground, grabbing Julien's trouser legs in her 'stumps' as she wrapped herself around, imploring him.

"Okay, stop. What the fuck are you doing?" Julien stammered, wiping his face clean.

Another low scream came from Mary as she pressed her head against Julien's thigh, clutching him tight in her faux dismembered arms. Eric frowned, too intrigued to stop her now. "Keep going."

"Uh...an...an t'were my case, I should go hang myself."

"If thou hadst hands to help thee knit the cord."

Mary let out another scream, then buried her face in Julien's crotch. Eric had just opened his mouth to ask why, when...

"What on Earth is going on back here?"

Mary sprang to her feet on hearing Johansson's voice, straightening her skirt and sleeves, rebuttoning the top of her blouse.

"I told you I heard something," Johansson hissed.

"That you did," Father Callahan agreed. "Eric, Julien, Mary."

"Father."

"Father."

"H—hi, Father."

Eric looked from Mary's muddied sleeves, to Julien's bloody arm, to Johansson's plain-faced fury at not receiving the same courteous acknowledgement they'd given Callahan.

Fuck him. He could deal with it.

"Well, answer me! I heard screams," Johansson fumed. "Mary, your uniform is filthy! What's all this about? Eric?"

"Your niece, that flies away so fast?" Eric mumbled under his breath. Somehow, he doubted Johansson would get the reference to the play's next line. He was right.

"Anything you have to say, you can say aloud," the teacher snapped. "One last time. What are you three doing back here?"

"We're just rehearsing a play," Mary insisted. "Miss Harley said we could rehearse wherever we wanted."

"On school grounds, I'm sure."

"What's the play, Mary?" Father Callahan asked.

"Shakespeare," Eric answered. "*Titus Andronicus.*"

Mary smiled in agreement, brushing the dust off her skirt, her blouse now rebuttoned.

"I don't think I've seen that one, Eric," said Callahan.

"Neither have I," Johansson snapped. "And this school has been producing a senior Shakespeare every year for a very long time."

"And always the same ones," Eric protested. "*Hamlet, Midsummer Night's Dream...*We just wanted to do something different. The state board approved it. You can ask Miss Harley."

"Mary was screaming, Eric." Johansson's voice was low and even as he lined up his target. "Did Miss Harley approve that, too?"

"It's in the script," Julien pointed out.

"I did not ask you, Mister Davids—what happened to your arm?"

"Huh? Nothing."

"You're bleeding."

"Oh! I...I scraped it on a branch."

"You should look where you're going," Mary threw in. "Stupid."

"And so, last time, what were you doing off school grounds?" Johansson asked, nostrils flaring as he took out a clean handkerchief and gave it to Julien.

"Thanks."

"May I see the script, please Julien?"

Jules nodded and handed the book to Father Callahan as he mopped away the blood with Johansson's handkerchief.

"What scene?"

"Page fifty-one."

Eric felt as though some deathly silence had encroached on them as Callahan thumbed through the book. Not a bird sound. Not even the crack of a branch. Nothing, as the priest took what felt like an eternity to find the scene.

"She hath no tongue to call nor hands to wash…" he read aloud. "Well, it is graphic, but I think—Excuse me, Mister—!"

Johansson had already grabbed the book from Callahan's hands. His frown deepened as he flipped back a few pages, examining the words. "Eric, this is a rape scene. The character's been raped, her tongue cut out and—"

"Thanks. I've read it," Eric growled. "I've read it several times. Have you?"

"That's not the point, Eric. I don't need to. And you watch your mouth. You're in enough trouble based on your music assignment, which I am *not* prepared to discuss just now—"

Pity, Eric thought. Why not? Why not get it all out, right here and now in one great, explosive argument and take Mary, Julien, and Callahan along with them? Johansson had wanted a reason, any reason to take him on for how long? It didn't seem to matter. Why not now, when Eric could cut his whiny moralising down for good, in front of witnesses?

"—and now *this*?"

"Tim," Callahan stopped him. "I think we should discuss this with Miss Harley present, don't you? I'm sure she knows what she's doing."

"There's nothing to discuss," Johansson insisted. "Trash like this…this abhorrent violence has no place on our school stage."

Eric gave Mary a forlorn look, hoping this discussion would be over sometime before 2050. The girl shrugged it off.

"Violence *is* an unfortunate part of our world," Callahan rebutted. "Christ himself understood that."

"He also condemned it."

"Like the play," Eric argued. "It condemns violence. The obsession with revenge. It's not like it's glorified or anything. That's the whole point."

"This has nothing to do with you, Eric," Johansson barked. "Be quiet!"

"It's all about him," said Julien. "This play was Eric's idea. We talked about it, and everyone wants to do it. And it's not trash. It's Shakespeare. It's classic."

"Exactly," Eric mumbled. "I don't see the problem."

It felt to Eric as if Mary, Julien and Callahan had melted away, leaving just him and Johansson locked in a fierce contest of stares, each unwilling to surrender to the other. Johansson was a fucking moron. Besides, what happened in drama was none of his business. He was supposed to be a music teacher, though Eric doubted he was qualified to do even that ever since he'd spent an entire lesson harping on why Stephen Sondheim had perverted the musical theatre form with moral ambiguity. What was his real problem with Sondheim anyway? Did the speed and nimble-ness of the man's lyrics break Johansson's little brain, or was it a 'thou shalt have no other gods before me' thing?

"You said Miss Harley approved this?" Father Callahan asked.

"She got it added to the list. Just for this year. Just for us."

Callahan quickly covered the smirk that crossed his face. Johansson didn't see it, but Eric did.

"Play or no play," Johansson continued. "The point is none of you are authorised to be off school grounds within school hours, for any reason."

Eric shrugged. "We just wanted some space."

"For that scene. We didn't want to freak anybody out." Any sweeter, and Mary's smile would have given her cavities.

"Back to class. Go."

They grabbed together their notes and started walking. Johansson remained in front, like some self-satisfied drill sergeant. Eric lingered back at Father Callahan's side. He didn't know what Callahan thought of their performing *Titus*. But Johansson was annoyed. That usually put a smile on the priest's face. When they rounded the corner of the arts block, Miss Harley was waiting for them, leaning against the classroom door.

"Where did you three get to?" she called.

Johansson barged forward before Eric could answer. "We found them about halfway up the hill in the park. Miss Harley, can I have a word with you?"

"You may, but I'd like a word with my students first."

Johansson opened his mouth, but she cut him off. Eric thought he heard Callahan suppress a laugh, though he couldn't be sure.

"What were you doing up there?" she demanded. "I told you to find rehearsal space. I didn't say you could leave school grounds."

"Sorry about that, Miss. There was some screaming in the scene, so we thought we'd go find some space," Eric explained. "We didn't want to worry anyone." He gave Johansson a piercing glare. "It's just a scene in a play."

"Look, I've had just about enough with your tone, Eric."

"Mr Johansson," Harley cautioned. "I'll take care of this, thank you."

"Miss Harley, if you'll excuse me?" Father Callahan offered them a slight smile and took his leave. Either he had more important things to do, or could no longer contain his amusement at Johansson's outbursts.

"What concerns me," Johansson growled, "is the text you've chosen for your class. What is this? *Titus Andronicus*?"

"That's right." She turned her attention to Eric and his friends. "Guys, wait for me inside, please."

Mary and Julien obeyed, but Eric wasn't moving.

"Eric," Harley cautioned.

"This play was my idea. I'm responsible."

"And I supported you. Go inside."

"The problem, Miss Harley," Johansson snapped, "is the scene they were rehearsing in particular, in which a young woman is brutally raped. Now, do you really think—"

"Mister Johansson, Lavinia is not only raped, she has her tongue torn out and her hands cut off in a direct reference to the legend of Philomel. I'm not sure if you're familiar? I should also like to point out that *Titus Andronicus* is a revenge tragedy, during which, all the main characters but one are brutally murdered, including Lavinia's rapists, who are baked into two pies and fed to their mother. Now, do you have any further concerns about the drama curriculum to take up my time, or can I get back to my class?"

Johansson looked ready to explode. The man had gone bright red about the cheeks and widow's peak, his nostrils flaring.

"Eric," Harley said quietly. "Go inside, now."

This time, he obeyed, shivering a little as he sat down at his desk beside Julien.

"Mate," his friend prompted. "What did she say?"

Eric sat silent, unable to remember.

CHAPTER SIXTEEN

"Hey, you're back."

Eric let his school bag slide to the floor. Joe was grinning like an idiot, holding out a drink for him. The clothes Eric had loaned him were too small. The T-shirt's once ironic logo stretched uncomfortably across Joe's much broader chest.

"It's four, on a school day. I'm normally back by now."

"How was I supposed to know that?"

Eric shrugged, accepting the drink. It was Joe's first full day of freedom. Eric wasn't sure if that made what he had to do now easier or harder. "I need you to do me a favour."

"What?"

"I need you to go back in the theatre room for a few hours."

Joe stared at him like he'd just been cut.

"Just for a few hours," said Eric. "I've got a friend coming over."

"Dude, no."

"Joe—"

"No! Don't!"

"Don't what?"

Joe swallowed, a hint of sweat beading on his brow as Eric advanced on him. "Don't tie me up again."

"I didn't say I'd tie you up." Eric's voice was a whisper, his face close enough now to feel the heat from Joe's rapid breath. "Do I need to?" Backed against the counter, Joe looked at the floor as he tried to steady his breath. He was still shaking. "Hey," Eric said, driving a finger up under Joe's chin. The man flinched as Eric prodded him. "I asked you a question. Do I need to tie you up?"

"No!"

"I said I've got a friend coming over. What am I supposed to tell him about you?"

Joe just stood there, quivering. Eric waited for the silence to weigh his captive down.

"Only for a few hours, yeah?" Joe asked.

"Probably. Maybe the night. Take some food if you want. Just stay out of sight. I can't explain you."

Joe nodded, slowly. "Okay, for you."

"Leave the clothes."

"Oh, fuck off!" Joe cowered as Eric raised a threatening hand.

Eric frowned, but it soon gave way to a grin as he appreciated the power. "I don't totally trust you yet, and I don't want you running off. Give me the clothes back."

Joe gave him a futile stare before stripping off the shirt and pants. He began to roll down the jock Eric had loaned him.

"Leave that on."

"Huh?"

"You can keep that, if you want."

Joe handed back the rest of the clothes. "What do you want out of me? Out of this?"

Eric shrugged. "Good night, Joe."

"You got this place all to yourself?"

"Til Mum gets back from LA, yeah."

Julien wandered through Eric's lounge room, running a hand over the velvet covered couch, grinning at the plasma TV Eric hadn't used since he was fourteen. "Sweet. Dude, next party's at yours, yeah?"

Eric scoffed at the idea. The image of Joe the drinks waiter was back. Not happening.

"Eric?"

"It's okay. I use my own stuff, mostly." He passed Julien a can of Coke from the fridge and led his guest back to his room, and his own plasma. "Wii, 360..."

"I'm not really into games."

"Me either." He collapsed on the bed, sitting up on a pillow as he grabbed the remote and flipped on the TV. The blue light of a blank channel filled the room as Julien paced around him. "Want me to throw a DVD on?"

"What? You don't have Blu-Ray?"

"I never saw the point. If the movie's shit, it's shit. Better picture's not going to fix that."

Julien flopped down on the foot of the bed and stared at the blank screen. "So, what do you do with it?"

"With what?"

"The cash. All the extra cash you make from clients."

"That's kind of private," Eric grumbled, crossing his arms.

"Okay. Well, what do you do with some of your other clients then? Don't give me names, just—"

"That's private too."

"Look, man. It can't all be private, or you wouldn't have told me."

"And I'm sorry I brought it up. I know it's not your—"

"No, no you don't. You can't just drop this on me, *take me on a fucking appointment,* and then tell me it's none of my business."

Eric held his tongue, doing his best not to huff. It *was* nobody else's business. He hadn't even wanted to tell Jules, but it was too late now.

His friend rolled over and gave him an expectant stare.

"What?" Eric shifted uncomfortably.

"You know you want to tell me. It's like, you know those people who carry around secrets for years, and they get all bottled up and give them heart attacks and shit?"

"Um, yeah?" Eric asked, starting to wonder if Julien was high.

"You wouldn't have said anything if you didn't want to tell me."

"Okay, fine. Guess."

"Huh?"

"What do you think I do? And get off my bed, you fag!"

Julien rolled over onto his feet and pushed himself upright, taking another sip of his drink. "Well, they take you to the opera and stuff, right?"

"That's not what you meant." An evil grin crossed Eric's lips. "What do you *really* want to know about? The sex or the money?"

"The money," Julien laughed, putting his Coke down.

"Ah, now that's—"

"Private? Come on, man. It's me."

"I was gonna say…look, never mind."

"*Go on.*"

Some part of Eric hoped his reluctance would convince Julien to drop it, but he knew better. Besides, if he couldn't trust his close friends…Christ, is that what they were now? "I'm applying to film schools in the States. Next year."

"What? Where? Like, New York?"

"Well, yeah. Most of the best ones are in LA, unfortunately, so I'm trying there, too. Mum doesn't want to pay for it. So I'll make my own way."

Julien put his Coke down. He'd barely sipped it. "She won't pay for you?"

"Nope."

"That's bullshit. Doesn't she work there?"

"Can we not talk about this anymore?" Eric grimaced. "That's what it's for, okay? You wanted to know. I don't do it for fun."

"Never said you did," Julien said with a shrug. "Hey, I'm not judging you!"

"Think it'd matter to me if you did?" The question had sounded so much gentler in his head. But it was out now, and Julien was already on his way out.

"Wait. I didn't mean it like that." He got up and followed Julien to the kitchen. "What are you doing?"

"Got anything else to drink?" came the mumbling of his friend from behind the open fridge door.

"Umm, wine? Some vodka in the freezer?"

"Not for me, for you."

"Huh?" Eric narrowly caught a can of Sprite that Julien tossed at him from the fridge.

"You're too uptight."

"Like I said, vodka's in the freezer," Eric said cracking open the can. "Just one, I've got a client tonight."

Julien grinned. "Busy boy."

Before Eric could move, Julien had taken a fish-shaped plastic sauce dropper out of his pocket and delivered three drops of clear liquid into the can.

"What are you doing?" Eric demanded. "I just said I've got a meet tonight! I can't—"

"Will you relax? It's just G."

"G is not going to help me relax!"

"Do you want me to go, then?" Julien put his can down on the bench and headed for the hall.

"No," Eric said, taking gentle hold of his arm and pulling him back.

Julien smiled as he gave his drink the same treatment he'd given Eric's and raised it high. "To selling your arse and chasing your dreams?"

Eric finally managed a smile. Toasting to prostitution with G-spiked soft drinks still in cans. It set new standards for classy.

❖

The two of them lay on the bed, each with an empty can beside them and another almost finished. Eric let his guest talk. Either the drug had been slow to react, or Julien had been sold some lame shit, which meant it probably hadn't come from Nerida. Eric had no idea how well connected his friend was, if at all. On the surface, the former athletic golden boy was perfect for Sydney. He had the strong jawline and a dark, handsome face, which Eric had learned was the fruit of a marriage between a young, naive Aussie on a gap year in Paris and the daughter of Algerian immigrants he'd met there.

Then, Jules had that generous smile, just sly enough to be charming. A perfect master of the corporate universe in waiting, except that Julian's greatest greed would only be satisfied by the adoration of an audience. That much was clear to Eric every drama class.

Not that money wasn't a factor. Jules's folks had money, all right. Eric doubted that the guy beside him, now so happily sharing his life along with his drugs, had ever really wanted for anything except to be recognised. To be praised on the strength of his talent. This at least, they had in common.

"That was the first time I saw Shakespeare. *Richard III* with Ian McKellen. The movie, I mean."

"I've seen it."

"It was on TV. I didn't even see the start. So I missed the whole 'winter of our discontent' speech. But the rest? I couldn't get it out of my head for days. Took me ages to convince Mum to get the DVD."

"Mum? How old were you?"

"Thirteen."

"You sat through *Richard III* when you were thirteen?"

Julien looked away, hiding a shy grin behind another sip of his drink. "Twenty-seven times," he mumbled.

"*What?*"

"Til Dad took the disc." Julien snorted with laughter, "He put it away somewhere and said I could give it a rest for a few weeks. I was pissed off!"

"Twen...twenty-seven times? What was *wrong* with you?"

"Nothing! It was McKellen, man. I studied everything. The way he limped, every little movement in his face. Mum got me the play to read as well, but I don't think I ever finished it. I just watched that guy so closely, every detail. It was like every frame of that performance was just for me. I used to act it out too, just by myself. What was I gonna do? Ask the guys from soccer to run lines? But I got bits wrong because I'd just copy the movie and not read the script."

"Of course."

"And I even..." Julien's embarrassed grin returned, all but hidden behind his drink. "It really felt like McKellen was my acting teacher, you know? I used to imagine he'd come and take over the class at St Joseph's. I wasn't even taking drama then. Only two guys were, and they were both fags and didn't care who knew."

"Umm, you know McKellen is—"

"Yeah, I'm not stupid."

"Just checking."

"So, I used to imagine he'd come and take the drama class, or just do a talk there or whatever, and then he'd spot me, right? And he'd see how good I was at playing Richard. Then I used to have this kind of fantasy that he'd take me under his wing. You know, train me privately until I was as good as he was. Maybe even send me off to some posh Shakespeare school in London or something."

Eric smiled, finally catching Julien's eye as the drug set in. Now, he was relaxing. Whether it was the chemical or the conversation, he couldn't say.

"Sounds stupid, but when you talk about the States?" Julien shrugged. "I get it."

"Somehow, I don't see McKellen sponsoring my application."

"Your clients' contacts aren't that good, huh?"

"My clients' *contacts* are none of your business," Eric smirked, gently digging Julien in the ribs, mostly to spare himself another plea to 'chill out.'

"Funny part was," Julien muttered, swallowing down the last of his drink. "Maybe a month later, I said to my dad, 'Hey, it's been a while, can I have my DVD back now?' And do you know what he says to me? He says, 'What d'ya need it back for? Haven't you got the whole bloody thing memorised?'"

"Bastard."

"The stupid prick had lost it!" Julien laughed. "And he didn't tell Mum. She was spewing when she found out. Said he'd thrown it out on purpose and *fuck,* she could yell! I mean, she just blasted him for about twenty minutes. Something about letting his son bring some culture into the family. I mean, she was *mad.* Maybe it's a French thing. I didn't get involved."

"What does your dad do?"

"He used to run his own business. Grease and oil chain on the coast. Hardly ever saw him when I was little. Pretty successful, too. He sold it six months ago. Put it all into the mines. We moved down here for Mum. She's in finance. They married right after she graduated, and she kind of put her career on hold for him for years. I mean, he's a fair bloke. Don't think he's not. But that was the start of my dad's introduction to theatre."

"Hold on," Eric frowned. "Your dad? Your *ex-grease monkey* dad?"

"And Mum wasn't taking no for an answer," Julien continued, cracking a fresh can of coke and adding a few more drops of G. "So, if a play came through Coffs and up the coast, Dad took me to anything I wanted to see. And I wanted to see—"

"Everything!" Eric finished with a wicked, almost admiring grin, refreshing his own drink and offering it up for enhancement. "Even *Richard III*?"

"Hahahahaha! Oh, man! No, but that would have been hilarious!" Julien replaced his drink on the bedside table and relaxed against the bed frame, loosening his top button.

"You feeling okay?"

"Yeah. Stuff's a bit weak is all."

In the silence that followed, Eric realised Julien's breathing had gotten heavier. Either his friend was tired, or the drug was doing its job just fine, if not necessarily in the way Jules had expected. He also realised they'd been lying on the bed together for almost an hour. It had bothered him at first, but now it felt comfortable in its own weird way. Maybe even nice. Julien had closed his eyes, and his chest was rising and falling now with each breath, the thick down of soft black hairs quivering slightly beneath the openings in his shirt. It didn't surprise him that Jules was so hairy. His arms and legs—

Julien had opened his eyes again, staring right at him, as sure as he'd been staring at the boy's chest a moment before. Eric swallowed. He wanted that moment to return. That silence between them. The few discreet moments they'd spent observing each other.

"So does the agreement with your dad still stand, now you're in Sydney?"

Julien smiled. "I wish. That was the trade. I get to go to an artsy school instead. Dad wasn't too keen on it at first, but like I said, he's a fair bloke. So they asked some contacts of Mum's in Sydney and found this place. Well, it was worth it."

"You could have studied drama in any school."

"But I wouldn't have met you."

"Your parents don't mind? You being out so much, I mean. Have you even been home in—"

"Either I'm in my room with the door shut or I'm out doing stuff." Julien stifled a yawn. "You think they'd really notice? That's how I like it."

"Me too," Eric admitted.

Just for an instant, the silence returned. This time, neither of them looked away.

"Is this the bit where I'm supposed to tell you you have beautiful eyes?" Julien asked.

"No. Because it's a fucking cliché, and I'd be a lousy director if I let you."

Julien snorted a laugh and collapsed against him, his head awkwardly propped against Eric's arm. "Ow," he mumbled into his host's sleeve before easing himself up onto Eric's shoulder. "Sorry, do you mind?"

"Are you comfortable?"

"Not really. But you're warm. And soft. You feel like a girl."

Eric eased his shoulder out from under Julien's head, lifting his arm so the boy could snooze against his chest instead. "I'll make you a deal."

"Mmm?"

"You don't tell anyone we did this, and if I ever do *Richard III*, the part's yours."

Julien mumbled something into the folds of his shirt.

Eric couldn't bring himself to actually hold Julien. But to have the guy's head resting against him, eyes occasionally glancing up at him from under tired lids. He couldn't help but smile.

"How about you?" Julien asked, stifling a yawn. "When did you know you wanted to be a director?"

Eric shrugged, trying not to throw the guy off in the process. "Polanski. *Repulsion, Rosemary's Baby, Chinatown.* He's just so good at keeping the balance, you know?"

"Balance?" Julien's eyes had closed now, and the word came out mute and half-conscious.

"Between fear and fascination. He keeps that suspense. Look at *Repulsion.* Catherine Deneuve's character? The whole point is she's repulsed by sex, but she's fascinated by it at the same time. It slowly consumes everything in the film, as she just—"

"Like you?"

"What do you mean by that?"

"Your clients..."

"Jules?"

"So tired."

Eric pretended he hadn't heard, going on to describe Polanski's every narrative trick, so calculated to secure the audience's fascination. The creation of a world falling apart within a movie frame. A little of what he'd—

His arm was around Julien. Had Jules put it there? Coiled himself within Eric's limbs so delicately he hadn't noticed? Was it the drug? His friend's skin, the perfect, smooth darkness of his hair, that obscure scent he used so carefully, now powerful under Eric's nose.

"What time do you have to leave?" Julien's voice was such a breathy whisper, Eric was unsure he'd heard it at all.

He ran his fingers over the soft black hairs of Julien's chest. Like they belonged there. Like they'd been invited. "Whenever you're ready to go." As Jules fell asleep in his arms, Eric found himself kept awake only by the wish that Joe would stop screaming.

CHAPTER SEVENTEEN

Eric felt underdressed, almost naked in a pair of jeans, T-shirt and leather jacket, as he stepped out of the cab in front of Margaret's house. He pulled the jacket tight around his body in the now pelting rain and trekked through the sodden forest of his client's garden. The droplets of water sparkled as they hit his eyelashes, like little shocks of electricity that fizzled to nothing. A few more hit his lips, tasting sweet and light as he licked them away. Leaves, bushes, and grass shone all around him in boisterous illumination, a botanical fanfare, heralding the arrival of their owner's favourite bit of tail.

Julien's G was good shit.

The delivery entrance was unlocked and ajar. The dim light seeped out into the wet darkness of the yard to beckon him. Eric slipped inside, shut the door behind him and hung the jacket up on the rack, leaving his wet shoes at the foot of the worn red brick steps that led up into the main house. He was at Margaret's in jeans and a T-shirt. Sure, there were always guys his age dressed this way at the opera. But in Margaret's company, it felt wrong, even if they were Armani, with a touch of...

Shit. The belt was from Bluefly. Wrong belt!

He flinched, almost stomping on Persephone as the cat darted between his legs and raced for the hall.

"Ah, there you are, Eric. Come in! Come in!"

Eric squinted as he stepped into the light of Margaret's sitting room. The room was so bright, it seemed to be ringing around him.

Even the air felt lighter, fresher than normal, with no trace of the musty nostalgia that normally hung over Margaret's furniture. Instead, warm aromas filled the room. Old polished furniture, good whiskey and fine chocolate. On the sideboard next to him sat an open bottle he didn't recognise and an open but untouched box of six sugary formations from some ritzy Melbourne chocolaterie he'd never heard of.

He didn't want to touch them. Didn't want to risk altering the blissful sensory load.

"I do hope you like those," Margaret said. "Artemis Mint. You've never really struck me as a chocolate person, but I think you'll find them a good excuse to indulge."

"They're perfect, thank you." Eric faced her and caught himself before his jaw dropped open.

Margaret was dressed in a flowing black evening gown, the top half of which was encrusted with faux silver and purple gemstones. The plunging neckline of the dress was broken by a similarly jewelled necklace, though Eric suspected *those* jewels weren't fake. Seven rings highlighted Margaret's hands, their stones bursting with colour against rose gold bands, and bony white fingers.

What the fuck?

"You, ah . . . said to dress down?" Eric stammered.

Was she setting him up to look like a slob? Ugh, note to self. Dropping G before visiting Margaret? Not such a hot idea.

"You're dressed just fine."

"But you look...I mean—"

"Purely for fun, I assure you." Margaret waved away his concerns. "I love this gown, don't you? I so rarely get the opportunity to wear it anymore. Perhaps I'm too old, but—"

"Nonsense," Eric said automatically. "You look amazing."

Margaret raised a hand and cradled his chin in her jewel-encrusted fingers. "You're very sweet, my dear." She kissed his cheek and retreated to the next room, leaving a dark purple lipstick mark on his face.

Eric rummaged deep in one of his pockets for a tissue and wiped it away, smearing his fingers in purple wax. "Is it seven thirty again?" he called, shoving the tissue back into his pocket, careful not to get lipstick on the screen of his phone. God, he'd even worn sneakers. Not for the opera. Jesus!

"We're not going out tonight, Eric."

"Oh?" The boy frowned, taking a sip of the whiskey. It was every bit as good as the aroma had promised. The flavour wrapped itself around his tongue and swirled its way down the sides of his throat, bitter and just a touch overpowering. He set the glass down and stared at the chocolates. Mint? He couldn't smell any mint.

"It's only *Tosca*, Eric. They'll do it again in a few years. With a better lead, one can hope." Margaret returned, smiling at him with a large, purple-wrapped box in hand.

"Margaret?"

"Happy birthday, Eric."

"Oh." He stared at the box, dumbfounded. "How did you know? I mean, thanks! You didn't have to do this. I didn't even—" He reached out and caught the present as Margaret flopped it down into his arms. It was heavier than it looked.

"I was just curious, really. You'd been seeing me for almost a year and never mentioned anything, so I asked my niece to do a little snooping on that 'Facebook' thing, and well, who knew? My lovely, sneaky boy! Eighteen tomorrow and didn't say a word."

Eric shrugged. "Sorry, I just didn't think it was—"

"Shut up and open it." Margaret grinned. "Come on, open! Open!"

He nodded appreciatively and began to undo the black bow that surrounded the package.

"My niece is about your age, Eric. You know, if it weren't for our rather unusual relationship, I think you two—"

"I've got a girlfriend, Margaret. Thanks."

"Do you, really? How interesting. What's her name?"

"Mary."

"That's very Catholic."

The bow finally slid free. The purple wrapping soon followed to reveal a plain white box.

"Her dad's very Catholic."

The lid of the box was stuck.

"But Mary doesn't know you do…visits?" Margaret reached for the whiskey and a clean glass.

"Huh? No. No way!"

"Mmm, good. Ahah! Finally!" she beamed, clapping her hands.

The lid came free and Eric reached for the black garment inside. The fabric was soft and velvety to the touch, carefully sewn into a tough under-layer to keep its shape. He lifted it out of the box and held it up in the light, trying to ignore Margaret's grin. The tunic had no sleeves, and was open at the front with silver buckles on straps to close it. Two more buckles hung on each side. They seemed redundant, though Eric was sure he could find a use for them if he tried.

"I know being a pup isn't really you," Margaret said, sipping her whiskey. "I could tell, last time, my love. It was all over your face. I hope that's more to your liking? The funny girl at the shop in Enmore said they don't sell many of these, but I thought, well…"

"Can I try it on?"

"My dear boy, I *insist* you try it on."

Eric carefully laid the tunic back in the box and stripped off his T-shirt. He picked up the present once more and slipped it around his shoulders, fastening the buckles in front of the mirror. He started at the top, but it seemed to pull the garment out of shape around his chest. He unfastened it and started again, this time from the middle. Better. The fit was more even now. Who knew Goth-wear could be so complicated? Where was Nerida when he needed her?

"Very handsome," said Margaret.

Eric tightened the last of the straps and turned around, inspecting himself in the mirror. The tunic's fit was okay around his slim form, though a bit more muscle would have filled it out. It also didn't suit the Bluefly belt or the blue jeans. He'd have to hit Gareth West up for some leather pants.

"Something the matter?"

"No, nothing," he insisted, turning to face the mirror again. He liked the way the tunic emphasised his shoulders. They could use it. It made him feel powerful. "I love it, Margaret. Thank you."

"Good, good," she said with a grin, clapping her hands together as though his modelling were something to applaud.

Maybe it was. He looked hot.

Margaret picked up the whiskey and her glass and took them to the overstuffed easy-chairs in the corner of the room. "Shall we sit down?"

Eric brought his drink and chocolates over, setting them down between the two chairs and trying to sit comfortably in the stiff tunic. With a little effort, it finally allowed him to relax, drink in hand.

"So, tell me about Mary," Margaret prompted, "and have a chocolate."

He obediently scooped one out of the box. "What do you want to know?" he asked, taking a bite. Okay, *now* he tasted mint, an explosion of mint that erupted over his tongue and fought its way through residual whiskey to stake its claim on his senses. The two didn't mix. Irreconcilable flavours amplified beyond any rightful intensity. The G was peaking. He put the whiskey aside.

"How did you two meet?"

"Church."

"Is she in your classes?"

"Yeah. Drama."

"Oh, drama? Good, is she?"

"Yeah. In our play—"

"And what does her father do?"

"Umm, I don't…that is I don't think…"

"Eric," Margaret cautioned. "Are you all right?"

Mint, whiskey, cat, crumbs of cheese, dust on the crazy tea set, Margaret's lipstick, her dress, the new fabric of his tunic, its metallic buttons. The smells, the sights. Each hurting more than the last. Lovingly choking him with the entrails of a world unravelled for his delight.

"I…"

"Eric?"

He couldn't answer. His eyes widened as they tried to process everything around them. Margaret. Her hair, her wall of makeup… fucking beautiful!

"You've been taking drugs!" Margaret set her whiskey down and skewered him with a glare.

He looked at her sheepishly. "Sorry, I had a friend over. I didn't ask him to bring it."

"What did you take?"

"Just a bit of G. It'll wear off soon."

"Fine." Margaret raised her hands in surrender, getting up and taking the whiskey bottle with her. "What's this play, then?"

"Huh?"

"You said Mary was in a play?"

"Oh, yeah. *Titus.*"

Eric heard her fumbling in the liquor cabinet. The clinking of bottles splintered in his ears like shattering ice until it mercifully stopped. Margaret returned with a richly detailed green bottle.

"*Titus Andronicus?*" she said, uncorking it. "One of my favourites."

Eric recoiled as the aroma filled the air. "Absinthe?"

"Why not?" Margaret poured them each a small nip. "If we're going to go down the road of sensory abandonment, let's do it properly. I daresay it's a better match for those chocolates, anyway." She lifted one of the glasses, and Eric responded in kind. "To murder, madness, and The Bard." Her absinthe was gone in one swift scull.

Eric instantly felt as though he'd poured window cleaner down his throat as the residual flavours of mint and whiskey vanished under the all-conquering green sea that sent him coughing uncontrollably into his palm.

"Only the best, you understand." Margaret grinned.

He forced a few nods between coughs.

"Are you in *Titus* as well, then?"

"Yes," he wheezed. "Demetrius."

"Ah, yes. I played your mother, way back when." Margaret topped up their drinks.

Eric set his down on the table. "Tamora? Really?"

Margaret closed her eyes and held her absinthe steady, inches under her nose. "Victorious Titus, rue the tears I shed, a mother's tears in passion for her son. Oh, by 'son', I don't mean Demetrius, obviously. Alarbus, Tamora's eldest. Poor thing gets chopped up and hewn to the gods within the first ten minutes."

"I know the play," Eric smiled, taking out his phone.

"What are you doing?"

"Keep going, I want to see," he urged her.

Margaret set her drink down, a mournful look crossing her face as she continued. "And if thy sons were ever dear to thee, O, think my son to be as dear to me! Sufficeth not that we are brought to Rome, to beautify thy triumphs and return, captive to thee and to thy Roman yoke, but must my sons—"

Oh fuck, somebody help me!

Margaret stopped and glared at Eric, who now held up his phone to play back the MP3. Joe's screams, now blended against the swirling notes of *Tosca's Ta Deum*.

"What on earth—"

"Keep going!" he urged.

Can somebody hear me? Fuck! Help!

"Eric, what *is* that?"

Somebody help me! Please!

"Just something I found on the Internet. Keep going, please?"

Margaret took a deep breath and continued. "Must my sons be slaughter'd in the streets, for valiant doings in their country's cause?"

God, just...somebody, please hear me? Oh, fuck!

The Italian choir was drowning out Margaret's performance and Joe's screams were quieting down. Eric quickly hit the button to repeat the track as Margaret kept going.

"Andronicus, stain not thy tomb with blood: Wilt thou draw near the nature of the gods? Draw near them then in being merciful: Sweet mercy is nobility's true badge."

Fuck! Help! Somebody help me!

"Thrice noble Titus, spare my first-born son."

Eric sprang to his feet, wrapping one bare arm around Margaret's waist as he grinned at her with evil intent.

Please! God, just...

"Patient yourself, madam, and pardon me," he read Titus's lines off the screen of his phone as Margaret tried to push him away with feeble, theatrical hands. "These are their brethren, whom you Goths beheld alive and dead, and for their brethren slain religiously they ask a sacrifice—"

Ta Deum and its juxtaposed screams were cut short by the colliding vocals of Lady Gaga and Beyonce as the phone shuddered to life in Eric's hand. He let go of Margaret's waist and glared at the screen. The number was blocked. He turned off the phone and put it away in his pocket. "Sorry about that," he mumbled.

"It has rather killed the mood, dear." Margaret downed her absinthe.

Eric saw no need to go into detail. He didn't know why he'd played his assignment. Though perhaps if Alarbus had had any lines, they might well have been similar to Joe's cries. Maybe on that level, it made sense.

"Your reading was adequate," Margaret acknowledged, pouring another shot. "Though, I don't think you're really a Titus, do you?"

Adequate? It was a cold read. What did she want from him?

"Not really. I like Saturni—"

"Aaron," Margaret cut him off. "Enterprising, charming, and ruthless. Like you. That's the part you should have pushed for."

Eric sat down, perching on the edge of the plush seat as he tried to imagine it. "I'm not really those things. And I'm not black."

"Oh! Have they got an indigenous to play him?"

"Well, no. I don't know who's playing him yet. I'm not sure Miss Harley's decided."

"I saw *Othello* a few years ago at the House. They had an indigenous in the lead. He was just marvellous."

"We don't have any Aboriginal students in the class."

"Well, for that school's fees, I shouldn't be surprised! Miss Harley…that wouldn't be Tracey Harley? How old is she?"

"I don't know. Thirty-two, thirty-three?"

"Good lord! Little Tracey Harley? Who would have thought?"

"You know her?" Eric asked.

"Helena tried to teach her ballet, many years ago. She would have been seven, eight? But those feet! So Tracey Harley went into the arts after all? My god."

"Well, she doesn't teach dance."

"It's as they say, Eric. Those who can't do—"

"She's a really good teacher, Margaret."

His client offered him a sympathetic smile as she sat down and topped up his glass. "I'm very pleased to hear she's done well. Yet, she didn't audition you for Aaron?"

"I didn't want it." He scooped up another chocolate. She was making him uncomfortable now. "So, I didn't audition for it."

"A pity."

"Mary wanted me to play Demetrius. Because of…you know."

"Lavinia's rape and dismemberment?"

"Mary wants me to do it."

"That's very sweet of you, dear," said Margaret, putting a hand over his.

Her hand felt warm to the touch, almost like velvet. The gentle wrinkles that had invaded her skin only softened it as she caressed his fingers. Eric shivered, but he didn't pull away. It wasn't an unwelcome feeling, but Margaret's hand seemed to glow hotter as it clasped him. He'd never had sex on G. Not with a client. Not with anybody.

"I would like to see you as Aaron," Margaret said, now sipping her drink rather than throwing it back. "Would you audition for me?"

Eric slowly withdrew his hand and took out his phone. Margaret finished her absinthe and sat back in her chair, hands folded patiently in her lap while he retrieved the file. He watched her head slowly tilt back until she was staring at the ceiling.

"Tracey Harley, teaching Shakespeare," she mumbled. "*Titus*, no less. In the masterful hands of high school actors. O cruel, irreligious piety!"

"Found it!" Eric cleared his throat and began to recite. "Stay, murderous villains! Will you kill your brother?—"

"No, no, no, no, no!" Margaret waved him silent and stood up. "Try act two, scene two."

Eric skimmed through the script. "The hunting party?"

"No. Three, then? Scene three."

"A very excellent piece of villainy?"

Margaret nodded and stepped toward him, one jewelled hand outstretched until its cool fingers brushed the side of his face. "My lovely Aaron, wherefore look'st thou sad?"

The rest of the words barely registered as Margaret stroked his skin. It felt like it was tingling. He fought the urge to push his tongue into his cheek, meeting his client's loving touch through the fleshy wall of his mouth. He heard the odd word here and there. The line about sitting under the sweet shade, the one about Dido and the wandering prince. But they made no sense. Just beautiful nonsense, almost musical as Margaret continued. He stood there, enraptured.

"Of lullaby to bring her babe asleep," she finished, placing a finger on his lips.

He heard the clock on Margaret's mantle go. Midnight. He gently lifted her finger with his tongue, sucking at the cool flesh of its underside, avoiding the polished nails. Remembering the line, he moved her hand away from his face. But he didn't let it go, instead letting his fingers dance around hers as he read. "Madam, though Venus govern your desires, Saturn is dominator over mine." Again, the words fell away. He could see them. Was reading them. He felt them fall on the musty air. But their meaning was lost as Margaret lifted their joined hands and caressed him underneath the tunic. "Blood and revenge are hammering in my head," he heard himself say as she unfastened his belt, her wearied, but still soft and tender hand finding refuge in the warm, smooth flesh of his lower abs, teasing the crease of his jockline. "Hark Tamora, the empress of my soul." He closed his eyes as she forced her hand into his jeans and caressed the inside of his thigh. He hadn't seen her remove her rings, but he couldn't feel them either. His sudden erection pushed his jeans tighter still. Saturn be damned. Venus wasn't taking 'no' for an answer.

"Don't stop," Margaret whispered to him. "My dear, beautiful boy, don't stop. Some music?" She nodded at his phone.

Eric was uncertain at first. But even as he stared at her, his thumb slid over the controls, calling up the edited version of *Ta Deum*.

Margaret grinned at him as Joe's screams filled the room. "This is a day of doom for Bassianus."

"His Philomel must lose her tongue to-day." He thought of Mary as Margaret's cool fingers ran over his cock. Joe had fucked her. Joe had fucked Mary. He'd hurt her. The size of him had hurt her. And she'd let him. She'd said nothing. Lose her tongue? Why not? She's not using it.

Margaret slid a finger up and down the length of his shaft. The coldness of her touch felt incredible. "Thy sons make pillage of her chastity?" she asked, stealing his line again.

Fuck! Help! Somebody help me!

"And wash their hands in Bassianus's blood...oh!" he gasped as she yanked open his jeans and pulled them down around his thighs. He fell back in the chair, arching his back as its plush upholstery prickled against his bare skin. He tried to lie back, but the stiff buckles of the tunic held him firm.

Margaret leaned in between his knees, grinning at him as her hands massaged his slender arms. He closed his eyes with a faint, appreciative sigh. He felt his cock twitching, thudding against the fabric of the chair. Margaret leaned forward and kissed him, lingering as she hovered. Her hands weren't cold anymore. Just soft. Soft and warm like her breath, her lips, the air around him.

"Ah, my sweet Eric, sweeter to me than life!" She kissed him again, pushing her tongue deeper as he put his arms around her. His sex batted angrily against the expensive fabric of her dress as she draped herself over him. She finally slid away, warm fingers drifting down the length of his body until she took him in her mouth.

Joe screamed again. Eric relaxed further into the chair as Margaret lapped at his manhood. Manhood. No longer a boy. All of eighteen. He closed his eyes and saw Mary standing naked in front of him, a clean kitchen knife in her hand, with Joe behind her, tenderly kissing her shoulders and neck.

Eric clasped her waist, running a hand down the flawlessly smooth skin of her thigh, across the cleft of her backside. Eric felt the pull on his erection become stronger as Joe began to suck on it. It got harder still as he kissed Mary, her bosom and nipples melting against his own as she guided his hand toward her sex. He traced the outline of its tender opening, gently spreading it with his fingers.

Mary quivered as Joe's tongue pushed between Eric's fingers and lapped at her clit.

Can somebody hear me? Fuck! Help!

Eric eased Mary away from Joe, wrapping his own arms around her, the tip of his dick now pushing against her breach.

"No," she whispered with a smile, playfully moving to one side as she continued stroking him.

Strong hands massaged Eric's butt as Joe spread them apart and forced his tongue into his master's arsehole. The boy shuddered, uncomfortable at first until Mary shushed him quiet, descending his chest with deep, wet kisses, down his stomach, until she spread her lips around his cock and began to suck him, her hands wrapped around the back of Joe's head, locking the three of them together. Eric ignored Joe's moans, letting the man push his tongue deeper inside him. He wrapped his own strong fingers around the back of Joe's head and held him fast.

He enjoyed the way Mary was touching him. She ran a finger over her moistened clit and held it up to his lips. He sucked at it, taking first that finger, then another, then lapping at her hand, suckling at her flesh, the three bodies, all of them joined as one organism now.

Mary was still holding the knife. Eric hadn't given it a second thought. She released his cock with a wink and beckoned him to turn around. He obeyed, and Joe returned his attention to Eric's cock, lapping at his master as hungrily as before.

God, just...somebody, please hear me? Oh, fuck!

Mary walked behind Joe and slapped his thigh. Joe rose, but remained bent in half, his body now tilted at ninety degrees to straight legs, dutifully pleasuring Eric as Mary caressed the curved muscles of his smooth, brown behind. With a playful grin, she took the knife and gently ran the tip of its blade over the small of Joe's back until it rested against his opening.

Joe shuddered, crying out in pain as she slid it inside him, though the sound was muffled by Eric's cock.

"Faster." Mary smiled at him.

Joe nodded obediently. Eric sighed, so close to coming.

"Don't." Mary eased her sex onto the knife hilt and slid it inside her, her weight pushing the blade deeper into Joe. She screeched with satisfaction as she fucked him, the knife securing a bloody communion between them.

Eric wasn't hard anymore. His cock fell from Joe's lips as the man looked up at him with a stupid grin, eyes rolling with pleasure as Mary fucked him. Eric could smell blood.

"Stop," Eric whispered. "Mary, stop it. *Stop it!*"

The girl stopped, tilting her head as if this were the stupidest request in the world.

"What are you doing?" He tried to rebutton his pants, then realised he wasn't wearing any.

Mary smiled and leaned forward, raising her arms in an ignorant shrug. Bloody stumps remained where her hands should have been, and buried within them were two kitchen knives. One with the hilt sticking out, the other with the blade.

"Mary—"

A long stream of blood spilled from her mouth onto Joe, who gasped in ecstasy as the gory baptism washed over him, rubbing it over his chest, his belly, his legs, his cock. Eric peered closer and realised Mary had no tongue.

"Eric!"

He startled, snapping straight to attention at Margaret's command. His host was standing in the doorway, waiting for him.

"Sorry." His belt was still fastened, his pants snug around his waist.

His client frowned at him. "Are you sure you're up for this evening?"

"Yes." He got up and strode across the room to her side. At least the tunic felt good.

Margaret gave him a critical look. "Let's go upstairs."

"Yes. Yes, anything you like, Margaret. It's your time."

"Yes, dear. It is."

CHAPTER EIGHTEEN

Oh fuck, somebody help me! Can somebody hear me? Fuck! Eric clumsily pawed at his bedside table until he managed to land his fingers on the whining phone and slap the alarm silent. He buried his face in the pillow, the sickly sweet aroma of mint and absinthe-laced spittle rising from a damp patch in the fabric. He pushed his face deeper into it. Anything to stop his head spinning. It didn't help. No G before a client meet. Never again.

He'd kill Julien.

It was only when he shivered with cold and pulled the doona up around his bare shoulders that he realised he was naked. He'd managed to get home, undress, and get into bed somehow. His cock ached as it stiffened under the sheet. He'd had a client last night. He remembered that much. Carmel? No, Margaret. The rest of the night suddenly came back to him, the memory of it alive and vivid.

Holy shit.

Oh fuck, somebody help me! Can some—

He groaned, yanking the phone off the table as the alarm went off again. He rolled over, trying to shut off the noise with clumsy fingers. Only now, did he recognise his edited *Ta Deum*. He didn't remember setting it as his alarm. In fact, he didn't remember setting an alarm at all. Joe's screams distracted him as he fumbled with the screen, failing to turn off the noise and instead bringing up Twitter. *Good morning dears,* someone had tweeted. *It's Fondle a Flemish Flying Fish Friday!*

A school day. Crap! He finally managed to silence the noise.

Joe was standing in the doorway, staring at him.

"What?" Eric asked, replacing the phone on the bedside table.

Joe shivered, looking away. "You taped it?"

Eric hadn't thought of this. He hadn't thought about setting Joe free, or that the man might hear the recording. "Yeah," he admitted. "It was for an assignment. I thought it might be interesting."

Joe's eyes were quivering. "Okay."

"For music."

"Okay."

"Do you want me to delete it?"

Joe shook his head, shifting uneasily between feet.

"Good."

"Do you want any more?" Joe asked. "Screams, I mean. I can do it again, if you want."

Eric turned his nose up, grimacing at his servant. "No. It had to be real."

Joe nodded, leaving the room.

Eric could smell cooking. Frying eggs, ham and fat. He pulled the doona tight around his shoulders as he checked the time. Almost seven thirty. He laboured himself out of bed and headed for the shower, soaping himself clean and washing away the traces of absinthe, G, mint, whiskey, chocolate, and Margaret that clung to his senses. He remembered now. Margaret had given him a present. It was folded over a chair in his bedroom. Black with silver buckles. It made him look powerful. He wondered if Mary would like it.

He winced, throwing water on his face as he thought of Mary, bleeding over Joe from the ragged stumps of her wrists, and the open, mutilated maw of her mouth. He'd imagined it all, not that that made him feel any better.

He dried himself off and slipped into his school uniform. The shirt was pure white—dull, dull, dull. The blazer, a safe, boring navy blue. The unholy robes of Christian Fellowship. He wanted to sling Margaret's present over the shirt or even underneath the boring ensemble, but he decided against it. He remembered the tunic being tight. Too tight to wear all day.

His captive was in the kitchen, heaping fried eggs, ham, tomatoes, and toast onto a plate.

"Hey," Joe smiled, taking the freshly made cup from the espresso machine and handing it to his master. "Happy birthday, man."

Eric had forgotten. Even thinking about Margaret's present hadn't reminded him. He sniffed at the coffee. It was very fresh and had notes of caramel that Joe somehow managed to keep intact. Satisfied it wasn't spiked, he took a sip. It tasted...good. Great, his captive was a closet barista. That could come in handy.

"Thanks," he mumbled, drinking more.

"I couldn't get you a present or anything, so I hope this is okay."

"Why would *you* want to get me a present?"

Joe shrugged, a broad grin piercing his face. "It's kind of embarrassing—"

"Tell me," Eric grumbled.

"Well, you kind of saved me, man."

"Saved you?"

"I broke into your house. That was shitty, okay? I know. But up til then, that's all I did. Break into people's places and steal shit. Then there was the drugs. I've had mates stabbed in front of me, all right? Watched them bleed to death because we're all too chicken shit to call an ambulance. You know how that feels?"

The image of Mary and Joe covered in blood returned. "Watch your tone," he cautioned.

Joe swallowed, nervously. "I just want you to know, that's not what I'm about. I don't need that shit anymore."

"Nice. What's your point?"

"It's you. You got me out of it. Knocked me out, tied me up and looked after me. I wanted to fucking kill you at first, but it gave me time to think. Then, you came back that night with your girlfriend and—"

"I said you do *not* talk about her!" Eric spilt some of the coffee as he slammed it back down on the bench.

"Jesus, I'm sorry!" Joe said, cowering. "I only mean that that night, I got a good look at myself. You made me want to be something better."

"Well, good. What do you want? A fucking diploma?"

"No."

The smell of cooking fat clashed against the freshness of the coffee, and Eric realised with horror that the fry up was for him. "Are you trying to give me a heart attack before twenty?"

"It's a big day. You're eighteen now, man. You know what that means?"

"Yeah," Eric muttered, straightening his school bag. "Two of my clients just lost interest."

"Dude—"

"I don't eat fried food, Joe. Make sure you clean up."

Chapter Nineteen

I still don't get why Lucius kills me."

"Toby, your character just killed Titus, Lucius's father," Miss Harley explained.

"Yeah, I don't get that either. Because Titus kills Tamora—"

"Tamora, who, through her schemes, has killed half of Titus's family—"

"But I don't see what Saturninus does that's so terrible. I mean, sure, he kills Titus, but this is after Titus has killed his own daughter, one of his own sons, Tamora's sons, baked *them* into a pie and fed them to everyone. The guy is clearly a psychopath. He's got it coming."

Eric groaned, letting his face collapse into his arms on the desk.

"Something you'd like to add, Eric?"

"They're all crazy," he explained.

But Harley wasn't looking at him or Toby or anyone else in the class. She was looking at the two figures now casting a shadow across the doorway. Johansson and Principal Wagner.

"Yes, Ms Wagner?" she invited. "What can we do for you?"

"Miss Harley." The principal smiled, her teeth almost as white as her severe crop of bleached hair. "Might we have a quick word?"

Harley nodded. "Guys, if you could all please find one of your scene partners, we'll be workshopping today. Thank you."

The teacher followed Wagner out, leaving the class to steadily dissolve into small groups.

Eric didn't move. He could feel Johansson's stare on his back.

"Hey, did you pull up okay last night?" Julien whispered to him.

He wasn't sure how to answer that. "Umm…yeah, thanks. Was good stuff."

"You weren't, like, uncomfortable?"

"Don't worry about it."

Julien grinned, heading off in Felicity Turner's direction.

"Hey," Mary whispered. "Happy birthday."

"Thanks."

"Eric?"

"Yes, Toby?"

"Do you really think Titus is crazy?"

"Yes."

"Do you think Saturninus is crazy?"

"Yes."

"But I don't get it. Saturninus is angry at Tamora and her sons for what they do to Lavinia, but then he kills Titus for killing her?"

"It's a revenge tragedy. These people are slaves to their feelings. They stab first and don't care about who deserves what or body counts or facts or reason or any shit like that. They're hurt, they're angry, and they want somebody to blame."

Toby gave him a quizzical stare. His eyes were large, brown, and as far as Eric could tell, devoid of any synaptic activity. "Are you free after school? Maybe just to hang out? Run the scene a couple of times?"

"I'm not playing Titus. Ask Darren for help."

"Darren's an idiot. And he's got football practice."

Eric couldn't argue with either point. "I'll think about it."

"Thanks."

Mary glared at him as Toby left them alone. "Why are you so mean to him?"

"I wasn't mean. I said I'd think about it."

"Okay."

He watched Julien squat beside Felicity's desk until their eyes were level. It seemed so calculated, right down to the warm grin

Julien was wearing for her benefit. The kind actors usually reserved for headshots. Felicity just gave him a shy smile. The guy had ditched his tie, just like they all did after assembly. But now the top button had come undone on his crisp, white shirt. Had he done that on purpose too? When Julien caught Eric staring, his grin tightened with a faint slyness, and Eric felt a shudder go right through him, knowing he'd been caught in a shy smile of his own.

"Eric?"

"What?"

But the voice hadn't been Mary. It had been male. And German. Steffen Koray looked down at them, his dark, Turkish features a stark contrast to Toby's pasty white complexion.

"You and Julien are Demetrius and Chiron?"

"Ah, yeah. And you're...Aaron?"

The exchange student flashed a grin of perfect white teeth. "Foreign guy. Feeling a bit typecast."

Eric couldn't help but smile back. Steffen was dark, handsome, charming, and on the rare occasions he spoke, his voice was rich and seductive but never campy.

Steffen and Julien had both arrived at Christian Fellowship on the first day back after summer. Steffen, right from the start, had preferred the sidelines. The complete opposite of Julien. In fact, besides some lengthy admiration from Nerida on his first day, nobody had paid much attention to the guy. He seemed to like it that way. Now, he was Aaron. The most fucked up character in the whole play.

"Where's Julien?" the German asked.

Eric gave them a lazy nod for Steffen's benefit. "He'll come over when he's good and done."

"You want to start without him?"

Eric shrugged. Not really. "Sure." He looked for Mary, but she was already gone.

"Come on."

The two of them tried to slip unnoticed past the teachers outside. No such luck.

"You'll stay on school grounds this time, Eric?" Harley cautioned him, interrupting her conversation with Johansson and Wagner.

"Yes, Miss."

"Miss Harley," Johansson began, "I really think—"

"Mr Johansson," Wagner interrupted him. "You're quite entitled in your own class to specify where and in what manner your students are to rehearse. I'll remind you that Miss Harley enjoys the same privilege. Boys."

"Hello Miss," Eric said quickly.

"Ms Wagner." Steffen gave her a polite nod.

"You two don't have any scenes alone, do you?"

"Julien said to start without him. He'll catch up."

Satisfied, Harley dismissed them as Johansson said something Eric couldn't hear.

❖

"What are you doing?" Eric demanded. "Shouldn't we at least go somewhere Jules can find us?"

Steffen wasn't listening. He waited until he was sure the chapel was empty then swiftly opened the door and strolled in. "Eric, come on."

"Steffen, what the hell—"

"It's quiet, so we can concentrate. Hurry up!"

Hell, if Callahan didn't want students in his office, he'd have locked it, which he never did. The corkboard of notes on the wall to his left was clear enough. Need to talk? See Father Callahan, who's out right now, but leave a message. Your personal crisis, reduced to a name and number on the corkboard for everyone to see.

"What scene do you want to do?" Eric asked.

The German shut the door behind them and rounded Callahan's desk, rummaging through the bookshelves.

"What now?"

With a victorious grin, Steffen pulled a fresh looking bible from the shelf and dropped it on the desk. It spilled open halfway through Leviticus.

"Looking for tips on dismemberment?"

"Better." The boy cracked open an inch-square zip-lock bag and tipped its contents out into the crease of the book's binding.

Thanks, Nerida.

Eric leaned forward and inspected the product. Using the bible for smoke paper was more traditional, though a bit westie, circa... Christ, his mum used to do that!

Steffen flashed him another smile and tore out a page. He rolled it into a tight tube and separated the snow along the crease in two neat lines. "Thin pages, so nothing sticks."

Eric watched the first line disappear. "Oh, irreligious Moor." He grinned as he accepted the tube and did the remainder.

Steffen tore the pages out and scrunched them deep into his pocket.

"I thought you said nothing sticks?"

"Better to make sure, and I hate Leviticus. All the out of date shit Moses was too lazy to burn when he retired." Steffen sat down on Callahan's desk and swung his legs over to face Eric, taking out a cigarette.

"Callahan's going to smell that."

"Probably," Steffen mumbled, the cigarette bouncing in his lips. "Aaron wouldn't care. Why should I? You want one?"

"No." Eric sauntered around the desk and sat down in the priest's chair, leaning back and flicking his gaze around the room. Steffen's coke felt good as it pumped through him.

A profile of the mysterious German was starting to form inside Eric's head. He knew plenty of Turks lived in Germany, but not that many who sent their children on exchange to Australian schools, surely? Added to that was Steffen's perfect English, Machiavellian streak, disdain for religion and fondness for cocaine. Immigrant family or not, his elusive classmate must have had some cash behind him. He was tempted to see if Steffen had ever come to Callahan's office for the usual reasons, but the counselling folders were locked away.

"Mary's your girlfriend?" Steffen asked, blowing out a mist of smoke.

"Yeah. Two years."

"She's pretty."

"She is. What scene, Steffen?"

"You like Julien?"

"He's okay. What scene?"

"You think he likes you?"

Eric hesitated. Like this was any of Steffen's business. "I guess. Look, there are no scenes with Demetrius in them and no Chiron. We've got to go back and get Jules."

"Sorry. Only had two lines."

"I meant to rehearse."

"But he's busy," the German laughed, "with Felicity. He won't come."

"What do you mean?"

"He likes her, man. He's seeing in pussy vision." Steffen extinguished his cigarette on the window sill, a sneer rounding out each syllable as he spat out the words.

"You do what you want," Eric muttered, getting up.

"But you like him?" Steffen slipped a mint into his mouth. It smelt strong, reminding Eric of Margaret—the chocolate, the absinthe. Or it could have just been the coke. "Yeah, you do."

"I said I did." Eric was getting annoyed now.

"You like me?"

"Huh?"

Steffen's lips tasted sweet as the fake sugars of the mint hastily smothered the cigarette smell. The boy nipped tenderly at Eric's lips, dabbing them with his tongue as he ran a hand over Eric's crotch. Eric pulled away, but it was too late.

"Doesn't take you long," Steffen grinned.

Eric tried to ignore the sudden bulge of his erection as he tried to work out what had just happened. Steffen was hot enough, but he felt suddenly sick. "I like girls, Steffen."

"Me, too." Steffen put an arm around Eric's waist and took him in a long, open kiss.

Eric didn't fight him, but he couldn't bring himself to slip his tongue inside, instead letting Steffen lap at him as he pleased.

He felt numb, impassive as he tolerated the intruder. He caught Steffen's hand as the boy tried to undo one of his buttons, smooth, cold fingers slipping over each other.

Steffen brought Eric's hand up to his face with a smile, then guided it down over the curves of his throat, slipping it inside his shirt. Eric felt the boy's heart quicken through his lightly furred chest, warm against the frozen touch of their hands.

"You kiss like a girl."

"What?"

"Soft hands. Soft lips. You like me, Eric?"

"Not like that."

"Why not?"

Eric froze as a loud click came from the door to the chapel. He tried to pull away as the handle shook. But Steffen wouldn't let go of his hand.

"You locked it?" Eric mouthed.

The German shrugged.

One final shake resounded before they heard Callahan's voice. "Hello? Hello, is there someone in there?"

Eric's heart pounded in his chest as he tried to pull away from Steffen once more.

"Relax," the boy whispered, holding him firm.

Silence.

Eric held his breath, waiting for the clink of a key, another shaking of the handle. But the only sound was Callahan's footsteps, moving away as Steffen took Eric's face in his hands. Eric scowled, knocking them away.

"Yeah, you like me." Steffen said, grunting as Eric shoved him back onto Callahan's desk, and leaped on top of him. "Eric?"

"Shut up." Eric pushed Steffen flat against the desk, one hand pinning him, the other mechanically working the buttons of his shirt.

Steffen tilted his head back with a faint sigh, his shirt hanging open. "Eric, if Callahan comes back—"

"I said be quiet," Eric wrapped his fingers around Steffen's face, gripping him tight. "You're the one who locked the door."

Steffen gasped, taking in the smell of Eric's hand. He relaxed into the desk, lying perfectly still as Eric ran his hands down the length of his body, over the fine hairs of his chest and down his deeply tanned stomach.

Eric toyed with it all, like it was his own property, slipping a hand inside Steffen's belt and running a cold finger over the boy's attentive cock.

"Is this what you wanted?" he asked.

Steffen smiled with appreciation as he twitched to Eric's touch.

"Then you do exactly as I tell you," Eric sneered, grabbing the German's wrists and pinning them to the desk above his head.

"Eric," Steffen whispered.

SMACK.

Steffen stared at him, taking Eric's hand and bringing it up to his cheek, where he'd been slapped.

Eric could see now that he understood, as Steffen grinned at him one last time.

❖

Eric had almost snapped his phone in half when Johansson had called his name. He didn't know why he'd been so nervous. It could have been the coke. He was still high, but coherent. At least, nobody had told him any different.

Reactions had varied when he'd flicked on the MP3 and Joe had begun screaming over the opera. An approving nod and grin from Julien, who'd failed to notice his disappearance from drama. A broad 'you actually did it?' smile from Nerida, and from Mary, just the gentle tilt of her lips as she recognised Joe's voice.

Johansson hadn't seen the artistic merit and had sent Eric to Wagner's office. He'd thought about making a detour by Father Callahan's once again. But no. Not in light of his recent German conquest.

He stared at the ginger cat clock that ticked on the admin block wall. Its tail and its annoying eyes flicked from side to side as it tapped out the steady rhythm of his wait. So tacky. So eighties. Was Wagner even in?

"Eric?" she called. "Come on through."

Louise Wagner had taught music for almost twenty years at Christian Fellowship, and it showed in her choice of decor. No less than five metronomes decorated the mantle behind her desk. The slightly dented flute she'd played in her own high school band hung proudly on the wall, and the window sills and filing cabinets held a number of the school's music trophies from the beginning of her tenure—earned by students long forgotten, who'd shuffled into safe careers, donned power suits and now beat the remnants of their former dreams into the pavement at Martin Place. A dozen certificates from institutions in Sydney, Melbourne, New York, London, Vienna and Chicago hung on the rear wall. Eric liked Wagner, but she loved to show off.

She sat at her desk, hands folded up under her chin, staring down at him from behind a pair of thick rimmed glasses. A cherry red scarf offset her crisp black suit, matching her eye-catching lipstick and nail polish. On anyone else it might have seemed cheap. On Wagner, it meant business.

"How've you been keeping, Eric?" she asked in a tone as far from congenial as Eric could imagine.

"Fine, thank you, Miss."

"How's your mum?"

"She's good."

"Been busy?"

"Yeah."

"I understand you've been helping Miss Harley with this year's play?"

"Kind of."

"I also understand you've taken on a rather experimental project in Music?"

"I guess."

"May I listen to it?"

He offered up the player. Wagner took it without a word, disconnected his earphones and plugged the USB into her laptop. A moment later, Joe's screams and *Ta Deum* invaded the office. Wagner gently pressed her hands together, fingertips under her lips as she listened. She didn't repeat the file when it had finished. She didn't look at him, either.

"What were the criteria for the assignment?" she asked.

The question caught him off guard. "Umm, take different sources of contrasting sound and digitally blend them to create a new piece."

"I suppose you pass." Wagner unplugged the USB and handed it back.

"Joh—Mister Johansson didn't like it."

"Neither do I."

Another long silence passed as Eric put the player away in his pocket. "He didn't put any limits on what we could use."

"Eric, it sounds like a man being tortured. Please tell me it's not."

"He isn't. He's just a friend. He did some screams for me, just for the assignment. That's all."

"Yet you told Mister Johansson you got it from the Internet?"

"I sort of lied about that. I thought it would be less trouble. Sorry."

"Not one of your classmates, is it?" the principal sighed. "It sounds like Julien Davidson."

Eric frowned. "What makes you say that?"

Wagner narrowed her eyes.

"Well, it isn't. You can ask him." Fuck this. If all he'd wanted had been shock value, he would have taped Mary. She would have done it for him, too.

"I see." Wagner straightened her glasses and made a note on her laptop. "Well, it's up to your teachers if they choose to credit you or not. I'm not overriding Mister Johansson's decision. But I will ask him to let you do the assignment over."

"If you say so."

"Listen to me. He's perfectly entitled to fail you for the semester if he feels your work is inadequate. The only reason I'm doing this for you is because your other grades are so high, and it would be an awful shame—"

"No…I get that, thanks. It's okay. I'll do it. For you."

"Eric," she muttered. "Why do you feel this need to antagonise him?"

The image of Johansson's arrogant, moralising face crossed Eric's mind, a small shower of gore exploding from its forehead. "What were you, he, and Miss Harley talking about?"

"I can't discuss that with you."

"It was *Titus*, wasn't it? Johansson doesn't want us to do it."

"Eric, *Mister* Johansson has some concerns about a couple of the play's scenes, yes. I understand he stumbled on Mary, Julien, and yourself rehearsing a rape scene?"

"It's post-rape," Eric pointed out. "You never see anything, just the result."

"The mutilated girl? Thank you, I have seen a production of *Titus*. Two, in fact. One of which did show the deed in graphic detail. I'm not convinced it's right for a Christian Fellowship stage."

"It's Shakespeare."

"Young man, there are a great many wonderful plays by far lesser writers that I could not allow to be presented in this school."

"Well, respectfully, Miss, don't you trust Miss Harley?"

"Pardon?"

"She's directing. I'm sure if you talk to her about it alone, she can make sure—"

"Eric," Wagner sighed, looking up at the door. "I've received three quite 'frank' emails from parents this week, all about *Titus*. In fact, I've a meeting in the next hour on the same subject. Do I need to fill in the blanks for you?"

"So? Just because somebody complains the loudest doesn't make them right."

Wagner got up from her desk, pouring herself a glass of water. She didn't say anything at first. She just stared out the window, watching the school populace as it broke for lunch, one class at a time. "Nice bit of logic when we're all fair and reasonable, isn't it?"

"Sorry?" Eric frowned.

"Eric, you know this school has always tried to foster its performing arts program, but not everyone in this community is as well read or open-minded as you. There are others, influential others with some sway over the budget and more particularly, the funding to the drama department."

"So, they're threatening to pull the money if Miss Harley doesn't pull *Titus*?"

"Not yet. But these flames are fed by attention, Eric. Best bushel them now, I think."

"You can't cancel our play!" the boy barked.

"Don't raise your voice to me." Wagner downed her water in one gulp.

"But…you can't."

"I've no intention of it. But certain heads must be allowed to cool. I'm going to ask Miss Harley to postpone *Titus* until October, the end of the school year. Trust me, Eric. The powers that be will pick fewer fights with next year's board positions up for nomination."

"Oh sure. Spring. Because, you know, there's nothing like Shakespeare's goriest, nastiest work for a festive spring play. I don't believe this!"

Wagner shrugged as the bell sounded for lunch. "So, you understand our little problem. I'm sorry to drop this on you, truly. But if you aren't prepared to wait another six months, it's unlikely your class will be presenting any play at all. Do you know what that could mean for your folios? What about your classmates, Eric? The ones who really need a senior play under their belts? What would it mean for them?"

"Let me talk to Miss Harley," Eric protested. "Doesn't it matter what she thinks?"

"Of course it does. I'm trying to represent all sides here. In the meantime, lock your script in a drawer and forget about it until October. The worst thing you can do right now is draw more attention to the issue than there needs to be. Let Miss Harley and I sort it out, please."

Realising that his fingernails were almost breaking skin, Eric unclenched his fists, which did nothing to soothe his rage. October? Who knew what could happen in six months? His classmates could move schools. Harley could cave and make them do something like…God, if she made them do *Merchant of Venice*, he'd take out a pound of his own flesh. And if she did keep *Titus*, she could totally recast the parts. Steffen could go back to Germany. Julien could—

"October," he whispered, silencing his panicked thoughts. "Okay, October." Fuck. They graduated in November. All the drama schools would be well into auditions. Nobody would care about the play. Damn their folios!

"I appreciate that, Eric. You're dismissed."

Dismissed? Like hell.

❖

"Hey."

"Hey." Eric shot Felicity a forced smile as he tried to listen to the voices behind Wagner's door. He waited for Roslyn the Fridge Shaped Admin Lady to go for lunch before he raised a hand to knock.

"They won't let you in," Felicity mumbled.

"Who's in there?"

"Mum and Dad. I tried talking to them already."

He leaned closer to the door. The voices were low, even muffled behind the frosted glass. He heard Wagner, and a man and a woman he didn't know. Felicity's parents, he guessed. "How long?"

"Fifteen minutes? Don't know how long they're gonna be."

Another voice, higher and more agitated. Miss Harley.

"What did your mum say about the play?" Felicity asked.

"Shhh," he hushed her, leaning closer to the door.

"They're kids!" he heard the strange man bark.

"Seventeen? Some of them eighteen?" That was Harley.

"What do we tell Rachel?" the strange woman asked. "About why she can't come and see her sister's play?"

"We'll be staging the stronger scenes in a way that ensures they're accessible to younger students."

"In your opinion?"

Eric froze. The new voice was angry and authorative, one that he and half of Sydney knew and recognised immediately. He started to back away, swallowing down the lump in his throat, his heart beating hard enough to hurt in his chest.

"You, Miss Harley," the voice continued. "You, who approved this work in the first place."

"Mr Weblock, I assure you, Miss Harley is—"

"Speaking, not just as a representative of the community, but as a Christian Fellowship parent…"

Eric jumped, almost losing his footing as the glass door slid open.

"Was there something you wanted, *boy?*"

He stared at Weblock's swollen red face and flaring nostrils, any words of protest or explanation frozen in his throat. The man had to recognise him. It was impossible that he wouldn't.

"Eric?" Ms Wagner called. "This is a private meeting."

He turned and bolted.

"Eric?" Felicity called.

He barely heard her. All he could hear was that man's voice, vibrating inside his head as he left the admin block behind, passing one empty classroom after another.

BOY. BOY. BOY. BOY.

Eric…

Now the guy knew his name! 'Boy?' The word had given him so much protection. Not anymore. He had to get to Mary. He had to reach her *now!*

❖

Mary was sitting behind the old groundskeeper's shed, staring vacantly into the bushland behind the school where they'd gone to rehearse *Titus*.

"Hey," he whispered.

"Eric." Her voice was so calm and controlled. But the undeniable hint of venom that lay under it made him shudder.

"Jesus."

"Just go away, please. I'm fi—" She slapped his hand away, giving him a furious, red-eyed glare, streaked with long-dried tears.

He flopped down beside her, the warmth of corrugated iron spreading in lines down his back as he leaned against the shed alongside her. She'd been so full of courage and curiosity that day, attacking the play—and Julien—with equal delight. Scary in her own way, but he'd loved seeing it. Loved how committed and fearless she'd been. Johansson had stopped them, and they'd all but laughed in his face. They couldn't laugh at Weblock. Even Mary couldn't laugh at him forever.

Why Weblock? Why did he have to get involved at all?

"You want to go for a walk?" he offered.

She shook her head.

Eric thought about putting an arm around her, letting her head lay in his lap. Right. Because all she needed right now was for some guy, even him, to come along and patronise her. Instead, he closed his eyes, lifted his face to the sky and basked in the sun's rays. "How'd he find out?"

When she didn't give him an answer, he wondered if his question had been too stupid to deserve one. It wasn't as if they'd been doing the play in secret. Maybe part of him had just assumed her dad wouldn't notice. Maybe Mary had assumed the same. Perhaps Weblock wouldn't have noticed until opening night and by then it would have been done, with nothing the bastard could do about it. Mary could sneer and spit in his face.

Sure. And maybe Eric's mum would be so inspired by LA and have so many amazing, famous contacts, she'd get him into AFI with a full ride. Not in a million fucking years.

"Felicity? Are her parents there?" Mary asked.

"Yeah. She was waiting outside Wagner's office when I left. I think she's pretty cut up—"

"Stupid bitch!"

The attacked stunned him. "Who?"

"Who do you think?" she snarled. "Stupid plastic cunt!"

"Woah, okay! What's wrong? How's this Fil's fault?"

Mary straightened her blouse as she stood up, arms crossed over her chest. "You wouldn't get it."

"Right," he answered, careful to check the tone behind his sarcasm. "Because ever since grade six, in all that time I've known you, I've never, ever been able to make you feel better. Come on!"

"No," she insisted. "It's all just bullshit. Don't worry about it."

"Hey," he put a hand on her shoulder, more like the hand of a big brother than a boyfriend. But wasn't that exactly what she needed right now? A hug would have really sent her over the edge. "Please, just tell me?"

"Her dad," Mary mumbled. "He's the one who brought it up at church, at the men's group. That's how Dad found out."

"Okay," he said patiently. "Still not seeing how Felicity—"

"And this morning, Dad says—he actually has the fucking nerve to say to me, *over breakfast* Eric, in front of Mum—'Jim Turner's girl told them she's in a play. *Titus Andronicus.* Isn't that good of her? To let her parents know what she's doing at school? Aren't they lucky to have such a *good daughter*?' and he's spitting the words out at me real slow, like I'm retarded or something!"

He nodded, slowly lowering his hand. "The implication being that you're not a good daugh—"

"*No shit!*"

He wanted to ask why she cared about being a good daughter to such a shitty father. "Are you going to be okay?"

Mary suddenly screamed through clenched teeth, beating at her sides and shaking her head. "I hate it, Eric! A year this shit has been going on! Remember that abstinence workshop?"

"What? Mary, that guy was an idiot!"

"*He* didn't think so. He did a fucking show on it, for God's sake! A whole hour on the bloody radio about why every high school should have one! And when Felicity came out with her stupid line about 'the sacred chamber of God', he just…I mean *fuck!* What side of a Mormon tampon box did she read that one from?"

"Mary…" he hesitated, not quite sure how to ask what he needed to know. "Are you safe at least? He's not—"

"No, he's not."

Neither of them could talk about what Mary had been through last year, during her Father's well-publicised row over four dodgy sponsorship deals. It had put him off air for two weeks and almost ended him entirely. Though he'd played it cool in public view, the stress he'd been under had shown in the form of bruises on Mary's arms. From what little Eric knew, her mother had endured far worse. But what was he supposed to do about it? Call the cops? A few threats from her dad would have had the charges dropped within an hour.

"Ever since that stupid workshop it's been 'Felicity' this, 'Felicity' that. Miss Fucking Sunshine. 'Why can't you be more like her?' I hate it!"

"Shhh," he hushed again, catching hold of her wrists and letting her nestle into him until she stopped shivering. "Come stay at my place tonight. Cool off a bit."

She shook her head. "Can't. We've...I've got plans."

"Not with him? Oh fuck! Mary, please tell me not with him."

"No." She eased herself out from his grasp. "I'd like to. Spend tonight with you, I mean."

"So blow off your...what are you doing, anyway?"

"I..." she suddenly looked profoundly uncomfortable.

"Hey! Are you guys okay?"

Felicity stepped out into the sunlight, which somehow made the light on the iron shed seem all the more bright next to the shimmering flax colour of her hair.

"Hi," Eric said. "We're okay, I think."

"Didn't you hear the bell?"

Mary straightened her cardigan, angrily brushing stray grass off her skirt.

"How'd it go in there?" Eric asked.

"It's okay. Wagner's totally on Harley's side. Don't worry."

"And your folks?"

"They'll be okay. I think they just talked it all out, you know? Mum's not so bad."

Eric wondered if Julien knew what Mary really thought of his blonde, good-girl crush. Or had he been too smitten to notice? *Pussy vision*, Steffen had called it. Maybe if they just let nature take its course, since nature did seem to be firmly on Julien's side, Felicity wouldn't remain quite the role-model Mary's father imagined.

They turned to follow Mary as she headed back toward class.

"Mary? Oh man, your dad," Felicity sighed. "He's intense, huh?"

"No shit," mumbled Mary.

"What do you mean, talked?" Eric asked.

"Huh?"

"You said they talked it out."

"Oh, right! I just know what Miss Harley said."

"Which was?"

"Just stuff. Some changes."

"Know what? Forget it." Eric shook his head. "I'll ask her."

"Eric," Mary stopped in her tracks and turned to face them. "Let her finish."

"Oh, I was."

"No, you weren't. What do you mean? What changes?"

"Mary..."

"Felicity?" Mary stepped forward, gradual and determined, her entire face flattened by the wash of sunlight, wind gently blowing her hair as she stared at the blonde girl. "Just tell me."

"Well, like the bit where Titus kills his youngest son? They're cutting that character."

"What else?"

"The bit where the boys rape Lavinia."

"Hey, maybe we should just—"

"*Eric!* Go on, Fil. The scene where they rape her? They want to cut that?"

"No. Just change it. So they beat her up instead."

Eric's mouth had gone dry, like he was awaiting some nearby explosion he couldn't escape. But Mary's lips were a steely line, her eyes fixed on Felicity. All trace of the surrounding world was absent to them now as she remembered everything.

"What did Dad say about that?"

"I don't know. He's like..." Felicity shrugged. "He's not happy. But Harley said she's going to craft it as a statement about, like, violence against women and stuff. But staged in a way that's more subtle. Not so in your face, you know? Mum and Dad think it's a good idea, and I think if Dad's okay with it and Ms Wagner's okay with it, your dad won't...you know."

"Won't what?"

"Mary…"

"Eric! Won't what, Fil?"

"Won't give us a hard time."

Mary nodded, slowly. "Right. No hard times for you. Or for Ms Wagner. Everything behind closed doors. Nothing to talk about. Nothing to worry about."

"Mary, are you okay?"

"Yes of course I'm okay, Eric. Why wouldn't I be? They're not going to rape me anymore," she laughed. "You're not going to rape me. You're just going to beat me up. Hit me with your fists, because that's so much better!"

"Well, it is, right?" Felicity asked. "I mean, it's in the script. Something horrible has got to happen, and it's not as bad as what's in there. Besides, it makes an important point. That's what art's all about, right?"

Felicity screamed as Mary launched herself at her, arms spread wide, teeth and claws bared. She stumbled back into the dirt of an empty garden bed, hands flying up to protect her face from Mary's short, vicious nails.

"Hey!" Eric swooped to grab Mary's arms. She whirled around and met him with a solid whack to the jaw. He cradled his stunned face as he staggered back. She'd hit him. She'd really hit him hard enough to hurt. But he couldn't break her trust now.

"I'm sorry," he heard her sob. "I'm sorry, I'm so…" She quickly backed off as he went to put his arms around her.

"Hey," he insisted. "It's me. It's just me."

She looked him over, cautiously watching him massage his wounded jaw. Then, all of a sudden, fell forward against him.

Eric hoped nobody would ask questions about the blotches on his shirt, damp from tears. His jaw, he could deal with. The office would ask questions, so he'd have to get some ice from the science lab. Easy enough. Mary had stopped shaking now. "Fil?" he asked.

The girl erupted from behind her hands, furiously skewering them with her eyes. "You crazy bitch! What the hell's wrong with you? You want to kill me?"

"Hey! Calm down, okay?" Eric turned his attention back to Mary, smoothing her hair with long, steady strokes. "Look, she didn't know," he whispered to her. "It's okay. She doesn't know. She didn't mean—"

"Doesn't know what, Eric? That your girlfriend's a psycho mole? You are so fucking busted, you crazy—"

"Hey!" Eric yelled. "Cool it. Now."

Felicity wiped her eyes, then brushed the dust from her skirt as she stood up, straightening her blouse.

"Are you okay?" Eric asked her.

She snorted, checking her soiled hands. "I guess."

He went back to stroking Mary's hair.

Felicity sniffed away a tear and turned to leave.

"Fil?" Eric called. "Listen. I'm really sorry. But you can't tell anyone about this. Nobody!"

"Oh, piss off, Eric!"

"I mean it! You just can't. Look, there's stuff you don't know, okay?" He felt Mary shudder in his arms. The last thing she needed was the gossip chain doing its worst.

"Like what?" the blonde challenged, folding her arms.

"*FIL!*"

She jumped back, startled by his outburst.

"I am so sorry. But between us, only."

She gave him nothing. Not a nod. Not even a dirty look.

"Jesus, have I gotta beg? *Please*, Fil! For me?"

The girl swallowed, straightening her clothes one last time, now looking mostly like her usual self. "Whatever."

The polite thing would be to walk with her back to class. But Mary needed him more than Felicity did. He watched the stunned girl go, cradling Mary's head against his chest. Finally stable, no longer shaking. The drying blotches on his shirt now felt strangely natural. She pulled away from him, her eyes mostly dry.

"Stupid," she muttered. "I feel so stupid."

"Are you sure you don't want to stay over tonight?"

She squeezed his hand. They didn't say anything as he walked her back to class, lingering back as she slipped inside. Maths, wasn't it? He'd lost track of the time.

The science lab in Kenny Block was empty. He snuck in, grabbed three pieces of ice, wrapped them inside a towel and pressed it against his face. Almost twenty minutes late. A few more wouldn't make any difference. He had to be sure. He rounded past the admin block, walking slowly as he listened for that voice. That awful, booming siren of self-righteous indignation and thinly disguised greed. But it was gone. The giant had stormed back to its castle to count its gold. He sneered, forcing the childish metaphor out of his head.

He felt the iPhone vibrate in his pocket. One missed call. When had it come in? It could have been during drama, music, when he'd been with Wagner, or when he'd been with Steffen or Mary. He hadn't even thought about it.

Hey, lovely. It's your mum. Listen, I know you're in school so I'll make it quick. I've got some exciting news. Just had a chat to Marcel. He's got to take off back to Paris for a few weeks—all a bit last minute—anyway, much as I'd love to join him, there's some hitch with the visas or some excuse like that. Also, says he needs some personal creative time, so you know what that means. Plenty more fish, eh? Anyhow, guess where I am? Tom Bradley International Terminal at LAX, and they just called boarding. So, surprise! I'll see you in about fourteen hours, baby boy. I'm coming home. Love ya!

Eric lowered his phone slowly as his mother's voice faded. Fourteen hours. Fourteen hours…shit! He checked the time on the message. Received three hours ago. Three whole hours? Midnight. He had til midnight, like this was some kind of bad fairy tale. Fuck!

"Eric?"

"What?" he barked, shoving the phone back into his pocket and rounding on Toby. "Sorry, what is it?"

"Just wondering about this afternoon," Toby said with a grin. "Where should I meet you?"

"I don't know, Toby. It's kind of awkward," he said, trying to walk away.

"I've got the house to myself, if you want to come over. Mum and Dad just had this case of really nice wine come in. But they're gone for two weeks. They won't miss it."

"Toby, I really can't. Mum's coming back tonight."

"Does she really need you there? I mean, I get that she's your mum and you want to see her, but it could be fun. We don't get to talk much, just you and me—"

"Toby!" Eric finally shouted. "I have other stuff on."

Toby stared at him, dumbfounded. Finally, he shrugged. "Maybe sometime soon then?"

"Yeah, see you around."

Chapter Twenty

That afternoon's double Maths period felt like the longest class of Eric's life. He'd considered cutting it but hadn't wanted to push his luck after the trip to Wagner's office. He'd caught Father Callahan's eye in the hall on the way out, though the man hadn't stopped him.

He'd gotten a text from Julien on the way home but had accidentally deleted it before having the chance to read it. The bus was late, and it was packed when it did arrive. He'd had to stand. An hour after school had gotten out, he'd arrived home to find Joe sitting on the hardwood floor in the kitchen.

"Do you like it?" the man asked.

Eric frowned, inspecting the kitchen. Apart from the smell of disinfectant, it looked like it had never been used. He opened several cupboards for inspection. Their once overflowing contents were in dozens of neat stacks.

"What did you do?"

"You said clean up."

Eric turned and glanced over the rest of the living area. It was spotless. Not a speck of dust on the furniture, and the balustrade leading downstairs had been newly polished.

"Umm...thanks, I guess," he murmured.

"You wanted it done," said Joe. "I didn't touch your bedroom. I will if you want me to, but I thought I should ask."

Eric grimaced as he caught the fresh smell of the wood polish. Shit. His mother would never believe he'd done all this.

"You do like it, right?" Joe asked, standing up.

"Joe, we've got a problem. Mum's coming home, *tonight*. I only just found out."

"Okay. You want me to pretend I'm a mate from school?" Joe suggested. "I'm a bit old, but I can try."

"I want you out, Joe," Eric blurted. "I need you out. I can't explain you."

The man stared at him, his eyes vacant, as though he could disbelieve the words away.

"Get out! Look, thanks for cleaning the place, okay? Now get your shit together and go!"

"Go? You're…you're really kicking me out?"

"Yes! I'll give you some money if you need it, but you have to leave."

Joe didn't move.

"What's the problem? It's what you wanted, isn't it? You're free. Now get out!"

"Dude, no."

Eric's eyes widened, a shrill cry rising inside him. "*No*?"

"I don't want to leave! I don't understand, man. I thought you liked…could use me?"

"I have, Joe. You're used, and now I'm done. Thanks, it's been great. Really interesting, actually. Now, go back to your life."

"My life?"

For the first time since he'd granted Joe any semblance of freedom, Eric saw the flicker of anger in the man's eyes.

"My life? Have you been listening to *anything* I've said about my *life*?"

Eric flinched as Joe stepped toward him. The man's chest stretched against the T-shirt he'd borrowed, huge arms bulging from its sleeves. Eric swallowed. He'd gotten careless, forgotten how big Joe was.

"I have *nothing* out there. Do you get that?" Joe snarled. "And you want to just cut me—"

Eric slammed his fist into Joe's jaw, sending the man sprawling into the kitchen. Joe fell against the cupboards under the sink with a loud bang and didn't move. But his eyes stayed open, staring at Eric feverishly as his lower lip quivered. It was bleeding. Eric took a clean tissue out of his school blazer and knelt down beside his captive, gently dabbing the blood away.

"Please?" Joe begged. "Don't just throw me out."

Eric stared at him, silent for a moment, until he took out his phone.

CHAPTER TWENTY-ONE

H e cooks. Cleans well. Makes excellent coffee."

Margaret circumnavigated Joe, inspecting him like she'd just acquired a new statue for the hall.

"I see. And gardening? Does he do gardening as well?"

"Probably. I haven't asked him." Eric ignored Joe's furtive glances. The man would do gardening if Margaret wanted gardening done.

"But what about your...arrangement?"

"Mum's coming back tonight. She doesn't want hired help."

"Why ever not?"

Eric drummed his fingers against his thighs as he scrambled for an explanation. Had something gone wrong in LA? Could his mother afford help? "She found Dad in bed with the help. That's why he left." He ignored Joe's confused frown.

"Well, she can get into bed with this one, can't she? Turnabout is fair play, after all."

"Can I talk?" Joe mumbled.

Margaret narrowed her eyes at him. "If you speak clearly, you *may* talk. Yes?"

"I...I need the work. I can't go home."

"And you can't stay here. I'm sorry, but your personal troubles are not mine."

"I can earn my keep."

"Eric," Margaret sighed. "Will you please try and talk your mother around? This is perfectly ridiculous."

Eric kept his eyes fixed on Joe. The man steadily kneeled forward until he was on his knees in front of Margaret, his head bowed. She frowned, roughly taking his chin in her fingertips and turning it for inspection.

"You said he was strong?" she asked.

"Yes," Eric assured her. He considered mentioning Joe's by all accounts huge cock, but thought better of it.

Margaret ran her fingertips through the dark curls of her potential acquisition's hair. The man nuzzled his head against her hand, letting her caress him as she pleased, almost like he was sniffing it. Eric watched her carefully.

She was smiling.

"Wait here, both of you." She smartly left the room, returning with an accessory Eric recognised. "I hope this fits you."

The metal collar, lined on the inside with soft fur, was a tighter fit on Joe than it had been on Eric, but Margaret managed to close the clasp all the same.

Joe tilted his head from side to side until it sat comfortably.

"How much?" Margaret asked Eric.

"Huh?"

"Must I repeat everything? He's yours. How much do you want for him? And how much to keep him?"

"Oh!" Eric was about to blurt out 'nothing, he's yours.' "Five thousand?"

"Five thousand?" Margaret snapped.

"Three! Three thousand, and he's yours. No less."

Yeah, sure. He could do with an extra three grand.

Margaret ran her fingers through Joe's hair again. "All right. Three thousand for you, and will he accept four hundred a week? I should think it plenty if his room and board are already provided."

"Four hundred? A *week*?"

"Well, how much were you paying him?"

Eric swallowed down a small choke.

"About that," said Joe.

"It's settled then."

"What are you going to tell Gerald?" Eric asked.

"Whatever I tell my husband, I doubt he'll hear it. All that lazy lump will see is cheap household labour. Stand up, you silly boy!"

Joe obeyed, the collar still snug around his neck, studying Margaret with his dark eyes as closely as she observed him.

"You're rather handsome, aren't you?"

"Thank you, ma'am."

"Young man, 'ma'am' is how one addresses the Queen. You may address me as Mrs Moss. If you want to call your employer 'ma'am,' I suggest you go work for Andrew Felton."

"Actually, you could," Eric muttered. "He just fired Viktor."

"Who?"

"Viktor. Ukrainian guy, obsessed with working out." At least, Eric guessed the man was Ukrainian. With their recent conversation, who could know?

"Details, boy," Margaret moaned. "You trouble me with details."

"Sorry."

"I suppose you're ethnic, too?"

Joe licked his lips nervously.

"Middle Eastern, by the look of you. What are you? Arab? Israeli?"

"Margaret!"

"Eric, I ask now, because I don't wish to disrespect your friend by getting it wrong later. Now, kindly stop interrupting."

"I'm a Leb, Mrs Moss. Lebanese, I mean."

"He looks nothing like an Israeli," Eric pointed out.

"There's such a thing as Arab-Israelis, boy. Must I remind you that every Israeli prime minister since the state's formation has been of Arab stock? Perhaps if you weren't such a stubborn, bone-headed leftist, you'd know that?"

Coppery blood seeped from Eric's tongue as he bit down harder, determined to stay silent. This wasn't about him. He wouldn't let her make it about him.

"Where are you from?" Margaret asked Joe.

"Bankstown."

"And what do they do to thieves in your culture? Cut off the hand, don't they? I'll keep that in mind."

Eric stared at his toes and shook his head. He wasn't strong enough to claw Joe off Margaret if things really snapped. In fact, he might have preferred not to.

"Take off your shirt," Margaret commanded.

"Huh?" Joe grunted.

"Your shirt? Lift!"

Joe flicked his eyes timidly at Eric, who just raised his hands. At this point, it would be easier for all of them if Joe just did what he was told. The man obeyed, shucking off Eric's T-shirt and tossing it to the floor, exposing his huge chest and tight brown abs. They met with instant approval.

"Bankstown?" Margaret asked. "Well, we can't let you go back there, can we?"

"Got nothing to go back to," Joe sighed as Margaret circled one of his nipples with the tip of a painted fingernail.

"Death for the cultural soul. Do you have a cultural soul, Joe?"

"I dunno."

The woman grinned, cupping her hands together. "I'll let you in on a secret. *Everyone* has a cultural soul. It simply needs tuning. Do you understand?"

"I guess."

"Do you like opera?"

"I dunno."

"I have two tickets for *La Traviata* next week, if you would like."

Eric snorted. Thank God it wasn't *Tosca*.

"Umm, that'd be, cool, I guess?" Joe stammered.

"Margaret, maybe something lighter?"

"Oh," the woman beamed. "I'm sure we'll find no shortage of light entertainment to keep him occupied 'til next week." She grinned at her new toy through bright purple lips. "Wait here." She took hold of her evening dress and gracefully ascended the stairs, disappearing into her bedroom.

Joe turned to Eric, colour draining from his face faster than he could speak. "Dude, I've changed my mind, yeah?"

"What?" Eric barked under his breath.

"She's a freak!"

"You'll be fine. Stop moaning."

"Listen, man, I will do anything, say *anything* to your Mum. You can't leave me here!"

"All done, Joe," Eric muttered. "You got used to me. You can get used to her. It's done, Joe."

Margaret returned with a wad of yellow fifties in hand.

"Eric, here you are."

The boy's eyes widened. Three thousand? All in cash? He accepted it gratefully and resisted the urge to count, at least until Margaret had turned her attention back to Joe.

She grinned and took the man's hand. "I think we're going to be good friends, you and I. Don't you agree?"

Joe looked up, meeting her gaze mournfully as she rubbed his hands between her own. "Yeah."

Eric swallowed, thrusting the money deep inside his jacket pocket.

"Eric," Margaret said.

"Yes?"

"You may leave us now."

Eric swallowed, watching Joe carefully. His former subject didn't move, petrified under Margaret's gaze. "Yes, ma'am."

CHAPTER TWENTY-TWO

The house looked cold as Eric approached it, but the darkness behind its windows promised desperately needed sleep. Sleep without company. Sleep without dreams.

He heard Julien's voice in his head. "Hey, dude." A few more words followed, but Eric couldn't make them out. He murmured a half-answer, only to find he couldn't make that out either.

The key slid smoothly into the frozen lock, but the deadlock was already undone. Had he left the house so quickly? It seemed like Joe had taken forever to get his shit together. Ironic for a guy who'd broken in with nothing but the intent of walking out loaded. And the son of a bitch had gotten what he wanted. Eric had to laugh.

"What?" came the faint echo of Julien's voice in his mind again.

He ignored it, focused on sleep. Sleep before his mother got home. Their happy reunion could wait until morning. He'd pop two pills and a herbal just to make sure of it.

"Think you're better than us, arsehole?"

Eric spun around to face the gravel-voiced speaker, but no one was there. No shadow, nothing at all. Just the arm that wrapped around him from behind, pinning him helpless against his attacker as a hand clapped over his mouth.

"No point struggling, mate. You've had this coming for a long time."

He knew the voice, but it was exaggerated, frightening. A silhouette crossed into the moonlight.

"Oh, Eric. You won't like this. You like to be the one in charge, eh?"

Eric knew that voice. Crisply accented like a bad Bond villain. It matched the silhouette.

Steffen Koray.

"Hold still, and we'll make this quick," the first—very Australian—voice mocked him from behind.

Eric hissed at them from behind a crushing wall of fingers, but his assailant was too strong for him to do anything.

Steffen looked down at him with a stupid, cocky grin. "You like things to be quick, don't you, Eric?"

It was in that moment that Eric realised just how little he knew about Steffen Koray. Someone fastened his hands with a tight cord. Then, he saw another face, right beside Steffen.

"I didn't want to do this, dude. You know, you're a pain in the arse?"

Julien. He was sure of it.

Eric tried to scream, but it was futile. Steffen slipped a blindfold over his face, and within seconds, he felt himself being bundled into a car.

CHAPTER TWENTY-THREE

M ove!" the gruff Aussie voice commanded as Eric copped a hard shove and marched forward.

"Fuck off!"

Not a sound from Julien. What was he doing?

Eric heard a lock turn. He screwed up his nose at the sickly scent of jasmine, so strong it made his nose itch. The boys edged him through the door, one foot in front of the other on the polished wood floor. If he could just get a hand free, just one, he could land a punch. Maybe two. Across the guy holding his arms? No. Across Steffen's smug—

"Happy birthday, bitch!" Nerida enveloped him in a hug and kissed his cheeks. The lights flared on while unseen hands whipped the blindfold off his face and quickly untied him.

"Uh...thanks?"

"Didn't scare you, did we, big fella?" Darren, his Aussie accent less of a gross stereotype now, slapped him hard on the back as he rounded on his 'victim.'

"Eric's not scared of anything," Steffen grinned.

"Not sca..." Eric tried to think over the laughter, whoops and hollers of a dozen of his classmates. "What the hell is going on? Julien?"

Mary offered him a sympathetic shrug from the end of the couch, where she'd perched with knees drawn up under her chin, trying to look small.

"What does it look like?" Darren laughed at him. "Happy birthday, mate!"

"Didn't tell anyone!" Nerida scolded. "You don't get off that easy, Mister!"

"You…who planned all this? Nerida?"

"It was Toby, mostly."

"*Toby?*"

At the sound of his name, Toby jumped up from the couch and came at Eric with a big, stupid grin. "I told you, you should have come to my place. I had it all organised."

"Then," Nerida took over, "you had to be a spoilsport and turn him down. So, we had to get creative."

"You had to *kidnap* me?"

Either Nerida didn't hear him, or she ignored the question. Where was Julien? Eric couldn't see him at all now.

"Was my idea," Darren admitted.

"Of course it was."

"Thought you'd like it."

"Not much!"

"Sorry, then." Darren rolled his eyes, took a long pull of his beer and disappeared into the crowd, at least six of whom Eric didn't know.

"I'll get you a drink," Toby said, retreating to the kitchen.

Eric couldn't deny the relief that rushed through him when Mary grabbed his arm and hauled him out to the back porch.

"Excuse us, guys?" She smiled sweetly at two boys Eric didn't know, their sunken, dark cheeks illuminated by a joint they were sharing in the dark. "Thanks."

The strangers left them in peace.

Mary's face was almost shaking as Eric stared at her, dumbstruck.

"I am…so…*so* sorry," she said. "I tried to stop them. I told them you'd hate it."

"Well, you could have warned me. But it's fine."

"I don't mean the kidnapping thing. I mean all of it. Toby's just…he's sweet, but he doesn't know anything about you."

"None of them do."

The girl cupped a hand over his on the railing. "So, you're not angry?"

"Not now. Where'd Julien go?"

Mary frowned, confused. "He said he'd try to stop by later, if he can get away."

"Mary, I heard him. He helped put me in that car, with Darren and—"

"That's impossible."

"It's not impossible. I *saw* him, Mary."

"He's got Toby's address. He'll probably show up later."

"Really?"

"He sent me a text."

"Jules didn't have anything to do with this? With Steffen and Darren?"

"Eric, what's going on? What do you mean, you saw him?"

"He wasn't there? Wasn't at my place at all?"

"Not that I know of," Mary all but growled at him.

"Must have imagined it," he mumbled.

"Yeah, you must have."

The sound of a sliding screen door interrupted them. Toby stepped through, carrying three drinks.

"Hey," Mary said with a smile. "Are those for us?"

Eric took a sip. Absolut Citroen. Toby knew him better than they'd thought. "Thanks."

"No problem."

"For all of it, Toby. This is awesome. I'm just...kind of overwhelmed." He forced a smile. Mary raised an eyebrow at him, but he ignored it.

Toby shrugged his thin shoulders, his blue eyes kind and sincere as he spoke. "Got to do something for your birthday, and if your mum's coming home, it's your last day of freedom, right?"

Eric managed to stop a reflexive grimace, but he felt it rising inside him, seizing hold of his throat until he forced it down. Last day of freedom? Not bloody likely. He'd make sure of it. Even if his mother tried her usual routine of obligatory interest in his life until she got bored, she wouldn't change anything.

"I'll be back." Before Eric could stop her, Mary slipped through the screen door and vanished inside.

Eric narrowed his gaze on Toby, who looked away, taking another sip of his drink.

"Still need some help working out what a 'revenge tragedy' is?"

"That was to get you over here. Had to get your attention somehow, didn't I?"

"I thought so. I never thought of you as dumb."

Toby let out a quiet, derisive snort. "You've got a way of making every compliment sound like an insult. You do know that, right?"

Eric looked up as he heard Julien's voice again, then realised he'd imagined it. 'Hostile dickhead?' He guessed he could be, sometimes. Often. That was what Toby meant, wasn't it?

"It doesn't matter," Toby continued. "Everybody likes you. They like how smart you are, and how you always say what you think."

"What do you think, Toby?"

"About what?"

"Anything."

"You're really asking me?"

"I don't know very much about you." Did he want that to change? Did he want to get to know Toby? Not really. But maybe, just a bit? "You don't have to answer if you don't want."

"I know about you."

"What do you know about me?"

"I know you're a lot nicer than you pretend. I like you, anyway."

Eric leaned against the railing, its wooden finish cold and smooth against the flesh of his hand, a sharp contrast to the warmth of Toby's fingers as they wrapped over his.

"What are you doing?" he cautioned.

The boy pulled his hand away, but didn't stop staring. It made Eric uncomfortable, like Toby was basking in him.

"You're a really sweet guy," Eric muttered. "Everyone says that."

"Really?"

"Toby." Eric didn't know why, but he planted a gentle kiss on the boy's forehead, brushing the dark brown fringe away from his eyes. "I like you too much to hurt you."

Toby's frown wasn't petulant, just determined and dignified, as he gave Eric a solemn nod.

Eric thought about telling the boy that some guy out there would be lucky to have him, or some patronising shit like that. But Toby had his answer. The one he'd expected. Eric could see it on his face, even as Toby turned away to hide it.

"I'm gonna go find Mary."

"Okay."

"Thanks for the party. I mean it." Eric left before Toby could answer. He barely noticed Steffen, leaning against the window in the dark, a silent, smoking witness to their conversation.

❖

After twenty-five minutes of conversation with Darren, Eric's mind was made up. He wanted to die. The first five minutes had been taken up with Darren's 'apology' for the kidnapping stunt, which constituted a second-by-second breakdown of how the bastards had made it happen. This had been followed by ten minutes about *Titus*, and Darren's oh so sincere humility at being offered the title role, and a further ten minutes on various agents and casting directors Darren had had meetings with since that audition, and the walk-on on *Home and Away* that was due to happen in Spring, or 'maybe after I've seen the script.'

Eric felt sick. Andy had once told him there were only three types of successful male actors in Australia. Second-rate soap stars, musical queens—gay or straight, it made little difference to the archetype—and thugs. It had seemed like a joke at the time. But now, as Darren continued, the thought solidified into horrifying realisation.

Unless you happened to be Hugh Jackman, you were screwed, and even then. *Les Miserables*? Musical queen. *Wolverine*? Thug.

If Hugh fucking Jackman couldn't break the Australian curse, what hope was there for mere mortals? Too isolated. Too insecure. That was Australia. That was why nobody who made it stuck around.

More strangers turned up. The room was swelling with posers and hangers on. He couldn't find Mary, which bothered him, even though he knew she could take care of herself. The repressed sexual ferocity of the guests had relaxed into a mellow atmosphere of sleaze. But this wasn't Eric's house. It wasn't his problem.

"Eric?"

"Huh?"

"I said you're a pretty good actor. You tried any agents?" Darren asked.

"I'm not an actor, Darren. I'm a director."

"Oh. Cool. But have you tried any agents?"

"I'm gonna go find Mary." He left before Darren could trap him with another word.

"Happy birthday, Eric."

He turned and smiled to Felicity, who gave him the briefest, coldest nod he'd ever seen, before disappearing into the crowd. He hadn't expected her to forgive him so quickly. Or at least, he hadn't expected her to forgive Mary, and him by extension. Why had she even shown up, then? Were things still awkward with her folks? Had she only said that stuff about *Titus* to make him feel better? Hell, it didn't matter. She was here. In fact, besides Darren, she was now the only familiar face in the crowd, which must have numbered at least fifty throughout Toby's house. He couldn't see Toby, or Steffen, or Nerida, or Mary. Conversations flared and vanished under the dull roar. A couple of fags from U Syd, who supposedly knew Steffen. A girl he recognised from church who was trying to pin her hair back while sucking down an appletini through a bent straw. A couple of jocks doing lines off the coffee table.

"Hey," he grabbed a random passer-by. "Any G around tonight?"

"Piss off." The heavily tanned girl shook him off and rejoined her friends, who'd monopolised the cocktail bar.

Plastic bitch. He checked his fingers for traces of wipe-off orange tan.

"Eric?"

"*WHAT?*"

"Scheiße!" A startled Steffen splashed the two drinks in his hands as Eric rounded on him.

Eric swallowed, giving Steffen an apologetic look as he accepted a drink. "Thanks."

"What the fuck is wrong with you?"

"Nothing." He took two long sips of it, watching one of the jocks bang the table and storm off as his friends yelled after him.

"Go have a cry then, ya poof!"

"He wishes!" one of Toby's friends yelled back, getting a laugh from the flock of girls around the bar.

The disgraced jock paused, muscles tensing as he clenched and released his fists, before apparently deciding it wasn't worth it. Coke mixed with 'roid rage. Part of Eric wished he had Viktor's number to pass on. He didn't so much like Viktor, but the guy's training was good. Old school. No drug cheats allowed. Right, like this loser would...

"Eric, you listening to me?"

He looked back at Steffen. "Sorry. I just wasn't expecting this."

"Is surprise party," the German said flatly.

"Yeah."

"You are surprised?"

"Uh-huh."

"Then is good surprise party."

"If they don't wreck Toby's place first," he muttered, watching the cocktail slappers' faces screw up as they drank some brew they'd whipped up with so much blue Curacao, it looked like Windex. Eric smirked. Scene from *Heathers* in three...two...

"You not like surprises, Eric?"

"I like them when I'm doing the surprising."

"That's why we do *Titus*?"

Shrug. "One reason, I guess."

"But it's not a surprise. It's another play. That's all."

"Well...yeah, but it's something different. Wakes people up, shocks them—"

"Bullshit." Eric hadn't seen the unmistakable contempt in Steffen's expression before. "Bullshit. You think a Shakespeare play shocks—"

"Some people, yeah. But that's not the point. This isn't about shocking anyone."

"But it is. Felicity told me her mum freaked out over it." Steffen shook his head, drinking more of his beer as he turned his gaze back to the slappers. "Fucking Australians, man. Just like the Americans. All sensitive about stupid shit that isn't real! Oh, no! Cocks and tits! Save the children! Blah fucking blah! You think stuff like *Game of Thrones* would ever get made if it were up to Australians?"

"So why are you here, Steffen?"

"Why Australia?"

"Why Christian Fellowship? You just killing time? Trying to piss me off? What?"

"Is…" the German hesitated, his face suddenly lit up with a stupid grin that hung open like a trap waiting to snap shut. "I need a reason?"

"No. Not really. But you've got to want something out of it. *Something*, Steffen!"

"Like you want to make movies?"

"Yes."

Steffen cocked his head toward the suddenly vacant porch. Without a word, Eric followed, pretending not to hear the shattering of a glass blender and the screaming of an over-tanned bogan girl behind them.

The porch was empty, and the air outside had gotten noticeably cooler. Eric could barely hear the party now, and for the most part, he was relieved. Relieved to be away from the conversations of strangers who'd swarmed to celebrate a guy they'd never met and would never care about. That was fine. It went both ways. All he heard was the click of Steffen's lighter as the guy lit a joint, had one toke and passed it to him.

"What are you? The new Nerida?" Eric accepted it, coughing as the smoke filled his lungs. Strong shit. He passed the joint back to the grinning German.

"Want me to shotgun you?"

"Huh?"

"You know," Steffen took a long toke and held it, leaning closer. Eric suddenly understood. "Oh, that's o—"

Steffen didn't give him a chance to refuse, passing the rich smoke between them. Eric didn't fight it. He never lost control of his breath either. Not even a cough this time.

Slow and controlled, Steffen ran a moist tongue over his lips as he withdrew. "You still like me?"

"I told you. Not like that," Eric whispered, hoping they hadn't been seen.

"But in school…"

"That was different."

"Different, how?"

"I liked…never mind."

"You liked controlling me." Steffen backed off with a cocky grin, relaxing against the porch railing with a knowing, confident ease. "That why you want to make movies? To have control? Make your own way?"

"No. I like telling stories. That's all."

"That's good. Or else, better to write books," the German scoffed. "Then you have control. Why put up with shit from actors and studios when you just want to tell stories? Why would you waste time with other people's stupid scripts?"

"I can still make them look how I want. Tell the story how I want."

"What is the stupid English expression? Like lipstick on your neighbour's pig?"

"Yeah? Funny. At least the pig is alive," Eric hissed, starting to get annoyed now. What the hell did Steffen know about it?

"Pfft! Alive? A script is words, Eric, dead words on a page. They don't change. Then you want to trust actors and editors to somehow bring them to life? Okay, *now* I tell you to write books instead. Then you can bring—"

"Books are dead! Like a stuffed animal. Pretty? Sure, beautiful even. Complete, finished, stuffed, and mounted on the wall. They're static. Scripts are always changing. They're ugly. They're real. They breathe, consume, bleed, sweat, fuck, and shit—"

"You mean they die slowly?" Steffen interrupted. "Getting infected and changed every time you let someone else touch them. You want to create stories? You want to direct somebody's script? So, you want to be a butcher! To cut and shape another person's ideas for people to consume."

"That's a pseudo-intellectual jack-off, and you know it."

"No, that's you. Creators? All murderers of ideas. Sometimes we're lucky enough to get lots of them, one after the other. Then I guess we all want to be serial killers. We must be crazy, you and me. Nobody thinks what we do is important, and even if they do, they sure don't want to pay for it. But we do it anyway."

"And that, like your 'butcher' metaphor, is bullshit!"

"*Bull-shit* is your *Titus*! Man, nobody's going to remember it next year. And nobody's going to remember you! Some Australian kid who wanted to be a professional liar? So fucking what? What difference does that make? Where's the next level, Eric? What's gonna make you so important? Why should anyone care?"

The image of balling his hand into a fist and slamming it against Steffen's nasty, toxic grin materialised and vanished in an instant, before Eric got hold of his senses. No. He wouldn't lower himself. "What do you mean, next level?" he murmured, the image of wiping Steffen's blood off his hands still with him.

"There you are!"

Eric looked up to see Mary wander over to him, her hair tied back into a smooth black ponytail, her milky breasts scooped neatly into two flawless shapes, filling out a black and red corset. A jewelled choker decorated her neck, and around her eyes, lips, chin, and cheekbones were the gentlest touches of unusually dark makeup.

"Later," Steffen excused himself, going inside.

"Nerida and Corrine did it for me. What do you think?"

Eric grinned. Suddenly, Steffen's pot felt better. "Looks hot."

"I have to give the corset and choker back, but for tonight—"

"Queen of the Goths." Eric stood up and wrapped an arm around her. "Does my sweet maiden wish to be ravaged?"

"Not in full makeup, thanks!" she laughed, pushing him away. "Besides, if you rip this, Corrine will kill you. Slowly. Probably with her teeth."

Eric had to admit, she probably would. Then Nerida would raise him from the dead, just so she could do it again. Why not? Nerida seemed able to procure every other pill and potion you could imagine. Surely raising the dead was no stretch.

"Did you talk to Toby?"

Eric nodded. "He'll be okay."

"Good."

He took her hand, kissing its long, painted black nails before twirling her around, arms wrapped around her waist as she let him encircle her. "Goth queen," he whispered. "You look like Tamora."

She grinned, head tilting back until it rested on his shoulder. Her pale skin and flawless teeth were cloaked in moonlight as she looked up at him. "The worse for her, the better loved of me," she crooned sweetly.

He gently nipped at the lobe of her ear and kissed the tender flesh behind it. Then her neck, slowly descending until she clasped his hands. "Let's go home."

Chapter Twenty-four

When the police had called him into one of the admin offices and questioned him about the party and what had happened to Felicity, Eric had told them the truth as he remembered it. The party had been for him. His eighteenth birthday, though he hadn't known many of the guests. Toby's parents had been out of town, leaving them the perfect venue, but Eric hadn't known any of this prior to his sudden 'invitation' from Steffen and Darren. He left out the part about the staged kidnapping.

He told them he'd spent the early part of the night talking to Mary until the Goth girls had taken her, leaving him to talk to Toby alone. He made up some lie about the conversation that bypassed any talk of their sexuality. He told them he'd last seen Felicity after suffering an hour, give or take, of conversation with Darren. He told them they'd briefly acknowledged each other with thinly veiled, mutual disinterest. He told them about the coke snorted off the coffee table, though he hadn't indulged. And about the girls blending cocktails. He didn't tell them about Steffen's thoughts, comparing the creative process to serial murder. He wasn't convinced that they'd care or understand. They'd probably just hear 'serial murder' and lock him up, or at best, call his doctor. He told them he and Mary had gone to his home, where she'd slept on the couch, a story his mother could verify to the satisfaction of both the police and Mary's parents, though he hoped that wouldn't be necessary. He told them Julien had never arrived.

A red-nailed hand gently tapped his arm.

"Eric?"

He looked up to see Miss Harley, her face road-mapped by a worried frown.

"Are you all right?"

"Tired."

Harley nodded and left him alone. She turned to write something on the whiteboard, revealing a tell-tale lock of grey hair peeking out from under its bottled black facade. To Eric, it seemed to be winking. Saying 'Yes, here I am. You were right. You're not going crazy, even if you're already there.' He dismissed the last thought as vanity. He wasn't interesting enough to be crazy.

Felicity had wished him a happy birthday and then she'd gone off with some guy who'd fucked her until she'd bled enough to be rushed to emergency. She'd been found wandering the streets at five in the morning, out of her head. Everything else he'd heard had been rumours. That her head had been shaved, and the hair stuffed and taped inside her mouth. That her nose had been sliced open or her thumbs cut off, like they did in the Yakuza. He didn't know what to believe. But nobody could deny it had gone down at his birthday party—the one he hadn't asked for, hadn't wanted, and now couldn't wipe from his memory, even if most of it had slipped away on its own. How had this toxic, steaming pile of crap come to be his problem?

"Where's Jules?" he asked Mary.

"Sick?"

"Do you know if he made it to Toby's?"

"No."

"No he didn't, or no you don't know?"

"I was with you."

"No Julien today?" Harley asked.

Eric shrugged.

Johansson and Principal Wagner cast shadows from the doorway.

Harley threw them a brief nod and continued. "As most of you know, *Titus* was one of Shakespeare's earliest plays."

Eric realised the two had stepped inside and were now closely watching Harley.

"Some scholars suggest this was why the play features such unusually graphic violence. Enfant terrible playwriting. A young writer pursuing the shock of the new. Some even call it the first true horror story in the English language. This reasoning has also been used to dismiss *Titus* as the work of what critics today might call an immature 'gore-hound.' In fact, many have gone so far as to dispute Shakespeare's authorship of it."

Eric heard light murmurs around the room, though nobody laughed out loud. Johansson and Wagner were silent.

"Can anyone tell me why we're attracted to these stories?" Harley asked. "What fascinates us so much about violence? Violent stories. Violent theatre."

Eric tapped his pen against the desk and looked at Mary. She was scribbling something in her diary. He couldn't make it out.

"Anyone?" Harley charged, her voice now bearing the first pangs of frustration as she looked up at Johansson and Wagner.

"It's safe," Eric explained. "We can act out negative emotions vicariously through the characters without consequences."

"But do you think everyone has those emotions? An urge or even a willingness to kill?"

"Of course. Anger's one of the most primal emotions. Anger and fear. It's how revenge tragedies work. We watch these people, empathise and get involved with their lives. When they feel joy at destroying an enemy, so do we. We feel vindicated, like we've overcome our own enemies somehow."

Harley smiled, her confidence renewed. "So, if that's the case, let's talk about those urges explored in *Titus* that we would never, ever consider. What about them? Things so horrible that the thought sickens us? Take the pies that Titus bakes for Tamora, tricking her into the cannibalisation of her own sons."

Only now did Eric notice that Johansson and Wagner had left.

"What's going on there?" Harley seemed to have ignored her colleagues's sudden departure. "What is Shakespeare hoping to achieve, and what are our feelings when we see that scene?"

"Consumption," Eric murmured.

"Sorry, Eric? Speak up."

"It's the consuming matriarch. Shakespeare understood society's consumption of people, its perpetual nature. Everyone is consumed by something. Love, money, religion, family, their pasts, their upbringing. Demetrius and Chiron are, too." He looked up at Mary, who'd put her pen down and now gave him her full attention, her stare perplexed and cautious.

"Go on," Harley urged.

"They're consumed by their mother's evil. Her ideas. Her values. Her morals, in that she has none. They can't separate from it. They're a part of her, permanently attached and controlled. So when this relationship is properly portrayed, we're horrified by their deaths in spite of their crimes."

"You're saying this symbiosis with their mother diminishes their responsibility?"

"Only in the minds of the audience and only if it's done well, but yes."

"And how has that informed your preparation to play Demetrius?"

Eric swallowed down the last of his nerves. "Actors can't afford to judge characters, so I don't judge him. Titus is a tyrant and a butcher. He's murdered their brother for his stupid religion. His whore of a daughter deserves what she gets—"

"Eric!"

"In the minds of those characters," he explained. "This is why so many people don't get or like *Titus*. All the characters are horrible, but they've all been wronged. They all have a real axe to grind against the world."

"You think Tamora's actions are legitimate?"

"She's my mum."

"And Demetrius is a part of her?"

"Yes. When she eats him, it's like a consumption of self."

"Excuse me?"

"And that's what Tamora is. That's what consumes her. The self, her own power, her wealth, her position. Me, me, me. When she loses it all, she feels entitled. So she starts consuming anything she can. She consumes Rome. Consumes Titus's empire. In the end, she consumes her own flesh and blood."

The room was silent as Harley leaned against the whiteboard, red nails tapping against the wall as she let Eric's words sink in.

Eric put a hand on Mary's. She pulled it away.

CHAPTER TWENTY-FIVE

"What are you wearing?"

Eric looked down at his black tunic, running his hands over the smooth velvet and cold silver buckles as Mary ogled him hungrily. "Do you like it?"

"Yeah, it's hot."

"Mum got it from this weird boutique in Santa Monica," he lied.

"Americans have all the cool shit."

"Because Australians lack imagination."

She snorted a laugh, downing the last of her Diet Coke. "You do know you're an Aussie, right?"

"I'm not an Aussie. I was just born here. There's a difference."

"Do you really want to get away that badly?"

He couldn't see any point in answering that question, just as he saw no point in asking why she'd pulled her hand away from him in class. Besides, it had been Mary's idea to come over, and with his mother away overnight in Melbourne for 'meetings,' they would have been stupid to pass up the chance.

"I still think you should come with me."

"Yeah, right," she laughed. "Even *if* we both got into the same school, what would I study, Eric?"

"Acting. Writing. Whatever you want."

"Yeah, that's really funny."

He took the glass away and wrapped his arms around her slim waist. She buried her face in the soft, black velvet wrapped around his chest, caressing the thin, barely formed biceps his tunic could never accentuate. He accepted her kiss as she pushed forward, almost lifting off the ground as she inhaled the scent of the velvet, the scent of him. He kissed her again, the movement so perfect, even graceful in its cliché, like some old silent film couple. Eric was sure Mary had risen to her toes to meet him.

"Do you know just how good an actor you are?" he asked.

She broke away from him with a smile. "Not as good as you."

He wasn't going to ruin things by asking what that meant.

It was after eight by the time Julien arrived. By then, Eric had cracked open a bottle of wine, only to feel foolish when the open-topped Mercedes roller-skate Jules called a car pulled into his driveway. Eric hadn't expected that. Jules never mentioned his car, which probably meant that under that topless, prestige exterior, it was a shit box.

Rather than turn down the wine, Jules had asked to stay the night, a request to which Eric had agreed against every impulse. They'd even hugged hello. Julien had hugged him in that weird, blokey, back-slapping kind of way they probably still did up in Coffs. It had been particularly awkward in the velvet tunic, which Eric had since stripped off and replaced with a GAP T-shirt he would never otherwise have admitted owning. He doubted Mary or Jules would care though.

Jules. When *had* Julien become Jules? Probably that day at the gym. The day he'd met Viktor. More importantly, it had been the day he'd met the other Eric. Eric, the character, the pretty boy you paid to have on your arm at the opera to disguise your gold-plated slide toward the grave. The boy who, after spending the evening as your fashionable accessory in full view of all your peers, would for the right price accompany you home to satisfy those needs you denied in such well-heeled company.

It would be a tough lifestyle to maintain now his Mum was back. But he had to manage. With the cash Margaret had given him for Joe, a few more appointments would give him all the money he needed. He also had to check in on Andy. Maybe Viktor had been rehired, all back to normal and fights forgotten. Eric could use an easy few hundred. One he didn't have to earn with an uncomfortably extensive knowledge of a client's sexual depravity.

Julien's hug had made him uncomfortable too. It had made his stomach turn, though that could have been the tightness of the tunic. Julien wouldn't be the only one staying the night. Mary, having tipped the remaining Glogg down the sink and ceremonially laid the bottle to rest in the recycling, was now totally off her face as she danced with Jules with near-full wine glasses in hand.

"Eric, come dance with us!" she beckoned, downing a large gulp.

"In a minute."

"Come on, man. We're celebrating," said Julien.

Eric was starting to regret his decision to stay sober. But it seemed a shame to waste it. "Do you want to go for a drive?"

They stared at him, morbid smirks crossing their faces. What? Didn't they trust him? He could drive if he felt like it, and he did.

"Sure." Julien fumbled in his pocket and tossed Eric his keys.

CHAPTER TWENTY-SIX

Eric had never seen the beach at night. He didn't much like it during the day, either. Sand caking his skin, endless tourists with tans too dark for their bleached blonde hair, and either the scorching sun or blustering wind, depending on when you had the misfortune to go. The unimaginatively named Palm Beach stretched north of Avalon, under the watchful gaze of Barrenjoey Lighthouse. This was where the great Aussie dream came to retire. To eke out its last days in clichéd disgrace, and then die. But tonight, they had the beach to themselves.

"Smile for me."

Eric curled his lips into a sarcastic grimace as Mary shoved the camera in his face.

"Okay, don't smile. Do something funny!"

"Jules, help me!" he called, pushing her away with a laugh.

"Nup."

"Jules!"

"Sorry dude. Busy."

Julien's shirtless form was stretched out on the sand, the stray white powder in contrast to his tanned complexion under the moonlight—a tan Jules was content to keep working on under the stars—while a drunk Mary harassed Eric with a mini DV cam. The sunglasses Jules had fished out of the glove box were just sarcasm.

"Eriiiic!"

"Put it away." He tried gently to prise the cam from Mary's fingers. Shit, why'd he even let her bring it? The last thing he needed was sand in his camera. She finally gave it up with an indignant pout and lay down next to Julien. Eric put the cam away in its bag.

Jules had liked the film. 'Dude, this looks awesome. Your lighting's great,' he'd said. It had made Eric proud. Not just of himself, but of his star, who'd been kind of brave, now he thought about it.

"Eric, come lie down with us," Mary called. "Take off your shirt."

"Why?" Eric was starting to like the beach after dark. The unearthly blackness of the ocean. The equally sinister sky marked only by a few stars.

"Why not, dude? It's good for you."

"What is?"

"Moon rays. They keep you centred."

There was a moment of silence before they all cracked up laughing.

"Where did you—"

"Forget it. I don't know where that came from."

"Byron?"

"More like Nimbin!"

"*Coffs.*"

"Fuck off!" Julien laughed.

"Are you high?" Eric asked, finally sitting down.

Mary began pawing at his shirt, until he finally peeled it off.

Eric suddenly imagined himself doing lines of coke off the creases of Julien's abs. Purely for the novelty of it—and for the brag factor, once Jules became famous.

"So, you really liked the film?" he asked.

"I told you I did, dude. You're sending that to the US schools, yeah?"

"I've still got to cut it together."

"When are admissions?"

"October," Eric winced. Just one more reason he didn't want *Titus* delayed.

"Plenty of time. You want to do any reshoots?"

"Can you two talk about something other than work, please?" Mary grumbled, kicking sand over Eric's legs. "You're boring me!"

"Your scenes were the best." Julien winked at her.

"You do know how to make me feel less bored, don't you?"

Eric shrugged, distracted by a baby sand crab trying to shuffle its way across a powdery mound, away from the three giant humanoids that had invaded and probably crushed its home. "Not really. It's pretty clean. Had to cut some of the more intense stuff out."

"Was fun, though. You had fun, right?" Jules was still drunk, his voice impish and insistent.

It had been fun. More fun than Eric wanted to admit. He couldn't remember all of it. Maybe it was better that way. Jules lazily turned his head and looked back at him through the sunglasses, lips parting to reveal those perfectly shaped teeth.

"What?"

Eric realised he was staring.

"I'll be right back," Mary promised, careful this time not to shower them both in sand as she got up and headed for the car.

"Nothing," Eric murmured so quietly, he was surprised Jules could hear. "Just…thanks for doing the project for me. With me."

"No problem, dude," Julien laughed. "That's what they look for, you know? All the schools? Intensity. They want to see that you're fearless."

"So how fearless are you?"

The smile fell from Julien's face. "What? What do you—"

"The US schools. I'll give you my list. I want you to apply with me. Both of you."

Julien took off his glasses, his eyes widening. Eric knew he was shooting long. Would Julien's folks pay his way? Would they keep him there? What about tuition?

Every question and doubt Eric had suffered in chasing his goal was repeating itself on Julien's face, crossing it like rivulets of water rushing for the lowest point of ground. If Jules did want this, how much would he give up for it? Eric had slept with people three times his age for it. He'd played nice, even when it had revolted him. What was Jules prepared to do?

"Umm…I don't know, dude."

"Don't know what?" Mary staggered back to them, a full wine bottle and three glasses in hand.

"Eric wants us to go to the States with him," Julien said quickly.

Mary stared at them both, her mouth curling up into a 'wtf?' sneer. Eric resisted the urge to wince. This had been a mistake. He should have asked her *months* ago. Privately. "You're both good enough to get in," he murmured.

"You and Jules, maybe! Jules?"

"Umm, I'd need time to think about it. We've got til October, right?"

"Eric, even *if* I got in, my dad would never—"

"*Fuck your dad!*"

Julien and Mary stared at him, stunned as the last word echoed around the beach. A light came on in one the houses nearby. For only a second, Eric felt as though he wasn't really there. Like it wasn't him on that beach, listening to these excuses. Like he was witness to a drunken conversation that had been hit with a sudden, cold shock of sobriety.

"This isn't about what he wants!" He fixed his girlfriend with a glare. If she wanted something, something just for herself, she would have to find a way to make it work. Just like he had. Damn it, he'd do it for her! October. Another five months. He could do that. Double his savings to cover her way. He could handle Margaret, Andy, Gareth West, Deborah…fuck, even Carmel Roukstein if he had to. And if Mary didn't get into the same school, so what? They could still work together. Still make beautiful and crazy alchemy together.

Mary's jaw slowly re-hinged itself into a confident grin as she poured three glasses of wine and passed two to the boys. "Fuck you, Dad!"

Eric nodded at her, slowly. "Again."

"Fuck you! Fuck you! *Fuck you, Dad!*" she bellowed.

"Yes!"

"Fuck your dad!" Julien joined in.

"Fuck Dad!" Mary screamed.

"Fuck Dad!" the boys echoed together.

They lifted their glasses with a celebratory clink and sculled the wine. Before Eric could move, Mary had thrown her wine glass toward the ocean. He heard a splash as it hit the shallow, black water.

"Fuck you," she muttered, "you evil cunt."

The boys shrugged at each other, then tossed their glasses into the waves.

❖

"So when do I get my camera back?" Eric hadn't even noticed Mary get it out again, though he wished she'd use it for something other than shooting a documentary on his non-existent abs, which appeared to be the stars of her show.

"You have the rest of your life for that, Mister Director," she grinned, tucking the camera under her protective arm. "Come on."

Eric and Julien stared at her as she ran for the water, camera lovingly cradled in her arms in a way that made Eric feel only slightly more comfortable.

"I think you lost your camera, dude."

"She'll bring it back."

"You're sure about that?"

Eric closed his eyes, letting his mind drift until he only heard the crash of waves lapping at his attention. He felt tired. Not sleep deprived. Just physically exhausted as he sank his body deeper into the cold sand.

"So, what? Your mum left you a message right before she got on the plane? "

"She did."

"Intense, man. You got it all out though, yeah?"

"There's nothing left. Not that she'd notice, anyway."

"Come on, dude," Julien laughed. "You're telling me she didn't say anything?"

"She doesn't know. She's not gonna know." Eric lazily flopped his head to one side, just in time to see Julien lower his sunglasses and look at him.

"What?"

Julien started to laugh. It was a sharp, almost cruel sound that made Eric want to sink deeper into the sand, his legs about halfway in now as he slowly wriggled them around.

"Lucky bastard," the jock finally mumbled.

"What do you mean, 'lucky'?"

"I mean your mum. The way you get around her."

"You mean the way she's totally disinterested?"

"Do you care?"

Eric swallowed, feeling the anger grip his chest, if only for a second. He sifted sand though his fingers, letting its cool texture calm him as he wet his lips to speak. "Your parents support you."

"Well, my Mum does. Dad I think just—"

"Julien? They love you. They'll back you, whatever you want to do. Don't take that for granted, because it isn't."

"I don't," Julien murmured.

For a moment, the only sound between them was the hiss of fine sand passing through Julien's fingers, as if he'd taken a moment to digest the thought before returning his gaze to the black sky.

"Heh, no matter what I want," he said, grinning like an idiot. "*Anything I want!*"

"Shhhhhhh. You want somebody to come down?" Eric realised he'd never seen Julien drunk. High, sure. But not really drunk. Not this drunk.

"You need wine," Julien grumbled, scrambling to his feet and brushing sand away. He put his hands behind his head with a wide yawn.

"You don't. Tired?"

"Maybe."

"Then get back down here."

"Huh?"

"Sleep on the beach. I'll wake you up if anyone's coming."

"You're the one still sacked out." Julien kicked a spray of sand across Eric's body.

Eric laughed, spitting sand.

"What're you gonna do?" Julien sat down next to him, leaning back on his hands. "Watch me while I sleep? Because that's kind of creepy."

"I don't know. Maybe film you?"

"Okay, getting creepier."

Eric couldn't resist a sneer. "Andy Warhol filmed a guy sleeping for five and a half hours."

"Ye-ah. Didn't he also film a guy getting a blow job?"

"Only his face."

"Still."

"I've filmed you doing worse."

Julien scooped up a handful of sand, pouring it from one hand to the other. "I guess. Hey, did you know Vik used to do films? Not the same kind, exactly."

"Vik?"

"Viktor. Andy's guy. The trainer."

Viktor? It seemed impossible.

"Movies? Really?"

"Porn."

"No way!"

"Yeah! Swear to God. Have you seen the guy without his shirt? Ripped as!"

"Okay, that I knew."

Still. Porn? Did Andy know about this? Had it been the spark of one of their many arguments? He cursed himself for being so judgemental. If the Ukrainian had the perfect bedroom body, why not use it?

"Where'd you find it?" he asked. "I mean. What kind is it?"

"Google 'Dmitri Novachek.' Mostly gay stuff. Couple of bi three-ways. Hey, did you even know it was possible to get your head—"

"Wait. He told you about this? Or were you just randomly—?"

"Sure he did. I mean, why not? You told me about your sex work."

"Jesus! Will you keep it down?"

Julien's grin fell open into a slack-jawed gape. He discreetly cocked his head toward Mary. "She doesn't know, does she?"

Eric half laughed. "Would you tell her if it was you?"

"No. You're different though."

"In what way?"

"In every way. You're kind of fearless. I like that about you."

Eric watched Mary splashing in the dark, shallow waves, his camera safely left on the dry sand. "I wouldn't tell her. I couldn't."

"I don't mean that. I mean going to the States by yourself."

"Yeah, but I'm not doing porn," he laughed. "Would you?"

Another stupid grin. "If it's art."

"Okay," Eric smiled. He couldn't pretend to be surprised. "So, next time you fall asleep naked? I'm gonna film every inch of you."

"Pervert." Jules tossed the sand over Eric's chest. "Shit!" he backed off as Eric got to his feet, shaking sand over both of them. "What are you? The walking dead?"

"Guys!" Mary called.

Julien shot him one last cheeky look as they staggered down the beach.

❖

"Hey, watch out for the water."

"Eric, I'm not stupid. Now, take off your clothes."

"Sorry?"

"I said strip. Lie down where the water can reach you."

He turned to Julien, only to get a non-committal shrug.

"You too," Mary grinned at Jules. "Don't worry. I'm not going to shoot your bits."

"So, why can't we keep our pants on?"

"Eric!"

Julien was already naked before Eric could object.

"I said lie down."

"Mary."

"Eric?"

He snorted indignantly. Maybe Mary was a director too, deep down. He wasn't sure how he felt about that.

"Hooolyyyy shit!" Julien screeched, his voice skimming a falsetto that almost matched Mary's giggle as he fell into the water. "Holy shit, that's cold!"

Eric struggled to keep breathing as he threw himself onto the sand and felt the frozen water wrap around his naked body. Jules wasn't kidding. Yet in some strange way it felt good. The night, the ice cold water washing over his skin. It felt wrong but equally wonderful, like a perversion of all that the beach was supposed to be. Kind of awesome in its own way.

"Maybe you should cuddle together for warmth?" Mary suggested.

"Oh, fuck off!" Julien laughed. "Are you filming this?"

"Not yet."

"Come on, Jules. I thought you wanted to be fearless?"

Shit! Stupid! Stupid thing to say! But wasn't some truth in it? When they'd been chatting on the sand, with Mary out of earshot, Eric had thought about reaching out and maybe just taking Julien's hand. Something small like that would have been okay, wouldn't it? But in front of Mary?

"That's *not* what I meant and you—"

"Just get a bit closer," Mary urged them, "so you're both in frame."

Eric could barely feel the cold waves now. He only saw the confidence in Mary's face as she adjusted the cam and lined up her shot. Sure, he knew what he was doing, and Jules was the best actor in school. He could swallow his feelings and do this. Just for her.

"Jules," Mary cooed sweetly. "Bring your other hand up to Eric's face."

"Are...are you sure about this, dude?" Julien whispered.

Eric finally reached out and squeezed his friend's hand. "Fuck, no."

❖

"You guys are pathetic."

"What's wrong?" Julien looked up at his director with a cold, professional gaze.

"It's like you've both got herpes or something," Mary scolded. "Will you just get your tongue in there and pash him, already? Don't be such fucking pansies!"

"Mary, I think maybe—" was all Eric managed to get out before Julien pushed his tongue deep inside his mouth. The taste of wine was still fresh on the boy's lips as Eric surrendered to this sudden burst of enthusiasm.

Then, as quickly as he'd attacked, Julien withdrew. "How was that?" he asked with method professionalism, though Eric was sure this wasn't what Stanislavsky had had in mind.

"Okay, I guess?" he got out.

"Cool. You want to just go for it?"

Hell. Eric flipped them over and pinned Jules to the sand, mauling him with open, ravenous kisses as the waves crashed around them.

"That's it. Keep going. Keep going!" Mary shrieked.

They did, all memory of their conversation now gone as they clasped at each other's bodies, kissing and exploring, the sensuality of the kiss now stripping away the fears and doubts that had paralysed them, all awkwardness and embarrassment forgotten. Eric had kissed men before. Clients, Steffen…but this felt good. Kissing Jules felt natural and right in a way he hadn't expected. The tight muscles of his stomach, the gentle prickle of black hairs that blanketed the toned indent of his chest, slender hips that gave way to the perfect curve of his firm backside.

Eric knew he was hot. It had been his living for the better part of a year. But Jules was something else. His physicality. The perfection of his body. As they lay naked and secure in each other's arms, Eric forgot Jules was even a man. He was a friend, so close and so intimate. Someone Eric trusted, who made him feel safe even exposed like this.

He yelped, sitting up as Julien grabbed his butt.

"What's wrong? Too much?"

"No, just…" Eric stammered, his breath slowly returning as he straddled Jules. "Just—"

"Umm…Eric?"

"What?" he looked down at his newly formed hard on. "Oh… I'm…Mary, is the—"

"It's off," she promised, tucking the camera away in its bag.

No porn tonight. Thank Christ. "Sorry," Eric mumbled, covering himself.

The fleeing tide now barely reached Julien's shoulders as he gave Eric a sympathetic shrug. "That's okay. It's a compliment, eh?"

"Huh?"

"Well, what do you reckon? Would you go gay for me?"

Eric swallowed. Jules was looking at him with a half-tender, half-cocky grin he wasn't sure he liked. "Guess I would," he admitted. "Probably. Does that bother you?"

"Nup," Julien glanced down the length of his body, gently squeezing the tip of his own manhood. He was hard too.

Without thinking, Eric reached out a finger and stroked the curve of Julien's ear, then traced over the boy's forehead, down the length of his nose to his lips, then the gentle curve of his jaw. So perfect it scared him.

"Kiss me," his friend whispered.

He gripped Julien's wrists tighter and embraced him in a deep, open kiss. This time, he didn't care about Jules grabbing his butt. In fact, he pushed harder against his friend's touch. Everything felt real. This perfect-looking person with so much talent. The perfect chameleon to play any part, including this one.

"Do you want me to fuck you?" Jules asked.

"No."

"Then fuck me, man. Shape me into what you want."

Eric laughed, quietly whispering into his friend's ear. "I already have."

Mary was watching them, the camera bag at her feet along with all of her clothes. It was the first time he'd seen her completely naked. She was silhouetted against the moonlight, like some pagan goddess as she approached them. Eric eased himself off Julien, now unable to take his eyes off her. He couldn't even tell if he was still hard. Without a word, she lay down in the sand between them, wetting her hair and slicking it back, taking each of them by the hand.

"Guys?" she whispered. "Please?"

It felt as though some unseen claw from Eric's stomach was reaching up to tear a piece out of his heart. The look Jules was giving him sure didn't help. It was longing, humble and inquisitive. Yes. He wanted to answer that look. He wanted them both. To take Julien in his mouth as he held Mary tight against their chests. But Julien's look had changed. His longing, his lust had changed. It didn't long for Eric's body anymore, at least not entirely. It longed for Eric's permission.

He granted it with a single nod, but Mary held Jules back.

"I want Eric to go first," she whispered.

Eric's stomach had ceased to be content with his heart and was now attempting to tear strips off the inside of his throat as he choked on words.

I…

Umm…

Well…

All these formed somewhere in the recesses of his mind as he gazed upon the invitation of Mary's modest but perfectly rounded breasts. Her soft, slender stomach stretched down to the neat, triangular down of hair that shrouded her sex, all of her flesh that perfect bluish-white under the moon. It looked all the more pale against Julien's dark complexion.

Julien was still erect, his hungry stare shifting between Mary and Eric with a mix of adoration and apprehension. What was Mary asking him to do, exactly? Was the request meant for both of them, or just for Julien? Was there such a big difference? Yes. In his mind, there was. This was not how he'd imagined his first time with Mary. Or with Julien. God, when had he started imagining a first time with Julien? He felt the thoughts slowly overwhelm him. He tried to stop…tried to just stop thinking and feel. But it was no use.

"No," he said finally. "I'm just…I'm sorry." He let go of Mary's hand.

She stared at him, but her disappointment quickly turned into a forgiving smile. "Do you think it'll hurt?" she asked Julien.

The nervousness drained from Julien's face as he ran a hand down the length of Mary's thigh, tenderly massaging her as he kissed her face and neck. "Only the first time," he promised.

Eric wasn't convinced.

Julien shuddered with a satisfied moan as Mary grabbed hold of his shaft. Eric felt his own suddenly go rigid as he watched his friends gorge themselves on their rediscovery of each other.

"There serve your lusts," Eric murmured. "Shadow'd from heaven's eye, and revel in Lavinia's treasury."

Neither of them heard him, his words smothered by Mary's sighs as Julien pushed inside her. As Eric stared out at the black ocean, he realised how much he missed Joe.

Chapter Twenty-seven

Dear Ms. Volger,

I trust this letter finds you in good health and that all went well with your recent business in Los Angeles. We appreciate your regular e-mail correspondence and active participation in your son's schooling, despite the distance. I am delighted to inform you that Eric's academic and artistic performance has been exemplary. He remains an active, well-liked and valued member of our school community.

It is with great regret that I must inform you of our decision to cancel the proposed senior production of Titus Andronicus, *originally selected at the request of your son and several other students. While Christian Fellowship encourages students to take risks in their creative work, many members of staff and the school community have questioned the play's graphic content, particularly in light of recent events involving one student who had been cast in the production. After lengthy consultation with parents and members of staff, the decision has been made to cancel the project.*

Students and parents will be notified as soon as an appropriate supplement to the senior drama program has been decided. Please be assured that as HSC exams approach us, the well-being of the students remains our top priority.

Yours in Christ,
Principal Louise Wagner
Christian Fellowship College

Eric folded up the letter and thrust it deep within his pocket. Johansson was a cunt.

Chapter Twenty-eight

In all his previous trips to Father Callahan's office, not once had Eric ever made use of the psychiatrist's couch the priest kept by the frosted window. But today, he needed to lie down. More than anything, he needed to stop moving or thinking. To stop talking or answering the questions in his head that people kept asking him with their stupid looks and pathetic headshakes of sympathy.

Why hadn't Wagner helped them? Why hadn't she fought harder? Maybe doing the play in October would have sucked, but it would have been something, even if it did get lost in a sea of end-of-school bullshit.

"Eric?"

Now, they might as well scratch it on the wall under the difference between Callahan and JFK. Eric's great idea for the senior play was a flop.

"Eric."

"Sorry," he mumbled, folding his arms over his head and holding the back of the couch.

"You know how I feel about wasting appointments made in class time. What class do you have now?"

"Maths."

"Not music, today?"

Eric grimaced under his sleeve. "Johansson said he'd mark me down if I missed any more classes." He wasn't giving up that

A. He'd suffered long and hard for it, even if the teacher was an arsehole.

"Are you happy your mum's back?"

"We haven't killed each other."

"Have you talked about what happened? With *Titus*?"

Eric ignored the question. Callahan was smart. He could figure it out.

"You didn't tell her, did you? You didn't even tell her you were doing it."

"Nothing to tell. No show 'til opening curtain."

"Why didn't you? Did you think she'd disapprove? Tell you 'no?'"

"I don't care what she thinks!" Eric barked, spinning his legs off the couch and turning angrily to face his counsellor, only to be met with the man's cautionary glare. Callahan was right. He'd already lost the play. He would at least keep his temper. His pride.

"You really don't like talking about your mother."

Shrug.

"I hear Miss Harley's decided to go with *Hamlet*?"

"*Hamlet*'s a cliché."

"There's a reason for that, Eric. Miss Harley's still directing. I think she'd be keen to have you in one of the leads."

"It's overdone!"

"It's a revenge tragedy. That's what you wanted to do, isn't it?"

Shrug.

"Eric, who are you really angry at? Mr Johansson?"

"Who else would you suggest?"

"He's not your enemy, Eric. He can see your talent, just like Miss Harley can. He'd be one of your biggest advocates if you'd stop antag—"

"He shut us down. It wasn't even his subject! He had no right—"

"Felicity was hurt, Eric."

"That's not my fault!"

"Nobody blames you."

"He does!"

"I doubt that. Besides, he's not the only one who had concerns over *Titus*."

"But he..." The words drained from Eric's voice, as if the air had been sucked from his lungs in one cold blast. "You spoke against me, didn't you?" He turned to face Callahan again. He had to see the man's face, his eyes, his lying, fat tongue as it patronised him, asked him about his feelings. Son of a bitch!

The priest didn't move. He sat there, leather-bound notebook in lap, a black pen neatly tucked into its cover, watching Eric's simmering rage. "This isn't about you, Eric. I read the play. I had a meeting with Felicity's parents the other day."

"Oh, Jee-sus."

"They read the play too, Eric. They had questions I couldn't answer."

"'Violence is an important part of our world. Christ himself understood that.'"

"Eric, when I said that—"

"Remind me, Father. What's the one, grave, unforgivable sin? The one that gets you straight to the ninth circle? Betrayal, isn't it?"

Callahan dropped his notebook down on the desk and crossed to the bookshelf with a stoicism that made Eric suddenly nervous. "You mean the betrayal of trust?" He reached up, pulled out a bible and dropped it open, next to the notebook, inches away from Eric's nose. It opened at the remnants of two pages, torn from the middle of Leviticus. "Yes, Eric. It is."

Again, Eric felt the colour drain from his face, the icy vacuum seize his lungs.

"Not everyone is as stupid as you think." the priest said quietly. "There's an impressive new scratch in my desk too if you want to see it."

Eric's mind raced for what he should say. Apologise? Tell Callahan it had been Steffen's idea? What had they done anyway? "I better go."

"Eric..."

Even with his back turned, Eric knew Callahan was straining to keep a cool temper. He could hear the unspoken commands, so entitled, demanding respect. Sit down, Eric. We're not done, Eric.

"That voice. The screams you used for your music assignment. That was Julien Davidson, wasn't it? What were the two of you doing?"

Against every impulse, Eric resisted the urge to turn around. "Go to Hell."

Chapter Twenty-nine

"M iss Harley? Miss Harley."

"I'm busy right now, Eric. What do you want?"

Eric tried to soothe his rage with a nervous swallow as he approached the desk. The light of a monitor showed up every wrinkle of Harley's frown. He hadn't expected his visit to be unwelcome. "What are you doing?"

"Drafting a letter of recommendation for Julien, if it's any of your business," she replied. "Which I suppose it is, since he's now looking at American schools. Not that you had anything to do with that, of course?"

"I might have said something. But if Jules wants to—"

"I wish him luck," she muttered. "I wish you both luck."

"Thanks." Eric nodded gratefully. Harley was on his side. Picking a fight with her wasn't going to get him anywhere.

"What can I do for you?"

"They pulled *Titus*, Miss."

"I'm the director, Eric. I was aware. What do you want me to do about it?"

"Maybe talk to Ms Wagner? Make her understand that this has got—"

"Talk to Ms Wagner? That is all I've done for the past three weeks! I've tried! I've done everything I can do, and I'm sorry, but we lost. Do you understand that?"

"But if we wait, let things cool off a bit, maybe til October—"

"*Eric!*"

He stepped back, startled by her explosion of temper, the faint strands of grey now threatening to pop out as she flicked the hair away from her face. He had never, ever seen her like this.

"I am not taking any more heat for you."

"I'm sorry." Eric heard his voice wavering.

"I know. So am I. I'm not angry. Not with you."

In the corner of his eye, he felt the one thing he'd tried to hold back on. Harley pushed a box of tissues across the desk, but he shook his head and wiped the tear away.

"Oh, for God's sake, Eric, it's just bloody high school!" Harley snapped. "If we do *Hamlet* or *Romeo and Juliet*, would that be so terrible? Would it matter?"

He closed his hand tight around the USB stick in his pocket. "I just…I wanted to be different."

"Believe me, you are very, very different."

"That's not what I meant!"

Harley closed her laptop and relaxed into her chair as the late afternoon sunlight crept through the blinds. "I think it is."

"What's that supposed to mean?"

"Do you remember what I said when you were in ninth form, on the first day of class?"

"The theatre is not about us," he mumbled.

"I said the theatre is not about *you*. The play is not about you. Not you, not me, nor anybody. It's about the work. The story. The collaboration. That bond with each other, with the audience. All the great actors get that, Eric."

"But I don't want to be an actor."

"I know. You never wanted to be in *Titus*, either. You wanted to direct it. But even the director's power is never absolute. If you can't get your head around that, do something else. Art isn't about controlling everything."

"I…I get that. I just—"

"Make sure you do! If it makes you feel better, you're very good at it. Look at your classmates sometime, Eric. Drama, music, the arts? At most schools, these are not exactly the cool classes to be in. Ask Julien about it if you don't believe me. Do you know how excited he was to be here when he arrived, in this class, where people cared more about his acting than what he did on the soccer field? You think the Central Coast gave him that? I mean it, Eric. I've taught in schools where drama teachers are treated like the lowest of the low, where the arts departments get no money and no respect. But here?" She finally smiled at him, clearly not caring about the light now showing up every trace of grey in her hair. "And that's largely thanks to you guys. How passionate you are. How you're willing to try anything, and I *love* you for it."

"Thanks," he said quietly.

She reopened her laptop and continued typing. "What've you got there?"

"Huh?"

"Your pocket. You're holding something. Your entire body's energy is focused there."

Only an acting teacher…

"My show reel. It's not ready."

"Put it on."

He pulled out the USB. It looked so small in his hand. So many hours of work. The stick felt cold all of a sudden.

"You really want to see it?" he asked.

Harley turned her laptop to face him. "If you'll let me."

He didn't watch the film as it played. He was too interested in Harley's reaction, if she had one. It was hard to tell.

"It's, umm…" the teacher began as the video fell silent.

"Yes?"

"Your lighting's very impressive. Your editing…it's suspenseful. I assume that's what you were going for?"

"Yes."

"It's good, Eric. It's not ready, but it's good." She handed back the USB.

"You…you didn't think the content—"

"I don't know. Is that the kind of movie you see yourself making?"

"Maybe."

"Then why are you apologising for it?"

Eric managed a half-smile, but he knew it was forced and empty. He could feel the tension spread across his neck and shoulders. He couldn't force it away. Rigor mortis on a stick.

"I'll see you in class."

"Miss? Do you know if Felicity's okay?"

"I haven't heard. I'd be happy to ask after her for you. Let her know you're thinking of her."

"No," he said. "That's okay."

Chapter Thirty

Fuck them! Fuck them, fuck them all! Motherfucking fucktards! What the fuck is wrong with them? Jesus, fuck!"

"Nerida?"

"What, damn it?"

"Will you please stop swearing?"

"Fuck off, Eric! How can you be so fucking calm? It was your fucking play!"

"I know that, and now it's gone. And your best impersonation of Dennis Hopper in *Blue Velvet* isn't going to change that."

She fixed her eyes on him, hands on her hips as she stiffened her back, hiding another barrage behind pursed lips. It was the first time Eric had seen those lips their natural colour. Nerida's hair was still dyed black, which made her face seem all the more plump and ruddy in a not unpleasant way. Mary had gotten so thin this year. He cursed under his breath, realising he'd just compared the two.

"Why are you so weird?" Nerida asked.

"What?"

"You heard me."

"Yeah, I heard you. *You* want to know why *I'm* weird?"

"Ooooh, no. No, we are not playing that game. This is not a competition, buddy. I look the way I want to look. I dye my hair, slap on a metric fuck-ton of makeup and half of Melbourne thinks I wear too much black. And I *don't* pretend it makes me special or different, or edgy. I do it because I like it! And when I want to, it all comes off. See?" She clutched the lapels of her blouse. "White!" She then slapped her thigh, sending a loud smack bouncing around the room. "Denim! But you? It's like a conversation with fucking IMDB!"

"Oh, come on!"

"What? It's true! I'm not convinced you're even capable of interpreting a single human emotion without a movie reference. It's not like anybody knows these movies!"

"You've never heard of *Blue Velvet*? Really?"

"*Eric!!!* For real? Can we not talk about the fucking movie?"

"What do you want to talk abo—"

"Your play, maybe? The one those fuckers cancelled?"

Sinking lower into her couch, he stared into its velvet upholstery, smirking as he noticed it was blue. Its shade darkened as his hands brushed over it. "I don't want to talk about that."

"So, you just don't care?"

"Of course I care!"

"Those fuckers! Those fucking zebra fuckers!"

"Nerida?"

"*I hope they get crossing chafe!!!*"

"Are you high?"

She stared at him, incredulous. "That's all I am to you, isn't it? Dispensary?"

"No, it's just—"

"Get out!"

He put his hands on his knees with a scoff and laboured to his feet. "Yes, Ms Desmond."

"What?"

"*Sunset Boulev—*"

"*DON'T EVEN!!!*"

"Nerida!" He grabbed hold of her hands.

"Let go of—"

"'Zebra fuckers?' You're acting kind of strange."

She let her head fall forward into his chest with a quiet, slightly exasperated groan of surrender. "I'm not high," she mumbled into it.

"Okay. Just checking."

She looked up, her cheeks flushed pink with sudden optimism. "You want some?"

"Please."

❖

The glass coffee table felt cold under Eric's legs. He wasn't sure if it was the temperature of the room, or the fact that they were laid out on the floor, legs resting well above head height on the table top, which had to be screwing up their natural blood-flow.

Nerida torched their third joint and passed it to him.

"So now we can't do *Titus*..." He choked a little on the fresh smoke as it filled his lungs. "What would you suggest? What's your favourite Shakespeare?"

"Ugh," Nerida rolled over, putting a hand on his chest and shaking him. "Plays and movies! Plays and movies! You know what I once heard somebody say, about writers whose characters do *nothing* but talk about plays and movies?"

"It's just a question."

"I heard it's because the writer's got no content. Nothing to call their own."

"Well, that's bullshit," he said. "Stories and media are just part of who we are. They're a human experience. You've got access now to every book, every movie, every story ever created. Stories are the content now, Nerida. They're the interpretation. So I'm asking you, what's your favourite Shakespeare?"

She rolled off him and took a long toke, holding it for a few silent seconds before giving him the answer he'd instinctively known she would. "Guess."

"*Macbeth*?" he pounded the carpet twice before realising first of all that they were not in a theatre, and secondly, that the floor wasn't made of wood.

"Guess again."

"*Titus*? Is it *Titus*, seriously?"

She looked at him, her eyes lazy, even bored as she blew out the smoke. "*A Midsummer Night's Dream*."

He snorted back a laugh. "Copious amounts of hallucinogenics?"

She pierced him with her green eyes as she rested her head on one arm, the joint still burning between her fingertips. "You really don't talk like a normal guy."

"Normal?"

"Yeah. Darren would never use words like that."

"You're comparing me to *Darren*?"

"No!"

"Fighting words, White."

"Will you chill out?" She passed him back the joint. "Okay, fine. Julien. Julien would never say that."

He took a long toke without looking at her. She had no way of knowing how much *that* particular comparison had stung. "It's just what comes into my head."

"It's a very pretty head, Eric."

He passed the joint back, not noticing it had gone out until it reached her fingers.

"I like *Midsummer* because nobody ends up with the person they think they're supposed to. Or they spend ages chasing the wrong person. And that's genuine to me. That happens, much more than this 'love at first sight' bullshit. I mean sure, I think love at first sight happens. Maybe often. But I don't think it's a good feeling. It's more like, 'I've met this amazing person and they don't feel the same way about me.' It's not a happy feeling, it's bloody horrible. In *Midsummer*, it feels honest. Like Shakespeare knew all of that was a farce. He knew we all fall for the wrong person."

"I don't know about that. It's kind of—"

"Depressing?" Nerida took out her lighter and reignited the joint. "It is if your happiness is going to depend on another person."

Eric let himself sink deeper into the carpet, the rubbery, synthetic texture of its fibres pressing into his back through the flimsy cotton of his T-shirt. "Sounds awful."

"What's yours?"

"What do you mean? What's my happiness?"

"Woah! I know you're stoned, but noooooooo, Socrates. Stopping you right there! Your favourite Shakespeare, dick! Like I have to ask…"

He shrugged, taking the joint off her again, ignoring the nausea that tugged at his stomach. "*Othello.*"

Nerida's head turned so fast, he half expected her to have carpet burns on her face. "Not *Titus*?"

"Nope. *Othello.*"

"But you wanted to do *Titus*. Fuck, Eric! We fought to do—"

"I didn't fight for shit," he reminded her. "Oh Jesus, I only said it as a joke! I thought I was proving a point. I didn't think Harley would actually *listen* to me! Turns out, I was right in the end. It's out of their precious, comfy league."

He could feel her stare burrowing into the side of his face, as though it could penetrate what Nerida now probably thought was his thick skull and get a glimpse of the deranged brain inside. A brain that was still ticking over. But it was the truth. He wasn't that cut up about *Titus*, specifically. Not anymore. The tears he'd fought back in front of Harley had been real enough, but they'd been tears for his lost project. The loss of something that was his, and that, he could always take back.

"I hate you," Nerida finally spat out. "I hate you so, so much right now."

"Please do not tell me you 'believed in' me." He toked again. "We just ate, and I'd like to keep it down."

"Oh, piss off! Do you know how excited you got everyone?"

He blew out a long billow of smoke toward the ceiling. "Hooray for everyone."

"Why's that so hard for you to understand? It's like I said to you. People go to theatre because they want to feel something, and violence does that. That destruction, like the tearing apart of everything that's pristine and pure and orderly." She gracefully reached over and took her turn with the joint. "Maybe it's like a sex act."

"A what?" he laughed.

"I'm serious! That extreme ecstasy. That sudden adrenaline rush. What's the word? Catharsis! I love that word, don't you? Sounds like, medical or something, and it is I guess. Like the removing of—"

"*Othello*," he cut her off. "I like because everyone ends up getting exactly what they deserve. There's justice in it. Man puts trust where he shouldn't, woman accepts judgement where she shouldn't, man is jealous of another man where he shouldn't be. They all put their trust in something that isn't real, and they all end up dead."

"Not all."

"Close enough. Now, imagine…just imagine if Othello had wanted proof. If he'd said 'Bullshit. Desdemona loves me, and I won't jeopardise that without proof. Show me this betrayal. Show me something.' What if he'd demanded a video? Proof, or it never happened." He held his hand up high above their heads, fingers cupped around the small, invisible form of a video camera, pointing down at them, opening every pore of their skin, widening their eyes, catching detailed changes in emotion. The tears of hash-induced tiredness. The faint puffs of smoke. The gentle smile of Nerida's colourless lips. "That's what movies are. When something goes down on film, it becomes an immortal record of a person, an idea, a story, and you can doctor it, change it, cut it together however you want. But you can't say it was never there." He watched the lights on the ceiling crystallise into focus within the curve of his hand.

"So the story becomes the new content," Nerida murmured. She was staring at it with him. "And what's in your head becomes real."

Eric wished they had an actual camera. Wished he was catching their conversation on video. Making this conversation real. She got it. Nerida White got it. "Whether it's real, like a memory," he said, "or fantastical, like a wish or a fear of something horrible."

"Dude," Nerida laughed. "You should totally bug Miss Harley to do *Othello*. Pitch this stuff to her. Tell her you want to play that angle."

"I talked to Miss Harley today. She said 'it's just bloody high school,' and she's right." He grinned as he closed one eye and tilted the mimed camera until it was directly focused on Nerida. "So why would I waste such a good idea on bloody high school?"

"It's a great idea," she said. "I mean, usually, somebody stages *Othello*, they try and do something new with infidelity, jealousy, all that. Which is fair. Without it, there's no story. You said it's your favourite, but I notice you don't mention that."

Eric's shot wavered. "Some guy who's so weak and insecure about a woman's love that he blames and murders her based on his wrong assumptions isn't my idea of a hero."

"So you don't empathise with him? Just a bit?"

"Jealousy is a nasty prick. Jealousy is paranoia that completely takes you over, and what good is it? Getting angry? Exploding into revenge? What do people think they're accomplishing with that? Defending their mate's honour? Seriously? By losing their shit and taking out all who stand in their way?"

Nerida rolled awkwardly onto her side, eyes darting over him as she shifted her legs on the table. Eric tried to reposition her face within the invisible view finder. Her white blouse had come undone at its top two buttons. The strong curve of her thigh stretched her blue jeans and sank deeper into the carpet as she tried to relax again, her head gently falling into the crook of her arm. She ran a hand through the carpet as though it were some giant, docile, shaggy pet to be stroked. "So you wouldn't get jealous? Not ever?"

"No," he answered, hearing the hesitation in his voice. "Not to that extreme."

"Of course not, you dick! Not to *kill* anyone, but there's a lot of other things you could do." She ran a cold finger along the flesh of his forearm.

In his other hand, the joint had gone out again. He could smell the traces of its scent. Taste the bitter, earthy vapour that remained on the air.

"What if it was me?" she asked.

"What about you?"

"What if I was yours? Would you be jealous? Would you defend my honour?"

He reached over and gently lifted the expired joint from between her fingers, flicking it harmlessly over their feet and onto the coffee table. "I didn't think you cared about honour."

She stared at him, impassive, green eyes catching his undivided attention for the first time. A ruddy pink flushed her cheeks, either from pot or their inverted position relative to the coffee table.

"I'd look after yours. I'd look after you." Her voice was calm and sure of itself. A voice able to put into words what Toby couldn't. But Toby, he'd seen that coming for ages. He'd known how to put Toby down gently. He'd rehearsed it in his head.

"Can you not record this, please?" Nerida said dryly, staring at him through his empty hand.

Eric grinned, putting the imaginary camera away behind him. "It's off."

"Your parents," Nerida continued, unsmilingly. "They're not together any more, are they?"

The question should have made him feel violated. Interrogated, somehow. But it didn't. Any trace of anger would go no further than the shallowest hollows of his brain. "My dad left us," he admitted.

"I'm sorry," she whispered. "I...no, forget it. It's nothing."

"You can say it."

She lowered her eyes at him, her mouth flat-lined into a resigned grimace. "I can't imagine not growing up with both my folks. I'm sorry. I should not have brought this up."

"Why? It's not like I'm unique. What did you want to say?"

She put her fingers into his open palm, stroking its lines as though she could read them. Perhaps she could. "My parents... they're kind of textbook, Eric. Totally in love, I mean with each other, and that's it. Nobody else. Not me. Not Beata."

"Your sister? Isn't she boarding in Italy somewhere?"

"Yeah," Nerida laughed. "I haven't seen her in a year. I haven't seen Mum and Dad in two months. 'Oh Nerida's a big girl, she wants her freedom and can handle herself. Yee Lin can keep an eye on her.' And let me tell you—"

"I know the fee—"

"Yee Lin comes in every Friday at exactly 9.35 a.m., while I'm at school, cleans the place, or so she says, then leaves. I think the last time I saw Mum and Dad was more recent than the last time I saw Yee Lin."

"Isn't that the way it should be?"

"Aw gee, thanks Mary Poppins."

"I only mean you must miss them?"

"That's not my point!" Her voice had taken on a growling, irritable tone, not to be interrupted. "Point is they don't give a shit. They're still together. And I mean *too-ge-THER*. Fuck, it's embarrassing! I don't mean embarrassing like your parents are supposed to be embarrassing, either. I mean grade nine embarrassing. Always kissing and holding hands when we're out in public. You probably think that's sweet. You do think that, don't you?"

"I didn't say—"

"Well you're right. Or at least, they think you are. But that's the way they think. Everything's so fucking perfect for them, their daughters can't possibly..." she paused, her hand now clawing gently at his palm, like she was screwing up some invisible paper. It was a nice feeling, in its own way. Nerida's touch was cool and smooth. Some of the smoothest skin he'd ever felt against his own. "I'm rambling," she said.

"I don't mind."

"Yeah, but I do. I only meant that I can't imagine what it's like to have your parents split. I didn't want to go off into this... whatever it is. That was totally selfish. I mean, I *can* handle myself. They're not wrong about me."

"That makes two of us," he muttered. "But my dad just started sleeping with other people. He still loved Mum. But he...did what he had to, I guess."

"But they—"

"Mum...didn't quite see it that way."

Nerida fixed her eyes on him as though she'd just reached some deep insight. "Is that why you don't believe in jealousy?"

"No."

Her gaze lingered on him, but she didn't persist.

"I just think people should do what they need to be happy without hurting anyone. That's the part that matters. Is that so hard?"

Nerida pushed herself upright and straddled him. He caught his breath, waiting for her to reach for the buttons of his pants. But she didn't. It was just the weight of her presence on top of his, tasting him, lavishing him.

"So," she whispered. "You're really not into Toby?"

"You know about that?" he laughed.

She grinned. "I do now."

Oops. Maybe Toby wouldn't mind.

"Are you sure we're not going to hurt Mary?" she asked.

He shook his head. "You know, when Mia Farrow and John Cassavetes make love on the floor in *Rosemary's Baby*, that's the last time they do it before he puts the devil inside her. Then she spends the next ninety minutes freaking out over whether she's imagining the whole thing."

Nerida smiled at him with big white teeth. "Too late."

He didn't ask which one of them she meant.

CHAPTER THIRTY-ONE

In asking me for my understanding of Hell, the question begs clarification before I can even begin. Do you seek my interpretation of damnation, or a more generic definition? Is Hell, as some would have us believe, separation from God, separation from the alleged light of a supernal patriarch, or a humanist notion of separation from the self-worth and purpose that drives us? If that self-worth and purpose, in fact, drives us to be better human beings, is this not in itself a manifestation of God, if we interpret that notion to be the God of monotheistic religion, in whom faith is a means to inspire this betterment of self and in turn, hopefully, the betterment of society?

On the other hand, if one is to interpret Hell as a literal and physical place of punishment, this brings into question the personalisation of such suffering, and if such personalisation might be tailored to one's sins or one's fears, if they are so divorced, one from the other. For instance, might a serial divorcee—an oft-ignored, still egregious offence to Catholic doctrine—be forever confined to the bonds of marriage?

So if one is to ask me my understanding of Hell, I am forced to consider both these interpretations of the point, first in terms of a literal concept, as I believe this bears great influence on the conceptual Hell of 'separation.'

If, in my understanding of Hell, I am to interpret it as a literal place, it is one where the same songs repeat on a perpetual loop because a cruel and faceless God has decreed it so. It is one of fluorescent lighting and consumer hoards seeking to further a lifetime's devotion to collecting crap from discount department stores. It is one where I can stand in the middle of this army of VISA-wielding zombies and scream, scream, scream, to within the edges of my life, knowing I'll be told to shut up before anyone asks what's wrong.

If, in my understanding of Hell, I am to interpret it as a literal place, it is one in which over-tanned women in ill fitting, visible bras cackle on mobile phones on their way from the gym to coffee and back again. And back again. And back again, until the time comes to collect their children from whichever institution of learning they have chosen to unburden them for any designated number of years, so that their coffee and gym ritual might continue unhindered.

If, in my understanding of Hell, I am to interpret it as a literal place, it is one of multiplex cinemas playing action movies on fifteen out of sixteen screens, twelve of which will be shown in redundant 3D to the zombies who emerge under the misconception they have enjoyed a cultural experience. It is one where anti-culture has become culture, where pop culture has no place because what was once pop culture has become passé, the domain of the Gen-X moderati to be afforded no voice. Too old to be cool. Too under-ripe for nostalgic exploitation. It is one where only the traditionally cultural and the deliberately uncultured can thrive, praised and cultivated for their elitism and anti-intellectualism, respectively.

If, in my understanding of Hell, I am to interpret it as a literal place, it is one where the zombies return home and burn offerings of meat upon the altar of gas and steel that dominates the hallowed quarter acre of their grassy chapel, for no smaller size will do. It is one where oversized skewers of flavourless seafood are dowsed in cheap beer. It is one where the inhabitants use a bastardised version of English in which two or more vowels are used where one would suffice. It is one where such considered intellectual notions as 'she'll be right, mate' are a declaration of policy. One where this apparent relaxation is accepted as an achievement and where any challenger is to be cut down as a heretical snob.

If, in my understanding of Hell, I am to interpret it as a literal place, it is one in which the unknown quantity, the shock of the new, is reviled as an attempt to pervert this perceived blissful apathy. It is one where one must adapt or be outcast. It is one where one must be white, of soul if not of skin. It is one where the zombie's own children come before all others, where all in the toxic mother's unfortunate wake must bow before her whim until this self-righteousness grows tedious, and the child is of an age to accept emotional abandonment, the same values now instilled.

It is one without a world to be seen beyond Bali or Fiji or Phuket. It is one in which complaining is a sanctioned neighbourhood pastime, led by the champions of radio airwaves with words crafted only to stoke fire within the malcontent zombie heart.

It is a place in which the zombie is too self-absorbed to understand that I am not, nor shall ever be, its 'mate.'

It is a place where I am powerless, in soul if not in practice, deafened by the roar of my silent screams.

It is a place into which I am born undeserved.

Know that my understanding must also reach beyond this manifestation to the Hell created by those who've attempted escape via financial means. Those sequestered in inner city mansions and townhouses, living off investments and patronising the opera just as they patronise any other person they happen to meet. For this Hell, dug as it is frequently into a wall of old minted cash, provides no shelter from the stirring words of the angry champions of the malcontent, determined as they are to leave no heart unhardened by their exploitative message of doom, for it is when the zombie—even the moneyed zombie—is at its angriest, that it is most easily controlled.

If, in my understanding of Hell, I am to interpret it as a state of mind, a point of separation from self-actualisation and achievement, from power over one's own fate, then know that each time I am confronted by this Hell, with each cackle of its vile accent, each flash of bleached blonde hair under fluorescent light, each sickening whiff of beer soaked prawn, I grow firmer in my resolve. My resolve to not be a zombie. My resolve to care. About myself. About my work. About others in whom my trust and love are not misplaced. About who I am and what I stand to leave behind. Each fresh scent of this Hell reminds me of what I must achieve. The challenges that lie before me, should I wish my art to be supported, unhindered by the cynicism of blissfully malcontent zombies. To work outside of this Hell.

And so in offering me this reminder, Hell, in its literal manifestation may confine me, but as a state of mind, perhaps it is the separation of God that drives me to be a better person.

❖

Callahan read the paper twice before sliding it back across the desk. "Quite an essay to write on your first detention, Eric. Not exactly Ginsberg, is it?"

Shrug.

"Is that how you really feel?"

"Sort of. I make it bearable, if that's what you're asking."

"Running away to America is not going to solve your problems."

"It might make them more interesting."

"More challenging, you mean? Your uni years are going to be tough as it is, Eric. Are you sure you want to lose the home field advantage?"

Eric fixed his eyes on Callahan, the words, his thoughts, were suddenly the clearest they'd been in weeks. "I make my own advantage."

Callahan nodded, opening his desk drawer and taking out a small, fresh envelope.

"What's that?"

"A letter of recommendation," the priest explained. "For wherever you feel is going to foster your…vision."

Eric grinned, ignoring the wryness of that remark and stuffing the letter away in his blazer pocket.

"You're free to go."

Wait. That was it? No more to be said about the incident with Steffen? No questions about his mother?

"And Eric?"

"Yes?"

"I'd prefer it if you didn't come see me again."

Eric swallowed, giving the only response he could. "Okay."

CHAPTER THIRTY-TWO

"D o you like it?"

Eric looked up at his mother, chopsticks hovering over dinner like an ibis's beak.

"I'm a bit out of practice," she confessed, smiling at him over the top of a near-full bottle of Chenin Blanc. Her white blonde hair hung loose around her freckle-pocked face for the first time since she'd arrived home. It was also the first time in months Eric had seen her without makeup. A flimsy pink T-shirt, probably from GAP, completed this reconnection to suburban simplicity. "You know, Marcel used to enjoy taking us to this place just up from the Viper Room on Sunset—"

"Can you not talk about Marcel?" Eric hadn't meant to snap. Maybe his mother's latest return to the confines of pedestrian Australian housekeeping, along with her rekindled interest in his life, was sincere. Maybe. "It's good," he mumbled, stirring some cabbage around on his plate. "Maybe next time a bit more ginger?"

"I'm sorry, love. Anyway, he's out of the picture. More ginger, you reckon?"

Eric tried not to wince as he crunched a mouthful of fresh ginger between his teeth. "Just a little."

"Did you cook much while I was away?"

"A bit." The Chenin wasn't a good match for stir fry. At least, not the way his mother had made it.

"I got a call from Father Callahan the other day," she continued. "Did you really tell him to go to Hell?'

"Why?" he mumbled, scooping up more chicken between the sticks and shovelling it away. "Did he need directions?"

"Look, if you want to be angry at me, that's fine. But you don't take it out on your teachers. Is that understood?"

He shrugged.

"Eric, answer me. Is that understood?"

"Yes," he growled. "I lost my temper. I apologised to him." Two…three full mouthfuls of under-gingered chicken passed his lips.

"How's school going, otherwise?"

Eric slowed his chewing and tried not to meet her eyes as he picked up his wine. "I get A's," he mumbled to the bottom of the glass.

"Well, that's good. And you've been okay for money?"

It didn't matter how the wine tasted. Right now there wasn't enough of it.

"Reckon I must have the only seventeen-year-old who's never asked his mum for money."

"I'm eighteen."

"I know, love. Been looking at uni?"

"Colleges, mostly."

The correction invited a glare from his mother as she poured them both more wine. "American colleges, you mean?"

"Some."

She sighed, setting the bottle down on the table with a loud bump. "So you really want to do that? Go off on your own? No friends? And then, what? Think you're going to walk into a job? America's not what it used to be, Eric. There's no money left. Not for bright-eyed walk-ins like you. They'll be looking after their own first. Can't say I blame them. You do know they're in the middle of a global financial crisis?"

"Everyone is," he muttered. "That's why it's called a global financial crisis."

"You know what I mean! I can't support you in LA. Definitely not New York. Who do you think is going to hire you? You'll be waiting tables, scrounging for tips like some Mexican!"

"That's racist."

"That's *fact*, Eric, and…look, I'm not having this conversation right now."

"We already had it. Then you left."

"That was work!" she snapped, setting her wine down.

"You found a job there."

"For a few weeks, Eric."

"Two months."

"You're not going to be able to fly home every two months! What are you, crazy?"

Eric slammed his wine down with a sharp thud.

"I'm sorry," she said, looking away. "That's not what I meant. It just slipped out. You know that's not what I meant."

Shrug.

"Wouldn't you miss Sydney? Miss everything?"

Shrug.

"I hate not seeing you. If it were up to me…It's just work." She reached across the table and took his hand.

To his astonishment, he let her.

"Or it was," she said.

"What?"

"Marcel—"

"*Can you not—*"

"No, listen to me. Do you know why Marcel's gone?"

Her fingers felt cold and amphibian, wrapped around his hand.

"I told him this'd be the last time. I missed you, baby boy. I got sick of missing you, sick of not being there. I don't want to 'not be there' for the next four years, Eric. What about when you finish high school? Go to uni? Get your first real girlfriend?"

"I've *got* a girlfriend," he sneered. "Her name's Mary. I *told* you about her."

"So, I want to meet her! That's the point! It's like I don't know who we are or what's happening in your life, and I don't want that to be us. You're all I've got, Eric. And being away from you? I hate it."

"I don't."

She dropped his hand as if she'd been burnt. "Do you mean that?"

"I don't hate it." He shovelled another chopstick-load of stir fry into this mouth. "It's the way it is. I make it work."

"What do you mean, you 'make it work?'"

He wolfed down another mouthful of chicken.

"Fine." His mother slowly rose from her chair, clearing her half-full plate and taking a near-full glass of wine into the kitchen.

Eric started to wonder if she would ever find out how he'd supplemented his income over the past six months, just how much he'd managed to accumulate in a relatively short space of time, and the argument he'd been most eager to avoid—what the money was for. His college fund.

A slip of blue cardboard landed in the centre of the table, a sheet of carbon paper stapled inside. Eric eyed his mother, his temper simmering beneath a rapidly thinning layer of politeness as he recognised it.

"There's still three repeats on that, baby boy. Going off your pills? Is that how you're making it work? Is it?"

"I had to."

"Why?"

"It doesn't matter. I'm back on them now."

"It matters, Eric! You know what the doctors—"

"Fuck the doctor!" His plate skittered away with one swift push, toppling his glass of Chenin. It spilt across the table, seeping through the cloth.

"Eric? Eric!"

He was already halfway to his room. How dare she! There was more to him than those bloody pills! Even she knew that! And the best part, he thought as he slammed the door shut behind him, was that yes, he had made it work. He'd stopped taking them. Nothing had happened. Nobody had died. The world hadn't blown up. Part of him wished something like that had happened. Maybe he needed more powerful pills.

"Don't you storm off on me!"

Another part of him wished he'd remembered to lock the door.

"And you will not use that language in this house. Is that clear?"

"See?" He sneered, snatching up the bottle and pouring one of the ugly green horse capsules into his hand. He swallowed it with a defiant glare. "Still taking them!"

"I know you stopped, Eric. The chemist hasn't seen you for two months. I checked."

He snapped the cap off the bottle, poured out the pills, and stuffed the handful into his mouth.

"What are you doing?" His mother shook him by the shoulders as the bottle slipped from his fingers.

He bit down on the pills, their sour taste spilling out over his tongue as she tried to dig them out from between his clenched teeth, tiny pieces of green gel cap spraying in spittle over her fingers. He finally let his jaw spring open and spat the mashed wad of pills into a tissue.

"There," he snapped. "Now I need a repeat."

For only the second time in her life, Karen Volger, or Delamont, depending on the asker's level of influence in the entertainment industry, tried to hit him. She was only stopped by his faster reflexes catching hold of her wrist.

Eric could see in her face that this loss of temper had hurt more than the first time. Immediately after that first outburst, she'd stopped, realising it wasn't her son she was angry with, but his father. Dad. Did she look at him and see Dad?

"I…" she began.

She would not apologise. He knew that much. 'Sorry' wasn't a word she understood. He straightened his shirt and pushed past her.

"Where are you going?" she demanded.

"Work."

"I didn't know you had a job."

"Of course you didn't."

CHAPTER THIRTY-THREE

Enter without knocking, Margaret had said. Through the delivery entrance, via the garden as usual. Her instructions had been very specific. He hadn't been able to hear from outside, but the *a capella* voice was now clear as he approached the living room. It was Margaret's voice, which had been met with some respectable applause over several years of theatrical service before she'd abandoned it.

He recognised the aria immediately. *Tosca*. Vissi d'Arte. But something was off about it. A lot of things were off. Margaret wavered on the top notes like she was unsure of her own ability to reach them. Every so often, a faint choke would punctuate her vocals, one compounded by an all too evident anger that escaped her with each flaw.

The door to the living room had been left ajar. She had her back to him. He stopped at the door, watching for a moment as Margaret summoned the energy for a peak in the score. This time she reached it. Not perfectly, but every bit as well as half the singers Eric had listened to in her company over the past year. She seemed smoother, more composed as she continued.

Eric realised he had never once heard Margaret sing an opera piece. She'd played him a private recording of her musical theatre standards, but this was new. Had Joe brought out some profound change in her? Something he'd never been privy to as the boy on Margaret's arm?

Yet, he was here now, wasn't he?

It also astonished him that Margaret would even own, much less be seen in a woollen dressing gown. Much less let *him* see her in it. She lapsed into silence, leaving her song unfinished.

"Sit down, Eric."

He quietly slipped through the door and did as he was told.

Margaret picked Persephone up out of her favourite armchair and sat down in her place, the cat now curled up in the lap of her begrudgingly tolerated owner-turned-invader. She didn't offer him a drink. Didn't even look at him. She just sat, an aged hand stroking the bony jutting of her chin.

"That was beauti—"

"No, it isn't." She said this with such a firm, quiet finality that it seemed rude to contradict her. "How have you been?"

Persephone's tail flicked from side to side again, like a badly synched clock.

"Fine. Busy." The silence soon became intolerable. "They cancelled *Titus*."

"Oh?"

"Apparently a play written in the 1590's is too controversial for the delicate sensibilities of a twenty-first century audience."

"That is a shame. So rarely performed," she said unsmilingly.

Eric ran a finger over the polished wooden armrest of his chair. Not a speck of dust anywhere. "How was…Joe?"

"You were right. He cooked. Cleaned well, then vanished."

"Margaret—"

She silenced him with a gently raised finger. "I just don't… What the devil were you trying to achieve?"

For a full four minutes, Margaret waited patiently for Eric to compose his answer, assuming he could find one he believed himself. As much as he resented this entrapment under the pretence of an appointment, dishonesty at this point seemed beneath him. Besides, on some level he'd known this discussion would be unavoidable. He'd realised it the moment he'd given Joe to her. Given, no less! The exchange of money had been Margaret's idea.

He struggled to reconcile events as best he remembered them. The events that had led to Margaret's unwitting participation in his project. He had the tapes, an editing process he'd barely finished. Julien's performance had been everything he'd hoped. More convincing than he'd even thought possible.

Over and over he'd watched it, editing it down.

The recording of his subject's screams—the project within the project, for music—had become difficult enough as they'd gotten to know each other, and the terrified cries of Joe, the character Jules had created so completely and convincingly, had become more than mere white noise. They'd become pain.

Eric realised this internal emotional betrayal was probably his own fault. His own part of the project. His own character, the nameless captor, 'Dude,' or whoever. An actor must feel the character. Know the character's heart. These had been Margaret's words. Would she understand he had gone off his pills to know that heart? The heart of a captor and a tormentor?

"It had to be real," he murmured.

"What?"

"It was for a film," he explained. "For our college apps. Jules, and me."

"Jules? Was that his real name? You lied about that too?"

"I'm sorry we involved you. Mum came home. It seemed like an interesting plot development. What would happen next. It made sense."

"Why didn't you just *tell* me that, Eric? Why the trickery? You didn't even bring a camera with you. You didn't film anything! What the hell were you playing at? I paid you—"

"I didn't ask for that! You offered."

"Not the point. You lied to me, Eric. I thought our relationship was—"

"And you *believed it*?" he shot back. Stupid bitch! Stupid! Stupid! "You truly believed that I'd taken a burglar prisoner? That I knowingly brought a burglar into your house, expecting you—"

"Worse than a burglar, boy. An *actor*."

"Didn't he tell you any of this?"

"Not a word. Never broke character. Oh, yes, that young man will go far. Very professional, I can assure you! He up and left me, Eric. Understood? He abandoned me! Just like—"

"Oh, don't! Just don't, okay? Gerald's never coming back, Margaret. Don't you think it's time you got over it? You're over fifty. Grow up!"

"Eric! I am only fort—"

"You are bloody not! Did you ever think maybe he topped himself because he couldn't stand you anymore?"

The accusation shut Margaret up tight. Persephone jumped down, made a run for the stairs and disappeared up into the bedrooms.

"How...dare you!" his host finally barked.

"I dare because you're no better than me, Margaret. Any of you. You all pay me, *pay me* to go out with you, to make you look good, to turn you on, to hold you and make you feel for a few hours like you're not quite so fucking sad, lonely, and miserable, but you know what? That just makes me better than any of you. I've got all the power, Margaret. You need me. Not the other way around. Because for a few hours, I can help you forget that you're slowly slipping away into nothing. But do you know what? At least I could respect you, because I thought we both understood that. Now, do we?"

Margaret's hands were shaking as she slowly pushed herself out of the armchair and crossed to the liquor cabinet, taking out a tumbler. She filled it with an oversized gin and sculled it down, immediately pouring another.

"No, really. I'm good, thanks," Eric muttered.

Margaret glared at him, filling a second tumbler with gin and clumsily thrusting it into his hand. It spilt over his fingers as he took it.

"Thanks."

"That was very hurtful, Eric." Margaret leaned against the liquor cabinet trying to regain her calm. But Eric could see her flashes of temper as she hastily poured herself another drink. "I know you've quite the flare for rudeness. But must you be so, *so* hurtful?"

Eric sipped at his drink, sucking gin off his fingers. "I'm just being honest."

"Really? I believed you before. Why should I believe you now?"

"Margaret...I believed it too."

"What?"

"While we were making the film. I went off my pills. I wanted to see what would happen. What I'd feel. Joe became real. When I.. sold him to you. He was real to me."

Margaret's face was blank as she listened to him. But her shoulders soon started to relax. She downed another gin—Eric had lost count now—and finally offered him the smile he'd been sure would never come. He'd only told her the truth, about Joe, Julien, and how he'd felt.

"You can have the money back," he offered. "I didn't spend any of it. Not a cent."

"My sweet, honest boy." She set her glass down and drifted over to him, cradling his chin in her fingertips. "Let me give you something real."

Margaret's nails seemed to effortlessly rip through his skin as she raked them across his face. He tasted the blood as it trickled down to his lips, the searing pain of his chin, cheek and forehead highlighting each spot into which Margaret had dug her claws. He clutched at his face to protect it. To stem the bleeding. But no second assault came, only the low clucking of Margaret's laughter.

He wanted to scream. To grab her by the throat and shake her, to throw the crazy bitch across the room. But the words, the actions, wouldn't come. He could only stand there, staring at her in morbid disbelief, nursing the cuts she'd made in his face.

"Oh dear," Margaret said, her aging visage now cracking into a hideous, self-satisfied grin. "Not so pretty now, Eric?"

He ran for the doorway, only to be blocked by his clie—*ex*-client. Definitely ex-client! She pushed him away with shocking force, sending him stumbling against the liquor cabinet. Eric grabbed the gin bottle and brandished it at her.

"What are you going to do with that?"

"Get out of my way!" he barked.

"So," she mocked, "this is what you look like when you have no control?"

Eric smashed the gin bottle against the cabinet and threatened her with the broken bottle-head. The cuts in his face were still bleeding.

"Oh really, Eric! Must we burden the evening with clichés? I thought you wanted to be a proper filmmaker." Margaret clapped her hands together and graciously stepped out of his way. "We used to be such good friends."

Eric didn't waste time wracking his brain for a smart-arse reply. Keeping the broken bottle trained on her, he backed into the lounge. He heard only a faint hissing before the teeth and claws punctured his ankles, and the furry ball sent him sprawling to the floor.

Persephone launched herself at the throat of the boy who'd fallen so far out of favour with her mistress. Eric tried to push the cat away, but only succeeded in cutting his own face with the bottle. Fucking cat! As crazy as its owner! He threw the animal away, flailing as he tried to wipe blood away from his eyes. He heard Persephone's low growl and brought the bottle-head down, hearing a high pitched screech as it landed. The room instantly fell silent. Wiping the blood off his face, he caught Margaret's horrified stare as she advanced on him. He threw the weapon away, scrambled to his feet and ran for the delivery entrance.

"Eric? Eric, get back here!"

Ignoring the pain in his face, along with the surge in his stomach that begged him to throw up, he burst through Margaret's garden to the relative safety of Mosman's leafy streets and ran.

"Eric? Eric! Don't think you can get away! Your life is over, boy! Everyone's going to know about this. All of them! You are dead! Dead!"

He didn't hear the rest. Nor did he stop to look at the smattering of onlookers who'd emerged from their overgrown palatial homes to hear the gin-soaked ranting of Margaret Moss.

Eric wouldn't let her be his problem anymore.

Chapter Thirty-four

From the safety of a cab, speeding onto the Harbour Bridge past the apartment blocks of Milson's Point, it occurred to Eric that Margaret probably had enough influence to make good on her threat. He probably had just ended his career as high class escort to Sydney's middle-aged-to-fading subscribers to the Great Gatsby dream. It wouldn't happen right away. Margaret was furious, but not so self-destructive she'd tell anyone the truth. She would craft a cover story, one that wouldn't fuel the gossip chain, bring her social disgrace, or afford her peers a cruel giggle at her expense.

But fuck! Did any of that matter? He had the money. Enough to cover himself for at least two years. But not Mary. What if Mary got in, too? What if they made good on their idea and went together? He couldn't pay for them both. Jules would be okay. His folks would fit the bill. But Mary…shit! He was bleeding again.

"Sir, you go city?" the cab driver asked.

It'd be okay. He'd done it here. He could do it in the States. He'd meet clients. Lots of them. Rich clients. Old money. Richer than Sydney. Rich enough to keep them there as long as they wanted. Enough money to buy off the pesky expiration of a student visa. God bless the untaxable profession. God bless fucking America.

"*Sir*, you go to—"

"Yes." Eric snapped out of his thoughts. "No, wait. Edgecliff."

"Edgecliff?"

"Yes!" He barked Andy's address. Yes…Andy. The man would be back from South America by now. He had to see Andy.

"All right, sir. Is all right. I get you where you want to go. You calm, okay?"

Eric relaxed into the seat. "Sorry." The front seat. Why had he chosen the front seat?

"No, you okay, sir? Blood?"

"I said, Edgecliff!"

The driver shook his head. "Okay. You the boss."

"That's right. I am."

For the first time that night, Eric felt a smile crack the corner of his mouth. He was only half conscious of the rest of the journey. The cabbie could have taken him anywhere. He doubted he would have noticed.

Eric could hear soft music coming from inside the house as he rang the doorbell a second time. Shadows flicked across the dimmed lights. Maybe candles? It was impossible to tell through the frosted glass. Eric had never seen Andy's house like this. He'd never shown up unannounced, either. He glimpsed a tall, athletic male striding up the hall, wrapping the fuzzy white flash of what must have been a towel around his waist. Whoever was inside, Eric had their attention. Viktor's attention.

"Eric," the man whispered, his accent thick as he opened the door, wiping the sheen of sweat from his forehead. "What...what are you doing here?"

Even in his pained state, Eric couldn't help but stare at the man's near perfect body. He'd never seen Viktor so naked before. The flimsy towel barely gripped the circumference of its owner's goliath loins. Yet since the Ukrainian...Croat, Serb...whatever... was here, back in Andy's service, Eric had to wonder if the new uniform had been part of the deal.

"Eric, you can't stay."

"I....I need to see Andy."

Viktor sighed, running a hand through his hair.

"Please, Viktor? It's important!" His head had started bleeding again. He could feel it.

"What happened to you?" Viktor frowned, putting a powerful but careful arm around his shoulders and ushering him inside.

Dozens of lit candles ran along the length of the hall. Some were set on candelabra, some just tea lights on the shelves or side board. The flickering light gave Eric a headache, or maybe it was a delayed symptom of Margaret's blow. Or had he accidentally swallowed some of the tabs he'd scoffed into his mouth to freak out his Mum? It didn't matter. He was sure Viktor was helping, at least in part, to keep him steady and upright. The man gently sat him down in the formal lounge, then disappeared to fetch disinfectant, several cold packs, a bowl of ice water, and a sponge. Gym junkie, compulsive liar, and first aid nurse. Brilliant.

"Cat," Eric finally murmured, though the man hadn't pestered him for explanation. "Cat scratched me."

"Big cat." Viktor dabbed the blood from Eric's forehead. "Big cat wearing nail polish."

Great. Now Eric, the great storyteller, couldn't even lie properly.

"Can...can I see Andy? Where is he? Please?"

"Shhh. You'll see him soon, eh? Calm down. Nasty cut there, my friend. Hold still."

Eric hissed in pain as Viktor disinfected the wound. "Is he okay?"

"You worry about you for now, all right?"

"Victor plea—Ow!"

"He'll see you soon. Now hold still, or I pin you down."

Eric raised an eyebrow, making no effort to hide his suspicion.

"There. Much better. You been drinking?"

"Not much."

"Good. So the bleeding should stop." The man packed up the first aid kit and took it away.

The smell of the burning candles and the flickering light didn't seem so irritating anymore. In fact, it was kind of soothing. Or had he just managed to calm down? To get over the shock of Margaret's outburst? He watched the light's hypnotic reflection on the far wall, knowing the same light was caressing his damp cheeks. His breath deepened, growing more sure and steady as he relaxed into the couch.

"Here." Viktor put a tall glass of cold water on the table in front of him and sat down. "You feeling all right?"

He nodded, taking several grateful gulps of water. "Thanks."

"Your friend, he's not with you tonight?"

Eric stared down into the grain of the teppanyaki table. "No."

"Shame. Nice guy. He trains with me now."

"I know," Eric's voice was barely a whisper. "Where's—"

"Andy, Andy, Andy," Viktor teased. "He's not *home,* Eric. Why? You not want to talk to me?"

"I didn't say that."

"But you never try. What? I'm not good enough? Viktor's not good enough? Not interesting? Not smart enough for you?"

"It's not that. I just don't *know* you. What would we talk about?"

The man grinned at him, casually crossing one leg over the other in a move that stretched the white towel to its limits.

"How's training?" Eric asked with a shrug.

Viktor laughed at him through a sneer that was somehow even more condescending than the question. "It's goooooooooooood!" he crooned, in a low, guttural voice that Eric would have taken for a Boris Karloff impersonation, if he'd had any reason to think Viktor knew who Karloff was. The man gave another laugh, loud and exaggerated, mocking his attempt at small talk.

Eric kept his breath steady, staring at the coffee table, refusing to rise to the bait. When he looked up, the Ukrainian's towel had fallen open. He ignored it, closing his eyes, focusing on the scent of candles, the faint smoke that teased his nose. Another sip of water. "How long's Julien been seeing you?"

"He came into the gym the day after I saw you guys there."

Of course he had. Eric didn't know why he'd asked. He didn't need to be thinking about Julien right now. He heard the quiet sounds of weight shifting on the couch as he felt Viktor sit down beside him.

"You want painkillers or anything?"

"No."

The warmth radiated from Viktor's body, like the man had just stepped out of a spa or sauna. He finally opened his eyes. Viktor was sitting a comfortable distance from him on the couch, his towel left on the opposite seat. "I…I wasn't expecting to see you here."

"My wife," the man muttered, "is busy tonight."

"Umm…okay?"

"No, Eric. Not okay. Very not okay. *Bus-y*." Viktor arched an eyebrow. "Fat guy, too."

"Oh," Eric drained the last of his water. Most guys probably would have gotten drunk in this situation. But not Viktor. It made sense to him, in its way. "Ah…sorry."

The man shrugged, looking forlornly at his fingers as they ran against the fall of dark hairs on his muscular thigh. "Terrible… terrible thing. But I come here. Try to relax. Not think about it. Yoga for an hour, then meditate."

Of course. Fucking Mr Health.

"Why so many candles?" Eric asked, suddenly wishing he had a joint.

"You know, I lit the first one. Then two, and three, and I asked myself the same thing. Candles? Why bloody candles? Why does anybody meditate with fire? Fire breaks things, Eric. A destroyer. A big, mean, ferocious thing that warms you for a little bit then consumes you. Turns you to ashes on the ground. That's fire. Then I lit another one just to make sure. Same thing. Burning smell? It was clean. I clean away the old life. My married life. I change everything. No distractions. Nothing familiar. No lights. Just candles. This…" Viktor looked around the room, as though the sight of so many flickering candles had illuminated a critical absurdity within his own argument. "I don't know. Is just me."

"I guess." Eric couldn't help noticing the stress still evident in Viktor's jaw, still clenched. Meditation? Yeah, right. "Why are you naked?"

"Feels natural. Relaxed. I need to be comfortable right now. Doesn't make you uncomfortable, does it?"

"No."

"Good."

Their odd silence made Eric very aware of his own breath. Smooth and steady. Inhale, exhale. He also felt that having Viktor sit naked next to him seemed a lot more natural than it probably should. Who else had seen Viktor naked? Thousands of people across the Internet, if Julien could be believed. If Julien could ever be believed. "Was this the first time? I mean, with your wife. How long have you known?"

"Maybe three months. I try to ignore it. She said it was done. Finish. Pfft! Couldn't ignore it anymore." Viktor paused, gently nudging Eric in the shoulder. "Have you got a girlfriend, Eric?"

"Yeah, I do."

"Julien said you didn't."

Eric closed his eyes and tried not to react. Why would Jules say that? Was it even a lie? What exactly was Mary to him now? What was she to either of them? "Depends where you sit, I guess."

"I sit here."

"No, I mean."

"You want me to put on clothes?"

"No, it's fine. Really."

Viktor nodded. "Do you not love her?"

He couldn't answer. How pathetic would it have been to say yes?

"Come on, Eric. Do you care for this girl or don't you?"

"Of course I care for her! Do you still love your wife?"

The man's tongue tut-tutted faintly from behind his sneer. "You think, she's with another man and I forget everything? It's not like the fucking trash magazines or movies. We built a life together, Eric. I will always have part of her with me." Viktor trailed off, running a thick hand over the fine black hairs of his ankle. "I meditate, is what I do. Meditate. Think about other things."

"Talk about other things?"

The Ukrainian shot him a mischievous grin. "You not get out of it so easy. Do you love her, Eric? Don't give me this 'care for her' bullshit. Love! Yes or no?"

"*Yes.* Jesus!" He snatched up the rest of the water and gulped it down. "I mean, I want her to be happy, whatever that means. That's the point, isn't it? Under all the bullshit, all the flowery emotions and weddings and kids and gifts and all of that crap, isn't it just 'I want you to be happy,' whatever that takes or whatever it is?"

"And you do not care that she fucks with another man?"

"I don't own her, do I?"

The grimness of Viktor's stare seemed to burn against the side of his face. Either that or he was too close to one of the candles.

"But you would do anything to make her smile? To make sure she's never unhappy again?"

He shook his head, his breath deepening at the scope of the question. "What? You mean forev—"

"Oh fuck that! Forever doesn't exist, Eric! Right now, what wouldn't you do to please her? Anything?"

Eric's mouth had gone completely dry. He looked away from Viktor's face only to find himself fixated on the man's smooth, pale chest, sculpted into powerful pectorals. He almost felt embarrassed to be staring at Viktor's nipples, yet they were the perfect focal point, permanently hardened by a coarse regime of brutal, repetitive exercise. Not the soft brown circles with cute sprouting hairs that marked the chests of Julien or Steffen. Nothing like Mary's perfect oval shapes that had stared down at him like dark, expectant buds that night on the beach. What wouldn't he do for her? She'd asked him to enter her, to be a part of her, and he'd refused. She'd even insisted he be first. She'd put him before Julien, and still he couldn't do it. Not with Julien there. Had he actually wanted to?

Viktor now sat mere inches from him, the two provocative dots on his chest now so close Eric could have touched them just by lifting his hand. He looked up, meeting Viktor's dark eyes again. Was he imagining the man's shaking? Maybe it was just his lower lip. Maybe Eric was the one shaking.

"Yes," he whispered. "Yes, I would."

Viktor leaned so close his breath washed over Eric's neck. The boy choked down a tiny gasp. Had he just felt the soft pad of Viktor's lips brush his skin as well? He closed his eyes as Viktor drew close to his ear.

"Then she owns you, whether you let her go or not. And you must make her happy."

He could feel the unyielding muscle of Viktor's forearm resting on his own, stirring in him a tempest of feelings. Curiosity, most of all. To touch it. To feel what it was like. Young skin, stretched over powerful muscle. Not like his own spindly wrists. Was that how Julien saw himself? What he wanted to be? Joe had had strong arms, and Eric had believed in them. Whenever Joe had threatened him or raised his hands to plead, Eric had believed in the strength of those arms. Maybe someday he'd have them himself. The one reward he'd take from the guidance of this stupid Ukrainian super jock whose wife had cheated on him with some fat slob.

"Eric?"

He opened his eyes.

Viktor had silently withdrawn. The man stared at him from his former position further up the couch. "You ever dream to fuck with me?"

His eyes widened. The tone of the question had been perfectly frank. Viktor's arms were open, hands turned to the sky as though the idea of Eric sodomising, or more probably being sodomised by, his client's reinstated servant was some simple, trivial inevitability.

"Not…not really."

"Why not? I single. You single."

"So?"

"So, maybe you crazy? I was in movies, Eric! Millions of women and men want to fuck with me."

"Yeah, I . . . I mean, I heard."

Viktor narrowed his eyes, a mischievous smile rising in his full, Slavic lips. "You did, eh? Then maybe we make a movie together some day?"

"Look, it's not that I don't think you're hot." Eric was about to point out to Viktor that the man's filmography probably didn't include the kind of films he planned to make, but decided against it. "Have you ever done…you know, more than the movies?"

"What? You think I'm some kind of whore?" Victor grimaced. "Ah, no judgement."

"None taken."

"No, Eric. Is just pictures. Movies." The man looked down at his strong hands again, rubbing his thumbs over one another as if he'd lived life without them and only just realised they'd grown on the edge of his hands. "Pointless," he mumbled. "All the men and women of the world want to fuck with you, and then it's done. Now, I clean house. For another guy. Because he wants to fuck with me."

"Viktor, Andy doesn't—"

"Listen, Eric." All trace of a sneer had vanished from Viktor's face, but it was still evident in his voice. His posture. The way he shifted his weight to one arm and cocked one corner of his mouth. The way he casually pushed aside his limp penis as he crossed his legs.

Eric couldn't help but look at it. That thick stocking of flesh hanging from the deep, manicured thatch of Viktor's dark pubic hair, which quickly evaporated into a thin trail as it ascended the ridges of his lower stomach, then disappeared completely into his navel, all skin north of that perfectly smooth.

"You like my cock too?" the Slav asked, without a trace of seduction or sensuality. "Sure, why not? She used to. Now I'm useless. *Everything* I'm doing is useless. This?" A loud smack echoed around the room as Viktor struck his abs with a hard slap. "All gone. In her—"

"I need to pee," Eric mumbled. He got off the couch and onto his feet, careful not to set his head bleeding again as he stumbled to the bathroom and closed the door.

❖

Eric stared into the mirror at the wound inflicted by Margaret's nails. It still refused to clot. He dabbed at it with a clumsy finger, which only made it worse. Or perhaps he'd imagined it. At least she hadn't hit him. There'd be no bruise. Just a fucking ugly...

He looked down into the porcelain basin and coughed, a few drops of blood raining into the sink as his head shook with movement. Finally, his bladder won out over his wounded vanity.

"Eric? Eric!"

"What?" He could barely hear Viktor through the locked door. Not over the sound of his peeing.

"Use the upstairs bathroom! The toilet? Is broken in there."

"Umm…thanks?" he called, thinking it was a bit late now.

He waited for the stream to stop and zipped up his trousers, instinctively reaching for the button and flushing the bowl before he realised what he was doing. It flushed just as it was supposed to. He stared at it for a moment, just to make sure.

"I think it's okay," he called. "I think you fixed it."

His response came back after a short silence. "Okay…good."

Eric cleaned his hands, letting another drop of blood, perhaps two, wash away with the water. He was starting to feel whole and normal again as he turned off the water. He stared at the blood on his fingers. Blood he was sure had not been there before he'd touched the tap. Fuck. He'd really made a mess. It seemed different though. Not the fresh, red nectar that had been ebbing, one droplet at a time from his scalp, but a blood that seemed harder, more congealed. More brown than red.

"Eric? Are you all right?"

He stared at the fragments of drying blood that mottled his fingers. Finely traced lines of gore, splayed in patterns over his fingertips. Whose blood could it be, if not his own? It reminded him of the last time he'd had blood on his fingers. After a night with…that night Weblock had set him bleeding. The pain had been excruciating. The awful feeling of warm blood trickling down his leg. The coppery scent, as he'd dabbed at it in disbelief. How his arse had punished him for the vile indignities it had suffered in pursuit of money. Given this thought, he might have treated Viktor's objection to being asked about whoredom with greater respect.

But all he could now see was the blood. And Weblock's bloated face. He wanted to see them joined in brutal, ritualistic communion. To violate Weblock as the man had violated him so often. To reach up and squeeze the man's black pit of a heart until it finally ruptured. To seize it at that moment before complete failure and tear it from its aorta. From the veins, arteries, and all the critical cables that kept the man's stinking, lying, odious form wandering around like the high and mighty. He would tear the bastard's heart out, feeling each tendon snap, down through his guts and out his arse in a brutal, forced defecation of the worthless life that it was.

Then he'd stuff the vile organ into the pig's throat and tie it there, like some Christmas dinner centrepiece, its wasted life snuffed out, not by greedy, gluttonous tradition, but by pure, honest justice. Such beautiful images. All clear to him in this single, lovely drop of dried blood.

Eric smiled, knowing exactly what to do.

He took out his phone and quickly called up the number. Steffen had the Swedish Chef as his incoming voice tone, and Eric caught himself just before singing along. 'Bork, bork, bork!'

"Hello?" the answer spared him.

"Hey, it's me. Want to help me make a movie? Something... next level?"

Another pause that felt too long, and then..."Tell me."

Eric took a deep breath, a lurid, grim smile staring back at him from the mirror. Viktor wanted to do something useful, did he not?

❖

"Eric! Your jacket?" Viktor handed it back with a stupid grin. "You're going to make great movies, Eric. Can't wait to work with you. Can't wait to see your name on screen. When clients talk about the great movie they saw, I'll say, 'Yeah, I know that guy.'"

"You might not *have* any more clients after this. You do realise that, right?"

Viktor shrugged, his smile unmoving. "Then I do something else."

Eric shook his head, finally unable to resist a smile of his own. "So, where is Andy? I thought you said he'd be ho—"

"I never said that. He's at Saint Vincent's. I took him there today."

Eric froze. Saint Vincent's? Oh shit. No! And he'd...how long had he been here? How much time...He rounded on Viktor in furious disbelief. "And you weren't gonna *tell me*???"

"You have other clients."

Eric turned his back on the house and ran.

CHAPTER THIRTY-FIVE

The corrosive, antiseptic sting of the hospital filled the waiting room and clung to Eric's skin, determined to remind him of where he'd waited the last two hours.

Waiting for what? Andy was asleep. At four in the morning, why shouldn't he be? But Eric didn't want to go home. It felt better to wait.

The boy sitting opposite him hadn't moved in two hours. Eric had seen him breathe a couple of times, but that had been all. A drizzling of blood had dried against the boy's face, and a vicious purple bruise shrouded one side of his lower jaw. He breathed again. Eric heard it this time, a wet, laboured sound like the scrape of copper over corroded iron.

Eric tried to sleep. Who was to say he wouldn't wait two hours more? But despite their heaviness, his eyelids wouldn't fall. He kept watching the boy, whose gaze had fallen to the floor as he pulled a grey hoodie up over his face.

"Are you all right there, love?"

A few seconds passed before Eric realised that the orderly, a weedy, rodentesque woman with greying dark hair that had been chopped too short in that strange dyke-spiked sort of way, had been addressing him. Or maybe she'd been addressing the guy in the hoodie. He wasn't sure.

"Excuse me, son?"

"What?" he asked.

The hoodie still hadn't moved.

"Is everything all right?"

"I'm waiting for somebody. Andrew Felton?"

"Visiting hou—"

"I'll wait."

The woman shook her head sympathetically, hands on her hips as she crossed over to him. "You can't wait in here."

Eric looked around the near empty room and swallowed. "Why not?"

"This is Emergency. Visitors don't wait here."

"If it's Emergency, why is *he* still here?"

The boy still hadn't moved. Eric couldn't tell if he was still breathing.

"Why's who still here?"

Eric finally heard the scraping of the boy's breath start up again. Was the orderly blind or just stupid?

"Who do you mean?"

"Over there. He's bleeding."

"I think you're confused, love."

"I'm not," Eric said through clenched teeth, shaking his head.

"Oops, hold still!"

"Huh?"

"You're the one who's bleeding. Wait here."

As she left his side, Eric looked back at the hoodie.

"It's gonna be okay." He wasn't even sure the boy could hear him. No, that was crazy. Of course he could hear. The room was dead silent.

The stranger lifted the bottom of his hoodie and shirt. Five angry stab wounds punctuated his stomach and chest, bleeding over skin that looked far too tanned for what Eric had seen of the face. His breathing still made the same wet, metallic sound. Scrape. Scrape.

"Worth it?" the boy asked, his voice a low growl.

Eric watched a trickle of blood melt into the boy's faded and tattered blue jeans.

"Totes," he said.

With a slow and deliberate nod, the hoodie got up and left the room.

"Here we are, put one of these on."

Eric cringed as the orderly tried to bring the band-aid up to his face. "I'm good, really."

"Are you sure?"

"Yes!"

"That wasn't you, then?" The woman pointed to the trail of blood leading to the door. The trail the boy had left.

"No, it was…it wasn't."

"Then, did you see who…? Oh, never mind. Get all types in here. Are you sure you're all right?"

Shrug.

"You've got to be honest with me. Have you been taking anything?"

He shook his head again. No sudden torrent of blood this time.

"Come on, love. What are you on?"

"Nothing," he hissed.

"Listen, if you're in trouble, you know we're here to help?"

"I need to see Andrew Felton."

"Are you family?"

He nodded.

"Mister Felton doesn't have any family listed."

Was she sure about that? Did she read it out of a patient manifest? Jesus! Got them all memorised, have you? Bitch! Eric sniffed away his tears.

"Hey."

He felt the strength of the orderly's arm wrap around his shoulders. He wanted to fall into it, collapse over the arm of the chair.

"Don't be like that. Come on. He's sleeping now. Come back after ten and go up to the visitor's lobby. I'm sure—"

"No! I want to see him. I have to." He sobbed, letting the tears flow. He wanted to bury his face in the woman's shoulder. Cry into her lap. But he would never beg. He wouldn't let anyone make him do that, not for anything.

"Shhh. I'll get you some water. Don't go anywhere."

Eric didn't plan to. He was alone. He'd only just realised it, but he had the Emergency waiting room entirely to himself. Sure, it was four in the morning, but this was Darlinghurst. Junkies, rent-jocks, and dirty jabbers. It should have been peak hour.

There should have been noise. At least inside his head, if not in the room. Margaret's shrill scolding, Joe's screaming, his mother's...anything. It had all become white noise, and he was too tired to make it out. The sounds were too complex, too painful for his mind to process or make solid. He started humming, just to make sure. Halfway down the stairs—

"Are you Eric?" The orderly was standing in the doorway, her arms now folded over a clipboard, held tight against her chest.

He nodded again.

"He wants to see you. Level ten. Room 1027. Keep it quiet."

For the first time that night, a wide grin spread across Eric's face. Dyke haircut or not, in that moment, no woman could ever have looked more beautiful.

If the antiseptic sting of the Emergency waiting room had burned Eric's nostrils moments before, the smell now hung around him like an over-bleached blanket, suffocating him as he bounded up the poorly lit hall to 1027. Was he making too much noise? Too bad if he was. Andy wanted to see him. Andy *wanted* to see *him*.

Locked door after locked door. Offices, storerooms, extensions to other wards. Where the fuck did they hide the patients? Where was—

1027.

A private room, bathed in warm light by corner lamps that filled out the shadows of Andy's face. The man looked not a day over forty. Eric suspected the lights had been moved at the patient's instruction.

"Why are you here, boy?"

Not the welcome he'd expected.

"I…"

Good question. Four a.m., stormed out of home, near-killed by an ageing socialite, dead cat—did it actually die? Had he really done that? Near-punch-up with a cab driver, nurse's strings pulled to even be allowed up here, and…fuck! Think fast, boy!

"I wanted to see you."

"Well, aren't you nice?"

As if he needed to feel even more pathetic. Nice? Not good, not bad, but *nice*? Pleasant? Tolerable? Inoffensive? All the terrible, miserable words he'd ever feared would describe him.

"I tried your house. Viktor was there, he—"

"Of course," Andy wheezed with a smile. "Where would I be without him?"

Eric decided this was a question best unanswered.

"What can I do for you? Sit down, boy."

Eric tentatively placed a chair alongside the bed and did as he was told. He suddenly felt cold. Exposed, as if the warm light of the room had been sucked through the window into the night air. All he wanted to do was throw his arms around Andy, nuzzle the man's neck, tell him how glad he was to see him, to be away from his mother, from Margaret, from school, from Julien and Mary. How much he hated it all.

Andy just stared at him.

"Are you okay?" Eric finally asked.

"Yes."

"But…why the rush to hospital? Why—"

"Eric. Let's not talk about me."

Eric tried to compose himself. Andy was right. If he wanted to tell Eric what was wrong, he would. Jesus! Wasn't he carrying enough burdens, written one by one down the lines of his normally flawless face?

"I think I hurt Margaret." He couldn't hold it in any longer, the tears that had longed to pool in the orderly's lap now flowed freely down his cheeks. Tears for himself, of course. Not Margaret. Nobody would cry for that bitch.

Andy looked away, staring at the blank ceiling as though Eric had just spoken in some foreign language he vaguely understood, but still needed a moment to process. "How?"

"I…I came over—"

"Good Lord, doesn't that creature ever get enough?"

"No! I don't mean like that. Mum and I had a fight and—"

"I have asked you not to talk about your mother."

"I...I'm sorry." It was hopeless. He couldn't think straight, much less relate his plight. How could he tell Andy about Joe? And he *had* promised never to talk about Mum. He buried his face in his knees, hands clutching his head.

Andy stared at the ceiling, waiting for him to finish.

"I should go," he sniffed. "Sorry I bothered you."

"Eric. What did you do to Margaret?"

"I told her, no more appointments. That I was done."

A lie. Even now, exhausted and trembling, he could play story teller. But as someone had once told him, the greatest virtues were usually the most dubious.

Andy had said that.

"What did Margaret do?" the man asked.

"She...she chased me out and stood on the footpath, screaming at me."

Eerie silence for a moment, and then a faint, muted clucking. Faster and faster until Andy finally erupted in a great belly laugh. Eric couldn't help but share it, the last tears gone from his face, the awful tension between them destroyed at the expense of whatever dignity Margaret had left.

"Oh, that's brilliant," Andy chuckled. "Well done!"

"She said she'd destroy me. That I was dead in Sydney." It was the truth, technically. Exactly how he felt. From the mouths of crazed socialites...

Andy stopped laughing. "Ah...and you'd like me to do damage control? Protect your name before—"

"No."

Andy turned to look straight at him, trying to sit up a little in the bed. "You do realise she can do it, don't you? Margaret Moss is that most curious of creatures, possessing remarkable charisma and influence despite being one of the most reviled people in the city."

"I know. Let her, Andy. I can't do it anymore."

Andy returned his attention to the ceiling, folding his hands over his chest. "That's very noble of you, but your American ambitions will be expensive. What will you do for money?"

Eric shrugged. "Pollo o pescados, señor?"

Andy laughed again. "Eric, that's racist."

"That's fact. I'll be fine."

A little of the warmth had returned to Andy's cheeks as he drummed his fingers on the bed covers. "How's Mary?"

"She's okay, I guess."

"And that nice fellow you brought over? Julien?"

Eric didn't know how to answer that. "They're both fine."

"Ah…" Andy offered him a sympathetic wince. "How do you feel about that?"

"They can do what they want."

"That's very grown up of you."

Grown up or stupid. He wasn't sure.

"Don't take this the wrong way, dear boy. I wondered if, well… He's very good looking, and you seemed so comfortable."

"You thought he was my boyfriend?"

Did he and Julien really look that close? Not as close as Jules had been with Mary, but closer than Eric had ever been to her. Fuck. Thinking like that was pointless. Childish.

"I think I hate sex, Andy. Women. Men. Any of it."

Andy raised an eyebrow at him. "Well, good. So do I."

"Really? But haven't you ever had somebody? I mean like, a real partner?" It sounded so clinical. Like a business arrangement.

"And compromise my independence? No thank you." Andy extended a fragile hand to him at last. "But I do appreciate good company."

Eric let Andy wrap his cold fingers around his. He suddenly couldn't stop, bringing his other arm around and nuzzling his cheek against Andy's chest for the first time. He felt the man's frozen hand run through his thick, dark hair, cradling him. The hand he'd been waiting for. He wanted to cry again.

"Tell me the truth, Eric. Do you think you'll get into school over there?"

"I have to," he whispered, muffled by the folds of Andy's hospital gown. "I don't know why, I just—"

"I didn't ask you to justify yourself. You don't owe that to anyone."

Eric let a tear slide down his face, then another. So much relief that he stopped thinking. "I love you."

Andy's breath stopped. The gentle heaving of his chest fell flat, and the gentle caresses through Eric's hair were suddenly still.

Eric realised what he'd just said. He desperately wanted to take it back. He knew the look Andy must now be seeing on his face. Pleading, begging for it to be unsaid, erased and forgotten.

"I think you should go, Eric."

He wanted to apologise. If he went out that door, left the hospital, would he even see Andy again? He didn't see how. He was going to America, maybe for good. Hadn't that been the plan all along? Did it matter what Andy thought? What any of them thought? Yes. Suddenly, it mattered a whole lot!

"Check your account in a few days," Andy said.

Stop, Eric thought. He wished Andy would just stop talking and hold him again.

"You'll find just over forty thousand dollars. You stay within your means, and it should carry you nicely for at least a year."

"Andy, no."

"You will not fight me on this. Is that understood? And you're to promise me two things. No more sex work, at all. I trust that won't trouble you?"

"No."

"And you'll return to Australia at least once during your first year to visit your mother. Are we quite clear?"

"But I thought—"

"Are. We. Clear?"

He couldn't help himself. He threw his arms around Andy one last time. "We're clear."

"Eric," the man murmured, staring at the ceiling, his voice so quiet it made Eric wonder if he'd heard it at all.

"Yes?"

"I'm proud of you."

Chapter Thirty-six

It was three weeks, four days, sixteen hours, and twenty-eight minutes before The Boy's next text arrived from The Master. It was short. Tawdry. To the point.

You're required tonight, boy.

Not even the usual 'Are you available?,' a courtesy that even The Master typically paid him. He didn't respond right away. He left it an hour, which he knew was stupid for the resentment it might breed within The Master. Was he waiting to be sure? Sure of what? What was left to be decided about this crazy idea?

He probably should have seized the opportunity immediately and set things in motion. Should have called his 'stunt double'—he was sure the term had never before been meant quite so literally—right away and made sure he was free.

When he finally did so, Viktor sounded annoyed, or at least irritated, as though The Boy had interrupted something of terrible importance and secrecy. But he had to come through. They had to do this. The Boy had promised himself that night at Andy's, staring into that drop of congealed, clotted blood.

He quickly spewed forth the situation, making clear the unexpected window of opportunity The Master had cracked open, and how uncertain he was of how soon they could expect another. No sooner had he finished this hasty flurry of clarification than the answer came back.

"When and where do you need me?"

With a grin, The Boy promised Viktor a text, hung up and called back his client.

"Boy," the cold greeting came over the line.

"Sir…" It was then he realised he'd never *actually* refused The Master before.

"I'll collect you from Milsons Point station at ten. Be on time."

"Sir? I can't make it tonight, sir." He counted the seconds of silence. Seven. An eternity to wait for the explosion.

"Yes, you can, boy." The response came with chilling evenness. "It will be well worth your—"

"No, I really can't. I'm sorry, sir."

"Are you refusing me?"

The Boy felt the quickening of his breath.

"Do you know what happens when you refuse me?"

For a brief moment, The Boy imagined what might indeed happen. Not just to himself, which made it worse. He swallowed his nerves, reminding himself of the plan.

"Please, sir. I have a friend."

Another silence. Four seconds.

"Continue."

"His name's Dmitry."

"Rusky?"

"No. Ukrainian."

"Don't split hairs, boy. Different dictator, same shit beetroot soup."

He didn't give the man another chance to argue, reciting the usual list of assets he knew would make Viktor sound like the most desirable catch of manhood The Master could imagine. Muscular, smooth, tall, but not overbearing. Age? Maybe twenty-six? No, twenty-seven. Definitely a fit, lean, peak condition twenty-seven. Letting honesty get in the way of the sale at this point was not going to help. The point was Viktor was hot. And a good fuck? The Master had no idea.

"Had him then, have you boy?"

The Boy froze, suddenly realising the implication of his gushing praise. Damn! "No sir! Not personally. But I've seen his movies." This he knew was a risk. What if The Master didn't want to be involved with a porn actor? It was too late now. "He's…" All he could do now was make shit up and hope for the best. "I sometimes imagine him, slid deep inside me, his tongue dabbing up and down my forehead, nose and lips. Then I just grab hold of these big, strong arms he's got and pull myself onto him, tighter and tighter. I imagine him kissing me and…you'll love him, sir. Honest, you will."

"You got yourself a little crush there, puppet boy?"

The Boy swallowed. Yep. Total overkill. "No, sir."

"You sure?"

"Yes!"

Eight seconds. A full eight, The Boy counted.

"Listen to me. I don't often say this, and I'm not gonna say it again. But you deserve to hear it. You've been a good boy. Don't think I haven't taken notice of that."

Good boy? What the…? "Sir?"

"Don't play games. You know who I am, boy. I know you saw me, and I know it was you. And at that school…What I'm saying is that your discretion is recognised and appreciated. You'll go far with that. Do you understand me?"

The Boy's eyes opened as wide as they could go. The guy was right. He'd been so caught up with worry over what The Master could do to him by knowing where he went to school. He hadn't stopped to think about the power he held in return. Maybe this whole game was unnecessary.

"Do you hear me, *boy*?"

"Yes. Yes, sir! I hear you."

"All I'm saying is that this guy sounds like a bit of a fantasy of yours, and I'd be a poor man if I rewarded your discretion by spoiling that. I had fantasies too, when I was your age."

The Boy couldn't think of what to say. Their conversation was growing more surreal by the minute. Fantasies? Of all the people to be talking about robbing him of his fantasies! He closed his eyes, only to be met instantly by the thought of Julien kissing his neck. For that brief second, he thought of not going ahead with the plan. Of telling The Master that yes, he would meet with him at the arranged time, and he was sorry for refusing.

But only for a second.

"Sir," he said. "You won't hurt me. I'm offering Dmitry to you because he'll do it for me, and I know you'll like him. No strings attached. No harm done."

Another silence, though he resisted counting this time.

"Tell 'Dmitry,'" The name was spat out sarcastically. "To be at the station at ten."

"He'll be there, sir."

He let The Master hang up first, then texted the details to Viktor. Then, he sent another text to Steffen.

Tonight. We're a go. Be ready.

Within just six seconds, the response came back.

Awesome.

Chapter Thirty-seven

For all the acquaintances in Eric's life who would have characterised him as anti-social, he had never felt so until that winter. His film was complete. His play was gone. They were rehearsing *Hamlet.* He'd accepted a small part to save face. His friends were…he wasn't sure what, anymore. He wasn't sure he cared. He would e-mail an intelligent-sounding question or two to admissions at a few of the film schools about once a month, just to keep his name fresh on their minds.

He hadn't heard from any of his clients. It seemed the Margaret Moss gossip kraken had done its work, quickly and conveniently ending his escort career. He hadn't phoned Andy. He couldn't handle that.

In three months, his mother hadn't mentioned their fight. He wasn't sure if this was some measured decision not to upset the tenuous repair of their frayed relationship, or simply her trademark detachment from anything remotely linked to his welfare. The exception to this, of course, was her unrelenting resistance to his move to America, which had also gone undiscussed throughout numerous mother-to-son bonding dinners and shopping excursions.

He didn't mind.

What else was he supposed to do? Hang out with Julien? Mary? He'd done that too, usually at the same time. Not that he'd had much choice in that. A few movies, a few more beach trips. It had felt strange, and he knew there'd been many more without him.

He'd hung out with Toby a few times. Toby, who, of all unlikely choices, had scored the title role in *Hamlet*, much to Julien's annoyance, though this outrage had been somewhat soothed when Miss Harley had offered him the part of Claudius. Jules liked to play the villain, or so he'd said.

Six months ago, Eric would never have believed him. Now, he couldn't doubt it.

Toby was a nice guy. The end of his infatuation with Eric had cleared the way for something that seemed like friendship. They'd run a few rehearsals together. Toby wasn't a great actor, but Eric wasn't going to tell him that. His poetry was better, even if he had been reluctant to share much of it.

Nerida could always put Eric in a good mood, and not just chemically. They'd hashed out a two-handed, abridged version of *Othello* one Sunday afternoon over three quarters of a bottle of Absolut Citroen and spent the following weekend equally drunk, clumsily filming it, a project made all the more awkward by their lacking someone for the title role. Nerida had tried to spin this as Othello being so wrapped up in his delusions of betrayal he'd ceased to be real himself, but Eric hadn't been high enough to buy that explanation. They'd fucked after that, which Nerida seemed to enjoy. She had a pierced clit. That was all he could remember about it.

He'd quit the gym and put on about five kilos. The doctor had blamed the new pills, but he hadn't stopped taking them. Who cared if he wasn't in perfect shape anyway?

Felicity never came back to school.

CHAPTER THIRTY-EIGHT

Miss Harley had been right when she'd said *Hamlet* would be a much safer bet for the senior play than *Titus Andronicus*. But Eric had known that long before his audition. He'd used the opening monologue from *Richard III*. It had earned him an annoyed look from Julien, but they hadn't fought over it. More importantly, it had netted him the part of Hamlet's father, which meant doubling on a couple of other small roles. Harley had even let him serve as assistant director. Wagner's idea, so he'd learned.

Harley had made a good call in casting Toby. He'd worked like crazy to deliver Hamlet's slow-rising madness with his limited acting skills. Darren, meanwhile, had pushed the 'might-be-gay' Rosencrantz and Guildenstern thing way to the point of parody, much to Steffen's annoyance. Nerida was throwing this creepy and, Eric suspected, very deliberate Oedipal tone under Queen Gertrude. Toby had missed it entirely, which made it more funny and adorable than disturbing. Meanwhile, Mary had taken all the fresh, bubbling crazy she'd been saving for Lavinia and transferred it expertly to Ophelia with very little need of help or direction.

His most important director's note, however, had been for the grade eleven guys doing tech, accompanied by a few choice bribes from Nerida.

The theatre was packed for opening night. All their parents and most of their siblings had made it out. All except Nerida's. Even Eric's mum had turned up, though nobody else had recognised her. He'd obliged her with a kiss and a hug and thanked her for coming.

He'd nailed the lines, let Toby carry the scene they shared, then sleepwalked his way through the rest of the parts easily enough. After all, he had nothing to prove when it came to his performance.

He slid in behind the side curtain as the 'play' scene began, and from there, picked out Weblock in the audience. Here…went…

Miss Harley stood beside him in the wings before he could move. As if this whole operation hadn't pushed his nerves to the fraying point already.

It had taken some sweet talk to convince her that a film would suit their modern retelling better than a play, an idea he'd seen done at least three times before. He'd mentioned this fact to Harley, who'd grudgingly conceded the point. He watched Julien and Nerida take their seats, greeted by Toby who sat at Mary's feet. The lines about laying his head on her lap bounced warmly back and forth as she smiled her way meekly through the scene. Toby had the rhythm of Shakespeare's comedy down. Eric couldn't deny him that.

The stage darkened as the film began.

Murmurs began to rumble through the audience. A few gasps, some stifled laughter, a few audible 'Oh my god's. The screen became suddenly lighter as the shot changed. Julien's face dropped in horror, Nerida just gave him a knowing smirk, while Toby remained in character, bitter eyes intent upon Julien until he glanced at the screen and jumped.

Mary's eyes were closed, offering him no reaction at all.

In the darkness of the wings on the opposite side of the theatre, he saw the bright glow of Steffen's smile.

Oh yeah, give it to me, you Cossack cunt!

Nerida's Queen Gertrude erupted into a most un-regal cackle as the hum of the theatre erupted into outrage and cruel laughter. Toby sat glued to the spot, eyes bulging, mouth gaping, frozen halfway between horror and hilarity before finally twisting into a gleefully scandalised grin.

Julien hastily looked back at Mary and gripped her arm. Mary however, only had eyes for Eric. Whether they contained amusement, horror, gratitude, or toxic resentment, he couldn't say. But they reminded him of the one thing he hadn't considered. Sure,

Mary would benefit from this little stunt, in the long run at least. But he hadn't exactly stopped to ask for her thoughts on it. What she might think of him…

"Wow." The voice behind him had been totally unyielding of emotion, surprise, horror, or praise. Harley. "Just…wow. Un-fucking-believable, Eric."

He turned to her, unsure whether to be proud or offended that his feat had earned such a flat response from his acting teacher. "If it were done when 'tis done—"

"Oh, shut up!"

He turned back to face the audience.

Weblock was gone.

"Every time, Eric," Harley continued. "Every little stunt you've pulled, I have been there, standing up for you, trying to protect you!"

He quickly scanned the auditorium for any sign of the man. He saw the wife, scrambling out of the stalls, chased by stares of astonishment and pity as she fled up the aisle and out the back. But she was alone. Weblock had to be ahead of her. That meant…at least it could mean…Oh fuck! He couldn't chance it.

"Eric, are you listening?"

He hadn't heard a word Harley had said. Steffen had already disappeared from the opposite wing. There was no telling what would happen if Eric didn't do the same.

"I said, Eri—Hey!"

He shot past Harley before she could stop him. Her yells faded to nothing as he weaved past dressing and rehearsal rooms. The dropped jaws and embarrassed sniggers that had met the video's first few moments had given way to loud belly laughs as students watched the action unfold on the stage monitors.

The stage door was off to the…wait, forget the stage door! That's exactly where they'd expect him to go. Where they'd be waiting for him. Fuck it! He bolted for the fire exit to his right. Some clichés were clichés because they just bloody worked. The alarm's blistering whine ripped through his brain before settling into its steady whooping. By then, he was already halfway across the car park.

A maze of car roofs and lumpy SUV's surrounded him in a way that made him feel like a wounded seal, alone in a shark infested sea. He should have kept moving. Every part of him willed his stubborn legs to move, but they refused. It was as if it the stillness of the night, the cold sight of dark metal hoods on all sides and the insistent whine of the alarm had somehow combined to freeze him in place. Or maybe, he reasoned, he just wanted a moment to bask in his achievement.

Fuck *Hamlet*. Fuck *Titus Andronicus*. They'd just ended the career of Barry Weblock, populist loudmouth, radio blowhard, former parliamentary hopeful, and all round arsehole. They'd launched their opening shot in the most spectacular, public way available to them and within hours, the handful of bloggers they'd emailed would finish the job. Weblock was done, and it felt damn good. So good, he'd almost started to laugh before he heard the scrape of shoes on bitumen.

He turned just in time to cop the fist already flying toward his face.

Chapter Thirty-nine

He knew he was in The Master's apartment before he realised he was tied up. He could smell the faint, stiff odour of ex-grammar school precision that clung to the furniture. Every piece that in his mind seemed testament to The Master's devotion to old world order, just as the smarting of his face was testament to the man's past as a boxer.

The ropes around his wrists and ankles weren't thick, but they were tight enough to keep him in place. For now, that place appeared to be on the floor. He slowly opened his eyes, only to stare on blackness, shards of light coming through a few cracks between the blinds. In a second of bleak humour, he wished that The Master had bound him to a chair like Joe. That at least might have brought his indignity around in some weirdly satisfying narrative loop.

Right, like this was some stupid movie.

Shit. Joe? No, he wouldn't think like that. In this place, he was 'The Boy,' and he would keep his real self safely locked outside. His true name, life and identity, would remain separate and all his own. Right now, 'The Boy' was in a shitload of trouble. The only sound in the room was the faint thud of footsteps on the carpet.

"So what now, boy?" the voice finally said. "Do we talk about the value of trust? What it means?"

He heard the man's heavy body settle into the sofa.

"Do we?" The Master asked again. "Do you know what trust means? *Eric?*"

And just like that, their masks were off. Characters shed. The Boy and The Master, both vanquished for good. His own opinion of this man, what he knew about him, the knowledge he'd pushed aside time and time again in pursuit of easy money, flooded his thoughts with hatred and anger.

"You hurt her…" he hissed. "She told me. She showed me!"

"Hurt who? Go on, you nosy little prick. Who do you think—"

"You know who!"

The man's breath seemed suffocatingly heavy in the darkness. "Do you think I'm stupid? Do you think I didn't know about you and her? Think I didn't tolerate it because I trusted you?"

"She hates you!" He drew as much venom as possible into the curse.

"And so do you, I suppose? I had thought I was wrong about you, when you decided to keep our little secret. Wasn't like me, Puppet Boy, to trust someone like that."

Eric heard the man's weight shift as he leaned forward in the couch.

"Hates me, does she? I don't suppose you'd oblige me with the name of a single sorry prick who likes me? They all hate me, Eric. And it doesn't matter, because they're all bloody shit-scared of me. You get a good look at the face of the next bastard who tries to nail Barry Weblock on illegal muzzies, tree huggers, or gay fuckin' marriage. What a joke! That's power, boy, and it starts with knowing none of that shit matters. I do not give a low flying sparrow's fuck if I'm liked, as long as I am respected. And yes, you bleeding heart little shit, that means feared! I can get on that phone right now and get the PM quaking in his fucking boots about an interview next week. *That's* what I am, Eric! That's the kind of control I have. I don't have friends, Puppet Boy. I have enemies and every single one of them is mine to control!"

"Was!"

"I am talking!"

"No, Barry! You *were* talking! Talking shit! That's all you ever do! Oh yeah, they were scared of you all right. A few words from those lips and *boom*! It's all over for whatever sorry fuck you don't like that day. Must have felt good, huh Barry? You're going to miss that all right! 'Coz right now, your golden words are worth shit, and you know it! Right now, you're just the fat old hypocrite who got caught on tape taking nine inches of Ruskie cock up the arse, so *fuck you,* you worthless, bullying, scum-sucking, fist-pumping cunt! You want to know what real power looks like, Barry? It's watching yourself get taken down in front of five hundred witnesses by that kid you used to screw without ever knowing it was coming. It's over, Barry! I beat you! I fucking beat you! *Deal!*"

"Then who's tied up on the floor, boy?"

Eric spat out a wisp of carpet fibre he'd inhaled, trying helplessly to lift his head. He heard Weblock relax into the couch again.

"You should get yourself on radio. That was quite a serve. I suppose I ought to be a bit offended by all that. Maybe I am, and maybe you're right. Maybe I can't make this mess blow away. Don't see how it makes any difference to you. So why do it, Puppet Boy? Why try to ruin me?"

Eric ignored the question. Weblock wasn't that stupid. Arrogant and wilfully ignorant, definitely, but not stupid.

"I wouldn't think too much about her any more, boy. You won't be seeing her again. Or anyone else."

Eric thought he heard the sound of a gun being cocked before the bang exploded and the pattering of gore blew over the couch and carpet. The noise panicked him. He could feel his entire body shivering as he tried desperately to loosen his bonds. 'Or anyone else?' What the fuck did that mean? Wait…had Weblock just blown his brains out, leaving Eric tied up with little hope of rescue? Weblock knew the value of good soundproofing, all right. This, Eric knew for a fact. He'd tested it enough times while his client had beaten him, caned him, and penetrated him. Now, he was trapped. Tied up and trapped in this hellbox apartment.

"Help!" Some small part of him felt foolish for screaming, but he was too panicked to care. His legs had started aching. "Can anyone hear me? Help! Please?"

"Eric!"

He caught his breath, just listening. Waiting for the voice to speak again. "Who's there? Who the fuck's there? Answer me!"

"Eric! Relax, it's me! It's me."

He felt fingers fumbling at the binds on his wrists until they fell free. The familiar hands of his liberator wrapped around his chest, holding him tight against their owner's body. Familiar lips kissed the back of his neck, shoulders and cheeks.

Steffen.

"You're okay. You're okay, except you're shaking," the German said. "Wait."

He felt the binds pull, then eventually fall from his ankles. Steffen put his arms around him again, hands closing around his, holding them tight.

"It's okay," the voice tried to sooth him. "I've got you."

"I'm fine," Eric whispered, though he knew he was still shaking. With Steffen's arms still around him, he rolled over, stretching out his leg as it started to cramp. He buried his face in his rescuer's shoulder and hugged him back, enjoying the simple security of another body around him. The cool leather of Steffen's jacket against his skin felt good, too. He felt Steffen cradling the back of his head, fingers lovingly threading through his hair. When his tears crested, Eric let them, welcoming the relief they brought. He nuzzled Steffen's neck, relishing the touch of the leather against his lips, then the thin cotton T-shirt. The natural scent of the soft, dark skin soothed him as it filled his nose. Again and again, he kissed his rescuer's face, running hands through the dense crop of dark hair.

He pulled their bodies tighter together, planting a row of soft kisses along the boy's chin, enjoying the roughness of his lips. He was drunk on the feel of the guy in his arms. Drunk on his smell and taste. He didn't know if it was just the exoticism of it, or if he was getting some perverse kick out of being here, in this horrible place.

In what seemed like the ultimate 'fuck you' to the man who'd brought him here and tried to destroy him, this would be the place where he'd make love for the first time, to someone he'd wanted from the first day they'd sat together in class. To someone he wanted so badly, he would forgive everything and focus on what they shared together right now. Their bodies, their wants…He felt his friend's name wrap around the tip of his tongue as it longed to connect with the object of his lust.

"Eric…"

"Please…" he whispered. "I want you."

"Eric!" Steffen snapped.

He opened his eyes, studying the dark look that had crossed Steffen's face.

Fuck.

All Weblock had put him through. The terror of it. The confusion. Being held so tight against Steffen's body. Being so turned on that his cock felt as though it would burst through his pants…

It had triggered him. Fuck! Fuck! Fuck!

He didn't wait to be told, instead lying perfectly still on the carpet.

"I saw him hit you," Steffen explained. "I caught a cab. Got here just in time. Then I waited."

"How'd you get in?"

"The way you showed me. Same way I used when I installed the cameras. This building's not so fancy. It's not hard if you're smart."

Eric nodded, nestling under Steffen's arm once more. Somehow, the rest of it didn't seem to matter. Was Steffen even telling the truth? And if he was, had he come here with any sort of plan or idea to get them out and away? He reached over and kissed Steffen on the mouth. Not with passion, but with affection and sweetness, letting the German suckle at him. Each touch bore the pleasant, gentle curiosity of strangers rather than two guys who'd spent the better part of the last hour quivering in each other's arms on the floor.

"You're fun, Eric. I'll miss you."

"Are you going somewhere?"

Steffen fixed him with a confused half-frown. "You are. America? Remember?"

"Right. So come with me."

"Come to Berlin. Cheaper. No crazy bible thumpers."

"Fuck off."

"Fuck you. I'm not going to America. What? You think we're boyfriends?"

"No!" The word seemed a lot more defensive than he'd intended. But still. Germany? Him and Steffen? Jesus! "I just... think you're super talented."

"Thanks. So does iSFF. Still got to send my application, but they liked my reel."

The outline of Weblock's head caught Eric's eye again as he sat up. "Good for you."

"We're not moving him."

"What?"

"He shot himself. It's got nothing to do with us. Nobody will know we were here."

"That's not—"

"Yes it is," Steffen interrupted, sitting up. "That's why we're so good together. I know what you're planning. What you're imagining when you create. I can make it happen."

"You certainly do that." Eric turned to see Steffen staring at him. But when he went to kiss him, the boy turned away.

"Just stop pretending you like me, Eric."

"I do like you."

"You like what I can do for you. That's not the same."

"Jesus, what's wrong? Don't you like me?"

"I just said I'll miss you."

Miss him? What did Steffen even mean by that? That he'd miss working together? Miss the sex? Pfft. What sex? They'd played up a few times. Gotten off, cleaned up and gone. "You wanna...I don't know..."

"No, I do not want to get a coffee with you, or go out to dinner, or see a stupid play. I'll see a movie with you, maybe, but for research. It's work. We work together. That's all. You don't care about being liked, Eric. You care about the work, and that I can respect. That's what I really like about you. It's the one thing that old fuck was right about."

"I am *nothing* like him!" Eric snarled.

"Not saying you are. Pass me my pants."

"Huh?"

"I need to show you something. Will you just pass them over?"

Given the choice between doing what he was told and continuing to be insulted, Eric tossed the pants to Steffen and stretched out, closing his eyes. He recalled how it had felt. How soft the guy's lips had been. The gentle prickling of the tiny, short hairs that furred his chest, the little cluster that formed around each nipple, where he'd so happily clamped his mouth. The shallow, neatly spread contours of his stomach. So like Julien.

His eyes opened. No. No, no, absolutely not. Thinking about Julien again wasn't going to help at all. Steffen had been there for him. Steffen had set him free and taken him in his arms and kissed him and made him feel wanted. But the face he'd imagined in the dark...the one he still saw when he closed his eyes. He wanted to say it was Steffen's, but he knew with gut-wrenching certainty that it wasn't.

"You need to see something," Steffen muttered, taking his iPhone from his pants and bringing up a video. "Some footage I got at your party. Taken with the same cameras I used in this place."

"Huh? At my party? What is this?"

"Please? I think you need to see it." Steffen passed Eric the phone, his face deadpan and humourless, all trace of a sneer now gone. "This is what you're in love with."

Eric played the file. Less than a minute into the video, he wished he hadn't.

Chapter Forty

"Two forty-nine Achilles, right?"

"Achilles Drive. That's it. You rented a car?"

"No, I'm gonna spend hours on the bloody bus, hauling luggage in a city I don't know! Yes, we rented a car." This sarcasm was followed up by the simple back and forth of Julien's breathing. "Can't wait to see you, dude."

Eric gazed out over the Los Angeles basin, his view spoiled only by the thinnest layer of hazy smog in the mid afternoon heat, clouding around the skyscrapers of downtown. "You too."

He hung up.

Two forty-nine was not the most upscale house Eric had stayed in since his arrival. Nor was its view the most spectacular. But it was more than enough. He had plenty of room and silence to work, privacy from the neighbours, and an ideal spot for his reunion with Julien and Mary. This, after all, was the Los Angeles they'd wanted to see. The vision they'd expected. Gleaming houses halfway up the hills. Giant, kidney-shaped blue pools. Each property uniquely designed yet strangely indistinguishable from the rest of the street. Not mansions. Not by LA standards at least, but easily as big as any of their homes in Sydney, and those homes weren't here. They didn't have *this*.

He picked up a fallen palm leaf from the patio and tossed it into the garden below. He then poured himself half a tumbler of orange juice, then a sliver of vodka, then more juice until he'd filled the glass. He rested the juice carton in one ice bucket, the champagne in the other. Toasting with mimosas was probably gauche, but it was too early for straight champagne and besides, who did they have to impress? Even if the neighbours could catch a glimpse, none of them were awake. Except maybe Mrs Duvall, a Hollywood native at eighty-seven years old who claimed to have known Rudy Valentino on a first name basis and slept with Billy Wilder. In a town defined by the stories it invented, Eric had no reason to doubt her word.

He quickly went back inside, checking the top drawer of the kitchen. Satisfied his iPad was still there, he undid the top two buttons of his shirt and fell into one of the chairs overlooking the skyline.

This was perfect. This was just the scene he'd imagined.

❖

"Oh…my…" Mary stammered.

"Holy fuck, dude! Score!" Julien laughed.

"You like?" He slid open the doors onto the patio, feeling the warm, dry air hit his face. The heat of the desert in Spring. Mild enough to soothe and invigorate him. That was how Julien looked now. Invigorated, probably by an energy most locals could no longer feel. The energy of LA and all it promised, as much Julien's dream as it had been Eric's.

"Eric, this is so great." Mary grabbed his hand. They'd never talked about her father's suicide. Never let it come into their relationship. She'd never mentioned it, or shown him one single tear. Not even one of relief, and he wasn't going to coax that tear by asking.

He led them out, picked up the bottle of champagne and began working the cork.

"Bit early for that, isn't it dude?"

"Not for mimosas," Mary said, opening the orange juice.

Eric smiled at her as she began filling each of their glasses a third full. "You don't have to—" The cork came free from the neck of the bottle with a loud, satisfying pop. "I've got it."

"Already done," she offered up the glasses.

"Yep, right in the pool. Nice shot."

"As long as it's not the neighbour's," he muttered, topping up their drinks and carefully replacing the champagne in its bucket. "So...to being here, I guess."

His friends lifted their drinks, but Eric knew he had only half their attention. The remainder, they'd divided between the city and each other. Mary wasn't even looking at him now. But that was fine. She was here.

"When do you start school? September, right?" Julien asked.

Eric waved him away. "Can we talk about this later? I'm on break."

"Gap year?"

"Half year," he smirked, sipping his cocktail.

"Sure. Later, if you want."

He winced as Julien slapped him on the shoulder.

"I'm just happy for you, dude. This is what you wanted. You worked so hard."

"Thank you."

Mary leaned on the railing, staring out over the city. "Eric," she whispered. "This is wonderful."

"Yeah," he agreed. "I've been lucky. Very, very lucky."

As they sat on the patio together, Eric found it harder and harder to stop staring at Julien. It made him uncomfortable, reminding him of everything he'd once wanted between them. It had to be somewhere near seven now, which meant he'd been drinking with Jules for almost five hours. An hour ago, Mary had hopped a cab, bound for Griffith Observatory. This had been fine by Julien, who had zero interest in astronomy or science or any sort. He and Mary were here for...was it five days or six? Enough time anyway. Their first time in LA as adults. The three of them together, no less. The possibilities were truly endless.

But first, they had one last play to perform. Eric had already rehearsed it so carefully in his mind. The sun had only just dipped behind the Bank of America building, and the entire basin had come alight in a hazy sea of orange. Julien's white shirt was bathed in it. Almost immediately after Mary had left, he'd unbuttoned it halfway down, so that Eric could see his chest and the top of his stomach. That was Jules, as fit as ever, and still as vain. Had this been deliberate? Of course it had. Julien wanted him to see the soft hairs on his chest. The ones he'd once touched. Was that all some great joke to Julien now?

Eric wondered if Mary enjoyed touching the little hairs as much as he had. He hoped so. He wanted her to be happy. Wanted them both to be happy, and though he chided himself for this admission, he couldn't deny it. Part of him wanted to toss his grand plan and take Jules in his arms, to kiss him as deep and open as they'd been that night on the beach. Only this time, with no nervousness and no doubt. Mary had given him the perfect opportunity to do it. To latently follow her directions from all those months ago and tell Julien that everything was forgiven.

But a pardon like that would send a clear message, 'Trample me as you will,' and that would be unacceptable. Nor would he allow Jules to simply forget him. Not ever.

"So, between you and me," Julien said, taking another sip of his drink, "how did you get to stay here? Really…"

"I told you, I'm house-sitting."

Eric wanted to take his hand. To feel the cold moisture on it. To taste Julien's wet lips in the dry Los Angeles air. But he wouldn't be distracted. Not by his feelings, or the gnawing sickness they stirred in his stomach.

"House-sitting? Okay, sure. But does it, like…belong to a client of yours, or—"

"The first one I stayed at was somebody Mum knew. Just a small apartment. Then people talked, and I started getting offers." This much was true. In his own way, he'd learned to navigate LA's own unique code of networking and favours.

"Shit, that's unreal. So your mum came around in the end?"

Eric shrugged. "What is it they say? It's easier to beg for forgiveness than ask for permission? Especially after your plane has landed. She didn't ask my permission to come here, did she?"

Julien flashed him another grin. "You must really love it." The sun had turned his tanned skin a gentle, sexy shade of brown. "I mean, how can you not?"

Eric had decided months ago that he did love LA. Despite all the bullshit with his mother and despite everything that it had been and represented, he was in a great place. A city that agreed with him. "I just wish I could stay."

"Huh?"

The sun was behind the towers of downtown now, peeking out between the Bank of America building and a neighbouring block.

"I don't think I told you. I didn't get in," he admitted, swirling his screwdriver with a satisfying clink of ice.

"What do you mean? How could you *not* get in? What, anywhere?"

"Not to Tisch, not to USC, not to UCLA. AFI…well, I never really thought I had a chance there, but I gave it a shot. My own fault, I guess. I should have applied to a few smaller names. Been more sure, you know? I had safeties, but I was just so sure."

"Weren't you using NIDA as a safety? Which, by the way—"

"Is stupid. Thanks. I know. I knew that when I applied. Now, *they* liked my folio. They must have. I actually made the first cut-off, but I didn't take the interview."

"You *what*? Eric!"

Eric felt the hard, sharpness of nails pressing against skin as he clenched his fists.

"How could you not at least give them a go? Shit, we could have gone together. Kept on doing projects together."

"What?"

Julien shrugged as he swirled his drink, taking another long sip of it. "I was going to tell you later, but I'm at NIDA now."

Eric drained his glass, crunching a piece of ice between his teeth as he stared at Julien. "I knew you'd make it. I'm happy for you, Jules."

"Thanks. Doesn't do much for you, though, does it? I guess there's always next year."

"What about Mary?"

Julien slurped on his drink as he lifted it to his lips, eyes not leaving Eric as he tried to gage the question. "You two don't talk?"

"Only about the things she wants to."

"And you didn't ask?"

"I've never pushed her, Jules. I'm not going to start. Did she get into NIDA with you?"

"She didn't apply. Not to NIDA. Not to the Actor's Centre. Nowhere."

"No?"

"USyd. Philosophy and social studies."

Eric stifled a laugh. Good for Mary. Pissing off her father, even in death.

Julien shrugged, taking in the warm air, eyes fixed on the sea, out past Santa Monica. "So, when you come back—"

"I'm not coming back, Jules. Not this year, anyway."

"Huh? You just said—"

"I only said I didn't get into the LA schools. I didn't get into NIDA either. Why the fuck would I come back?" He tried not to feel too condescended by his friend's raised eyebrow.

"Ah…well, Eric, there's this thing called immigration that usually doesn't—"

"Oh, I'm not staying in the States. But I'm not—"

"Jesus, mate. Out with it! You're killing me."

"I got into Concordia."

"Heeeey….New York? That's pretty—"

"No, not Columbia, you dick. Concordia. Montreal. Not my first choice, but it's good. Better than staying in Sydney. They still make heaps of movies in Canada."

"Yeah?" Julien grinned. "Comment est votre français?"

"Oh, shut up!" he laughed. "Concordia works in English. I'm more worried about freezing my ass off."

Ass? When had he started saying 'ass?' Oh. He knew. Right after that New Year's party, where he'd tried to pick up that girl who was an assistant to some famous agent and she'd told him to 'Watch your accent. Nobody will take you seriously until...' God. Wait until they heard his French.

He put a hand next to Julien's on the railing and watched the sun finally disappear. A faint green tinge flashed over his eyes. Beautiful. The sunset, the city and, though he hated to admit it, Jules, who looked at him with a disarmingly sexy half smile. Eric couldn't help but suspect it was the same smile he'd shown the selection panel at NIDA, though it was unlikely Jules had stroked the backs of their hands, the way he was doing to Eric now.

"Won't pretend I'm not disappointed," said Julien. "I miss you, mate. We both do."

Eric met him with a grim smile of his own. "I'm glad the folio piece worked for you. Maybe Australia has more balls than I thought."

Julien shook his head, the smile never leaving his face. "Balls? Sorry, you lost me."

"I mean, I got to interview with a couple of the schools here, and they just didn't know what to make of it. They didn't like your character. The Joe character. Said he was neither a hero nor a villain. They just didn't get him. Stupid, huh? And after all that work you put in? I'm really glad NIDA got it."

"But this place...Concordia?"

Eric gently eased his hand out from under Julien's fingers, giving them a friendly squeeze as he let go. "Oh, they loved it. *Loved it.* They thought it was in-your-face, uncomfortable to watch, scary. I told them what an influence Polanski had been, and they got that right away. Then when they saw we'd been working on *Titus,* I think I got points for the...demonstration of both classic and modern styles, or something. Anyway, I got the universal, art-snob 'mmhmmm' of approval, you know?" He quickly went back inside, fetching his iPad from the kitchen drawer. He smiled at Jules as he returned, slipping it out of its cover. "They said I was a risk, but a worthwhile risk. I guess the Canadians are just braver about that shit. It probably didn't hurt that I'd recut the thing either."

"Which I guess you're gonna show me? You are going to show me, aren't you?" Julien grinned.

Eric called up the file and passed the pad to Julien. "Of course. You can even have a copy, if you really want one." He watched his friend's face closely as the movie played. A faint grimace here and there. Some of the scenes they'd done with Mary, in particular. But for the most part, a broad smile.

"Hey, what was that?"

"What's what?"

Julien continued watching for a moment, then looked up at Eric, his face suddenly confused as pained cries emanated from the tablet's speaker. He hurriedly turned the sound down. "What *is* that?"

Eric shrugged. "I guess it's the girl in the scene. I didn't add any extra sound. I don't know. Do you think it needs something pretty? Like an opera or something?"

Julien's face fell as he watched a few seconds more. "But that's not me, is it? Can't be!"

"Looks like you, doesn't it? It's Joe. It's the same guy you see in the rest of the film."

"But I don't remember this! When did we…? No…no, Eric, this is fucked. How did you get this?"

"Does it matter?" He sat down in one of the spotlessly clean white chairs that surrounded the table. "Great performance, Julien. Really out of your comfort zone. I really…well no. I wouldn't say I 'admire' it, exactly. But it took guts, real balls to do what you did. I mean what goes down there, in those shots…that is totally not you. I mean that is *nothing* like the guy I know."

"Eric? W*hat the fuck,* man?"

"See, there was this one woman on the selection panel at UCLA. She didn't think Joe was threatening enough, that he was too sympathetic when he needed to be scary. What do you think, Jules? Felicity looks pretty scared, eh? Hah! See? Canadian already."

Through his tan, despite the orange sunlight reflecting off his skin, Julien had gone a deathly shade of grey. "I…Fuck! I *don't remember* this, Eric! This didn't happen! You believe me, right? You've got to!"

"I believe you. I believe your every word, your every action, every nasty, selfish fucking emotion on your face in that film. You're brilliant, mate. To me, you *are* Joe. No doubt about it. You've got an amazing career ahead. What does it matter whether you actually remember the scene or not? We got the shot, Julien. That's all that matters. It's as real as the shot. You can ask Mary's dad about that."

"Oh, you are so *fucked* in the head, Eric! This is sick. *Sick!* You are the most evil motherfucking cu—"

"*Hey!*" His sharp rebuke silenced Julien. "It's not sick. It's art. What are you? Johansson? If you're going to be that prissy, half of what we filmed is pretty sick. That's not the point."

"*How did you—*"

"It doesn't matter. What should concern you is that I have it."

"Yeah? Does it concern you that it is totally fucking illegal to film somebody like this without—"

"See, now you're boring me."

Julien, contrary to the bravado of his words, slumped down into his chair and pushed the tablet away.

"Yes it is 'totally fucking illegal' as you so eloquently put it, to film someone without their knowledge. But can we keep some perspective on this? Who's committed the greater crime here? Now, let's just say I do believe you, when you say you don't remember it—which I don't, but we'll come back to that. That doesn't matter, because I remember. Or at least, I know when and where it was shot. That night at my party, at Toby's place. You remember going to that, don't you?"

Julien glowered at him from beneath low eyebrows, not saying a word, his breath growing heavier each time he inhaled.

"Of course, I didn't even see you there. You arrived late. This would have been after you freaked Margaret out by leaving, which was very mean of you, by the way. She's a lonely woman."

Julien didn't move or make a sound.

"Now that I have your complete attention, let me explain what has to happen in this scene, along with what's *not* going to happen. I have in my possession the full, uncut footage of what went down in that room. The how and why is none of your business, and if you honestly don't remember or would rather not remember, I'll happily make sure you never have to see it."

"I hate you," the boy whispered.

"You can hate me. I'm not your friend. I'm your director now, and if you fail to follow my directions in any way, that footage goes straight to the New South Wales police. Copies will also go to Felicity's parents and to NIDA, and I'll be the last director you ever fucking work with. Are we clear?"

Nothing.

"Jules?"

"Yes."

"I recognise that look, Julien. You're looking for an explanation. A way to excuse yourself. To tell me why you did what you did and hope I'll understand. You can save yourself the effort. Do you know how many times I had to watch that shit? Guess."

Julien's only response was a loud swallow. The outline of it rippled down the flesh of his throat. He was visibly sweating now.

"Enough," Eric whispered. "And that's what I don't get. Every time I think 'That can't possibly be him. He'd never do that to someone. Why would he…why would *anyone,* but especially him, get a girl so fucked up she cuts off her own lips and goes wandering the streets until dawn with four fifths of a face? What could possibly make him do it?' And then," he leaned close enough to see a bead of sweat collect just above Julien's eyebrow. "Then, I understand it perfectly. I don't like it. But I understand it." He sat back in his chair and opened the top two buttons of his shirt. The night air felt good as it hit his hairless chest. "She scares me sometimes." He kept his gaze firmly fixed across the basin, unwilling to see Julien's reaction, the need in it that he knew was there. "No, she does. There's darkness inside of her that I won't ever fully get. I can't hope to, and I don't want to. If you're smart, neither will you. God knows how far it's gone since her old man topped himself. She never talks about that, you know? Not a word. Not even about what we did that night at the play. See, I respect that darkness. I also know how powerfully alluring that is for people like you and me. People who aren't afraid of the dark, just so long as it doesn't get too real on us or too scary. But it's exciting when those lines blur, isn't it? Exciting and ugly. What did she do, mate? Did she threaten you? Plead with you? Threaten to do something to herself?"

"Look, she—"

"No," Eric waved him off. "These are rhetorical questions. I don't want to know, Julien. Like I said, she scares me sometimes. Often. But I want *you* to know. I want it absolutely clear in your mind. I've seen it all. I know stuff about her that you never will."

"What do you want from me?" Julien's voice was raspy and hollow. Less than a whisper.

"I don't really think I'm the needy one in this situation, do you?"

Julien slowly shook his head.

"Not a good feeling, is it?"

"You..." Julien looked away again, toward the skyline, where the city's twinkling blanket was slowly coming to life, one light at a time. He brought his fingers up to his lips.

Eric thought he could see the vaguest hint of tears start to form. But Julien wouldn't let them. Was he even capable of crying? Eric suspected not. Not in real life, at least.

"You're not going to do anything to her, are you? I mean, with that footage. You're not going to hurt her?"

Eric carefully lowered his voice as he saw the back light of the neighbour's house turn on. He recognised the hairline of the owner's assistant over the fence. The tall guy, at least as tall as Viktor. "Julien...what do you *want* from me? Just answer."

"You said you had the whole thing?"

He nodded.

"Fine. Don't ever use it to hurt her. She doesn't have to be a part of it, man. This was my fault. I should have told her no."

"Look," Eric interrupted. "I don't want to know how much you remember or think you did, or didn't do, or why, or how, or any of that. What I have is on film. Nothing else. Don't worry. I'll make sure she's never implicated. I'd never do that, Julien."

All colour vanished from Julien's face.

"So this thing is official now?" Eric asked. "For real? You love her?"

"What?"

"Easy question, Julien. Do you love her?"

"Yes. I'd do anything for her."

"Yes, apparently you would. I believe you about that. That's the one thing out of your real, out-of-character mouth I don't question. That's what saves you, Jules, from me, at least. I've had this footage for six months. Sure, I used it to spice up the film. But in that, it's still fiction. I could have taken it to the cops at any time and told them it was real. That's if I was *really* pissed at you. Now do you believe I don't hate you?"

Julien's head was shaking again.

"I still love her too. And I was in love with you. But you knew that already, didn't you? I never made you deal with it, but you're not that stupid. You know, and as much as I hate it, and say to myself 'dude, you are a fucking moron,' you both still mean a lot to me." He heard the neighbour's back door shut with a satisfying slam. "What would Polanski make of that, do you think? What would Shakespeare have thought?" He leaned closer, beckoning Julien into his confidence. "So, what I want is for you to keep loving her and believe me when I tell you it'll be hard sometimes. Hold her when she cries. Don't ever be checking out another person while she's with you, even if she's doing exactly that. Don't ever talk about her father. Play with her silliness. Praise her intelligence. Love her dreams, and if you ever hurt her, if you are ever the cause of a single tear that falls onto her face, I promise you, that footage will get out."

Julien was looking down between his knees now, licking his lips uncomfortably.

"Look at my face, Julien. Stare into my eyes the way you did on the beach." He smiled as the boy did as he was told. "This is what I look like when I have total control." He leaned back in the chair, looking back at his subject with an all-knowing smile. "I wish you could see your eyes now. They're Joe's eyes, Julien. Joe's eyes. And while we're being honest with each other? I've missed them."

About the Author

Christian Baines was born in Toowoomba, Australia. He has since lived in Brisbane, Sydney, and Toronto, indulging an insatiable wanderlust, a love of dark mythology, and a passion for stories that lurk outside the norm wherever he can.

His written thoughts on travel, theater, and gay life have appeared in numerous publications in both Australia and Canada. His first novel, *The Beast Without,* was released in 2013, followed by his erotic short story, "The Prince and the Practitioner."

Puppet Boy is his second novel.

Books Available from Bold Strokes Books

Every Unworthy Thing by Jon Wilson. Gang wars, racial tensions, a kidnapped girl, and a lone PI! What could go wrong? (978-1-62639-5-145)

Puppet Boy by Christian Baines. Budding filmmaker Eric can't stop thinking about the handsome young actor that's transferred to his class. Could Julien be his muse? Even his first boyfriend? Or something far more sinister? (978-1-62639-5-107)

The Prophecy by Jerry Rabushka. Religion and revolution threaten to bring an ancient civilization to its knees…unless love does it first. (978-1-62639-440-7)

Heart of the Liliko'i by Dena Hankins. Secrets, sabotage, and grisly human remains stall construction on an ancient Hawaiian burial ground, but the sexual connection between Kerala and Ravi keeps building toward a volcanic explosion. (978-1-62639-556-5)

Lethal Elements by Joel Gomez-Dossi. When geologist Tom Burrell is hired to perform mineral studies in the Adirondack Mountains, he finds himself lost in the wilderness and being chased by a hired gun. (978-1-62639-368-4)

The Heart's Eternal Desire by David Holly. Sinister conspiracies threaten Seaton French and his lover, Dusty Marley, and only by tracking the source of the conspiracy can Seaton and Dusty hold true to the heart's eternal desire. (978-1-62639-412-4)

The Orion Mask by Greg Herren. After his father's death, Heath comes to Louisiana to meet his mother's family and learn the truth about her death—but some secrets can prove deadly. (978-1-62639-355-4)

The Strange Case of the Big Sur Benefactor by Jess Faraday. Billiwack, CA, 1884. All Rosetta Stein wanted to do was test her new invention. Now she has a mystery, a stalker, and worst of all, a partner. (978-1-62639-516-9)

One Hot Summer Month by Donald Webb. Damien, an avid cockhound, flits from one sexual encounter to the next until he finally meets someone who assuages his sexual libido. (978-1-62639-409-4)

The Indivisible Heart by Patrick Roscoe. An investigation into a gruesome psycho-sexual murder and an account of the victim's final days are interwoven in this dark detective story of the human heart. (978-1-62639-341-7)

Fool's Gold by Jess Faraday. 1895. Overworked secretary Ira Adler thinks a trip to America will be relaxing. But rattlesnakes, train robbers, and the U.S. Marshals Service have other ideas. (978-1-62639-340-0)

Big Hair and a Little Honey by Russ Gregory. Boyfriend troubles abound as Willa and Grandmother land new ones and Greg tries to hold on to Matt while chasing down a shipment of stolen hair extensions. (978-1-62639-331-8)

Death by Sin by Lyle Blake Smythers. Two supernatural private detectives in Washington, D.C., battle a psychotic supervillain spreading a new sex drug that only works on gay men, increasing the male orgasm and killing them. (978-1-62639-332-5)

Buddha's Bad Boys by Alan Chin. Six stories, six gay men trudging down the road to enlightenment. What they each find is the last thing in the world they expected. (978-1-62639-244-1)

Play It Forward by Frederick Smith. When the worlds of a community activist and a pro basketball player collide, little do they know that their dirty little secrets can lead to a public scandal…and an unexpected love affair. (978-1-62639-235-9)

GingerDead Man by Logan Zachary. Paavo Wolfe sells horror but isn't prepared for what he finds in the oven or the bathhouse; he's in hot water again, and the killer is turning up the heat. (978-1-62639-236-6)

Myth and Magic: Queer Fairy Tales, edited by Radclyffe and Stacia Seaman. Myth, magic, and monsters—the stuff of childhood dreams (or nightmares) and adult fantasies. (978-1-62639-225-0)

Balls & Chain by Eric Andrews-Katz. In protest of the marriage equality bill, the son of Florida's governor has been kidnapped. Agent Buck 98 is back, and the alligators aren't the only things biting. (978-1-62639-218-2)

Blackthorn by Simon Hawk. Rian Blackthorn, Master of the Hall of Swords, vowed he would not give in to the advances of Prince Corin, but he finds himself dueling with more than swords as Corin pursues him with determined passion. (978-1-62639-226-7)